THE MERMAIDS SINGING

ESTI JEDEIKIN

This is a work of fiction. All of the characters, organizations, and events portrayed in this novel are either products of the author's imagination or are used fictitiously.

Published in the United States by Holocene Press, an imprint of The Holocene Company, San Francisco, California
www.themermaidssinging.com
www.holoceneco.com/press
Printed in the United States of America

ISBN-13: 978-0-9827059-3-3
ISBN-10: 0-9827059-3-X

In loving memory of

my mother, Helen Kleinberg Caplan,
who nurtured my love of books

and

my husband, Leon Jedeikin,
who encouraged me to write

Eva sat with her back to the enormous desk, chair swiveled to face the plate glass wall, drinking in the sight of the city. It was a view that never bored her, especially on clear, cold nights when the blackness of the river contrasted more sharply than usual with the patchwork of lights of the office buildings around her and the bright ribbons of streets and expressways crisscrossing the city. That view from her office, on the corner of the twenty-fifth floor of a prestigious building, was nothing less than spectacular. It never failed to amuse her that she, of all people, could call this view her own. She, who, at age forty-three, should have been supervising student dissertations on Jane Austen and Thomas Hardy, not running a jewelry empire with offices on four continents.

Deep in thought and totally oblivious to her surroundings, she turned away from the view to face the luxurious office—the dark parquetry floor covered with a magnificent Persian rug; the massive antique oak desk; the soft leather armchairs flanking a heavy brass-and-glass coffee table in one corner; the single 19th-century English landscape over the bar hidden in an intricate Oriental sideboard; the few well-chosen ashtrays and *objets d'art*; the luxuriant potted plants and the mass of fresh-cut yellow daffodils in a simple Baccarat vase.

Eva considered the flowers her one real extravagance. Everything else in the office had doubled and tripled in value since she had purchased it, and could be considered a good investment in aesthetics and comfort. The flowers were replaced twice a week—no profit in that, just the sheer pleasure of spring all year round. A constant reminder that no matter how beautiful the gems and metals she dealt with every day, nature's offerings—especially yellow daffodils in early spring—were far more beautiful.

Can't shake off the influence of the Romantic Poets, she thought ruefully, and smiled as she looked at the daffodils and automatically thought Wordsworth.

The phone rang on her direct line, startling her out of her reverie. Only her children, housekeeper, partner, and a few close friends had the number. She hurriedly picked up the receiver, with a tentative and slightly worried "Hello?," so different from her usual, assertive business manner.

"Honestly, Mom! What are you doing in the salt mines at ten p.m. on your birthday? I couldn't believe it when I called home and Mary said you'd gone back to the office after having dinner with Jonnie. Why aren't you out celebrating?"

Eva smiled at her daughter's inimitable straight-forwardness. Sharon was not one for beating around the bush. She said what she felt, sometimes with negative consequences; but Eva always warmed to the bluntness—it was so different from her own reticence in personal matters.

"Hello, sweetie! It was nice of you to remember. What's new?" Knowing her eldest child all too well, she doubted that her birthday was the only reason for Sharon's call from her Cambridge dorm. Sure enough, the conversation soon focused on a friend of Sharon's who was looking for a job; Eva promised to see what she could do. She ascertained that Sharon was fine, did not need extra money, and was planning to stay in Cambridge during the summer to take some extra courses, but would, of course, be home for Passover.

"Oh, Mom, I almost forgot! I have regards for you from someone from your deep, dark past! He gave a talk here last week as part of the Business Management lecture series. He's from San Francisco. Robert Miller. A computer whiz. Do you remember him?"

Eva felt the color drain from her face. She clutched the edge of her desk, as if to regain her balance.

"Yes," she said faintly, trying to find her voice and hoping Sharon couldn't hear her heart thumping.

"You don't sound too keen, Mom. Actually, he seemed quite nice. And he was very interested in how you are and what you're doing. He didn't know about Dad," she added in a subdued tone, still having trouble accepting her father's death so many years ago, "so I guess he really knew you way back when."

"Yes, it was a long time ago," Eva said pensively. "How did he know you were my daughter?"

"Well, it was really weird. It was a small class—about twenty or twenty-five people—and he was staring at me while our prof was introducing him. Then, before he spoke, he asked us to introduce ourselves and sort of nodded when I said, 'Sharon Goodman.' After his talk and the question and answer session—he was super, by the way—he came over and said, 'You must be Eva Goodman's daughter; your face is just like hers.'"

"Go on," Eva urged, needing to hear more.

"Well, he's obviously been out of touch for a long time. He started asking about you—then suggested we go for a coffee so he could catch up on the Goodmans. He didn't even know we had Jonathan, and he was shocked to hear about Daddy. He seemed very concerned about you and how you've managed, and he was tickled pink to hear about the lady tycoon you've become."

"Oh, my God!" Eva groaned. "I can just imagine the picture you painted! How is he? How does he look?"

"Well, he's nice-looking, distinguished, but you know that, I guess—dark brown eyes, salt-and-pepper hair with more salt than pepper. Friendly face that's somewhat sad until he smiles. Nice smile. Are you interested?"

Eva smiled and said drily, "He's married and has a daughter about your age, so no thanks. But it's nice to hear that he's well." She suddenly wanted to end the conversation, feeling she was on treacherous ground. Sharon, intrigued, obviously wanted to continue.

"Well, you'll have to tell him yourself. He said he might look you up if he's ever in Minneapolis."

Don't look me up, Rob, Eva entreated silently. You've been out of my life for so long and I've learned to live without you. Please don't come back now and complicate things.

"Are you still there, Mom?" Sharon asked quizzically. "Are you okay?"

"I'm here and I'm fine," Eva answered firmly, "but I must get back to my desk. I have tons of paperwork to get through. Thanks for remembering my birthday, honey."

"Okay, Mom. Happy birthday again. You're working too hard, you know."

Eva smiled. "No, I'm not, honey. Besides, I really like what I'm doing and it's good to be busy. We'll celebrate my next birthday in a couple of years. People over forty should only count by fives anyway. Take care of yourself, Sharon."

"I will. Goodnight, Mom, kiss Jonathan for me."

Eva's face was a study in contrast as she slowly put down the receiver. She was shaken, but talking to her daughter always warmed her heart. Sharon had been a ray of sunshine from the day she was born—funny, charming, honest, with Dan's blond curls and blue eyes, and Eva's strong, feminine features and natural grace. Sharon had her father's outgoing nature and social ease, his firm determination and drive, but tempered with a kindness that was uniquely her own. She'd always been able to make Eva smile, even now when the "regards" from Rob Miller had thrown her completely off-balance.

Eva gently massaged her temples in an attempt to still her racing thoughts, at the same time breathing deeply to try to assuage the palpitations in her stomach.

So much time has passed, she thought, and my life is on such an even keel. I can't go back. I mustn't go back. I'm a different person now.

She had to concede, without false vanity, that the differences wrought by time were largely internal, and that the well-dressed, elegantly coiffed, definitely attractive businesswoman reflected in the office window had changed in style only, not in substance. She was wearing a dove-gray turtleneck cashmere sweater dress, black high-heeled shoes that accentuated pretty feet and slender ankles, and a magnificent double strand of enormous rose-colored pearls—a gift she'd bought for herself during her first highly successful buying trip to Tokyo. That was right after she had decided not to sell Dan's business but rather to run it herself.

Anyone seeing her still-youthful figure, her jet-black, shoulder-length, severely cut hair, elongated gray eyes, straight patrician nose, strong jaw, and surprisingly sensuous mouth would have said she was in her mid thirties. Eva, used to her looks, was less impressed. In the harsh light of her dressing room she could see the fine lines around her eyes, the deepening lines bracketing her mouth, the not-so-few gray hairs, the slight droop of her neck muscles, and the incipient loss of firmness and tone. She didn't care. Men still looked at her—after all, a pretty young widow who had succeeded in turning a small, successful business into a large, successful enterprise was sure to arouse male interest. But although she had male friends, and could flirt outrageously at parties and discreetly at business lunches, she invariably went home alone, pleading the fact that she had a live-in child as ample excuse for squelching any amorous overtures.

Her few short-lived involvements with men in the five years since Dan's death had seemed meaningless and trivial compared to the challenge of running the business and increasing its scope. Eva had not lied to Sharon—she did love her work: the buying trips to Asia and to Europe; the thrill of finding young new designers who created fabulous jewelry with gold and gemstones; the satisfaction of seeing sales increase and profits grow.

What little time was left, she devoted to family. Sharon had left for college two years earlier, but Jonathan, almost nine, promised to keep her busy for years to come.

Thank God for Jonathan, she thought, pushing away the insistent memories of Rob that kept trying to intrude. Jonathan is my agenda for at least the next ten years, he and Sharon. There's no room for anyone else.

She tried to get back to the work spread out in front of her, but found it impossible to concentrate. "What the hell? It's my birthday," she said aloud, shoving the papers aside and rising abruptly. I'm going to celebrate, she thought, going to the bar and pouring herself a generous snifter of cognac. She raised her glass to the reflection in the window. Cheers! she toasted herself, sinking into one of the soft leather armchairs, knowing she shouldn't because with the quiet and the cognac would come memories. She gave in anyway, and let them wash over her.

ONE

Nobody that good-looking could possibly be nice, thought Eva, as she coolly watched the tall, handsome, blue-eyed, Nordic-looking stranger slowly circling the room, stopping to engage in conversation here and there. She knew most of the people in the large, opulent living room. They were all connected with the university, and she supposed that she had been invited by virtue of being one of the faculty's younger and brighter doctoral students.

Either that, or out of spite. She suspected that Dean Williams, her host, had known of her brief but stormy affair with his protégé Andrew Harper, and had invited her to tonight's reception knowing that Andrew and his wife would be there and hoping to cause Eva a bit of discomfort.

As if on cue, Veronica Harper entered the room and made a beeline for the handsome Viking, who obviously was no stranger to her. Eva turned away in disgust. It figures, she thought. Any friend of Veronica's must be a creep.

She took a glass of white wine from the tray of a passing waiter, edged herself into a quiet corner, and surveyed the passing scene. Every academic luminary Mrs. Williams could dredge up was in the room, plus anyone who had ever made a sizeable contribution to the university. The men were in black tie, the women in basic black Diors with pearls or in colorful Pucci chiffon on silk. Eva felt dowdy but defiant in her black wool crepe skirt and white lace blouse. For the hundredth time that evening, she wondered what she was doing here and how soon she could leave without being rude, or at least without being noticed.

"You don't seem to be having a wonderful time," said a laughing voice on her left. Eva found herself looking up at a very blue, twinkling pair of eyes.

"I'm not," she said flatly. "I'm being polite and hypocritical, like my mother taught me to be."

"You're not doing a great job of it, I'm afraid," he chuckled. "I've been watching you for the past half-hour and you look bored to tears."

Eva's elongated gray eyes opened wide and she exclaimed in a perfect imitation of Veronica Harper's gushing tones, "Oh, my *dear*, I am *so* sorry! What would Mother say?"

His chuckle turned into a belly laugh. "*Touché*," he said, "I asked for that one! Why don't you like her, or is that a rhetorical question?"

Eva's face became serious and she blurted defiantly, "I don't like her because she's a phony and a bitch, and because I was once madly in love with her husband."

"And then what happened?" he asked quietly, a glimmer of surprise in his eyes at her candor.

"Oh, the usual naïve undergraduate/sophisticated professor kind of affair. I thought he would leave her for me—she really is a bitch, you know—but he quickly brought me back down to earth, explaining that he could never accomplish all the 'creative' things he's doing without Veronica's unswerving 'support and encouragement'—read, 'money' for that, and you have the picture."

"And you're still furious," the man stated, leading her on.

"Yes, in a way, but at myself, not at him. I later found out that he has a fling every year with one of his undergraduate students—usually a pretty one. In my year, I had the good fortune to qualify. I suppose I was an idiot—a naïve Jewish girl from an unsophisticated middle-class background. So I learned the hard way. It happens to a lot of us. But we survive." Eva wondered why she was confiding all this to a total stranger whose name she didn't even know. She decided it was a combination of the wine and her excruciating boredom.

As if reading her thoughts, he said, "My name is Daniel Goodman, by the way, and you're right about surviving, except I give credit to my unsophisticated middle-class Jewish background for *helping* me survive—it gave me the kind of vision I needed to cut through the bullshit."

This time her eyes twinkled. "You look like a Norse god, and you're Jewish!? My mother would love that!"

"It's her daughter I'm interested in! Does she have a name?"

"Name? Name! Yes! Eva, Eva Rubin. Pleased to meet you." She smiled and extended her hand. He shook it solemnly.

"Well, since I already know your darkest secrets, why don't you tell me even more about yourself?" he asked.

Boy, he's persuasive, she thought as she found herself talking in detail about her family, her ambition to write, her love of English literature in general and Victorian novels in particular, the doctoral program she was immersed in. Finally she stopped, realizing that she had been doing all the talking and still knew nothing about him.

"What about you? Any deep, dark secrets I should know about before I tell you absolutely everything about myself?" Eva demanded.

He laughed. "People think I'm a businessman, but I'm really a playboy. I specialize in seducing bright, beautiful brunettes but I pretend to deal in gemstones and jewelry."

After some probing, she found out that Daniel's initial description of himself was not inaccurate. His father had been a watchmaker and jeweler, while Dan had branched out into diamonds and precious stones. He had "done very well," as his mother liked to tell her friends in her canasta group. But mostly his energies had gone into making sure he remained a bachelor, to the despair of his mother's friends who had, one by one, reconciled themselves to seeing their daughters marry less magnificent specimens than Daniel. In the twenty years since his fifteenth birthday, he had sampled every possible type of woman—younger, older, blonde, brunette, redhead. And he had loved every minute of it.

A veritable bluebeard, she thought. Nice, after all, but definitely not my type!

"My dear Daniel, you are being positively rude by not circulating!" exclaimed Mrs. Williams, intruding on Eva and

Daniel, who had been busily exchanging their life stories. "Eva darling, will you forgive me for taking this charming male away from you? It really isn't fair to the other ladies for you to monopolize him, is it now?"

Jane Austen would love her, thought Eva. A veritable Lady Catherine de Burgh. She smiled sweetly at her hostess and said, "Not at all, Mrs. Williams, I was just about to make my excuses and leave your beautiful party. Thank you for having me. It's been a lovely evening, but I have a paper to finish and we students have to deliver our work on time!"

She smiled at Daniel and added in the same little-girl tones, a hint of satire in her voice, "It was a pleasure to meet you, Mr. Goodman. Do enjoy the party; the best people are here!"

She left quickly, easily finding her wool coat among the furs. She had arrived so late, she'd had to park two blocks away; Mrs. Williams would not have appreciated having a rusty little yellow Mini Minor parked in front of her magnificent home anyway, and Eva was glad to have to walk to her car. It gave her a chance to breathe in the cold night air and clear her head. Daniel is right about the ability to cut through the bullshit, she thought, vowing never again to subject herself to such an evening, no matter what the departmental pressures were.

Her phone was ringing as she unlocked the door to her apartment and she rushed to answer it; late-night calls always scared her.

Dan's voice responded to her breathless "Hello?" "How could you abandon me like that to all the dragon ladies? I thought you were a nice, kind-hearted Jewish girl!"

She took a deep breath, counted to three, and said firmly, "Daniel Goodman, the dragon lady has yet to be born who wouldn't succumb to your charms, so I won't feel guilty for 'abandoning' you. You're a big boy and you can take care of yourself. I'm not your type and you are most certainly not mine. I enjoyed meeting you. You made a devastating evening tolerable. Have a wonderful life! Goodnight and goodbye."

Eva could hear him chuckle as she put down the phone slowly. She stood still for a moment, deep in thought, then shrugged her shoulders, undressed, and put on a warm flannel nightgown.

Bluebeard should only see me now, she thought with a grin as she got under the covers and almost instantaneously fell asleep.

TWO

At 9:15 a.m., Eva's doorbell rang. It was the florist, delivering an enormous basket of daffodils, tulips, irises, and daisies, fluffed out with baby's breath. The card read, "Try me! I can also make a tolerable evening devastating. Will pick you up at 7:00. Dan."

The nerve!, she thought. He probably expects me to swoon just because he's gorgeous and has just spent $50 on spring flowers in January…He's right! I'm swooning. She resolved half-heartedly not to be home that evening, but 7 p.m. found her bathed, made-up, and debating whether to pin up her hair or leave it down.

Loose, she decided. It makes me look younger, and maybe he'll realize he's too old for me. Not knowing what he had in mind for the evening, she had not really known what to wear, but humor had prevailed when she looked through her wardrobe and realized that for years she'd been buying books, not clothes. To hell with him, she thought. I'm not one of his sophisticated ladies, and besides, my Dior is at the cleaners. She put on a heather-colored tweed skirt, a soft mauve angora V-neck sweater (at least it's a low-cut V, she noted with satisfaction), and plain low-heeled black pumps.

"My God, you look like a teenager! People will think I'm a cradle-snatcher, going out with a seventeen-year-old!" he exclaimed when she opened the door.

She drew herself up to her full five feet, five inches, seeming pitifully small compared to his six-foot-two-inch height. "I'm almost twenty, if that makes any difference, and we can order in Chinese food if you don't want to be seen in public with me," she bristled.

"No, no, you'll do!" he said, taking her long black mane in both hands. "You have gorgeous hair, you know; don't ever cut it."

Oddly flustered, she turned to get her coat while he surveyed her apartment. In a typically run-down building in the heart of the student ghetto, her tiny apartment nevertheless had a certain charm. It was obviously furnished with hand-me-downs and on a shoestring, but bright posters, hundreds of books, and a lot of straw and macramé gave it a cozy, welcoming air. He smiled with satisfaction, but not surprise, when he saw his flowers in the center of her coffee table. Since success with women was something he had come to expect, a young, obviously not-wealthy university student, no matter how pretty or brilliant, should be a pushover.

Eva was looking at him intently, as if she could read his mind. Then her serious expression changed to a light-hearted smile as she said, "I'm famished! Are we going to eat, or are you going to spend all evening checking out the decor?"

Since she did not comment on his off-white Mercedes sports car—usually the first topic of conversation when he dated a new girl—he decided on a change of tactics.

"I took the liberty of making a reservation at L'Etoile," he said, naming one of the city's fancier and more expensive restaurants, "however, we can go anywhere you like."

But instead of the anticipated, "Oh, no, L'Etoile sounds lovely," she said, "I'm not really dressed for anything that fancy—do you like Italian food?"

"Love it! Where did you have in mind?"

"There's a little *trattoria* not far from here. I know the couple who own it, and the food is really good. And cheap," she added, knowing full well that cheap didn't matter to him.

"Lead on, Macduff!" he agreed easily.

Well, at least he knows one line from Shakespeare, she thought sarcastically. Probably the only one. She knew she was being bitchy and unfair, but he rubbed her the wrong way with his debonair manner and his calm assumption that everything would go his way.

The restaurant was a typical Italian neighborhood eatery, frequented by students and less affluent faculty members. It had the usual red-and-white checked tablecloths, candles stuck in empty Chianti bottles as table centerpieces, heavy utilitarian china, and outstanding food.

Mr. Rossini took their order after exchanging a few friendly words with Eva, poured their wine, and then made himself scarce, sensing that the handsome young man in his well-cut business suit was an important date, not one of the university types he disapproved of, who spent their lives at his tables, drinking cheap wine and discussing philosophy.

At their quiet corner table, Daniel and Eva had the easy camaraderie that usually marks old friends. Dan found himself talking about his work, about the beauty of the stones he dealt in, the intricacies and rivalries of the jewelry business, his ambition to expand the business, the problems he had had working with his father, who left Germany with his wife and young son right after Hitler's rise to power but who continued to think in terms of a small corner jewelry store even though he had succeeded finan—cially in his new homeland. Eva talked about her parents, who also escaped Europe in the nick of time, and her mother, who felt that nice Jewish girls should marry and raise children and who did not understand Eva's academic aspirations or her love of a language and culture that were still somewhat foreign to her parents. She told Dan about her work at the university giving poetry tutorials to first-year undergraduate students, and about the dissertation she hoped to write, on Victorian women writers.

She was surprised and delighted to learn that Dan knew more than one line of Shakespeare, that London was his favorite city, that he loved theater and music and poetry, and that he shared many of her tastes. She mentally kicked herself for having been so judgmental and critical at first, and thanked whatever instinct had prompted her to keep her sarcasm on a tight leash.

Mr. Rossini reluctantly interrupted their cozy tête-à-tête. It was almost midnight and he wanted to close the restaurant. They were both startled and a little embarrassed to realize that so many hours had gone by. Dan hastily paid the bill and left a generous tip. The portions had been prodigious and Dan was amazed by the amount of food Eva consumed. He suspected that she spent more on books than on groceries and suddenly felt an overwhelming desire to feed her, as often and as abundantly as possible.

Watch it, old boy, he thought. She's too young for you, and you aren't her type.

Eva's thoughts paralleled his. Let him not make a pass. It's been such a nice evening, but he's too old for me and I'm not his type. I don't need another painful romance, it's not the right time to get involved, and besides, he's not the right person.

As if sensing her sudden reticence and feeling somewhat confused about his own emotions, Dan was quiet as he drove Eva home. Once they had arrived, he made no move to escort her into the building. They thanked each other for an enjoyable evening, but neither mentioned the possibility of another date.

"It's probably way past your bedtime," he said, lightly giving her a friendly peck on the cheek, "so I won't keep you up any later. Good luck on your thesis—I'd like to read it when it's done."

Exit Daniel Goodman. The End, she thought as she let herself into her apartment. Well, at least I won't have to eat for another week or so. She could not shake off a niggling feeling of disappointment. The evening had gone so well, but had ended on such a flat note.

Past my bedtime, indeed!, she huffed, then giggled as she remembered her fear at how she would handle an out-and-out pass. Should she call him? No, she shelved that idea, deciding that a man of his advanced years would not understand the more casual social mores that existed in her crowd. She realized with a start that he was only eight or nine years younger than her mother.

Too old. Definitely too old, she told her reflection in the mirror as she brushed her teeth. She tossed and turned that night but when she did sleep, in restless snatches, she dreamt of blue eyes and green London parks.

THREE

The week that followed was excruciating for both of them. Eva kept hoping Dan would call. She made every excuse to be at home as much as possible, in case the phone rang. She would not permit herself to call him, but did not really understand the sudden reticence that held her back. Eva had always been comfortable around men, possibly because of her closeness to her father, to whom she was both a daughter and the son he had lost when his wife gave birth prematurely with no medical assistance in Hitler's Germany.

Aryan doctors, even if they lived next door, were not allowed to treat Jewish women. By the time Dr. Liebermann arrived, it was too late to help the baby and almost too late to save Eva's mother. Hermann Rubin decided then and there that he and Hilda must leave Germany. His decision saved their lives and created a new one—Eva, the daughter he doted on. Her every talent was nurtured and encouraged. Eva, the Rubins' only child, had grown up confident in her abilities, unfettered by the shackles imposed by the '50s on young American women, or by the pseudo-morality that dictated virginity, helplessness, and the absence of intellect. She was an excellent student, a voracious reader who was not afraid to lead her class in science, and was chosen senior class president and valedictorian in her graduating year.

To the amazement of the other girls, boys liked Eva, though she maintained a certain distance, did not fall in love, and refused to be "pinned." She went to college when most of her classmates were getting engaged, completed a four-year Bachelor of Arts degree in two years, and had no trouble carving a niche for herself in a new town on a campus full of strangers. She was never shy

15

around men, treating them with the open friendliness that marked most of her relationships. And yet here she was, bowled over by an older, sophisticated, out-and-out roué, afraid to call him lest he think she was forward! Eva recognized the incongruity of her behavior. She almost called Dan a few times, but hung up as soon as she had dialed his number.

It's rejection you're afraid of, you hypocrite, she chided herself. Suppose you call and he doesn't remember who you are or is simply not interested?

She rationalized her behavior by telling herself that her interest in Dan was a dead-end street. She had been burned once by a suave older man. Why place herself in such a position again? Besides, it would take four more years to complete her doctoral program and she could not allow herself to be side-tracked, especially by a man fifteen years her senior who might want children right away. Eva laughed inwardly at her own mental contortions.

She only found out later that he hadn't called because he was scared to. Scared of the emotions that she had stirred in him, haunted by her gray eyes, her mane of thick black hair, her trim, feminine figure, her throaty, sexy laugh. Daniel Goodman had spent the greater portion of his adult life avoiding emotional entanglement with women. He loved women and reveled in their physical beauty, their smell, their grace, their sexual appeal. But he dreaded tying himself down to one woman, waking up and seeing a head full of hair-rollers and a face smeared in cold cream.

The thought of fatherhood absolutely terrified him. He liked kids—when they were someone else's—and was welcomed with whoops of joy by his married friends' children, who worshipped "Uncle Dan." Actually being someone's daddy was something else, he told himself, visualizing a little black-haired, gray-eyed toddler's sticky little hand holding on to his finger. Eva was not even his type! He favored tall, willowy blondes or redheads, preferably not Jewish and definitely not intellectual.

Who wants a bright wife? he asked himself. He groaned aloud, realizing that he was thinking of Eva as his wife, not just about how to get her into bed without her falling in love with him, or him having to declare that he loved her.

And then Dan suddenly brought his entire social whirl to a halt, without making a conscious decision to do so. When other girls he had dated called him, mystified and hurt at not hearing from him, he made excuses. He'd been busy, had to go out of town, wasn't feeling well.

But finally, after a week of agonizing about Eva, he took a deep breath and called her number. She picked up the phone on the first ring and he found himself tongue-tied, having convinced himself that she wouldn't be home.

On her second "Hello?" he blurted out, "This is Dan Goodman. Can I come over to see you? I mean, for a drink or a cup of coffee?"

She laughed. What a great laugh, he thought.

"Sure! Come right over! It's a little past my bedtime, but if you don't mind, I don't." He glanced at the onyx Cartier clock on his nightstand and realized that it was after ten. What the hell? He really wanted to see her.

"I'll be right over and I won't stay late," he promised.

"I hope you don't mind curlers and cold cream," she said mischievously.

Oh my God!, he thought. "No, no, that's fine, I love curlers!"

He hung up, feeling like a teenager, and drove like a maniac to her apartment, rehearsing what he would say, telling himself he was a fool, resenting her for making him feel this way, and hoping she would look awful in curlers.

"Where are the curlers?" he asked when she opened the door.

"I don't use curlers—my hair is too straight and so there's no point. But I could buy some curlers if you really want me to."

"No, no, I hate them. I was joking!" Damn her, she made him feel so gauche. Standing there barefoot, in a voluminous red velour robe trimmed in black, with no makeup and that magnificent mane of hair, she looked like a witch from Arthur's Camelot. Morgan le Fey. He was enchanted.

"Cognac or coffee?" she asked. "I'm having cognac."

He noticed the snifter on her coffee table next to a well-worn copy of *Pride and Prejudice*. The flowers he had sent were gone, dead by now, he supposed.

"Cognac sounds great," he said, a little more relaxed, raising an eyebrow when she brought another snifter and an expensive bottle of Remy Martin.

She noticed the look and smiled. "I'm a secret lush. It's one of my few vices—good cognac."

"Another dark secret," he bantered and sipped appreciatively. Eva curled up in her armchair, facing him, and raised her glass in a silent toast.

Neither of them knew what to say next.

"You're probably wondering what brings me here," he finally said.

"No, not really. I was actually wondering what was keeping you away," she replied honestly but guardedly, her defenses up.

He took a deep breath. "To be honest? *You* were. You scare me. You're all wrong—too young, too smart, too poor, too inexperienced, and too nice. You aren't tall. You're Jewish. My mother would love you. And you're gorgeous, to boot. You're all the things I was never going to find, all rolled up into one person. I was safe until now. It's not fair. You're ruining all my plans. I think I'm in love with you. I think I want to marry you. My God, I even want to have children with you! Me! I never wanted children—or a wife, either, for that matter." He stopped for a minute, then added quietly, "That's why I haven't called."

Her cheeks became flushed and she put down her brandy snifter carefully. He was afraid she'd laugh at him, but deep down he hoped that he had gotten to her, that she would melt a little. She'd been so damned cool and self-assured until now.

And then her anger took him by surprise. In all his fantasies about her, he'd never once imagined her angry.

"You have a bloody nerve," she said, her voice trembling but controlled. "You're a sanctimonious, egotistical snob! Did you think for one wild moment that because you sent me flowers and took me out to dinner, I would be falling all over you, hoping to get married? I have no intention of getting married for years and years, or of having children. And even if I did, what makes you think I'd pick you for my husband?"

She got up from her chair and paced to the window, putting some distance between them, took a deep breath and continued, eyes flashing with indignation.

"As a proposal, that stank! As a proposition, it was even worse. I think you'd better leave, but finish your cognac first, because it's too good to waste."

He was chastened, but admired her spunk. She was terrific when she was mad.

"I'm sorry!" he said humbly, displaying the little-boy smile that had melted more than one heart. "Can we start all over again? Forget my inexcusable behavior. I don't know what got over me. Please—come back and finish your drink. I'll be good. I promise." Eva sat down reluctantly, warming her glass in her hands, her guard still very much up.

They chatted for a few more minutes, with Dan doing his utmost to put her at ease, asking about the book she was re-reading for the tenth time. He convinced her to go out with him the next evening, assuring her again that he would be a good boy and that she'd like him when she got to know him better. She had to smile. He was so frankly charming, though his charm was the very thing that made her leery.

He did not try to kiss her goodnight, but took her chin in his hand, tilted her head up till her eyes met his, and said very gravely, "Just remember one thing! Darcy turned out to be a really nice guy—and he got his Elizabeth in the end. Thought it would be fair to warn you!" He flashed a wicked smile at her and trotted down the steps.

Damn him, she thought, hearing his car roar away, he's even read *Pride and Prejudice*! Talk about unfair!

FOUR

Their courtship was strange. They were each battling private demons—she, her fear of getting involved and of being hurt; he, his fear of getting involved and of being hooked. Neither wanted to admit that they were falling in love; each tried to deny the physical attraction that enhanced their friendship and camaraderie, which was evolving with every hour they spent together. He traveled more often, forcing himself to be away from her. She spent unnecessarily long hours at the library, willing herself not to be home when he might call. Each fantasized about making love to the other, but neither wanted to push the physical aspect of their relationship beyond their occasional, increasingly passionate goodnight kisses. Eva and Dan always met in public places—restaurants, discos, museums, parks, when the weather was good. Neither wanted to let the other feel too comfortable or too at home.

Eva had hesitatingly agreed to a big, fancy night on the town to celebrate the eve of her birthday. She was rushing out of the faculty library to go home and change when she literally bumped into Dan, who was coming into the building to look for her.

"Oh my God, I know I'm running late but I didn't miss our date, did I? I thought you said seven at my place and it's only a bit after six," Eva blurted out.

"No, you're not late, I'm early. I want to talk to you and I figured I'd find you here. Can we go for a walk?"

"Not if you expect me to be beautiful and glamorous by seven," she said lightly, but with a sinking feeling in her heart.

"Screw beautiful and glamorous, I want to talk to you," he replied insistently. They walked across the snowy campus uneasily, not touching. What have I done? she wondered, trying to suppress the sick feeling in the pit of her stomach at the thought of losing him.

"I can't take this anymore, Eva. You've become the focus of my life to the exclusion of almost everything else—and I'm scared of you. I'm afraid to touch you because I think you'll rebuff me. I'm afraid to say I love you because you may laugh at me. I want to impress you and charm you and bowl you over, and I feel you don't want any of that."

He stopped abruptly, turned toward her, and cupped her chin in his cold hand, lifting her face to his. "I don't want to wine you and dine you tonight. I want to take you home and make love to you. Please let me love you."

He was surprised to see her eyes glistening with tears. She kissed him gently, stroked his face with the back of her small warm hand, and said in a husky voice, "I thought you'd never ask…"

They walked silently to his car, hand-in-hand, afraid to shatter the moment with words. He drove with one hand holding hers, parked the car in its garage space, then led her into the elevator and into his apartment. They threw their coats on the couch and shed the rest of their clothes en route to the bedroom, still not saying a word. He took her in his arms, their nude bodies pressing against each other, the desires and needs of the past few months exploding, affirming their feelings for each other as they made love with an intensity that was new and frightening to both of them, over and over, until all they could do was lie in each other's arms and try to catch their breath, caressing each other as though they were afraid to let go.

"I love you, Eva. Will you marry me?" he asked softly, tracing the outlines of her eyebrows, nose, and mouth with his finger.

"Um-hmm," she said, not trusting herself to articulate more.

"Is that a yes or a no?"

"It's a yes, you dummy, but you can still back off if you want to think about it some more."

"Back off!? I'm crazy about you! I adore you!"

She closed her eyes and took a deep breath, then looked him straight in the eye. "I love you, too, Dan. I'm glad you said it first—I wouldn't have had the guts to do it. You scare me, too. You're so damned self-assured and attractive, and I get the feeling you always get what you want. But I'm glad you want me. I think it would have broken my heart if you hadn't wanted me."

They made love again, this time with the slow, measured pace of two people who have all the time in the world. A gurgle from her stomach brought them back to reality.

"My God, have you had anything to eat today?" he demanded, sitting up abruptly.

She thought for a moment. "Let's see—coffee for breakfast, an apple at lunch time; that's it, I think."

"You must be starving. It's almost midnight! Hot pastrami. That's it! Don't move."

She heard him clattering around in the kitchen, setting the table, calling the all-night deli around the corner and placing an order she knew they'd never finish.

Smiling, she got into the shower, turning on the water full-blast and scrubbing herself with a loofah until her skin tingled. She felt high, elated and happy and contented—with just enough apprehension at the situation she found herself in to assure her that she hadn't died and gone to heaven.

When she walked out of the bedroom wrapped in his burgundy terry robe, she saw that the table was set with fine bone china, crystal wine goblets, and linen placemats and napkins.

"Isn't this a bit fancy for hot pastrami?" she asked teasingly.

"It's almost your birthday. Sit down," he commanded, helping her into her chair as though she were a fragile china doll.

"God, you're beautiful," he whispered as he breathed into her ear, gently lifting her hair and kissing her neck. "Happy birthday," he added, placing a small gift-wrapped package on her plate.

She took off the silvery paper and gingerly opened the small black velvet box. Nestled in white satin was a wide, heavy, antique gold band set all around with oval garnets ringed in twisted gold.

"It's beautiful, Dan, thank you," she said, swallowing the lump in her throat.

"We'll trade it for a diamond, don't worry," he added quickly, misreading the huskiness in her voice for disappointment.

"Oh, no, we won't!" Eva exclaimed. "I'm not a diamond person. This is beautiful."

He took the ring and slipped it on the third finger of her left hand.

"There!" he said in a satisfied tone. "Now you're mine, and you may not avoid me any longer."

The doorbell interrupted their kiss.

"Damn it! It's the delivery boy from the deli! What timing!"

She laughingly pushed him to the door, saying, "Go on—you promised to feed me. I'm starving!"

FIVE

Although they spent most of their time in his apartment—the bed was huge and there was a dishwasher—Eva refused to move in with Dan. He accused her of being prudish and of caring too much about what people would say. She insisted she was neither, trying to explain that she needed a place of her own, at least for now, in this transitional period between singlehood and married life.

Dan pushed for an early summer wedding. His mother would be back from Florida, and Eva's parents could fly in from New York without braving the Minneapolis winter. She wanted a late summer wedding—spring was tied up with exams, final papers, her tutorial responsibilities, and staff meetings to plan the next school year. He backed down, sensing that she would not budge because her work at the university was more important to her than his ideas about their wedding.

He was furious when she sequestered herself in her apartment for two weeks before her exams, emerging only to have dinner with him every day. She unplugged her phone, stocked the fridge with yogurt and coffee, and pored over her books eighteen hours a day. He was proud as a peacock when she got straight A's, a scholarship for the following year—not that she would have needed that once they were married—and increased teaching responsibilities.

When Eva emerged from her marathon study session hollow-eyed, ravenous for sleep and mindless entertainment, Dan wondered if he could take four more years of this until she got her Ph.D. But when he lay in bed, with Eva's warm young body curled up next to him, her hair fanned out in disarray around her sleeping face, he felt a contentment he had never known before. The girls he had dated before Eva had been "broads," not women. He had purposely shied away from earnest bluestockings when he studied gemology, preferring his own kind of intellectual pursuits, which did include reading, theater, music—but never the type of women who seriously pursued a career in any of these fields.

Eva was a new breed of woman for him—independent, somewhat aloof, bright but feminine, devoid of the cloying phoniness of the '50s, yet having none of the shrill, strident militancy of the newly emerging feminist movement of the '60s. She fascinated him: cool, collected, reticent, with flashes of fire when her guard was totally down, right after making love, or late at night after hours of discussing hopes and dreams, childhood memories and adult concerns. She found in him a boyish vulnerability that belied his rakish playboy exterior. Yet he was a man of the world, so different from her fellow students, whose greatest concern was having philosophical discussions over carafes of cheap red wine and figuring out how and where to get laid.

Their respective parents were delighted about Eva and Dan. Millie Goodman had had only two fears with respect to her son— that he would never marry, or that he would marry a *shiksa*, a non-Jewish girl. Although Millie observed only the major Jewish festivals, her milieu was Jewish, and she dreaded being one of those women whose friends pitied her for having a non-Jewish daughter-in-law and grandchildren who called her "Grandmother." She wasn't thrilled when she learned that Eva planned to continue her studies and was in no rush to have children.

"She'll change her mind," she assured the ladies in her canasta group. "My Daniel isn't a kid anymore, and he shouldn't wait too long."

Eva's parents, initially concerned at the fifteen-year difference in age, were won over when Dan and Eva spent Passover with them. Dan was surprised to learn that while they certainly were not rich, Eva's parents were comfortably established. He had assumed that Eva supported herself because she had to.

"It figures," he said to his prospective father-in-law over cigars in the living room while Eva and her mother cleaned up after dinner. "She's so bloody independent!"

"Don't fight it, Dan. That's the way she's always been. She's an only child of parents who lost a child before she was born and couldn't have any more after. She spent half her childhood training us not to spoil her. I remember how hurt we were when she got a paper route at age eleven so she wouldn't have to get an allowance. We told her we wanted to give her an allowance, that it was our responsibility and privilege as parents, but she assured us that it was better for her to be financially independent! She could have gone to Barnard here in New York, but she opted for Minneapolis because she got a bigger scholarship and was accepted into their Ph.D program right after getting her B.A.. Don't try to change her. She won't let you."

"We'll see," said Dan determinedly, and Hermann Rubin shook his head with a fond smile. Dan was underestimating his daughter's tenacity. Perhaps stubbornness was a better word. But he'd learn, and he'd learn to accept her.

Eva and her mother came in from the kitchen, and Eva placed a fond kiss on the top of her father's head before sitting on the sofa next to Dan. There was a special bond between the two, Dan noted, a kinship that extended beyond the usual father-daughter relationship. Eva and Hermann were in cahoots when it came to keeping worry and care away from Hilda's sheltered life. Hermann had spent years shielding the woman he loved after the trauma she had undergone in Germany, and Eva joined forces with him as soon as she was old enough to understand that her mother was somehow different from her friends' mothers—more timid, less assertive, more protective of her family, and somewhat awed by her husband's and daughter's sense of adventure and fun.

They all chatted about current events for a while before Eva and Dan said their goodbyes and went back to the hotel where they were staying. They were taking an early flight back the next day, and Dan was looking forward to having Eva to himself again.

The controversy over the wedding had been resolved fairly amicably. Dan's mother had wanted a large, fancy wedding in Minneapolis. Eva's parents wanted a small, dignified wedding in

New York. The couple compromised by convincing everyone that a small, quiet wedding in Minneapolis was best. They made a storybook couple—Dan, tall and incredibly handsome in a gray morning coat, Eva radiant in a simple, long, empire-style gown, her hair gathered in a soft chignon, a gorgeous bouquet of daisies, daffodils, and baby's breath in her arms.

They spent the day before the wedding moving boxes of books and knick-knacks into Dan's apartment. Eva had sublet her apartment and sold all her furniture to one of her poetry students. She bade a private, wordless farewell to her little hideaway while Dan loaded the last box into the station wagon they had borrowed. After they returned from a carefree two-week honeymoon in Carmel, they had their first real fight, when Eva began unpacking and arranging her books.

She had ordered bookcases, paying for them with the money she got for selling the furniture in her apartment. Figuring that her brick-and-board arrangement was hardly appropriate in Dan's ultra-sleek glass-and-chrome apartment, she had chosen plain black-lacquered bookcases and asked the deliverymen to position them along the far wall of the living room. That meant removing a large modernistic painting that she didn't much like anyway.

"What the hell are you doing?!" Dan exploded when he walked in that evening. She stopped in mid motion, two volumes of Dickens held aloft, the floor littered with opened and empty boxes.

"I wasn't expecting you so early," she said, trying to mollify him, not quite understanding what was wrong, except that the living room was a mess. "I'll be finished in half an hour. Why don't you change and get comfortable, and then I'll figure out what to have for dinner." She hadn't realized how long she'd spent unpacking and browsing through the books. Each book had her name written inside, followed by the date on which it had been purchased. There was "Eva Rubin," with dates going back to the early '50s, written in a clear, child's handwriting. Many were worn, hardcover volumes scrounged from flea markets, garage sales, and second-hand bookstores; others were brightly colored paperbacks that had seen much use. The only matched sets were Dickens and Shakespeare, given to her by her parents when she graduated from elementary school and high school, respectively, and an old set of Jane Austen's six novels she had bought in Tottenham Court Road on her memorable first visit to London.

To Eva, each book was a memory. To Dan, they apparently seemed like so much clutter.

Her suggestion about dinner seemed to anger him more. He liked neither the bookcases nor their placement, and he was livid that she'd removed his painting.

"Don't you think it would be polite to at least consult me before you start turning my apartment upside down and spending my money on furniture I may not like?" he fumed.

Eva turned scarlet and bit back a sharp retort.

"I'm sorry," she said quietly, a small tremor in her voice the only sign of her extreme agitation. "I thought it was *our* apartment now, but even so, I should have checked with you first. I'll send the bookcases back tomorrow—I paid for them, by the way."

She turned her back to him and started putting the books back into boxes, holding back tears, clenching her lips tightly so they wouldn't tremble. Something in the tilt of her neck, and in her slow and methodical motions as she repacked the volumes warned him that he had better not say anymore, but he stalked dramatically into the bedroom, slamming the door behind him. He stayed there for over an hour, watching the news, then the sports, hoping she would come in and they could make up.

But she did not come in, and when Dan finally emerged from the bedroom to see what on earth she was up to, Eva was not there. The bookcases were empty, the boxes re-taped and neatly stacked; her jacket and keys were gone, but her handbag was still in the bedroom. He hadn't heard her leave. How far could she go, with no money or credit cards? She was probably just walking around the block to let off steam.

By 10 p.m., he was even angrier but somewhat concerned. He rationalized that if she had walked far, she would have a long way to come back, and that she probably didn't even have a dime to call home. He killed an hour by making himself a sandwich and cleaning up the kitchen after his makeshift supper.

At 11 p.m., he got into his car, noting that her little Mini was in the garage, and went looking for her. She wasn't in her usual spot at the university library, and the little office she shared with another tutor was locked. Nor was she at the coffee shop near the campus. I'll try Rossini's as a last resort, he thought, wondering what he would do if she wasn't there. She wasn't, but she had been, Mr. Rossini told him, looking at Dan sharply. She'd seemed upset, the *piccola ragazza*, and had ordered a glass of red wine, then a cappuccino, telling Rossini she'd pay him tomorrow because she'd forgotten her handbag.

"You have big fight?" Rossini asked rhetorically.

"Yes, sort of," Dan admitted, somewhat shamefaced.

"You go home, she'll be there soon. You make nice, she is a good girl."

Rossini seemed both sympathetic and suspicious at the same time. Women were illogical, after all, but he had a soft spot for Eva and what he considered her Italian look.

He was right. She was home when Dan got there, freshly showered and curled up with a book in one of the big leather armchairs, barefoot, wearing a soft, flowing robe. She looked up when he came in, but said nothing. He walked over to the chair and put his hands on her shoulders, looking straight into her eyes.

"I'm sorry," he said simply. "I had no right to talk to you like that. But do me a favor—next time throw a book at me, but don't walk out. I've been looking for you all over the place."

Eva dropped her eyes and said in a low voice, "I wasn't walking out. I was just walking, and I didn't realize how late it was."

She looked over to where the modernistic painting was propped up against the sofa. "I'll hang the painting back up as soon as they move the bookcases."

"Damn the painting. I never liked it anyway; and the bookcases are really okay, leave them where they are."

The bookcases stayed, but Eva moved them into the hallway near the kitchen and only unpacked the books when the school year started and she actually needed them. They settled into a comfortable routine, each learning to bend a little to accommodate the other. Eva paid more attention to trivial details, like having food in the house, and Dan learned to call home when he stayed late at the office. They were both very busy—Dan with his growing business and Eva with her teaching load and her dissertation. Their social life consisted mostly of each other. His bachelor social whirl came to an abrupt stop when they got married, and her university friends seemed boring and pseudo-intellectual to him—not that Eva had much use for most of them, either.

Dan was a morning person, jogging, showering, shaving, and dressing for the office before having breakfast with Eva, who had usually just gotten out of bed. She was a night owl, reading and writing for hours after watching the 11 o'clock news with him. They usually made love at three or four in the morning, when she was just getting into bed and he was waking up, most of his night's sleep over.

He once figured that they spent an average of two to three hours a night in bed together, and he teased her about it. "I used to spend more time in bed with girls I wasn't married to than I do with you," he once remarked wryly.

"Yes, but it's quality time that counts," she retorted with a mischievous smile. "How many girls gave you quality?"

"Let me see…" He started counting, first on one hand, then on the other hand, then on his toes. She playfully threw a pillow at him, ending that exchange.

Their next serious disagreement was about when to start having children. Dan did not want to wait. He was over 35, had sown all the wild oats he wanted to sow, and wanted to play baseball with his son before he was too old and decrepit.

"What if it's a girl?" Eva retorted tartly over a cappuccino at Rossini's. They were having the same discussion for the umpteenth time and she still had a niggling suspicion that for Dan, having a family was a way of tying her down and curtailing her independence.

"Then I'll play baseball with *her*," Dan insisted, pooh-poohing her theories about his male chauvinism. "Listen to me, Eva," he pressed. "You don't have to stop teaching, and you won't have to stop working on your Ph.D. We'll buy a house and hire a nanny—an English nanny, if you want—but let's not wait any longer. Please!"

Eva looked down at the checkered tablecloth. She'd used up all her arguments and they didn't make too much sense, even to her.

Maybe I'm scared that a child is more of a commitment than I'm prepared to make, she thought, too much of a responsibility. Maybe I really want a baby, but the idea—and the insistence—should come from me, not from him. That was the traditional way, wasn't it? Maybe I'm not being honest with myself. I'm certainly being unfair to Dan.

She looked up at him. His eyes were soft and he looked as though he would cry if she said no. Damn it, she thought, who can say no to a look like that?

She smiled at him and said in a low voice, "You're right, Dan. I'm being a stubborn fool. I'll go off the pill and we'll see what happens. Maybe I just can't picture myself as a mother—it wasn't in my five-year plan!"

"You'll be terrific, you'll see," he beamed, and called Mr. Rossini over to order a bottle of Asti Spumante.

"We're celebrating," he confided to the older man. "We're going to have a baby."

The Italian's face lit up and he patted Eva's head in approval. *"Auguri, signora! Primo maschio!"* he wished them, leaning toward Eva and pouring the sparkling wine into her glass. "When, *bella ragazza?*" he asked.

"Oh, in ten or twelve months," Eva said, and she and Dan both laughed at the expression on Rossini's face.

SIX

Eva calculated that the nausea hit on the second day of her pregnancy and the sleepiness on the third. She lived on melba toast, plain yogurt, weak tea, and sleep. She crawled into bed at seven in the evening, waking at nine in the morning and napping another two hours a day—at her desk, in the library—anywhere she could be immobile for more than fifteen minutes. The doctor assured her that as soon as the baby started moving, the nausea would pass, and he was right; but she despaired of ever getting back to a routine of sleeping four out of twenty-four hours, and worried about falling behind in her reading.

"*I'm* the one who's supposed to look radiant, not you!" she griped to Dan across the breakfast table. "Here you are—on a Sunday morning, yet, looking like you should be on the cover of a male version of *Vogue* and I look—and feel—like a hippopotamus the morning after an orgy."

"Come on, hippo," he said, patting her rear as she shuffled by to get more tea, "we're going house-hunting in half an hour."

She groaned and went to get dressed. A house, a baby, a *nanny*, for goodness' sake!

"I'm not ready!" she called out from the shower, noting that her toes were no longer visible, hidden by the hard, round mass protruding so strongly in front of her, seeming to have a life of its own whenever the activity inside started.

"It's okay—you have twenty minutes," Dan replied, purposely misunderstanding her meaning. His self-assured manner was a cover-up for his own mounting fears of impending parenthood.

This would be the first house they were actually going to look at together. Dan had seen a few but hadn't liked any of them, and

Eva flatly refused to even consider anything that was not central and reasonably near the university. The real estate agent's description sounded ideal—an old-fashioned house in Kenwood, built before World War II; four airy bedrooms on the second floor; a living room, dining room, modernized kitchen, and den on the main floor; a nice yard, quiet street, good school district; reasonable price—almost too good to be true. But true it was, and Dan and Eva wandered from room to room, touching the wood paneling in the shelf-lined den, noticing the detail on the ceiling moldings, almost feeling the warmth of future fires in the formal marble fireplace in the living room and in the Delft-tiled fireplace in the den. They would have to paint and furnish, but otherwise the house was in move-in condition, and Eva mentally thanked the previous owners for not cluttering up the house with floral wallpaper and sculptured broadloom.

They signed the offer to purchase on the spot, agreeing to the asking price, and closed the sale on the day of Eva's birthday. Her birthday present was a key ring—a heavy silver "E," with the key to the new house. Since the baby was due in three months, they spent a whirlwind month making the necessary changes to be able to move in well before Eva's due date. The house was furnished sparsely, but warm nonetheless. Dan conceded reluctantly that his high-tech decor, which was suited to a bachelor apartment, just didn't go with the old-fashioned wainscoting and satiny oak floors. For the den, Eva commandeered the two leather armchairs and painstakingly stripped and refinished an old mahogany desk she bought at an auction.

It may have been the house, or a hormonal readjustment, but she seemed to have rediscovered all her old energy—and then some. Her flair for making a place cozy emerged again after being dormant for months in Dan's sleek apartment, which she had never really made her own. She started with the baby's room, which she painted yellow and furnished in white—and refused to listen to her mother-in-law's warning that it was bad luck to fill the drawers with baby garments until after the birth. Then, with the house more or less in order and her energy level still high, she went back to her books and her research, determined to complete everything she had set out to do before the baby's arrival.

"Do you think she'll bring home jerks?" Dan asked anxiously, cradling his newborn daughter awkwardly, his forehead furrowed with worry.

"Not unless she grows some hair first!" Eva laughed. Dan looked clumsy and huge, holding the seemingly fragile six-and-a-half-pound baby as if she were made of eggshells. "But if she ends up looking like you, and I suspect she will, the jerks will come swarming, never fear!"

"Well, she won't be allowed to date before she's twenty, so at least they won't be pimply teenagers."

"Let's not get Victorian all of a sudden," Eva chuckled, scooping the baby out of her husband's arms. "How do you like the name Sharon?"

He considered for a moment. "Yes, it's pretty—it sure beats the pseudo-WASP crap my mother prefers!"

"Sharon Judith Goodman," Eva said, rolling the name around her tongue. Dan had been so convinced they were having a boy, they hadn't even considered girls' names. "I like that," she continued. "It's a good, strong name with traditional overtones. She can be anything she wants with a name like that."

"My daughter, the doctor!" Dan teased.

"Why not?" Eva replied.

"Because I'll be surrounded by lady Ph.D.s and M.D.s…. Have a heart—how much can one poor male cope with?"

"You'll manage," Eva said drily, then looked down at the baby, who had opened her eyes and was making sucking noises.

"I think the future Dr. Goodman wants to eat," she said, pulling down the shoulder strap of her nightgown and offering the baby her breast.

Dan watched Eva nursing the baby, marveling at how easily women became mothers; noticing for the first time in months how beautiful she looked, how small and soft and delicate she seemed with the mound of pregnancy gone, but with the remaining roundness of her body and face adding a vulnerability to her features that he'd never noticed before. He wanted her so badly, he almost felt jealous of the baby nuzzling her breast, as he would have liked to at that moment. Eva looked up at him and smiled, recognizing the expression on his face, one she had had to ignore during the last months of her pregnancy. He touched her cheek with the back of his hand, then ran his fingers through the softness of her hair.

"You look like a Madonna," he said huskily. "Didn't anyone ever tell you that Madonnas are not supposed to be sexy?"

"Jewish Madonnas are different," she said, bending over to kiss him softly. "Give me a few weeks and I'll show you."

SEVEN

There wasn't much opportunity to show Dan anything in the following weeks, or months. With his personal life settled into an established routine, and having changed from man-about-town to husband, father, and homeowner, Dan embarked on an expansion program at Goodman & Son that he had dreamed of for years but that his father, who wanted to keep the business small, had always thwarted.

"There is so much more to the jewelry business than my father was prepared to undertake," he explained to Eva. "With our connections in Europe and in the Far East, we shouldn't be supplying local stores only. The whole of North America is wide open, and people are starting to discover and to appreciate jewelry the way the Europeans always have."

Eva concurred and was delighted at Dan's enthusiasm and interest, but she had not bargained for his frequent absences necessitated by the expansion. She didn't mind the effect on their social life. She'd always disliked parties, and the crowd Dan had mixed with before their marriage—typified by Veronica Harper—certainly was not to her taste. She still had two or three close friends at the university and usually saw them on her own. That was fine—they were not Dan's cup of tea. What she did mind were the many nights she spent alone, and that her husband was not there to share in the wonders of Sharon's development. Dan was in New York when Sharon's first tooth appeared and in Los Angeles when she took her first step. He thought it was cute that her first words were "Daddy, bye-bye," but he refused to concede that Eva's unhappiness and hurt about his absences were understandable.

"Look, I'm doing it for you and Sharon, for God's sake," he said angrily when Eva finally tried to have a serious discussion about his plans for a three-week trip to Japan.

"The business is making more money than ever before; I've hired three more salesmen, an assistant, and another secretary. If anything should happen to me, you and Sharon won't have to worry about money. What more do you want?!"

"We want you at home, that's what we want," Eva replied, turning her back to him to hide the tears and swallowing hard to keep the tremor in her voice inaudible.

"And when I am home, you're busy with your goddamn thesis! You're a fine one to blame me, Mrs. Lady Academician. How many hours a week do you spend at the university and in that bloody den?"

We always come back to the same sore spot, Eva thought tiredly. She turned to face him and took a deep breath. "It isn't more than 9 to 5," she said. "Sometimes it's even less than that. And the work I do is at night after Sharon is in bed, or after you've gone to sleep. You knew I was going to be writing a thesis when you married me. I'll be through in a couple of years, and I'm trying very hard not to let it interfere with my family life. I'm only complaining because there seems to be less and less family life for my schoolwork to interfere with!"

Dan refused to be mollified, but he did make a point of spending more time with Sharon when he was in town. As things settled down in his office, he traveled less frequently but still spent more evenings at the office than he used to. He'd come home early, have dinner with Eva and Sharon, tuck Sharon in and read her a bedtime story, then go back to the office for four or five hours.

On the one hand, that suited Eva very well—she had the extra hours she needed to work on her dissertation without the attendant guilt of depriving Dan of her presence. But after a while, the evenings apart started bothering her. The thought even crossed her mind that maybe Dan wasn't spending all of those hours working.

"Are you trying to prove a point, or are you seeing someone?" she asked bluntly one evening when he came down the stairs after putting Sharon to bed.

He stopped in his tracks. "Don't be an idiot, Eva. I have tons of paperwork to do. I'm not running a little corner store."

"Why don't you bring some of the paperwork home and work here? The den is as much yours as it is mine, and I rarely sit at the desk."

"No, my dictation would disturb you and it would mean dragging papers from the office to home and back to the office. I won't be home late," he promised, giving her a peck on the cheek.

When he started staying out till 12 and 1 o'clock in the morning, she started wondering what was going on in earnest. At first pride wouldn't allow her, but she finally tried calling his office when he wasn't home by eleven. After the phone rang eight times, she hung up slowly. Maybe he's on his way home, she thought. But the office was not more than 15 minutes away, and at midnight he still hadn't shown up. Eva sat curled up in one of the chairs in the den, more and more convinced that there had to be a woman in the picture. When he walked in at 2 a.m., she was waiting, torn between worry about a car accident and anger at his not calling to say he'd be late.

"Where the hell have you been?" she fumed.

"In the office," he replied coldly.

"Don't lie to me, Dan. I've been calling for the last three hours."

"Oh, checking up on me, are you? Well, don't," he said angrily. "I'm tired and I'm going to bed. Good night."

"Wait a minute, Dan, please," she pleaded, following him up the steps to their bedroom. "Something is very wrong. I don't know what it is, but I'd like to talk about it. If you're unhappy with me, tell me why. If something is bothering you, tell me what. Maybe there's something I can do. But please don't shut me out."

"There's nothing wrong. I'm just very busy and I have a lot to do and you'll have to be patient. Now let's go to bed. I'm bushed." He started to undress.

"Is it another woman, Dan? Because if it is, I'd like to know. I can't deal with what I don't understand."

"Don't be an idiot, Eva."

"I'm not an idiot, Dan. Don't treat me like one!"

He glared at her and walked into the bathroom, shutting the door firmly, and shutting her out. She stood there for a moment or two, listening to the shower running, then went slowly back downstairs and threw another log on the fire. She sat there brooding until the log burnt down, then poked the embers around, shut the firescreen, turned off the lights, and went upstairs.

She checked on Sharon first and found her, as usual, sleeping on the floor, curled up in her comforter, her thumb firmly wedged into her determined four-year-old mouth.

She smiled and lifted the sleeping child back onto the bed, smoothing the blonde curls. Sharon was a carbon copy of Dan. Her eyes had remained blue and her bald head had become a mane of soft, ash-blonde hair. Eva sat on the bed for a few minutes looking at her child, then got up and wearily walked to her own room. Dan was fast asleep.

Another cherub, she thought grimly, as she climbed into bed and switched off her lamp. Sleep did not come easily as she tried to figure out where their marriage was heading, attempting to pinpoint exactly when things had started to go wrong. I'll think about it tomorrow, she finally decided, and smiled as she thought of Scarlett O'Hara. I never thought I'd be echoing her, of all people, she said to herself with an inward smile, glad to discover that she could still smile at something. Maybe this is just one of those rough patches marriages are supposed to go through, and maybe things will improve with time. But God help us if they get worse.

Things did begin to get worse just when she thought they were finally getting better. Her thesis was finished. Typed, proofread, corrected, agonized over one final time, and then submitted. If all things went well, and there was no reason why they shouldn't, she would get her doctorate at the spring convocation. She hoped her parents would fly in from New York, although her father had not been too well lately, and Dan's mother would be back from

Florida. Maybe after graduation, she and Dan could go away somewhere for a week or two; they had not taken a real vacation in years, and it could be a six-year anniversary present to themselves. At least their relationship had not deteriorated in the last year. Dan was still away a lot but when he was home, he was more attentive. Something of the *brio* we had at the beginning of our romance is definitely missing, she thought, but perhaps that's just familiarity and habit taking their toll on the spontaneity and excitement of discovering each other when the relationship was fresh and new.

…"Yes, Daddy, of course I understand. Just take it easy and don't push yourself too hard. We'll send pictures, and we'll see you in a couple of months when we come to New York."

…"Okay, Daddy. I love you, too."

Eva put down the phone slowly and rejoined Dan and Sharon at the breakfast table. They were both attacking their Sunday pancakes and maple syrup with gusto.

"My parents can't come for convocation," she told Dan. "Dad isn't well—the doctors think he may have had a mild stroke without realizing it. They're doing all kinds of tests. They haven't told me because they didn't want me to worry…. Dan, he must be really sick not to come," she added with a worried frown. "My Ph.D. means an awful lot to him and he wouldn't miss an opportunity to be with Sharon. He also wouldn't let me talk to Mother, which means she isn't controlling her worries and he doesn't want me to know how worried she is."

Dan covered her hand with his, sharing her concern. He really liked his in-laws, especially Hermann, with his quiet sense of humor and instinctive understanding of people.

"Maybe it's not that bad. Why don't you fly out and see for yourself right after the ceremonies are over?"

"I may do that," she answered, the thought of some sort of concrete action making her feel better. "Can you come, too? Maybe we'll all go, rather than waiting for the summer."

"You know how busy I am right now, Eva," he said gently. "But why don't you take Sharon with you? I can manage on my own."

She looked at him sharply, wondering whether he was genuinely concerned or whether he was clearing the decks for other reasons. Don't be a bitch, Eva, she told herself. He really cares and he's being damned nice about it.

Sharon had been surveying the scene, listening to each of her parents in turn, and she finally settled the issue.

"Papa Hermann wants to see *me*, I know."

Dan and Eva both smiled and the tension of the moment was broken.

"I'll make the arrangements tomorrow and Papa Hermann *will* see you, pussycat," said Dan, ruffling her curls.

"Good!" Sharon replied emphatically. "Then he'll get all better."

It was clear to Eva when she saw her father that he would not get all better, and that he was far sicker than he had let on. She and Sharon had taken the first available flight—Eva had literally dashed out of her cap and gown and was at the airport an hour after becoming Dr. Goodman. The convocation ceremony itself, an anticlimax after the grueling year of writing, rewriting, and defending her dissertation, was certainly overshadowed by her concern for her father. That concern was well founded, she now realized. Hermann had aged drastically in the few months since she'd seen him, and the tests he was undergoing were much more extensive than he had told her.

"I'll be all right, *ketzaleh*," he assured her, reverting to the nickname he'd always used when he'd comforted and kissed away childhood fears and hurts. His "little kitten" was not so sure. Neither were the doctors she spoke to. Initially they suspected heart trouble; now they were looking for a possible malignancy. It didn't sound good, either way.

"How are things going with you, Eva?" her father asked probingly. "You look tired and sad. Is everything okay with you and Dan?"

He may be sick, Eva thought gravely, but he hasn't lost his acuteness or his ability to hit the nail on the head. She hadn't even hinted at any troubles between them.

"I *am* tired, Daddy. It's been a hard year and I'm concerned about you. But I'm all right."

"You didn't answer my question," he chided her gently. "I'm not your mother, Eva. Me, you can tell, you know."

Her eyes stung with tears, but she smiled. "I never could fool you, Daddy, could I? No. Things are not so good. I don't know what's wrong, exactly. Dan is very busy. He's away a lot. He's always resented my work, though he's proud of my getting the degree and of my position at the university. He won't talk things out, though I've tried. It's almost as though he doesn't want things to get better."

She stopped, but then went on, in answer to the question in her father's eyes. "I don't know if it's another woman. I suspect there may have been other women over the years. Maybe there is someone now. There are a lot of hours in the day when he isn't in the office and I don't know where he spends them. Or with whom."

"What are you going to do about it?"

Eva got up abruptly, and walked around the room, stopping to touch familiar knick-knacks, pausing in front of a watercolor she'd always loved, wishing her mother and Sharon would get back from their shopping expedition and that this conversation would end.

Hermann lay on the sofa, legs covered with an afghan, propped up on large pillows. He watched her intently, following her progress around the room, his heart aching for his troubled, beloved child who seemed, for the first time in his memory, not to know what to do next.

Eva finally flopped back into the armchair next to the sofa and said wearily, "I don't know, Daddy. I really don't know. I've tried to figure out what I can change in myself to make him look at me the way he used to. And I don't know. It's not that he's making any demands I can respond to. We haven't even had an argument, to speak of, in the last few months. I feel like a part of the furniture. I'm there, but that's it. The only response I can elicit is an occasional brief burst of anger. It's like he's gone, and only his body is there. And that isn't always there, either," she added with a grimace.

"Does he want a divorce?" Hermann asked, concerned that some of the problems he had anticipated when first meeting Dan seemed to be coming true.

"Divorce! He won't even talk about anything being wrong, let alone want to deal with solutions," Eva blurted.

"Do *you* want out?" Hermann asked quietly, studying her intently.

Eva looked up at him, her expressive gray eyes a mixture of pain and confusion. "I don't know, Daddy. Something has to happen. Something has to change. We're in a kind of limbo, and it can't go on for too much longer."

Sharon's voice in the hallway startled her, and she quickly composed her face, smoothing her father's blanket as if to erase the past few minutes.

He looks so tired and worn, she thought, angry at herself for unburdening a burden he could not pick up for her. Should not pick up for her.

"I'll be all right, Daddy," she assured him softly, stroking his cheek with a light hand. "We Rubins are tough stuff and this will resolve itself one way or another. I'll be fine."

"Okay, *ketzaleh*. I believe in you," he smiled at her, sensing how difficult it was for her to talk about her problems. "Go make us a cup of tea while I see what my favorite granddaughter brought me." He looked affectionately toward the doorway at Sharon, who was tiptoeing in with a small gift-wrapped box for him.

Eva left the two of them to their own tête-à-tête, and went to the kitchen to help her mother unpack the groceries. She glanced at herself in the hall mirror, seeing for the first time the weariness and sadness that were so apparent to her father.

Time to do something about it, Eva, she admonished herself, although still not clear as to what the "it" really was, but agreeing with herself that the situation could not continue the way it had been going up until now. Here comes a showdown, Dan Goodman, she thought. I just have to figure out a way to reach you so you'll talk to me. But you are not shutting me out any longer.

EIGHT

Dan was not at the airport to meet them, though he had said he would try. Eva took a limousine home, trying to console Sharon, who had spent the flight planning her reunion with her father and drawing pictures for the occasion.

The house smelled of warm cinnamon-and-apple pie when they walked in. Mary was bustling about the kitchen, preparing Sharon's favorite foods for dinner. She hugged Sharon, then Eva, then Sharon again.

"Mr. Goodman is on his way to Los Angeles. He left this morning and asked me to give you this note."

"Oh," Eva said guardedly, "he didn't say anything about going away when I spoke to him." She slit open the envelope with her finger and read the hastily scrawled message:

> *Dear Eva,*
> *Something came up that needs my direct supervision. Will be in Los Angeles for the next few days. Kiss Sharon for me—I'll bring something back for her, to make up for my not being there to greet her.*
> *Dan*

And what about me? Eva thought bitterly. How will you make it up to me?

Mary was looking at her sympathetically, but questioningly. Eva arranged her face into a smile and told Sharon, "Daddy had to go away for a few days, honey, but he sends you a big kiss." Better not say anything about a gift in case he forgets.

Sharon's face fell for a moment, but then she squared her shoulders and, with a bright look, announced, "Well, I'll have time to make some more pictures. Don't be sad, Mummy, he'll be home soon."

Dammit, thought Eva, am I that transparent! She shooed Mary upstairs to give Sharon a bath, then went to her room to shower and change. Well, you can't have a showdown with someone who isn't here, she said to herself, so that's one item deferred—for now, at least.

She tried to talk to Dan when he got home a few days later, just in time for supper. It was Mary's day off and Eva was in the kitchen preparing a salad when she heard Sharon's whoop of joy as an airport limousine drove up to the house. Dan was relaxed and smiling, the business in Los Angeles apparently had been resolved to his satisfaction, and he was expansive and talkative as he played with Sharon, following Eva around the kitchen as she prepared two thick steaks for the barbecue—one for Dan and one for her and Sharon.

We look like the ideal middle-class American family, she thought, as they ate their dinner on the patio in the deepening dusk, polishing off the remains of one of Mary's famous apple pies. Sharon finally announced dramatically that she would put herself to bed with her new California bear and imperiously summoned both her parents to her bedside to tuck her in and kiss her goodnight.

She's making sure the family remains a single unit, Eva thought with wonder, trying to figure out how much of Sharon's behavior was instinctive and how much had been analyzed in that bright little head with its super-sensitive emotional antennae.

She turned to Dan as they walked down the wide stairway side by side and said, "Come, I'll buy you a drink on the patio—it's such a beautiful night."

"All right," he agreed, to her surprise, not pleading fatigue or work, or having to get up early. "Make mine the usual."

They sat quietly in the growing darkness, with only the yellow mosquito lamp casting a soft glow, sipping their drinks slowly. Dan wanted to know about her father's condition, now that Sharon was safely tucked away and Eva could talk openly. His eyes softened as Eva described Hermann's appearance and his undaunted conviction that this was a temporary illness, a trouble patch to be gone through and overcome, as he had overcome so many other troubled times in his life.

"He's concerned about us, Dan," she said softly, sensing that the mood and the timing were appropriate for saying the things that had been running through her head for months now.

"Why? What did you tell him?" Dan asked sharply, sitting upright in his chair.

"Nothing—he asked me if things were all right between us—you know how perceptive he's always been—and I had to admit that everything was *not* fine, but that I don't really know what's wrong. What *is* wrong, Dan? I wish you'd give me a hint, so I could figure out what to do."

"There's nothing wrong, Eva," he declared flatly. "I can't believe we're having this discussion again. You're paranoid."

"I'm not paranoid, Dan," she answered quietly, trying to keep the edge of anger out of her voice. "And I'm not stupid, either. Whatever we had in the first years of our marriage is either gone or it's in hiding somewhere. We're friends sharing a house and a child—I wonder what we'd be sharing if there were no child. We make love—occasionally—and it's purely physical, even when it's good, because *you're not here.*" She took a deep breath, then added softly, "Where are you, Dan? Where are you going? I'd like to know so I can be there with you. Please say something!"

"There's nothing to say, Eva. We've been married six years, we're in a rut, in a groove—a comfortable one. You're doing your thing. I'm doing mine. We have a terrific kid; maybe we should have more. You want the excitement and the electricity of a new relationship and that just doesn't last in the day-to-day of marriage and making a living. Stop longing for something that isn't there or you'll spoil what there is…" He drained the last of his Scotch and rose from his chair.

"Don't go in on account of me," he added, as she got up to join him. "The last few days have been rough and I'm tired and going to bed. Don't forget to lock the patio doors. G'night."

Another impasse, she thought, as he went inside. It's a stalemate. Whatever move I make, he moves his king and we're back to a draw.

She wondered if he was right. Maybe she *was* being paranoid. Maybe these kinds of doldrums were an integral part of marriage. But she couldn't really believe that, especially remembering the crackle of electricity that had always existed between her parents, changing throughout the years from a deep physical and emotional attachment to an even deeper commitment and loyalty and love. Dan feels that way about Sharon, she thought, he's not in a rut when it comes to her. The more he's with her, the more he loves her. He certainly can't say the same for me. Oh, God, don't let me be jealous of my own child!

Eva finished her cognac and went into the kitchen to clean up the supper dishes. It was too early to go to bed and she knew Dan would be asleep, or feigning sleep, curled up on his side of the bed, his back to her, unapproachable. She set the table for breakfast, debated the merits and demerits of baking some cookies, decided against starting a new mess, and went into the den. It had become "her" den. She realized that for the first time in years, there was no work on her desk that had to get done.

She would be teaching a new course in the fall as part of the new Women's Studies interdisciplinary program. The subject was the position of women in the 19th century as reflected in literature, but since that was so close to the topic of her thesis, no extensive background preparation or reading were required of her. She had submitted her reading lists and course outlines and had purposely left books and notes in her office at the university, determined to take off the month of July and maybe even a bit of August. She had not bargained for the feeling of emptiness as she wandered around the room with nothing specific to do. Writing a thesis is like having a baby, she thought. You're on a high at first, and then come the post-partum blues. Hers had been deferred up until now because of her father's illness and her fears for her marriage, but they hit with added force as she found herself confronted with two big problems and no solutions to either.

I will not brood, she decided, scanning the corner bookshelves where the brightly jacketed bestsellers of the last five years were stashed. Dan liked his books in hard cover, mostly action and spy stuff, which she liked too but had not had time to read much while immersed in her studies. She pulled out a new Le Carré novel and sat in her usual armchair to read. Reading was a trusted and true escape. It had always worked for her, and it did not fail her now as she became immersed in Smiley and Karla and the machinations of the world of foreign intrigue. When she put the book down, it was 2 a.m. Definitely not too late to go to bed, she thought, switching off lights and checking the locks. Sleep came quickly, to her great relief, but there were no solutions there, either. I guess it will just have to be limbo for now, she thought, wondering what would happen next, because limbo never lasted. She wondered if what was ahead wouldn't be worse, and whether the disjointed and troubled time she was now going through would be seen, in retrospect, as a time of relative peace and tranquility.

NINE

Eva was browsing in the lingerie department, debating the merits of the deep wine-colored robe compared to the soft peach. She decided on the wine—it was sexier and more dramatic, and Dan would like it—and was signing her bill when a saccharine voice behind her said, "Eva, dear, how *are* you?"

Steeling herself for a few minutes of aggravation, Eva smiled sweetly at Veronica Harper and replied, "I'm fine, Veronica. How are you?"

"Very well, dear, thank you. Fancy meeting you here. I thought lady professors were not into sexy lingerie, but I suppose one needs all the help one can get when one is trying to hold onto an errant husband."

And who should know better than you? Eva thought sarcastically, biting back an angry retort that she knew would get her nowhere, wondering what Veronica was leading up to.

"Of course, seeing as Daniel seems to prefer blondes these days... Oh, dear, I think I've spoken out of turn," Veronica said, seeing Eva's surprised expression. "But it *is* common knowledge, though I suppose the cliché that the wife is always the last to know still holds true, even in these enlightened days. I am sorry, Eva, if I've hurt your feelings, but you really should do something about Dan and that pretty assistant of his. I must run off now. I have a luncheon engagement and I'm already late. Do keep well, my dear—and good luck!"

Eva stood rooted in place, holding her package in front of her like a shield, her face a stony mask from which all the color had drained.

Bitch, she thought bitterly. *She's been waiting for an opportunity to pay me back all these years, and she finally got her chance. Thank you, Dan, for making it all possible.*

An elderly saleswoman approached, a concerned look on her face. "Are you all right, ma'am? Do you want to sit down for a few moments?"

"No, no, thank you, I'm fine," said Eva hastily, leaving as quickly as she could without actually running out of the store. She sat in her car trying to remember what Dan's assistant looked like. She had met her once or twice on the rare occasions when she dropped in at Dan's office, but could only recall an unclear picture of a fair, wholesome-looking, pretty Midwestern girl. *The kind you see on TV commercials,* she thought, *not usually Dan's type, but then I wasn't his type, either. Maybe his type now is anything different from me.*

Eva drove home mechanically, thankful that Sharon was still at school, but did not know what to do with herself once she got there. She began to dial Dan's number, then stopped when it dawned on her that she had no idea what to say to him. Sitting in one of the big armchairs, she realized that she had known for a long time. Not just suspected—known. The loose ends, the attitudes she could not pinpoint, the long hours away from home—it all fit now, as the pieces of the puzzle fell into place.

"Barbara Wallace. Who'd have imagined it?" she said aloud, trying to recall what she knew about the woman who was possibly well on her way to taking her place. Aside from the fact that Barbara was from a small town in the Midwest somewhere, Lansing maybe, and that she was good at her job, Eva knew nothing about her. She must be good at more than her job, she thought grimly, wondering what course of action—or inaction—she should take.

Dan resolved the question by calling to say he would be working late and would grab a bite downtown.

"Good," Eva said, "I'll buy you dinner. When shall I pick you up?"

He began to protest that it wasn't necessary, that all he was planning was a sandwich at his desk, but Eva cut him short.

"Dan, I have to talk to you. It won't wait. What time?"

There was something in her voice that he'd never heard before and any further discussion was squelched.

"Six-thirty. I'll be downstairs."

"See you then. Bye."

They were seated at a quiet booth at Rossini's. Eva hadn't said a word since Dan had gotten into the car. He finally asked in a gentle, almost humorous, tone, "All right, Eva, what's bothering you? You look upset. Let me guess. The University Press decided not to publish your thesis after all."

"Don't patronize me, Dan." She raised her eyes and locked straight into his, trying to fathom what was behind the boyish good looks and where she stood in his heart and mind.

"Tell me about Barbara Wallace, for starters," she said quietly.

Dan looked surprised. "Barbara? What do you want to know about her?"

"Anything that will explain why Veronica Harper is feeling so sorry for me as she busily spreads the news that you and Barbara are having an affair."

"Veronica is a class-one bitch and you know it," Dan protested. "She's been dying to get her claws into you for years, and not without reason, if you recall. She saw me in Los Angeles with Barbara, jumped to the wrong conclusion, and couldn't wait to tell you."

"Los Angeles? Barbara was with you in Los Angeles? I didn't know that. You didn't say anything about her being with you."

"I'm sure I did, Eva. You were very distraught about your father at the time and you don't remember. It means nothing," he added placatingly. "She's my assistant and we had a big contract to negotiate in Los Angeles and she came along. That doesn't make us lovers."

"What about all the late nights at the office? All the trips to New York and the Coast? What about how far away you've been, even when you're home? There's a lot of smoke for no fire, Dan," she said, her eyes downcast, nervously folding and unfolding her napkin.

He took her hand in his, playing with the heavy garnet ring and the simple gold band beside it.

"Eva," he said gently, stroking the long, tapering fingers, "I love you. Just accept that and trust me. I know I've been neglecting you lately; I'll try to change that. I'm flattered that you're jealous, but I hate what it's doing to you. Please, Eva."

"You're not convincing me, Dan," she began to say, then stopped as Mr. Rossini approached their table.

"Telephone for you, *cara mia*," he said, smiling at Eva, waving toward the bar and chatting with Dan while Eva went to the phone, a worried expression on her face. Only Mary knew she was here, and she would only be calling if it were an emergency.

"Dan, we have to go; it's my father, he's had another stroke. My mother just called the house and Mary called me here. I have to get to New York as fast as possible."

Dan was a dynamo in action. They drove home and called Eva's mother immediately. Hermann was in intensive care, his condition critical. The doctors suggested that his daughter come home immediately. Eva threw some clothes into a suitcase while Dan made flight arrangements. He held her hand all the way to the airport, hugging her tightly at the departure gate. She had insisted that he stay at home with Sharon.

"He'll pull through, Eva. He won't forego seeing Sharon grow up. Call me when you've seen him. If you need me, I'll be there on the first flight tomorrow."

How things fall into their proper proportions when a real emergency hits, Eva mused, leaning back in her seat, safety belt fastened, as if that would make the time pass more quickly. Her concern for her father had pushed everything else into the background. Normally a nervous flyer, she had not even noticed the revving of the engines as the plane began its takeoff.

Images of her father flashed behind her closed eyelids, like a disjointed rough-cut film—pictures of Hermann taking her to the zoo, to concerts, to ballets. The highly cultured and educated Berliner reveled in what New York had to offer, disagreeing vehemently with some of his countrymen who denigrated what passed for *kultur* in America. He felt fortunate that he could raise a child in a city that had all the cultural offerings of his native Berlin, with none of the restrictions and humiliations the Hitler years had brought to his beloved homeland.

Hilda disliked crowds and had never lost the fears instilled in her by the brown-shirted men who had terrorized her in her late teens and early twenties. Since she often opted for staying home, Hermann turned to Eva for companionship as soon as she was old enough to walk. The slim, dapper, obviously European professor and his beautiful jet-haired little girl became regulars at the Metropolitan Museum and at the Museum of Modern Art. Eva could still see them—she in a bright red empire-line coat with a matching tam, white kid gloves, frilly socks, and black patent Mary Janes; he in a dark suit with his gold fob watch—when Hermann took her to see the "Nutcracker," her first ballet, at age five. They had ended the afternoon with hot chocolate at Rumpelmayer's, which became another of their regular hangouts.

As she grew into a serious, studious, but often rebellious teenager, she and her father became even closer. He was her buffer in arguments with Hilda, who found it hard to accept the breezy casualness of American youth, the Elvis craze, the rock albums, the freedom. But he was also her conduit to understanding her mother's fears, the sheltered background she came from, growing up in an aristocratic Jewish family that had occupied a place in Berlin society for generations.

Hermann was the upstart young professor of mathematics, with no "background" to speak of. The Heschels were not thrilled at their daughter's choice of husband. They were even less thrilled when he took their beloved Hilda away, leaving Germany for the U.S. just before the doors clanged shut. Her mother and father, Hermann told Eva gravely when she was old enough to understand, were the only survivors of two large families. The Rubins—parents, aunts, uncles, and cousins—were among the first Berlin Jews to be deported to the East, the Nazi euphemism for their efficient death camps. The Heschels were luckier, by the standards of a society gone crazy, where luck was measured by how many extra days, weeks, or months one was permitted to live. They had been sent to Theresienstadt, the Nazi "model camp," and had two relatively "good" years there, before being sent to Auschwitz to be gassed.

Eva remembered the Eichmann trial. Hilda left the room whenever the news on television turned to the man in the glass booth in Jerusalem. But Eva and her father had watched, mesmerized. Hermann had broken down only once, when a woman who had been his student in Berlin testified. She had survived Theresienstadt, and it was through her that the Rubins had learned the fate of Hilda's parents and sisters. Eva was in high school at the time and could not understand her fellow students' lack of interest in the Eichmann trial. But then, they were Jewish-Americans—with parents who were mostly second- or third-generation. She often wondered whether any of her classmates had mothers like hers who woke up crying some nights for relatives who had vanished and would never return.

Eva wondered how her mother would cope if Hermann died. For the first time, she forced herself to consider that possibility. Her own loss would be indescribable—but she had Sharon, her work, and maybe she still had Dan. Hilda Rubin's life had centered around her husband for more than thirty years. Eva realized with a shock that her mother was still a young woman, barely into her fifties. What would she do with the long years ahead if Hermann did not recover?

The captain's voice announcing their descent to La Guardia interrupted her thoughts and she hastily organized herself so that she could be one of the first to disembark. Within minutes after landing, she was in a limousine speeding toward the hospital. The expression on her mother's face as they embraced in the anteroom of the Intensive Care Unit told Eva that she had not come a moment too soon.

"You can go in only for five minutes at a time, once an hour," Hilda told her daughter in a shaky voice. "He slips in and out of consciousness. He's been asking for you."

A kindly nurse bent the rules and allowed Eva to go to her father's bedside right away. Eva was appalled at Hermann's appearance, the tubes attached to various parts of his body, the heart monitor beeping in the background. She pulled up a chair next to his bed and gently stroked her father's cheek. His eyes fluttered and he smiled weakly when he recognized her.

"*Ketzaleh*, you came…"

"Shhh, Daddy, don't talk, keep your strength."

Hermann closed his eyes and seemed to slide into sleep, but a trace of a smile still lingered.

Back in the anteroom, Eva ascertained that her mother had been there for hours, with no food or rest. She would not go home, not even for an hour, so Eva went down to the coffee shop and brought up two black coffees and some plastic-wrapped sandwiches, which neither of them ate. They were not allowed to see Hermann during the still night hours, but they maintained their vigil in the waiting room, napping lightly between snatches of conversation. Hilda was remarkably controlled, not wanting to deplete her daughter's reserves of strength, reconciling herself to the possibility that this could be the end. At 7 a.m. she was allowed in to his room briefly and found Hermann resting quietly, but looking no better than he had the night before.

Eva went in at 8. Hermann opened his eyes as soon as she sat down and gave her the same weak smile that had raised her hopes the night before.

"Am I dying, *ketzaleh*?" he asked.

"No, Daddy, you're going to be fine. You'll pull through," said Eva in a choked voice, her eyes swimming in tears.

"Don't cry, Eva. Don't cry...take care of my Hilda, she's not strong...kiss Sharon, my baby Sharon..." His breathing was becoming ragged and Eva stroked his hand.

"I will, Daddy. Don't talk. I love you."

Hermann smiled at her again. A wide, happy smile that lit up his whole face. He held her hand and squeezed it weakly, then closed his eyes. His breathing became inaudible and Eva was startled when she realized that the monitor was no longer beeping, and that the green dot on the screen had stopped its jumping movement and was traveling in a horizontal line, making a continuous, insistent noise, like a kitten crying.

"Doctor!" she screamed, her voice reverberating in the quiet room.

A resident was at Hermann's bedside in seconds and quickly assessed the situation. He pressed the intercom and called urgently, "Code Blue! ICU 16!"

Eva was shunted aside in the organized onslaught of doctors and nurses rushing to Hermann's bedside with an array of machines.

A nurse escorted her out and said gently, "We'll let you know how he is in a few moments. Give the doctors a chance to get his heart going again."

Eva nodded, unable to speak, and she and Hilda clung to each other, wordlessly, sustaining each other.

They knew by the way the doctor walked toward them that it was over.

"I'm so sorry, Mrs. Rubin. There was nothing we could do. He went into cardiac arrest. We tried everything."

Hilda crumpled into Eva's outstretched arms, huge sobs wracking her small frame. The doctor stood by, not intruding on their grief, but waiting to see if his services would be required.

Hilda slowly straightened herself up. "I want to see him," she said quietly. She stilled the protest rising to Eva's lips. "You stay here, Eva. I just want to say goodbye."

Eva nodded mutely, suddenly witness to an inner strength she had never known her mother had.

Hilda came out a few moments later and gently took Eva's hand. "We'll go home now," she said softly. "We have a lot to do."

Dan and Sharon arrived within hours of Eva's phone call. Hilda and Eva had bathed and changed after crying themselves out and were able to handle Sharon's grief with calm dignity, soothing her with the assurance that, yes, Papa Hermann was gone, but the wonderful memories she had of him would always be with her. She proved to be a godsend during the *Shiva*—the ritual week of mourning prescribed by Jewish law—following the small but dignified funeral. Eva was amazed at the number of people who came to pay their respects to her father's memory. Dozens of colleagues, some of them Holocaust survivors, students he had tutored without payment, neighbors, old friends.

Sharon won everyone's heart with her serious explanations. "My grandfather is dead, but he still lives here," she would say, pointing to her heart, with all the gravity a five-year-old could muster. She fussed over her mother and grandmother, helping

Dan take charge of the situation, making the transition easier for both women with her bright chatter and bubbling affection.

"Oma, I'll call you every Sunday," she promised gravely as they all embraced Hilda before departing for the airport, bringing a smile to her grandmother's still-puffy eyes.

Hilda had insisted that they leave when the *Shiva* was over, refusing both Eva's and Dan's exhortations to come and stay with them for a while.

"Hermann is dead, Eva, and I have to learn to live with it. The sooner I start, the better. I don't want to run away from my home, from my memories. He is more here, in this apartment, than any—where else, and I want to stay here for now. I'll visit you as soon as I can, when I'm whole again, when I can come as a visitor, not as a burden."

"You'd never be a burden, Mother," Eva said quietly, embracing the small, frail woman she had always considered weak, marveling at her inner resources, kicking herself mentally for having underestimated her mother for so many years.

"You know, she's a true aristocrat," Dan said later as they were circling the airport prior to landing. "I always knew she had breeding, but I never saw the steel backbone behind the correct manners and self-effacing personality. She'll be all right," he said, squeezing Eva's hand. "And so will you," he added, noting the sheen of tears that suddenly brightened Eva's eyes.

In later years, when Eva tried to recall the period after Hermann's death, she could only remember the feeling that there was a hole in her heart, or in whatever part of the anatomy it was that lay between her ribs and hurt constantly.

Outwardly, she functioned well. Her classes were popular and well-attended. She had a way of conveying her enthusiasm and love of the material she was teaching to even the most obtuse of her students. The house ran like clockwork, thanks to Mary; and Sharon had settled comfortably into her kindergarten class. Dan was busy and somewhat preoccupied, but Eva decided to let it be. She felt brittle and fragile, despite outward appearances to the contrary, and wanted no part of rocking the boat, for any reason. Neither Eva nor Dan ever referred to their conversation at Rossini's when Eva learned of her father's relapse, and Barbara

Wallace's name never came up again. If Dan was having an affair, Eva did not want to know about it. At this point in her life, she did not care. The effort it took to live each day at a time, to maintain a cheerful façade, to function as she felt she had to, took all her energies. She did not want to look for additional minefields.

She missed her father terribly. She had called home every Sunday since moving out to Minneapolis, but her father had called her at odd times during the week, whenever he felt like it, to talk about her studies and her social life, and later about Dan and Sharon. She realized how much she missed his friendship, his advice, his ability to listen to her dreams and goals and problems from an objective but caring vantage point. She missed his warmth and humor, and while she didn't wallow in grief, the emotion accompanied her constantly.

Sharon was the only one who seemed aware of her grief. Every once in a while, Eva would look up and meet her daughter's steady, level gaze, and Sharon would say, "You're thinking of Papa Hermann, I can tell. Was it a nice memory?" Eva would smile and hug her. At times she would share the memories—Sharon especially loved the stories about the outings with her father in New York when Eva was a little girl—and at other times, Eva would just smile and nod and change the subject.

TEN

Eva's favorite room in the house had always been the den, especially on cold nights marking the onset of winter, when she lit a fire and curled up in the armchair near the fireplace with a book or her thoughts. With Sharon tucked safely in bed, Mary in her room with her television set, and Dan out of town, Eva reveled in the cozy silence, punctuated only by the crackling of the blaze. She put her book aside, too abstracted to concentrate, letting her thoughts wander as she stared at the fire.

The front door chime startled her out of an aimless reverie. The mantle clock indicated that it was almost 10—too late for a neighbor to be dropping by. She hurried to the door, peering cautiously through one of the small beveled glass panes, then opened it to admit the young woman waiting patiently, her head bent forward.

"Barbara! What are you doing here? Is something wrong? Dan isn't here—he's in New York."

Eva heard the panic punctuating her voice. Something had happened to Dan. Why else would Barbara Wallace be here, on her doorstep?

"I'd like to talk to you, Mrs. Goodman. It's very important. May I come in?"

Eva nodded and led her silently to the den, directing the obviously distraught and troubled girl to the other armchair as she sat in her favorite one by the fire.

At a loss for words, Eva waited for Barbara to begin.

When she stayed silent, Eva said gently, "Is something wrong? You seem very upset…"

Barbara lifted her head defiantly, anger kindling in her eyes. "Yes, something is wrong. It's wrong of you to hold on to Daniel against his will. You should give him the divorce he wants, and not threaten him with turning his daughter against him. He has a right to rebuild his life with me, and you shouldn't try to stop him. You should let him go now, so he can marry me before our baby is born illegitimately…" She burst into anguished sobs, covering her tear-streaked face with her hands as Eva stared at her, stupefied.

So this is what it feels like when your world comes tumbling down around you, Eva thought numbly as Barbara's sobs slowly subsided. She dug a tissue out of the pocket of her robe and silently handed it to Barbara, got up, and poured two stiff cognacs, handing one to Barbara and taking a gulp from her own glass as she sat down.

This can't be happening, she thought. It's like one of Mary's soap operas. I don't know what to say or do. Barbara had wiped her eyes and blown her nose and Eva sat back, assessing her "competition." A tall, slim, leggy blonde. Young, not more than twenty-three or twenty-four. Homecoming Queen-pretty—big, blue eyes, now rimmed in pink from her tears, and a small, pert nose, a vulnerable-looking mouth, a soft Midwestern accent. Very all-American. And very different from me, Eva thought, won—dering what had attracted Dan to someone so different.

"I think we'd better get a few things straight, Barbara, and let's try to be civilized about it." Eva's voice was husky but controlled, her inner turmoil totally contained. "You see," she went on gently, "I don't really know what you're talking about. I've suspected that you and Dan have been having an affair for quite a while. I even heard rumors to that effect, but he's always denied it. He's never asked for a divorce—he's never even wanted to discuss the possibility that our marriage was in trouble. Does he know you're pregnant?" she asked, with sudden insight.

"No," Barbara said in a low voice. "I didn't want to tell him until it was too late to have an abortion. I want his baby, even if he doesn't marry me. I love him very much. I want to give him all the things you haven't given him. He's the center of my life. You have your career. I only have him."

Tears of pain stung Eva's eyes as she understood what Dan had found in Barbara that he hadn't found in her. She got up and stood in front of the fire, struggling with her emotions, and finally turned to face Barbara, her features composed, belying her inner turmoil.

"You can have him, Barbara," she said in flat tones. "He's not mine to give, but I would never stop him from leaving. He can have his divorce, and he can see Sharon whenever he wants—I wouldn't punish *her* by separating them. You might want to ask yourself why he's been leading you on—making me the villain of the piece by presenting me as the obstacle to your happiness. But that's your problem, isn't it? Having a baby to hook your man is the oldest trick in the book. I don't know if it will work for you. It might. Dan is crazy about children. Now if you don't mind, I'd really like you to leave. I'm sure you know where to reach Dan. You can tell him he's as free as he wants to be. Maybe even freer."

She could see that Barbara wanted to talk, that she was more shocked by Eva's frank revelations than Eva had been by hers, but Eva wanted no part of any further discussion. Dan has created a hell of a mess, she thought angrily, so let him get himself out of it any way he can. She showed Barbara to the door, double-locked it, and returned to the den. I could sit by the fire all night, she mused, doing a midnight vigil straight out of Henry James, but I won't. I'll think about it tomorrow, like Scarlett.

Mechanically, Eva went through the routine of checking the doors, turning out the lights and looking in on Sharon. She took two of the sleeping pills the doctor had given her while they were sitting *Shiva* for her father and got into bed, staying as close to her own side as possible. She lay back, waiting for the pills to take effect, forcing herself not to think. She could feel her eyes closing as her body relaxed, seeing Dan's face in front of her, the way he'd looked the first time they met.

I should have listened to my instincts then, she thought, as sleep overtook her. Anyone that good-looking can't be nice... what a bastard he's turned out to be!

ELEVEN

"So, as we can see, both from *Emma* and from *Pride and Prejudice*, falling in love and getting your man is, in Jane Austen's terms, a learning process as well as an emotional experience. It's only when Elizabeth and Emma learn to recognize and understand their own shortcomings that they can have a meaningful relationship with the men they come to love."

Eva brushed away a lock of hair from her eyes, looking up from her notes and over the heads of the undergraduates in her 19th-century English Lit. class, just in time to see Dan walk in and take a seat at the back of the room. She looked down, shuffling her notes, dreading the confrontation that was coming. He had never come to one of her classes before, and she was so glad he hadn't come in earlier. The day had been difficult enough with a full load of classes, a faculty meeting, and consultations with individual students. The sleeping pills afforded an escape at night and enforced activity during the day helped her maintain a calm façade, but she knew that this moment had to come and supposed that the sooner it was over with, the better.

She gave the students their reading assignment for the following week, reminding them that an essay was due in two weeks, dismissed them five minutes early, and then sat down to gather her books and papers as the room slowly emptied.

When she looked up again, only Dan was in the room, still sitting in the last row. He's been home and changed clothes, she thought, noting his corduroy slacks and sheepskin jacket. I wonder if he's packed his bags. He was looking at her steadily and she met his eyes with a level gaze, remaining seated at her desk.

He approached tentatively and said in a tight, controlled voice, "I think we should go somewhere quiet to talk."

Eva gestured toward the first row of seats. "It's quiet here," she said evenly. "We won't be disturbed. Classes are over for today."

Dan sat down in the nearest seat with a stricken expression. "I owe you some explanations, I know, and some apologies, too, if that would do any good."

"You owe me nothing, Dan," Eva said coldly, the anger smoldering in her eyes a contrast to her calm tones. "You're a heel and a cad. You've been stringing along a fairly naïve and sentimental girl who has now pulled a fast one on you, and you've taken flagrant advantage of my own stupid tendency to stick my head in the sand when I didn't like what I was seeing."

Dan lowered his eyes, chewing on his thumbnail as he always did when he was worried or distraught.

"What are you going to do?" Eva asked in gentler tones, feeling her voice thicken with unshed tears.

"I don't know, Eva. I was going to ask you the same question. Do you want me to leave?"

Eva got up abruptly, pacing up and down, her hands shoved into the pockets of her blazer.

"Do I want you to leave?!" she echoed in amazement. "Do you have a choice? Does it make any difference what I want? You're having a baby, Daniel Goodman—what are you going to do about *that*?" She turned away from him, facing the blackboard, her eyes swimming.

He got up and put his hands on her shoulders, turning her around to face him, and looked down at her with anguish.

"You're the one I love, Eva. I've never realized that more clearly than I do now. Barbara was a fling—oh, I know it went on for a long time." Seeing her cynical expression, he continued hastily, "But only because I really didn't know how to extricate myself without causing a lot of pain. She worships the ground I walk on, and that did a lot for my ego. I know how immature that sounds, but you've always been so self-sufficient and self-contained, a success in your own right. 'Mrs. Goodman' wasn't enough for you; you needed it to be *Dr.* Goodman. I'm not knocking that, Eva," he added quickly as she bridled and took a step backward, "but it made Barbara's self-effacement and total, well, servility, almost, that much more attractive. Please try to understand."

"Oh, I understand, Dan. I understand all too well," Eva replied bitterly. "But all the understanding doesn't alter the facts. She's pregnant, and I gather she isn't about to have an abortion. Not that I blame her. How do *you* propose to handle the situation? Maybe she should move in with us and we can all be one big happy family—one daddy, two mummies, and two children! How are you going to explain that scenario to Sharon, let alone to the rest of the world?"

"I'm not suggesting anything like that, Eva. I may be a heel and a cad, but I'm not a total louse. It's my child and I'll support it, and Barbara if necessary, but I don't want to lose you and Sharon. I don't want to leave. What I'm trying to ask is, don't throw me out, though God knows I deserve that. I want to stay and make it up to you somehow, if I can. The affair with Barbara is over—I decided that before all this exploded, and that decision won't change. I can't dump her now, and I can't and won't dump the child. I just don't want you to dump me. I want you to love me, though that can't be too easy right now. I want to come home."

"It won't work, Dan," Eva said definitively, taking a deep breath to steady her voice. "It was hard enough to suspect I was sharing you with someone else. To know the truth is harder." He started to protest, but she stopped him, putting her hand to his lips. "Don't tell me I won't be sharing. There's nothing more intimate than having a baby with someone. You may not love Barbara, but when you feel that baby move, she won't be Barbara, or Eva, or anyone in particular. She'll be the person carrying *your* baby inside her, and I know how much that will mean to you. And after the baby is born," she continued, painting a word picture that he could envision only too vividly, "you'll share all the wonders of the first smile and the first tooth and the first steps and the first words. Are you prepared to cut yourself off from that? Am I prepared to ask that you do? No, Dan. But this situation is irrevocable. We can't go back to being Dan and Eva and Sharon anymore. There are two more people in the equation now."

"What will we tell Sharon?" Dan asked, wordlessly acknowledging her position.

Eva sighed. "The same thing one always tells a child when parents split up. Mummy and Daddy weren't happy together, etc., etc."

"But we were, Eva. We were very happy together," he said softly, stroking her hair, marveling anew at its thick smoothness.

"Wrong, Dan," Eva replied, moving out of his reach. "We haven't been happy for a long time. I've never been what you wanted. I'm not servile and self-effacing. I wouldn't know how to be even if I wanted to. I'm not good for your ego—and, you know what, you're not good for mine, either," she added with sudden insight. "I've always had to downplay my own achievements and accomplishments, when what I wanted to do was bring them home to you like trophies. But I knew my professional successes wouldn't make you proud, they would just make you unhappy.

"So you go your own way, Dan, and I'll go mine. Let's be civilized about it. I don't want fights and recriminations any more than you do. Just tell me when you're coming to pick up your things. I don't want Sharon to be there when you do that. We can talk to her together, if you like, but not today."

Eva quietly gathered up her things and walked out of the classroom and into the deserted hallway. She stopped at the door and stared at Dan, slumped in a seat that was much too small for his large, athletic frame. He looked up at her pleadingly, but she shook her head slowly, tears welling up despite her desire to control her emotions...and she walked away.

TWELVE

The next few weeks, with all their bustle and huge changes, threw Eva into an emotional whirlwind. Sharon was devastated to learn that her dad was moving out. Even though he'd been away a lot, there were still the morning snuggles and the goodnight kisses when he was home. She obviously wasn't buying the "Mummy and Daddy weren't happy" angle as the reason for Dan's departure, but she didn't probe and Eva was relieved. She would not have known how to explain the very complex situation they found themselves in to a five-and-a-half-year-old child. Eva wasn't sure she could even explain it to herself, so she forced her mind to deal with other subjects in the wee hours of the night when sleep was so elusive.

Dan surprised her by moving into a small, furnished apartment in an unpretentious building. She had expected that he would move in with Barbara, at least until the baby was born.

"I meant what I said, Eva," Dan explained when he brought Sharon home one cold Sunday after they spent the day together. "It's over with Barbara and me; in fact, it was never much to begin with. The only tie between us now is the baby."

"That's a pretty big 'only,' Dan," Eva said, a tinge of sarcasm in her voice. She was tempted to ask how Barbara felt about the new arrangement, and actually found herself feeling sorry for the girl, especially after catching a glimpse of her in a crowded department store one Saturday. Barbara looked haggard and tired; the freshness that had been such a hallmark of her good looks seemed to have disappeared.

Although she felt that Dan was being unfair and cruel, she knew him well enough not to be too surprised by his reaction.

He'd been duped, taken in by one of the oldest stratagems used by calculating women, and he wasn't the type to buy the ruse. The very fact that anyone would even try to hoodwink him was enough to arouse his anger and enmity. That was how he dealt with people, in business and in life. Had Barbara been more astute, she would have understood that the same quality that made Dan's handshake a binding promise would forever jeopardize his esti-mation of anyone who didn't "play by the rules." She had gambled and lost, lost Dan at any rate. She would still have her baby, but Eva doubted whether that would help Barbara in getting Dan back. What a mess, Eva thought. One marriage and one affair in ruins, two wounded women, and two children who would probably bear the brunt of the pain and loss.

She wondered where Dan came out in this painful equation. She saw him often since he spent as much time as he could with Sharon—more time than when he lived at home—and they usually exchanged a few words when he picked up Sharon or brought her home. Dan was tentative with her, and she was polite but distant with him. Sharon had enough to deal with without witnessing her mother's raw emotions. Eva tried to ignore her own anger and pain by keeping frenetically busy, resulting in a state of numbness that was somehow easier to deal with. She began to work in earnest on turning her doctoral thesis into a book, and found that by immersing herself in the problems and condition of women in the 19th century, she could largely ignore her own.

Nights, however, were bad. A few hours of heavy sleep triggered by sheer physical exhaustion, followed by hours of sleeplessness and the introspection that was so natural to her but that she fought hard to stave off. Eva always had a strong sense of physical and intellectual self-worth. An attractive, bright, and basically giving person, she had always been surrounded by people who either loved, liked, or at the very least respected her. Dan's betrayal cut much deeper than mere sexual infidelity; she now questioned and doubted the very things she liked most about herself—her ambition, competitiveness, and intellectual curiosity; her ability to give of herself emotionally; to be supportive; to love. She could not accept the facile explanation that the root cause of their problem lay in his emotional immaturity. That's a cop-out, she thought. There has to be more to it than that. There has to be a side to all of this that I caused.

She found that as long as she herself had not found the answers to these questions, she was unable to share the problem with anyone else. Very few people seemed aware of the fact that Dan was not living at home. Eva never spoke of it, and those who did know found no opening for discussion with her. One or two close colleagues had approached her with a sincere, "I heard about you and Dan, Eva. I'm sorry. If there's anything I can do to help..." But these approaches were shunted aside with a firm but unmistakable "Thank you," and a change of subject on Eva's part.

She did not want help, did not really know how to handle people's well-meaning offers of assistance, and dreaded being pitied. It's excessive pride, an inability to publicly concede failure, she admitted to herself; but knowing all that still did not pave the way to simply putting her head on someone's shoulder and crying out her grief. Had her father been alive, he would have forced her to do just that, to let out some of the pent-up emotions, to give in to simple human pain—the pain of rejection and humiliation, the sense of having lost something precious and irretrievable. On her own, she simply could not cross that barrier of pride, could not permit herself to break down, even in the privacy of her bedroom and in the loneliness of the night.

Eva was in her office at the university, marking final term papers, raising her eyes occasionally to gaze at the still-bare trees outside her window, reveling in the sunshine that finally exuded warmth as well as light. It had been a long, hard Minnesota winter and the weather had matched her emotional state. One level of her soul could not help but respond to the miracle of budding crocuses and melting snow banks that marked the first hesitant inroads of spring, but the rest of her feelings still seemed locked in the deep freeze she had imposed upon them.

Outwardly, she was fine, her life ticking along in an orderly, organized fashion. Her book was completed and had been accepted for publication by Harvard University Press—no mean feat for a young scholar. She'd been offered a post-doctoral year at Harvard but had turned it down, pleading family obligations. She and Sharon had settled into a different kind of daily routine, one Eva found comfortable, though she suspected that Sharon would have preferred the old life better, not realizing that the old life would not, could not, ever come back.

She was unprepared for Dan's sudden appearance in her office. He'd been hurt when Eva returned his birthday gift unopened. It was a small, flat, elongated box, no doubt containing an exquisite something that he hoped would help make amends, but Eva wanted no part of it. She knew that he had also bought the soft angora sweater "from Sharon," but that she could not return it without hurting Sharon's feelings. So she made a point of wearing the sweater only on days when she was sure not to see Dan. Today was one such day.

Sharon was at her grandmother's and Eva was going straight from the university to dinner with a few colleagues who had insisted on celebrating the publication of her book. Dan had entered her office quietly and she sensed, rather than heard, his presence. She looked up but continued to sit rooted at her desk, demonstrating none of the cordiality she tried so hard to show when Sharon was around. This office was her turf, and she resented his intrusion.

"Can I buy you a coffee, Eva?" Dan asked. "I have to talk to you, and you probably don't want me in your office."

She nodded curtly, piled the papers neatly at the corner of her desk, and put on her coat.

"I hope you don't mind the staff cafeteria. It shouldn't be crowded now, and I have to be back here in an hour."

"No, that's fine," Dan said, strangely abstracted. Eva's curiosity was aroused, despite herself. Barbara must be due to give birth any day now, she thought. Maybe he's had a change of heart and wants to marry her. Maybe now he wants a divorce.

"The baby died," Dan suddenly blurted out, the minute they were seated in front of their steaming Styrofoam cups of coffee "Barbara went into labor early, but that wasn't the reason. I was there with her. All kinds of things were wrong internally—organs and lungs that hadn't developed properly. It was a little girl. She lived three hours. The doctors assured me there was nothing any—one could have done."

He was crying quietly, but openly. Eva sat in shock, surprised by the intense grief that washed over her.

"I'm so sorry, Dan," she said softly, impulsively taking his hand and squeezing it. "How is Barbara taking it?"

"She was totally hysterical when they told her. She really wanted the baby, whether or not I was part of the deal. They sedated her heavily and she'll be out for hours, but it'll be very hard when she wakes up. I don't know what to do. I've created such a mess and caused so much unnecessary unhappiness just to boost my stupid male ego."

He ran both hands through his thick blond hair in a gesture of despair.

"The baby's death wasn't your fault, Dan. Oh, God, I feel for you—and for Barbara. I can't imagine the pain. I'm sorry, Dan. Really sorry." Eva's voice broke and they both sat silently, staring at the untouched coffee, not knowing what more to say.

"I'd better get back to the hospital," Dan said gloomily. "I should be there when she wakes up."

He shoved back his chair abruptly. "Thanks for listening, Eva. I appreciate your reaction. Another woman would be chortling at the ultimate revenge, but you're not like that. You're very special. I'm only sorry it took me so long to recognize it. Kiss Sharon for me. I'll come and see her in a few days, when things settle down a bit."

Eva nodded mutely, too affected by his words to even attempt a reply. She watched him leave the cafeteria, head bowed, shoul—ders stooped; the full weight of real grief was touching him for the first time, as he realized the enormity of everything he had lost.

She sat there for a few minutes, then got up quickly and made two phone calls to cancel her plans for the evening. She wanted to pick up Sharon and take her home, just so she could be with her, and to thank her lucky stars that, no matter what else might happen, her little girl was healthy and bright—and alive.

THIRTEEN

Eva saw very little of Dan in the next few months. He rarely came in when he picked up Sharon or when he brought her home, but Sharon reported, "Daddy was very sad for a while, but he's better now." Eva knew from her mother-in-law that "that woman" had left Minneapolis and gone home to her family. Probably to pick up the pieces and rebuild her life, Eva thought with compassion. But in Millie Goodman's book, Barbara was the scarlet woman who led her son into temptation and ruined his life. She did not blame Eva for what happened, although she felt that Eva should have fought harder to keep her man, but she certainly would not lay any blame on her golden boy, either. Her Daniel was merely a victim of circumstances, not a protagonist.

Eva smiled patiently and said little when these outbursts arose, which mercifully was not often, as Sharon usually was there when Eva and Millie were together. However, Eva jumped at the opportunity to get away when her publisher called, inviting her to Boston to launch her book. She took Sharon with her so they could extend the trip and make it a real vacation, and then called her mother, who was delighted to come and stay with them in Boston, and then drive up to Maine to open up the small cottage that Hermann had bought when Eva was a child. The cottage, which had been the Rubins' haven from sweltering Augusts in New York, hadn't been used in years, but was clean, well-maintained, and in move-in condition, the caretaker assured them over the phone.

Leaving Sharon on the beach with her grandmother, Eva took long, brisk walks at the edge of the water and began to feel human again for the first time in a year. They swam very little—the water

71

was icy even on the hottest days—but the sun and sea air were therapeutic. It had been a year of trauma, pain, and loss for each of the three, so the total relaxation and lack of responsibility that the place and the time almost forced upon them was welcome. On the drive back to Boston to catch their respective flights home, they sang and told jokes, and giggled like three schoolgirls. Eva and Sharon hugged and kissed Hilda after escorting her to her gate, then went on to board their own flight, an eye-catching study in contrasts: Sharon's sun-bleached hair resting against her mother's tanned bare arm as the little girl snuggled down in her seat after takeoff.

"What a fun holiday we had, Mummy," she murmured as the hum of the engines lulled her to sleep. "If only Daddy had been there too…"

It took another six months before Eva agreed, with great trepidation, to try a reconciliation with Dan. She could ignore the pressure from her mother and mother-in-law, but Dan's persistent yet careful wooing was harder to withstand, as was her loneliness. It was Sharon's deep need for her father, though, which really got to her in the end.

Sharon's comment on the plane had forced Eva to admit to herself that the child was deeply disturbed by her parents' separation. As happy as she was with each parent individually, and as cordial and friendly as they were toward each other in her presence, what Sharon really wanted was a home with a Mummy and a Daddy in their properly ordered places. She longed for breakfasts and dinners around a family table, with holidays and birthdays observed in the kind of togetherness that two separate ménages simply could not provide.

Sharon connived and manipulated shamelessly, with determination and planning that belied her six years. She would invite Dan to "come in for a drink with Mummy" when he brought her home and then insisted that he stay until she went to bed "so you can tuck me in and kiss my teddy and me goodnight." Eva tried to circumvent her daughter's maneuvers, only to find herself outsmarted. It was funny, but it also broke her heart, especially since Sharon never complained or verbalized her needs; she simply persisted in her matchmaking efforts with her parents.

Sharon had an avid ally in Dan, who made no bones about where he wanted to be. Sitting with Eva in the living room one Sunday evening after a day of skiing with Sharon, Dan suddenly stopped describing the day's events and started pacing about the room, scrutinizing every painting and every piece of furniture. Eva felt uncomfortable and guilty. She knew he was still living in the same furnished apartment—"nothing great," according to Sharon—while she lived in a comfortable, cozy home.

"Dan, if there's anything you want to take out of the house, please tell me," Eva said in embarrassed tones. "I don't need all this stuff—I hardly use this room anyway."

He stopped pacing and gave her a long, hard look. "I don't want to take anything out," he finally said softly, "I want to put something back in. Me! Don't you think it's been long enough— that I've learned my lesson, that it's time you forgave me?"

"It's not a matter of forgiving you, Dan. I forgive you. I think I forgave you a long time ago. But I've made a life for myself, by myself. It's very calm and even-keeled. There's no pressure to be what I'm not, or to conform to someone's image of what I ought to be. I don't feel guilty doing my own thing now. I don't feel inadequate anymore..." She stopped and covered her face with her hands, not prepared to let him see what dredging up all the old hurts did to her.

He gently pried her hands away from her face and sat next to her on the sofa. "But don't you understand that I'm not like that anymore? Don't you think I've learned something from all that's happened? I don't want the Eva who never existed, who I tried to make you into because I was an ass and a fool. I want *you*—you the way you are—Dr. Eva Goodman—wonderful person—not *Mrs.* Daniel Goodman—plastic adjunct. You were never inadequate—I was measuring you with a cockeyed ruler and by absurd, archaic standards. *I* was inadequate. But I've learned! Eva, I promise you—I've learned. Give me a chance to show you I've changed. I'll make you fall in love with me again. You used to love me—and I'm a better person than I was before. Really, I am. Let me show you. Just give me a chance!"

"And if it doesn't work?" Eva asked warily.

"It will work, I promise you; and if it doesn't, I'll do whatever you want. I'll leave the minute you ask me to."

"I'm not ready, Dan. I'm scared. I don't want you to make love to me. I'm afraid to share my life with you."

"I won't push. We'll do things at your speed. Pretend you're single and let me take you to the movies. We can hold hands and stop at that if you want. Let me court you. I won't move in until you're comfortable with the idea—or, better still, until you really want me to."

Eva looked dubious, but nodded yes.

"All right, we'll try it for a while and see where it takes us. But the door isn't open yet. You've only got a foot inside."

"That's all I want! I'll do the rest. Never fear."

They did it her way—a slow, almost tentative courtship at first. Movie evenings, followed by leisurely, informal meals out, followed by a nightcap at home in front of a crackling fire before Dan left to return to his apartment. Some of their outings included Sharon. Eva was heartbroken to see the eagerness and excitement with which the child latched on to these opportunities for family togetherness. She felt guilt-ridden at depriving Sharon of the closeness to both parents that their daughter so obviously craved.

It's ironic, she thought to herself as the three of them wandered through the museum one Saturday afternoon, how I'm the one who is turning out to be the "bad guy," how I've become the obstacle to our being a family. Both Dan and Sharon were careful not to press her, but she resented the kid gloves with which they handled her. She questioned her own motives, wondering whether the beating her ego had taken throughout the "Barbara episode" was still governing her actions now, whether pride had not become too big a factor in the scenario. Eva and Sharon were sitting in the cozy little breakfast nook off the kitchen on a sunny Sunday morning when Sharon looked at Dan's empty chair and, with a woebegone expression, said softly, "I wish Daddy was here and we could be a family again. Why won't you let him come home, Mummy? He's so lonely, and I miss him so much!"

Tears stung Eva's eyes and she felt her throat closing up. She weighed the pros and cons in her mind for the thousandth time, then dismissed them abruptly as she rose from the table and said huskily, "He can come home if he'd like to, Sharon. I don't want either of you to be unhappy anymore. Not because of me."

Sharon let out a whoop of joy and ran into the kitchen to call Dan. Eva poured herself another cup of coffee and couldn't help smiling as she heard Sharon's part of the conversation.

…"Daddy, Daddy! Mummy said you could come back if you want. Come right away and bring all your clothes!"

…"Yes, she's right here, I'll get her." Sharon walked into the breakfast nook carrying the phone in one hand, its long extension cord trailing behind her, and handed the receiver to Eva with her other hand, a look of triumph in her eyes.

"Daddy wants to ask you if you really mean it. Tell him you do!" There was a beseeching look on her face and Eva gave her a reassuring smile as she took the receiver.

"Hi, Dan," she said hesitantly.

"Eva, do you mean it, or is this a figment of Sharon's active imagination?" Dan asked tensely.

Eva smiled. So Dan was also aware of Sharon's tremendous need to have them together again.

"No, I mean it, Dan. You both want you to move back in, and I don't know what I want, to be perfectly frank. But this is be–coming a ridiculous situation, and I don't want to be the bad guy anymore. Come home, Dan. We'll make it work."

The whoop on the other side of the wire matched Sharon's in enthusiasm and outdid it in volume.

"I'm coming right over! Don't move! Don't do anything! Bye!" He hung up and Eva could imagine him grabbing his keys and making a dash for the car.

She had barely managed to refill the percolator when Dan's car roared into the driveway and Sharon went running out to greet him. She watched the two of them through the window, Dan scooping up Sharon and carrying her, his hair tousled, wearing faded jeans and an old fisherman knit pullover, still looking like a college quarterback as he loped toward the house.

He'd put Sharon down in another room, since he walked into the kitchen alone. Dan paused for a minute, looked at Eva, then crossed the kitchen in three long strides, enveloping her in his arms and hugging her tightly, neither of them saying a word. She'd almost forgotten how tall he was, and she felt tiny and fragile in his arms—and more scared and leery than she'd ever felt before. Sensing her mood, Dan gently tilted up her face with one hand, stroking and smoothing her long hair back with the other hand.

"Don't worry, pussycat. It will be good. I promise you it will be." He kissed her forehead gently, then her mouth with increasing passion and hunger. She found herself responding, the loneliness and suppressed needs of the past months overwhelming her, washing away the fears and doubts, at least for now. She held Dan's face with both hands, kissing him back with a fervor that surprised her, hoping she'd found her place again, this time for good.

FOURTEEN

Eva often wondered where the next three years went. The family routine had been re-established quickly and fairly easily. Dan *had* changed. He was solicitous and caring in a way he'd never been before, spending every free minute at home. He brought work home when he was overloaded rather than staying at the office, and shared plans, dreams, and the occasional setback in a manner that was new to him and fascinating to Eva. To the surprise of both of them, she made some business suggestions that worked well for him. Always possessed of a good eye for color and shape, she came up with some new design ideas for jewelry that proved highly marketable. Dan kidded that she ought to give up her academic career and join him in the business.

That suggestion remained a lighthearted joke, for Eva was making a name for herself in her field—this time, with Dan's encouragement and help. The book she'd published on women in the 19th century became a minor best seller, then a major best seller when it was reprinted in a paperback edition. Women's Studies, as interdisciplinary courses, were becoming popular at many universities, and Eva often was invited to lecture or serve on panels at conferences and symposia. She enjoyed her newfound fame, limited though it was to academic and women's circles. Also, she found she had a distinct flair for public speaking, which was simply an extension of standing in front of a classroom trying to capture the imagination and involvement of students—something she'd been doing well for years.

To Sharon, her parents' business and academic successes meant little. She reveled in having both of them together again, and if Mummy traveled more, Daddy was away less. They were rarely both away at the same time, but when that happened, she had Mary and her grandmother, both of whom spoiled her rotten. Sharon had now begun a campaign for a baby brother or sister, as if needing affirmation that all was well with her parents, and that enlarging the family would prove it.

Dan was ready. The trauma of the death of his second child—conceived with a woman he did not love, but his child none-theless—had affected him deeply. And he'd nearly lost Eva, too, realizing only when it was almost too late how much he loved her, how unthinkably empty life without her would have been.

They never talked about Barbara and the baby, although he sometimes felt that they should, if only to clear the air of a palpable presence that never really went away. But Eva never broached the subject even obliquely, by a crack or a comment. She never asked for details, as other women might have done, as Barbara had done consistently when he was having his ill-fated affair with her. It was as if Eva had chosen to erase that painful year from her life, to bury it and pretend it had never happened. He tried to apologize on more than one occasion, to reiterate his love for her by stressing that Barbara had meant nothing to him beyond a foolish escapade. He'd learned not to, sensing the distress he was causing Eva when he simply brought up the topic.

But Dan was troubled by a nagging awareness that the matter still had not been cleared up between them, and by the distressing possibility that it never could be. Eva had built a wall around that part of her emotions and he despaired of ever scaling that wall, or ever knocking it down. Things were good between them now and he was leery of rocking the boat, but he knew things were not as good as they should be, or could be, and in moments of introspection, he grieved for the loss of something intangible and indefinable between them, something that had been there, but would likely never return.

Eva knew what that something was, but she could not share the reason with anyone. She no longer loved Dan. It was that simple. She *had* loved him. His rejection of her would not have been that painful if she hadn't, but somewhere along the way, that love had died. And it wasn't only because of Barbara. That had been the final blow; but it started earlier, when Dan refused to accept Eva the way she was, when he tried to cast her into a '50s mold of wife, mother, and housewife, a stereotype that she could never adapt to.

She still cared about him deeply; he was still her closest friend, she rejoiced in his happiness and was saddened and concerned by anything that troubled him. But love, love in the deep, gut-wrenching sense, the love that two people who are soul-mates share—that had disappeared. Maybe it had never been given a chance to grow; or maybe her pride, her overly strong sense of self, had killed it. She didn't know, and would not allow herself to dwell on the reasons. That didn't matter. Their life together was good. Sharon and Dan were the central characters in her life, and she and Sharon were the center of his. They both loved their work. The proverbial "money and in-laws" were no problem. Sharon was happy. They were a family again. Leave the drama and the passion to the Heathcliffs and the Catherines, Eva thought. That isn't for real people like us; that only happens in novels.

Deep down, she yearned for the romantic, all-encompassing love she knew she'd never have with Dan. But rather than confront her need and seek fulfillment, Eva smiled pensively at what she called her "foolish notions," and firmly closed the door to that possibility, focusing instead on the calm, well-ordered pattern of her life.

FIFTEEN

"You can let go of the armrests now," said a laughing voice in the seat next to her. "You can even open your eyes. I think the pilot has things under control and no longer needs your help in keeping the plane up in the air."

Eva opened her eyes and slowly unclenched her white-knuckled hands from the armrests, forcing herself to relax. She was returning from Chicago on the early-morning flight in order to be on time for her first class of the day. She had just participated in a three-day seminar at the University of Chicago and, although that kind of city-hopping had become a fixture in her life, she remained a nervous flyer who was especially terrified of takeoffs. Landings were somehow more natural—people returning to the element in which they belonged—although she closed her eyes at those times, too.

Eva glanced at her traveling companion, whom she'd been too preoccupied to notice before. The face looking at her with an amused grin was a friendly one. Nice features: twinkling brown eyes, soft, curly brown hair graying at the temples and lightly sprinkled with gray throughout, deep smile lines at the corner of the eyes, a straight, strong nose. Early forties, she thought. Some kind of professional or businessman, she figured, noting the well-cut suit and subdued silk tie. She smiled back tentatively.

"Can I get you a drink, or coffee, or something? You seem very nervous," he asked solicitously.

Nice voice, low-pitched, West Coast accent with a hint of something different that she couldn't identify.

"No, thank you, I'm fine. It's just takeoffs that get to me. And landings, a bit. And I'm not too crazy about the part in the middle, either," she added with a self-deprecating smile.

"Do you fly often? It must be rough on you if you do." There was nothing prying or overly familiar about his question, just the amiable chit-chat one encounters during air travel, and Eva answered readily, glad of the distraction from the engine noise.

"I try to minimize it," she answered, "but I seem to be spending more and more time on airplanes these days, and I still can't say I'm getting to love it."

"Let me guess," he said, taking in her sleek chignon, slim figure, stylish suit and silk blouse, and the few unostentatious but obviously good pieces of jewelry she was wearing, "you're a manager of a classy department store, going back after a buying trip in the big city."

She laughed. "You're about 180 degrees off the mark," she said. "I teach English at the University of Minnesota, specializing in the 19th century." She glanced down at her clothes and grinned. "I guess I should be wearing a high-collared lace blouse with a cameo and high-buttoned shoes."

He glanced down at her legs, neatly shod in soft black high-heeled boots, and added hastily, "No, no. You look great just the way you are. It's just a game I play, trying to guess what people do by the way they look. I'm usually wrong, but it's a great way to kill time when you do a lot of traveling. I don't know if you've ever noticed, but there are all kinds of interesting types of people flying around this country."

"Now let me play your game," Eva said with a twinkle in her eye, "and let's see if I can guess what you do!"

She gave him a measured look, deciding he was very attractive in a non-movie-star kind of way. "You obviously travel a lot, but you don't look like a salesman. Too well-dressed. And doctors and dentists don't travel that much. You're either a lawyer with a far-flung practice or a business tycoon who travels around making deals all over the country," she said firmly.

It was his turn to laugh. He has a sexy laugh, too, she noted.

"You're a worse guesser than I am! No, I'm a figure-outer and trouble-shooter for a large computer company. With computers starting to make a real impact on businesses, even smaller ones, we have customers all over the place. I usually set up the systems for them when they decide to computerize, then supervise the staff training and check things out whenever anything goes really wrong. Kind of a far cry from English literature!"

"Oh, but at least you're not a dentist…what a disappointment that would have been."

They both laughed, realizing at the same time how comfortable and easy their banter had been, wondering where it would go from here, and pausing awkwardly for a moment. He broke the ice by extending his right hand.

"I'm Robert Miller, by the way, Rob to my friends. Now that we know what we are, we should exchange names!"

"Eva Goodman," she said, shaking his hand gravely.

"Oh, my God, you're the lady who wrote the book! I've actually read it. I didn't realize I was sitting next to a world-famous author."

"You're not," Eva replied, laughing at the expression on his face, "and I'm surprised you read my book—not too many men do, unless they're in that field."

"Well, to be honest, there was a big discussion at our house on feminism and women's roles and so on, and a friend of my wife's was carrying on and on about how the roots of the feminist movement go back to the early 19th century. She quoted your book a few times, in very supercilious tones, so I started reading it just to be able to talk back to her, and then found it really interesting."

So he's married, Eva thought, her disappointment at that revelation outweighing her delight that he'd liked her book. Probably has four kids and adores his wife, who is stunning and bright and a superb tennis player.

Rob noted the change in her expression and asked with concern, "Have I said something wrong? I really did like the book. I'm not just being polite."

"No, no," Eva said hastily. "I was just continuing your little game and filling in the background of wife, home, and family." She surprised herself by describing the mental image of his marital and familial bliss.

His response was a bitter smile. "No," he said almost pensively, "I'm afraid you're wrong again. It isn't like that at all. I'll tell you about it someday."

Eva found herself warming to the implication that there would be a "someday," that this attractive stranger who had come into her life in such a haphazard manner would possibly not be exiting so quickly.

"What will you be doing in Minneapolis?" she asked, shifting the subject to a less sensitive area, but also eager to know.

"I'm going to be a regular in your town for the next year or so," he said, partially answering her unasked question. "We're setting up a system for Abcor," he added, naming one of the large companies in the city, "and I'll be spending two or three days a week there. They've rented an apartment for me in some fancy building and they're laying on a company car and all kinds of perks. The commute from San Francisco isn't too bad, so I'll be seeing a lot of the two airports this year. It'll give me unlimited opportunities to play my 'what you are' game," he concluded with a wry smile.

"Welcome to our town," she said in a light tone. "If you can take our winter, hats off to you."

"San Francisco winters are pretty dreary," he replied, taking the lead from her and keeping the tone casual.

The two very self-consciously chatted about nothing in particular until the seat belt light came on and the pilot announced their descent. Eva felt the familiar flutterings that always gripped her before landing, but realized that she was clutching her armrests again when Rob placed a warm, steady hand on hers and said calmly, "Don't worry. The pilot knows how to land this thing with his eyes closed, and the visibility is great. We'll be fine."

She smiled weakly, trying to be convinced, supremely conscious of the touch of his hand on hers. She wondered if the electricity she felt was in her imagination only, or whether he sensed it, too. If he did, there was no indication. His gesture was a friendly one with no apparent overtones or undercurrents, a simple reaching out to a fellow passenger in distress, much as one would reach out to comfort an anxious child.

Suddenly she wanted him to know that this was not her normal demeanor. That she was a strong, self-reliant person who coped well with most things, but had a minor but controlled phobia about flying. She forced herself to open her eyes and found him looking at her with amusement.

"I'm not always like this, you know," she said tartly. "I'm actually quite fearless about most things. Flying just doesn't happen to be one of them."

The warmth of his smile almost obliterated the scream of the jets as the plane thunked down smoothly and the pilot turned on the reverse thrust.

"I'm glad I'm seeing this side of you first," he said, giving her hand a friendly squeeze. "It would be very intimidating to see you as the totally put-together person you seem to be—a weakness here and there is very endearing."

"I'll make sure to dig up a few more of them," Eva said in a lightly bantering tone. The plane was now taxiing to the gate, and she knew that the tightness in her chest was not caused by any phobia, but by the proximity and warmth of this stranger next to her.

They parted at the baggage pick-up, he leaving to meet the Abcor rep who would be greeting him, she to grab a cab to the university.

"I'd like to see you again, Eva," he said seriously as they shook hands, not a hint of flirtatiousness in his voice. "Can I take you out to lunch one of these days?"

She nodded with equal seriousness. "I'd like that. Call me at the university. I'm in my office first thing in the morning and most afternoons." She thought of inviting him home to dinner with them, to meet Dan and Sharon, then quickly dismissed the thought, sensing that he would possibly be an aspect of her life that she would want to keep completely separate and apart from her family.

"Until we meet again, then," Rob said, looking at her intently, still holding on to her hand.

"I've got to run or I'll be late for my class," Eva said gently, releasing her hand. She returned his gaze for a brief moment, then turned quickly and left the terminal, not daring to look back.

SIXTEEN

Eva heard the phone ringing as she reached her office the next morning. She ran the last few yards, hastily unlocking the door, hoping the ringing wouldn't stop.

Her breathless "Hello?" was greeted by the warm, sexy laugh that had haunted her dreams last night.

"You didn't have to run. This is about the sixtieth ring, and I had no intention of hanging up until you got there and answered! You did say first thing in the morning, didn't you?"

She laughed back, not knowing whether to be relieved or scared that her fantasy of his calling her had come true.

"I plead guilty. I'm a little late. Sharon, my daughter, had an accident with some spilt milk and that held us up a bit."

It occurred to her that she had not mentioned a daughter, or a husband, either. The same thought seemed to cross his mind.

"Do you realize that I know nothing about you, except where you work and what that work is, and that I've spent the past twenty-four hours thinking about you? Do you have about three hours for lunch so we can exchange biographies? Please say yes!"

She smiled. "Yes, I'd like that, but I'm teaching till 1. Is that okay?"

"Anything you suggest would be okay. Where do I pick you up?"

Eva gave him directions and put down the phone, her heart pounding like a schoolgirl's. A schoolgirl with a crush, she thought wryly, chiding herself for embarking upon something she should have nipped in the bud, but fully intending to embark on it anyway.

Lunch turned into a four-hour marathon at which they exchanged the kind of details that people normally require years to learn about each other.

"You go first," he said after their food was served and the waiter had left them to their own resources, realizing that their booth would be occupied for quite some time. "Name, rank, and serial number, then everything else about you, starting from the day you were born. I'd like to know it all."

Eva smiled and plunged right in, wanting to get through the preliminaries as quickly as possible, to get to know this "stranger" with whom she felt more at home than with people she had known all her life. Her eyes brimmed with tears when she talked of her father Hermann, and Rob reached across the table to wipe her eyes with his white linen handkerchief, then took both her hands in his.

Eva paused and took a deep breath, wondering how to broach the "Barbara episode." She lowered her eyes and said quietly, "Dan and I were separated for a while about four years ago. We…had things to work out. Then we got together again. It seemed the right thing to do at the time, and maybe it was."

Rob raised one eyebrow and gave her a bemused look.

"That's a wealth of detail to cover, the last four years," he said. Then, noting her expression, he added hastily, "I'm sorry. I really don't have a right to pry."

"You aren't prying. It's just that it's a period in my life I find very hard to talk about. I've never discussed it with anybody. I try not to think about it myself—though I'm normally very big on interior monologues…I'll tell you about it another time."

She felt the color rising in her cheeks as she realized that her words were an almost direct statement of expectation that there would, indeed, be another time; but Rob had either missed it or chosen to ignore it for now. They were both silent for a moment.

"It's your turn now," she nudged, gently but playfully. "Don't think I'm letting you off the hook after such a comprehensive autobiography of me."

"I wouldn't dream of reneging," he smiled, matching her playful tone, "though I do confess to having a problem with where to begin."

When she looked puzzled, he said softly, "You see, my father was German. A Prussian, in fact. Miller used to be Mueller—that got to you, didn't it?" he added, noting her suddenly guarded look. "I thought it would. But it gets better, I promise. My mother was Jewish, from a wealthy and very assimilated Berlin family—your parents would have known them. When they got married in 1930, neither family was overly thrilled, but these things happened and nobody was disinherited. The problems started when I was a couple of years old, after Hitler came to power and started passing laws about marrying Jews. My mother wanted to leave Germany, but my father felt he couldn't—ties to his family and to the family business, and to Germany itself.

"He arranged for a quiet divorce and my mother and I left Germany for the States—we came to San Francisco because my mother had an uncle there. I grew up thinking I was an orphan—which I was by the time the war ended. What I didn't know until years later was that my father had stayed in Germany because he was working for British Intelligence while forging a very brilliant career in the German High Command. My mother knew, but she was bitter that my father had chosen that over her. She reluctantly conceded that he was a hero—I was even allowed to keep his picture in a silver frame in my room with the posthumous medal the British awarded him—but I don't think she ever forgave him."

"That explains the accent," Eva commented, trying to dispel pictures of the little fatherless boy his words had conjured up. "There was something indefinable, but familiar, in your speech—it's the barest inflection of German. Someone who's spoken German all their life would pick it up, but I didn't."

He nodded and continued talking about the growing-up years, which were as typically American as hers, with the same qualifications of an immigrant parent, the same burning ambition to excel in school that Jewish refugee parents passed on to their kids. He spoke of his interest in computers and cybernetics, of the good years at Harvard and M.I.T., of the work he was doing now, which he loved.

"Do I note a singular lack of personal detail in your narrative, or is it my imagination?" Eva asked drily.

He smiled sheepishly. "I plead guilty to evasion—but only because I don't really know how to present my situation." He took a deep breath and plunged right in.

"I'm married, have been for the last thirteen years, to a beautiful socialite from a good San Francisco family. Her greatest concerns are her bridge games and her hairdresser appointments." He looked sheepish. "I know it's the oldest line in the book to say 'my wife doesn't understand me'—but she doesn't. Doesn't give a hoot, in fact. The whole marriage is a façade and a charade."

"Then why stay in it?" Eva asked bluntly.

The pain in his eyes was all too apparent. "We have an eleven-year-old daughter who was brain-damaged at birth. She's a gorgeous, adorable child who will never grow beyond a mental age of six or seven. Rhoda barely acknowledges her existence unless other people are around—then she plays the role of a doting, caring, but stricken mother. It's quite an act. I've asked her for a divorce but she won't hear of it—that just isn't 'done' in her circle, and even if she were to agree, she would never let me have custody of Jeannie. That would spoil her image as a sacrificing mother. And I won't leave Jeannie to the care of a nanny, though she has a wonderful one. So here I am," he shrugged, with the resignation of a person who has considered all the options for getting out of a marriage and found all of them wanting.

He showed her a picture of Jeannie—an exquisite dark-haired child with enormous blue eyes and finely etched features, sitting on a little satin footstool in a frilly white lace dress. It was a picture of stillness and repose. One got the feeling that the photographer had not had to struggle with a fidgety child, but had simply told this little china doll how to sit and when to smile. The smile hovered around the lips, but didn't reach the eyes, which were strangely vacant.

Eva took a picture of Sharon out of her wallet—a shot she took that summer when Sharon and Dan had been playing touch football in the park. It showed a lithe, sturdy, *alive* little girl, cannoning down the park, screaming with excitement, long blonde mane flying behind her in disarray, pink sneakers and white denim overalls streaked with mud and grass stains.

Rob looked at both pictures, shaking his head. He handed Eva back her snapshot and said gruffly with a catch in his voice, "She's lovely. You don't know how lucky you are."

"But I do," Eva said softly, giving the photo one final glance before tucking it back into her wallet. "Sharon kept me going through a lot of rough patches. She's very special. I am where I am largely for her."

They were both silent for a moment, then Eva looked at her watch and reluctantly brought them back down to earth.

"It's past 5 o'clock, Rob. Don't you have a plane to catch?"

"I wish I didn't, but I do. Let me drive you back to your car. Will I see you again next week?"

Eva nodded. "I'd like that. You know where to reach me."

They drove in silence back to the campus, both at a loss for words, not feeling comfortable enough yet to give verbal expression to the electrical current crackling between them.

She directed him to the parking lot and he parked alongside her car, switched off the motor, and turned to her.

"Thank you for a very special afternoon, Eva. It's been a long time since I've enjoyed anyone's company so much."

"Me too," she said. "It was lovely." Then she grimaced and laughed.

"Listen to us! Two little old Victorian biddies thanking each other for a lovely tea! I like you, Rob. I'd like to get to know you better. I'd like to be your friend. Let's dispense with the inanities and be honest. I'll count the days until you're back."

He took her face in both his hands, started to say something, then changed his mind and kissed her gently on the lips, then on the eyes, then on the lips again, with mounting passion. She responded in kind, swept by a physical desire the likes of which she had never known, twining her fingers in his hair, caressing his ears as his mouth hungrily sought hers, tongue exploring, hands searching out her back, her neck, caressing her breasts, hugging him to her in an all-encompassing embrace.

They pulled away from each other reluctantly, shaken by the swell of emotion and desire that had risen so suddenly to the surface of their consciousness.

He looked into her eyes and touched her lips with his forefinger. "One day I'd like to make love to you," he said in a husky voice.

"'One day' sounds too far away," Eva retorted lightly, brushing his cheek with the back of her hand. "Let's make it sooner. I'll see you next week. Now go, or you'll miss your plane."

She hopped out of his car and into hers, quickly started the engine, and drove away, not looking back. She didn't need to look back, knowing somehow that whether she looked back or not, he would always be there for her.

SEVENTEEN

Rob called her every morning. The quiet hour between 8 a.m. and 9 a.m. that she had always devoted to going over her notes and preparing for classes was now devoted to him. They talked about everything except their spouses. Rob's trip to Minneapolis was delayed by a week, leaving them both frustrated yet somehow relieved. Neither quite knew what was going to happen. The only thing clear was their need to consummate the growing attraction between them, and give some sort of physical seal to the emotional tie that was deepening daily.

Rob called from the airport to tell her he had arrived and was heading for the executive apartment the company had rented for him. It would become his home for the two or three days a week he would be in Minneapolis.

"I don't know if there are any etchings, but I'm assuming there are," he said with a low chuckle. "Will you meet me there in an hour?"

"I certainly will," Eva answered, not bothering to conceal the happiness behind her usual façade of reticence. "I've cleared my day and I'm all yours." I think I really mean that, she thought to herself, rummaging through her papers, looking for something to keep herself busy for the next half-hour.

She found a parking spot near the apartment building and was knocking on his door in five minutes flat, her heart racing He opened the door immediately and took her in his arms with the hunger of a man who has finally found water after days and weeks of thirst. They stood near the door, kissing for countless minutes, until Eva finally broke away and said, laughing breathlessly, "Are you going to keep me here all day, or do I get to see the etchings?!"

He took her by the hand and led her wordlessly into the bedroom. He guided her to sit on the bed that had been turned down, putting a finger on her lips to keep her from saying any—thing as he began to unbutton her blouse. He undressed her slowly and methodically, placing each article of clothing neatly on a chair, caressing her, not saying a word, not letting her undress him. When she was totally naked he undid the knot of her hair, letting it cascade down her back before placing her gently on the sheets. He then quickly undressed, dropping his clothes on the floor with mounting urgency. He was fully erect and she could feel him throbbing against her as he lay down beside her.

"Eva," he whispered, his voice roughened by passion. "Before we make love, I want you to know something. I don't just like you. I've thought about you constantly. 'I like you' is ludicrous. It means nothing. I love you. I want you more than anything else in the world."

It was her turn to hush him by pressing her lips to his. "Don't talk now, make love to me. I want you."

Their lovemaking lasted for hours, in turn urgent and passionate and then slow and gentle, like the changing rhythms of a stormy, then quiet sea. Neither had ever experienced the emotional heights and depths that accompanied their physical desire for each other, or the fundamental peace of mind and total relaxation of body and spirit that lingered and stayed with them long after the ecstasy of physical pleasure was over. They talked little, not wanting to disrupt the non-verbal communication established through the touch of a hand, the smoothness of skin against skin, the soft moans of pleasure each evoked from the other.

"Aren't they expecting you at the office?" Eva asked much later. It was early afternoon and they had not left the bedroom.

"No, I told them I'd get in this afternoon and would be there tomorrow morning. We have the day to ourselves. I'm glad since I've been fantasizing about spending a day with you—and the reality beats the fantasy." He caressed her shoulder, then ran his finger lightly down her breast, pausing to caress her nipple, which was suddenly erect with renewed desire. They kissed again at length, until Eva pulled away with a slight laugh.

"Unhand me, sir! We can't keep on like this; we'll both end up in the hospital!"

"Umm…" he replied absently, pulling her toward him again, "but what a way to go! I want you even more."

"I want you, too, Rob. That's what scares me. I've never felt like this with anyone, and frankly I'm terrified. It's like stepping off a high cliff—and I'm scared of the landing."

"Don't worry; I have a parachute. Just let me love you. The details don't matter…"

"But they do matter, you know," Eva said later as they sat cross-legged on the big bed, munching on the thin-crust pizza they had ordered in.

Rob looked at her quizzically.

"The details. The ones you said don't matter. They do matter," she added by way of explanation. "Not now, but they will later," she continued gravely.

He burst out laughing. The same low, throaty, incredibly sexy laugh she had found so attractive from the start.

"You sound like a world authority on love affairs—I thought the *Victorian* era was your specialty!"

She made a face at him. "The Victorians weren't so Victorian, you know. There was every kind of hanky-panky going on under those staid exteriors."

"Eva," he said, suddenly becoming serious, "just know one thing. This isn't 'hanky-panky.' I'm not sure what it is or how to define it, but it's not a fling or a flirtation, or even 'only' an affair. I know it sounds crazy, because we hardly know each other—but I feel like I've known you all my life. Like I've been looking for you all my life, and when I found you, I recognized you. I'm not making any sense, I know, but when you sat down next to me on the plane, my heart gave a thump I was sure you could hear. I think I fell in love with you right then and there." He noted her skeptical look and added in a rush of words, "Don't look at me like that. And don't doubt what I'm saying. This isn't my normal come-on, and I'm not a philanderer, anyway."

She smiled. "I'm sorry. I've always been a skeptic, and what little experience I've had in this area has made me more of one, I guess. It just sounds so…well…incredible. Love at first sight is for poems and plays, not for real people." She shook her head. "You liked what you saw, I'll grant you that. Maybe you have a thing for brunettes. The fact that I was terrified of the takeoff amused you and endeared me to you—you saw the vulnerable little woman every man wants to protect. I don't usually project that kind of image, but at that moment I was too busy trying to overcome my fears. You couldn't have 'fallen in love' with me then—you were simply attracted. So was I, when you started talking to me. But I could have turned out to be a miserable bitch. How were you to know?"

Waving a wedge of pizza in a gesture of futility and frustration, he said drily, "For twenty-five years I've been looking for this woman, and when I finally find her, she gives me a lecture in logic! Where is your spirit of romance? Don't you realize that we must have been lovers in a previous lifetime? Romeo and Juliet? Antony and Cleopatra? No, they didn't have happy endings—quick, name a couple with a happy ending! All right, don't," he added, as she shook her head, smiling. "I'm not going to waste any more time convincing you, not with words anyway. But I do warn you that this is just the beginning of something very special, so buckle your seat belt and prepare for a wild ride. I'm not going to let you go."

"That's okay," she answered quietly, "I don't really want to go anywhere."

"Good," Rob replied, vigorously dumping the rest of their meal back into the carton. He paused, then added roguishly, "And it's the eyes that did it. I have a thing about gray eyes with thick black lashes. What else does a woman need?"

"Not much!" Eva agreed with a laugh as they embraced again.

EIGHTEEN

Tuesday mornings in Rob's apartment became the focus of both their lives in the ensuing months. Rob started flying in to Minneapolis the night before so the mornings could be longer, especially as the harsh Minnesota winter set in, with an increased risk of flight delays and airport closures. Eva's schedule, always flexible except for her actual class commitments, easily accommodated fewer hours in her office and in the library. For the first time in her life, she was doing the bare minimum that was required of her academically. She'd prepared her course outlines and lecture notes over the summer. Although she corrected papers and exams and re-read her notes for each class the night before, she got by very well, her solid years of serious research and work adding a depth to her teaching that few of her colleagues could match.

Her home life, however, was harder to juggle successfully. She hated the subterfuge and scheming that having a double life suddenly entailed. Sharon, thank goodness, was not affected. Sharon's place in Eva's life and heart had been established from the moment Sharon was born, and was strengthened by all the years when she had been her mother's only mainstay and sole source of strength. Nothing, not even Rob, could change that, and Eva's growing love for him did not have to bring any change to her relationship with her daughter. That was a different love, if on a parallel track, a love she could keep separate, although she did long for Rob to meet Sharon.

Dan was another matter. At first he did not count, and Eva felt no guilt about her intense physical desire for and growing emotional ties to another man. She'd be discreet and she'd make sure Dan wouldn't find out about her affair—not in the lingerie department of a department store, at least, she thought tartly. She remembered the pain and the humiliation all too well, and had no desire to "pay him back" in kind. On the contrary, she bent over backward to create plausible reasons for being absent. Tuesday mornings were not a problem. She was ostensibly at the university library and could not be reached. When Rob took to staying Wednesday nights, she "created" a weekly study group that met on those evenings, giving herself a few more precious hours with him, meeting him at his apartment at 6 and going home at 11, hoping Dan would be in bed and asleep, or working late in the den if he was still up.

It wasn't easy, and it got increasingly difficult as the months flew by and the relationship between Rob and Eva intensified in every way, to an extent she had never dreamed could exist outside pulp novels.

"It's like being thirsty in the middle of an oasis," she explained to Rob one Wednesday evening, in the always-difficult last hour before she went home and into the dark tunnel of not seeing him for another five days. "I want you and long for you and dream of touching you and being with you and making love to you. Like a Bedouin thinks of finding water, except that I'm sitting right in the middle of an oasis—but it's not the oasis I want. The well is lemonade, and I want water; the trees are date palms, and I want figs…

"And Dan is so goddamn nice and good to me. He senses that I'm going through some sort of crisis, but he can't figure it out. He's also scared that I still haven't forgiven him for what happened with Barbara, and he's waiting for me to pay him back in some horrible way that he can't bear to think about. So he's doubly nice to me—patient, solicitous, caring—and terribly anxious to make things right by making love to me. And that's hard, too," she added thoughtfully, her voice tinged with pain.

"How many times can you have a headache, or be too tired, or not feel like it? Our sex life was never that wonderful after we got back together. Not for me anyway, though I think for him it was somehow better. I'd built too many walls during the bad years, walls even I couldn't break down, although I did try, initially. But now it's worse, because I don't want him to touch me. I only want you." Eva shook her head, as if that would help sort out her muddled emotions and guide her through the minefield of her conflicting feelings.

"There is one solution, you know," Rob said quietly. "We've talked about it but we always reach the same impasse. You could leave Dan, and I could leave Rhoda. Then you and I could 'officially' meet and fall in love and live happily ever after. Neither of us would be leaving for another person, ostensibly, and that's probably easier to take... They'd survive, you know," he said gently, smoothing the troubled furrows in her forehead with his index finger.

"And what about our children, Rob?" Eva sighed. They'd covered this ground before. "Can I put Sharon through that trauma for the second time in her life? She's not even ten yet. And can you do that to Jeannie, who's even more dependent than Sharon? I'd at least have custody. You know you wouldn't..."

"Well, there are only two other options, Eva," Rob continued, tacitly agreeing that all the obstacles she had raised were very real and just as insurmountable as they always seemed. "We can go on like this for as long as we can, and hope that a few years down the road, the realities will somehow change. Or, we can break up now before we hurt each other any more—I don't know if I could do that. You're the center of my life now. I can't imagine you not being part of it..."

"You'd survive, and so would I," Eva said grimly, the pain in her eyes a contrast to her brave front. "People do survive, you know." She wiped her eyes with the back of her hand. "Here I go again, leaving you on a miserable note, when I promised myself that I'd be light and bright and sparkling. I'm not too good in the sparkling department lately," she added with a woebegone look, "but I'll be better next week, I promise."

He said nothing, looking at her with questioning eyes.

"Yes, I'll be here, Rob. You know that," she answered his unspoken question. "You're a habit I can't—and don't want—to break. I love you. You know that, too, and you know how much. And whatever happens, that won't change. Count on that, my love. That won't change."

He held her in a long, tight embrace that conveyed his needing and wanting and loving in a way that words could not. She kissed his mouth lightly, smiled at him, and let herself out, leaving behind a whiff of her light cologne and the prospect of five long, empty days until he saw her again.

NINETEEN

That summer Eva dreamed, for the first time, a dream that would recur again and again in the years to come. She was on a ship, leaning against the guardrail, her hair loose and waving in the soft breeze. Rob was on another ship, sailing right alongside hers, impossibly close, so that they could hold hands and stroke each other's face, laughing together at some shared joke. Slowly, at first imperceptibly, the two ships moved like points on almost but not quite parallel lines, inexorably parting as they traveled forward. Soon their heads could no longer touch, yet they still held hands. Gradually their arms stretched out in order to maintain contact until the moment when, even leaning forward as far as they could over the guardrail, their fingers touched for the last time.

Now their contact was only visual, and as they both realized the full import of the growing space between them, they did not say a word. The scene moved in the slow-motion manner that only dreams can have. Each seemed oblivious to everything except their lover's strained, taut face and sad eyes, and the hopelessness of the situation.

Rob's face got blurry as he was carried further and further away from Eva. Then the ship itself became just a small white dot in the sparkle of the sun upon the water, and finally disappeared from view...

Eva's heart gave a physical thump of pain as she awoke in her own bed. She lay very still, as if moving her body would make the painful dream come true. She could not shake off the sense of foreboding and the wave of sorrow that washed over her as the scene played itself out in her mind, over and over.

Neither of us made a move, she thought, recalling the dream-like calm of the scene, the total silence of the players. We were so close at the beginning; either one of us could have climbed over to the other's ship. Later, either one could have jumped overboard and swum to the other. But we just let each other go... We let ourselves be separated from each other without making a move to stop it. We accepted the separation with such sorrow, but such fatalism. Why? What does it mean?

The sound of Sharon leaving her bed and going to the bathroom interrupted Eva's thoughts.

I woke her, Eva thought, recalling the many times during the "sad year" when Sharon had awakened and come to her mother's bed at precisely the moment when Eva's spirits were at their lowest ebb, in the long, dark pre-dawn hours when even the smallest problem loomed large and insurmountable.

Through half-closed eyelids, she watched Sharon peek through the open door into the bedroom, as if to assure herself that all was well and that both her parents were where they ought to be. She's like a little mother hen, checking on her brood, Eva thought, smiling in spite of the residual pain of the dream. Sharon saw the smile and crept quietly to her mother's side.

"Are you okay?" she whispered, not disturbing the quiet rhythm of Dan's breathing.

"I'm fine, sweetheart," Eva assured her, stroking the child's soft golden curls. "Why are you up?"

"Couldn't sleep. I was feeling sad. Can I snuggle?"

Eva's look, seen through the dim illumination of the clock radio and the hint of early dawn stealing through the curtains, was mildly reproving but receptive.

"Just this once," she whispered as Sharon crawled in next to her, wriggling into a comfortable position in the curve of her mother's body. "Go to sleep, *ketzaleh*, everything will be fine."

Sharon seemed reassured, the warmth of her mother's body lulling her to sleep within minutes. Eva stayed awake, the sleeping child in her arms only partially alleviating the dread that the dream was an omen that was going to come true.

Eva moved within the shadow of the dream for the next few weeks, wondering whether she should share it with Rob. She had not held back with him in any way up until now. Thoughts were verbalized as soon as they came into her mind when they were together, or were shared as soon as possible over the phone if they were apart. For some unfathomable reason, this dream was different.

Eva often had long mental conversations with Rob. These took place anytime and anywhere—in the shower; in bed at night as she slowly watched daylight filter into the room; driving her car to work; pushing a cart down a supermarket aisle; waiting in line at the bank. He was with her always, listening to whatever she wanted to say, sometimes interjecting a wry comment, sometimes nodding gravely in understanding, sometimes just listening. He became her alter ego, playing devil's advocate to her reasoned mental arguments as to how they should plan for their future. When she made a case for putting their own needs and desires first, he would draw her a vivid picture of the effect this course of action would have on their respective children. When she expressed her fears at being locked in to her present situation forever—at first because of Sharon, and ultimately because she could not find it in herself to hurt and devastate Dan—he would plead with her to put their happiness first, to picture the long, lonely road of life along two separate paths.

Rob and Eva never agreed, in the conversations in her mind; their diverse opinions and reactions were the two sides of the schizophrenic coin their lives had become. The dream was merely a reflection of all that; one didn't need Freud to interpret it. But its progression pointed to where her head was at. She and Rob could not travel along two parallel tracks that almost touched each other, forever.

Because the tracks were *not* parallel. Sooner or later, now that their paths had crossed and intersected, they would have to either merge or diverge; diverge as they had in her dream, as they did in Frost's hauntingly poignant poem *The Road Not Taken*. Which would be the road not taken? Eva had no answers. All courses were fraught with peril, anguish, and pain. Going on as they were now was becoming increasingly difficult; the emotional frustration of being in a time-limited limbo was taking its toll on both of them. The prospect of a final and complete break was one neither wanted to face: after all, they had no friends in common, lived in different cities, worked in different milieus. Walking out of each other's lives, walking away from the few hours a week when they physically shared the same space, severing the telephone link that bound them on days they could not be together, would be like death. Irrevocable.

No one in his or her right mind opts for death, or for walking away from someone who is the core of your existence, Eva thought, her face a study of determination and defiance. How can I let go of him? How can I tell him to let go of me? But on the other hand, how can I not...?

"What's wrong, Eva?" were Rob's first words when he met her at the apartment on a Tuesday in early fall.

She smiled wanly, marveling yet again at the acuteness of his perceptions of her. She thought she looked well, and had taken extra care with her appearance that morning. She returned his embrace and said lightly, "Does anything look wrong? I thought I looked kind of nice."

She pirouetted, her pleated skirt flaring out, baring slim legs shod in high-heeled black leather boots, the soft cowl-necked cashmere sweater framing her face, her hair pulled back severely, accentuating her high cheekbones and incredible gray eyes.

He surveyed her critically. "You don't look 'kind of nice,' you dummy! You look stunning. You always look stunning—even in clothes, though I like you better without them." His light-hearted tone changed suddenly. "You've also lost between five and ten pounds in the last few months, something of your sparkle is missing, and there's more sadness in those magnificent eyes than there was when I met you almost a year ago. It's been rough on you, hasn't it?"

To her surprise, but not to his, tears welled up in her eyes, coursing unchecked down her cheeks as she moved into the safety and warmth of his arms. He held her for a few quiet moments, rocking gently until her sobs subsided, patting her face with his handkerchief, kissing her damp lashes, tasting the salt on her lips as he put his mouth to hers, tongue meeting tongue in a soft caress that quickly changed to mounting passion. She could feel his erection as he unhooked her bra and fondled her lush, warm breasts, taking her erect nipple into his mouth, kneading her breast with one hand while the other unhooked her skirt and slid under her panties, finding the wetness between her legs, touching her clitoris, then slipping his finger into the warm slickness of her vagina until she moaned with desire.

She quickly undid his belt and opened his fly, then pulled down his shorts and released his engorged manhood, which sprang at her, throbbing against the smoothness of her skin. He sat down at the edge of the bed, still kissing her as he pulled her lace panties off over her boots, but not releasing her skimpy garter belt or sheer stockings, holding her buttocks and caressing her thighs as she stood facing him, kissing her navel, then burying his face in the soft curls of her Venus mound.

She lowered herself onto him, straddling him, moaning with pleasure as he filled her, then pausing for a brief second when she had taken his full length into her vagina and holding back, for she could have peaked right then and there. Then slowly, to a rhythm only she could hear, she moved up and down his hard shaft, stroking his back with the tips of her nails, entwining her fingers in his hair, playing a counterpoint on his face with the tip of her tongue. Their eyes locked together so as not to miss the slightest nuance of the pleasure they were giving each other. He met her downward strokes with upward thrusts of his loins as her rhythm quickened, then became a blur of movement that he stopped with a final, almost brutal thrust as he entered yet deeper into her and exploded in an orgasm so intense, he gasped as the semen spurted out of him in a seemingly unending continuum.

He could feel the ripples of her climax taking over where his left off, enveloping his organ in wave after wave of contracting wetness, the internal movement belying her outward stillness as she clutched him in a total embrace, not an iota of space between them. She came for an eternity, a second wave following, then a third. His semi-hardness rose to meet her, her contracting vagina insistent, wanting more, rekindling the passion that he had been sure was used up. By the time she collapsed in his arms, spent, he wanted more. Without breaking their hold on each other, still deeply embedded in her female warmth, he stretched out on his back, pulling her along with him, then rolled over, covering her body with his, closing her legs so that he was squeezed inside her to a threshold of near-pain that was almost as exquisite as an orgasm itself would have been.

He unhooked her garter belt, stroking her belly, then her breasts as he slowly thrust her into a sexual adagio that matched her previous rhythm. Her legs opened gradually as he thrust even deeper, her hands seeking his buttocks, caressing him as he pushed into her with mounting insistence. They climaxed together this time, the spurts of his orgasm matched by the waves of her own, their wordless sounds of pleasure blending into one perfect harmony.

He withdrew slowly, wanting to draw out the pleasure. She moaned softly as he detached himself from her, then smiled up at him as he stretched out at her side, his head propped up on one hand, looking down at her with a blend of love and desire that sexual release had in no way blunted.

"Now tell me what's wrong," he said softly, his finger pushing back an errant lock of her long black hair, then caressing her mouth. "I haven't forgotten the look in your eyes; it's still there, in fact, peering out from behind the satisfaction and smugness over your magnificent performance! Talk! I'm listening."

She started haltingly, finding it surprisingly hard to articulate thoughts and fears that were so crystal-clear in her own mind when she was talking to herself. She told him of her recurring dream, seeing the pain intensify in his eyes at her vivid description of the growing distance between them, of the dream ending with the final disappearance from sight.

"I don't know what's stronger at this point, Rob, my impatience, my wanting to get this schizoid phase of our lives over with, or my fear at what the end of this will bring—regardless of what choices we make. I feel boxed in—almost doomed, if you want to be melodramatic about it. My head tells me that the kind of involvement we have today has got to change. It has to either evolve into something more permanent and more open, or it has to die. It may peter out slowly, like it does in my dream, or it may explode in one big bang—but either way, it will be very painful.

"My heart tells me to just enjoy what there is and let the future take care of itself. But that's not working for me. I'm fine when we're together, or when we talk on the phone. As long as there is contact—even if it isn't physical. But when I walk out of here and close the door behind me, or when I put down the phone, knowing I won't hear your voice for another twenty-four hours, something dies a little…" Eva stopped, finding it hard to go on, her voice choked up. Rob held her close, stroking her hair, his eyes misty at the description of the emotions that were tearing her apart and so closely paralleled his own.

"What do you want to do, Eva?" he asked quietly. "You've given it a lot of thought—too much, maybe. You've got all the alternatives spelled out, and you've obviously considered the ramifications. Pretend it's only up to you, that whatever you decide goes—what's your choice?"

Eva looked up, startled. She had expected the kind of debate and back-and-forth discussion they always had in her mind. Those discussions never had a definite conclusion; rather, they had a different conclusion each time. Here she was being asked to make a choice, to articulate what she really wanted, to stop dodging the issue, as she realized she had been doing in her own mind; to take a stand.

She looked at Rob for a long moment, then said slowly, "I want you to leave your wife. I want to leave Dan. I want us to have a life together."

Her eyes held his, trying to read his thoughts, to fathom what was going on in his head, to know where she stood.

Rob took a deep breath, then said in a tentative voice into which he tried to inject a note of levity, "Well, that was straight from the shoulder—are you asking me to marry you?"

She could not go along with his bantering tone and shook her head sadly. "No," she replied with a catch in her voice, "I can't do that. You're married, and so am I. But I'd like to get to the stage where I *can* ask you, or you can ask me—I'm really not hung up on who asks whom," she added with a forced smile that didn't quite reach her eyes.

He got off the bed, wrapped a towel around his waist and walked over to the window, standing in a shaft of afternoon sunlight that looked deceptively warm. They had been seeing each other almost a year. His project in Minneapolis was coming to an end—he'd already dragged it out longer than necessary, but Eva didn't know that. The leaves had been turning from green to fall colors when he met her, and now they were turning again.

In many respects, the year had been the happiest in his life, but he recognized as clearly as Eva did that that was because they'd been able to have the best of both worlds, to live in a bubble of having their cake and eating it, too. They had each carved their lives into two distinct and separate portions, creating this oasis of love and passion and sheer happiness that was central to both their lives, yet was, at the same time, as unreal as the dreams he'd always had of meeting a woman who would affect him precisely the way Eva did.

He glanced at her, sitting on the bed wearing his shirt, hugging her knees, her hair cascading down her back, watching him unwaveringly with those piercing gray eyes, waiting for him to speak, her face inscrutable. His eyes locked with hers as he weighed again the consequences of what Eva was asking for, knowing that she would accept whatever decision he made, that the ball was now in his court.

Eva had committed herself to him to an extent that was unprecedented for her. She was prepared to go through whatever pain and trauma was involved, as long as they could be together at the end. She had put her cards on the table, ready to accept rejection if necessary, but determined to resolve the dilemma, one way or another. Did he have her guts? He wasn't sure.

"Eva," he finally said softly, "I need time to think. Not that I haven't thought about it, you know I have, probably as much as you have." She dropped her gaze, but not before he saw the unavoidable flicker of pain that he knew his procrastination would arouse. Then she looked up again, her eyes masked, her face impassive, not saying a word, waiting for him to go on.

"I have to at least broach the subject with Rhoda, to see where I would stand with Jeannie. You understand that; I know you do. Give me this week to think and to explore. I won't keep you dangling beyond that."

She nodded mutely, and got up slowly, heading for the bathroom. He intercepted her, holding her tightly in his arms, feeling her firm breasts through the fabric of his shirt.

"And I *am* hung up on who asks whom," he whispered gruffly in her ear, "so let me do the asking when the question can be asked. I'm old-fashioned."

She tightened her embrace, then let go, still not saying a word. He heard the shower running and was tempted to join her, then thought better of it. She was hurting, he knew, feeling rejected while trying to tell herself that he wasn't saying "no" to her, just "later." He watched her get dressed, her neat, compact motions so different from the passion-fueled ones of an hour ago. Her tailored clothes and the severe hairdo she was re-creating, pulling her hair back into a sleek chignon, changed her back into a proper, well-to-do, modestly dressed woman, so different from the voluptuous nude he had been making love to earlier.

She turned away from the mirror and faced him, her words echoing his thoughts, as they so often did.

"There!" she said in a light tone, patting her hair, "I've returned to my other persona, so I can go back to my other world." Her smile illuminated her face, still not reaching her eyes as she chucked him affectionately under the chin, kissing his cheek softly, then embracing him hard as her emotions got the better of her.

"Rob," she said huskily, the beginning of tears in her voice, "don't call me this week. Give yourself real time away from me and decide what you decide. It's a big decision, and I'll love you regardless. I'll see you next week, my love." She paused, as if about to say more, then shook her head and extricated herself. "Stay here. I'll let myself out."

He heard the door close softly behind her, and forced himself not to run after her and tell her to come back. You've got one week, buster, he told himself grimly, and you'd better start making some heavy decisions.

TWENTY

That week was the longest Eva had ever lived through. She was distracted and distraught to the point that Dan insisted she stay in bed one day, convinced she had some sort of flu. Rob had respected her request and did not call. She wondered if that was as hard on him as it was on her, and figured that it probably was. He doesn't love me any less than I love him, she repeatedly told herself, but he has a lot more to lose than I do. She found herself staring at Sharon, trying to put herself in Rob's shoes, to picture what life without access to her child would be like, then realized she was psyching herself up for rejection, trying to rationalize a choice she was almost sure he would make, as if that would lessen the pain.

By Tuesday she had gone through every possible scenario in her head, trying to prepare herself for any possibility, alternating between optimism and despair. She had made her choice and was prepared to face the consequences, convinced that in the long run she was opting for the better way. She even envisioned Dan meeting someone else, finding happiness with a woman who could commit herself to him totally, maybe even having more children—something she had adamantly refused him for years.

She took a long, hard look at her closet that morning, unable to decide what to wear. She smiled to herself as she realized that she didn't know whether to dress for a funeral or for a celebration, and finally opted for a soft, full gray suede skirt and matching silk blouse, and the strand of pearls her parents had given her on her sixteenth birthday and matching pearl studs her only ornaments. She debated whether to leave her rings on, the antique garnet ring Dan had given her when he proposed, and her narrow gold wedding band. She decided to leave them on. Time enough to take them off later, if that's what's to be, she thought. She took a small, flat package from under a pile of sweaters at the back of her armoire and tucked it in her purse, then went down to join Dan and Sharon for breakfast.

"You look nice, Eva, but peaked," Dan said, surveying her with a proprietary look. "Are you sure you're well enough to go to work?"

"I'm fine," Eva said, sipping her morning cup of strong tea and deciding against toast, urging Sharon to finish her cereal so Daddy could drive her to school because it was getting late. She had a few quiet minutes to herself after they left, but no patience for the morning paper. She gave Mary a few instructions about dinner—such is the double life, she thought wryly to herself—then drove slowly downtown, knowing she would be early. She wanted to get to the apartment first, to see Rob's expression when he first walked in.

He wasn't expecting her to be there when he let himself in, but wasn't really surprised to find her curled up on the couch when he walked into the apartment.

Eva knew what his decision was before he said a word. The heaviness of his step and the droop of his shoulders told her all she needed to know. Dark circles under his eyes indicated that his week had been even harder than hers. She stood up and went to the bar to pour them each a stiff Scotch. As she handed him his drink, she said in what she hoped was a light tone, "I know it's kind of early in the day, but come and drink to the loser anyway... I know...it's what I expected."

He sat down morosely in one of the armchairs.

"Eva, I talked to Rhoda. She knows about us. She's known for a while. Not details—just that there is someone else in my life. She doesn't care if I have one affair or twenty—she apparently doesn't lack for male company. However, she was very clear on what the outcome of a divorce would be. She'll fight me tooth and nail—not over custody of Jeannie, she'd get custody—but even over the most minimal visitation rights. And she'll drag Jeannie into court if necessary. She said that and she meant it. She was very calm but adamant. Eva…I…I can't do that to my baby, not even for us. Please understand."

Eva sat quietly, her eyes downcast, slowly swirling the Scotch in her glass, trying to assimilate her reactions to Rob's words. She realized that she had expected this to be the outcome, and that she would probably have made the same choice herself if their future meant giving up Sharon. What she hadn't expected was the sheer physical pain of actually facing a future in which Rob would be only a memory.

She wondered, would there ever be a time when thoughts of Rob would not be accompanied by an overwhelming sense of loss? No, there would never be such a time, she decided; the loss would always be there, accompanied by the inevitable questions of what it would have been like if his decision, and the circumstances, had been different. If Jeannie were an ordinary little girl like Sharon, in eight or ten or twelve years, when she grew up, custody or visitation rights would no longer be an issue. But Jeannie will always be a child, will never be able to make her own decisions or take a stand opposing her mother. She will always need Rob, and her needs will always exceed and preempt mine. And rightfully so, Eva conceded.

She looked up, meeting Rob's steady gaze. He hadn't taken his eyes, which still begged for her understanding, off her.

Eva put down her untouched drink and walked over to the window that looked out at the park across the street. The grass, still green, was strewn with fallen leaves. How appropriate, she thought. Rob hadn't moved from the armchair. She could feel his gaze boring through the back of her head, trying to read her thoughts, waiting for her reaction. She turned toward him slowly, her eyes locking with his, and whispered, "I understand."

"I knew you would—but it doesn't make things less painful, does it?"

She shook her head, unable to speak.

Rob got up quickly and took her in his arms,' suddenly unable to bear even the few feet of distance between them. She returned his embrace, then pulled away with a shaky laugh.

"I don't quite know what comes next. I guess I should go."

"No, not yet, Eva! Please stay," he pleaded.

"The longer we put off saying goodbye, the harder it will be, Rob. You know that."

"But there's so much I want to say to you," he said urgently. "I want you to understand why I decided what I decided. Why I had no choice. I want you to know that I'm hurting, too; knowing that I have to do this but also knowing that I'll never forgive myself for cutting you out of my life."

"I know all that, Rob," Eva said softly. "You don't have to say anything. I've been hearing your thoughts in my head all week."

She looked around the room and added in a tone meant to sound bright and normal, "Do you realize that we've never used this room before?"

"Don't make small talk, Eva," he growled at her, "and don't give me that chipper, 'all's well' tone of voice. We've never played games—let's not do it now. Let's say what we feel—honestly, even if it hurts. This isn't a social date. It's our last time together. Do you realize what that means, for chrissake?"

Anger overtook her, augmenting the pain, and she could barely control her voice.

"Yes, I realize what it means! And I realize that I'm probably responsible for bringing the issue to a head. I also know that once I walk out that door, I will never see you again and it will be like leaving a part of me behind. I know what I'm going back to—a charade of a marriage with a man I like and respect but don't love, a life filled with all kinds of wonderful things, except what I want most—you! I know all that, Rob," she added, her voice growing softer, "but talking about it won't make it easier—it'll make it harder. And no," she responded to the question in his eyes, "I don't think it's a good idea to make love now, knowing we'll never be together again. The last time was very beautiful, all the more so because neither of us thought in terms of that being the last time. Leave it at that, Rob. Hang on to the memories. That's all we can have."

She turned away abruptly, willing herself not to cry. He came up behind her, burying his face in the back of her neck.

"You're right. I'm sorry. I'm a first-class jerk. Do you want me to leave first?"

"No," she said. "I'll go first, but there's something I have to give you before I go."

She took the flat, elongated, gift-wrapped box out of her handbag and put it on the coffee table, then took his apartment key off her keychain and put it on top of the box.

"There. I won't need the key anymore. Don't look at me like that, please. This isn't a farewell gift. It's something I got for you a while back. I wanted to give it to you next week on the anniversary of the day we met, but I guess I knew there might not be a next week. I know that the choice you made was the only one you could make. If I were in your shoes, I would have made the same choice. We usually think alike. Please accept it, Rob," she continued in a rush of words, not wanting to give him a chance to protest, as she knew he would. "I want you to have something from me. It's not to remember me by. I know you'll remember me without it. It's for me to know that something from me is going with you. I know that doesn't make sense, but please humor me, even if you don't quite understand."

He nodded his acceptance of the gift but made no move toward the coffee table.

"I have something for you, too. And the same speech applies," he said ironically, going into the bedroom and coming out with a small volume bound in soft crimson leather.

"I found it in an antique book shop in New York and I thought of you. I'm sorry it isn't gift-wrapped."

Eva slowly opened the book to look at the title page. It was a volume of Shakespeare's sonnets, printed in the 1800s, inscribed in masculine Victorian handwriting, the ink faded.

"To my Beloved, may I remain in your heart forever.
R. March 1875."

"I was tickled by the coincidence of the man's initial and the date. It was meant as a birthday present for you, but I guess the inscription is even more fitting now. Don't forget me, Eva," he added, his tone becoming more insistent, "and please know that I'm always there for you if you need me. Promise you *will* call me if the going gets rough or if there's too much for you to handle."

Eva shook her head slowly. "No, you know I won't do that. I can't even think of that as an option, or this parting will be that much more difficult. One of the hardest things for me to accept when my father died was the fact that no matter how much I wanted or needed him, the only place he would ever be was in my own mind. That's where you have to be now, Rob, in my head—and in my heart. But that's all. There's no more physical you for me, once I walk out that door, and you have to accept that there's no more Eva for you, except the one in your memories. Otherwise you'll be waiting for the phone to ring, or for the postman to come with a letter, and that's unbearable."

Eva slung her handbag over her shoulder, holding the book tightly, the stricken expression in her eyes belying her outward composure. She kissed Rob lightly on the mouth, then put her finger to his lips to stem anything he might wish to say.

"Goodbye, my love," she said huskily.

He took her upturned face in both his hands, looking at her intently, as if trying to memorize every feature.

"Goodbye, my Eva. I love you." He kissed her softly, then let her go, reluctant to let the moment end.

He heard the elevator humming down the shaft, then stepped quickly over to the window, determined to catch one more glimpse of her. There she was, walking away, drawing her jacket around her to ward off the chill of the cool fall air.

Turn around and look at me, Eva, he willed. She paused in midstep, as if she'd heard his thoughts, stood perfectly still for what seemed an eternity, then shrugged, squared her shoulders, and walked out of his life with crushing finality.

Rob turned away from the window and picked up the box from the coffee table, tearing off the paper. A slim gold Patek Philippe watch was nestled in the satin interior of the leather case, with a small white card tucked under the alligator strap that read, *"For Rob, with all my love, Eva"* in her square, strong handwriting. There was no engraving on the watch itself, nothing that would have to be explained or hidden.

She'd known in her heart for a long time that they had no future together, that circumstances would eventually separate them. Her nightmare about the two ships had been a prophecy—

she'd hastened a showdown by taking a stand and by demanding a decision, but it would have happened anyway eventually, and she'd known it almost from the start, long before he would admit it to himself.

You'll be all right, my Eva, he thought. You're smart and you're strong and whatever you decide to do with the rest of your life, you'll do well. But I won't be there to see it, or to share it with you because of one little girl who can't go it alone the way you can, who will never be able to go it alone, and who needs me more than you do.

He went to the window again, hoping against hope that he'd see Eva walking back to him, knowing it would resolve nothing, but hoping nonetheless. The street was empty, as he knew it would be. The only person in sight was a gardener raking dead leaves in the park across the street. Rob stood at the window for a long time, knowing she would never come back, knowing the phone would never ring and the postman would never come.

He would be in Minneapolis again next week to wrap up things before going back to San Francisco full-time, but he would not return to this apartment. He quickly gathered up his few personal effects and tossed them into a suitcase, and left his and Eva's keys on the table, with a note to maid service to close up the apartment and give the keys to the janitor. Then he took one last look at the impersonal place that had been his haven of happiness for almost a year and walked out, shutting the door behind him with irrevocable finality.

TWENTY-ONE

The memory of that final day with Rob would always be disjointed for Eva. She drove around aimlessly for hours after leaving him, trying to figure out what to do with the rest of her day, with the rest of her life. When the aimlessness of both her thoughts and her movements finally got to her, she went home. Mary was not surprised to see her, the woebegone expression on Eva's face confirming Mary's belief that Eva "had a bug" of some sort. She bundled her off to bed and Eva went meekly, suddenly overwhelmed by the emotional exhaustion the week had wrought. To Eva's surprise, she kept dozing off, awakening briefly when Sharon tiptoed into the room, then again when Dan came in and quietly put a hand on her forehead to check her temperature. She looked up at him, her eyes glistening with unshed tears.

"You don't seem to have any fever, but you sure look like hell. You should have stayed in bed today, you'd have been better off," he chided.

Eva nodded mutely.

"Mary and Sharon are busy preparing a supper tray for you—chicken soup for your flu and veal something-or-other—feel up to it?" he asked.

"Just the soup, please. Don't let them go to too much trouble."

She almost added that she was all right, that she wasn't sick, just a little tired, but she decided against saying it. Staying in bed felt good just now; it certainly beat facing the world, though she knew she'd have to do that too, eventually. She slowly sipped the hot broth under Sharon's watchful and motherly gaze, then allowed herself to be tucked in, half-shutting her eyes as Sharon and Dan tiptoed out of the darkened room, telling her to try to get some sleep.

But she didn't sleep. She lay absolutely still, her eyes shut, re-living every moment she had spent with Rob—the meeting on the plane, their first lunch, the first time they made love, the long conversations about everything under the sun—their pasts, their present. Very rarely did we talk about the future, Eva thought, almost as though we knew from the start that there wouldn't be one. That a brief but wonderful *now* was all we would ever have.

She went over her year's worth of memories like a miser looking over his collection of precious gems or hoarded artifacts—picking up each one, scrutinizing it slowly and carefully, memorizing its size and shape and feel, then wrapping it up carefully and putting it away, sharing with no one. She knew that periodically she would look over this memory or that one; that some would come into her mind unbidden, triggered by a phrase, a sound, or a smell. With her natural ear for words, she re-membered their conversations verbatim—the serious ones, when Rob had spoken of the anguish of learning about Jeannie's condition, and when she had talked of the pain of her father's death or of the incident with Barbara; and the light-hearted, foolish talk in the relaxed and glowing aftermath of making love. It was all there in her mind, a storehouse of scenes that would be her only legacy of the past year.

She wondered if the memories would ever fade, lose their sharp, bright edges and become misty and sepia-colored, like the old photographs in her parents' albums. No, they would not, she decided, as the gray light of a chilly dawn filtered in through the blinds. She would hang on to them, come what may. She had loved Rob in a way that was new and unique, that she would probably never experience again. He was gone from her life—a decision forced upon them by the circumstances of his child's needs and his wife's calculated disregard; but the memories were hers, and if that was all she could ever have, she would treasure them as the only inheritance of a precious year. One she would never be able to pass on to anyone else, but one she would depend upon for sustenance. She was determined that the memories—her only link with Rob—would be a source of strength, not a cause for sadness. She would focus on the beauty and the pleasure of the time they had together, not on the pain of parting. But, like someone splurging before embarking upon a long and rigorous diet, Eva allowed herself the indulgence of replaying in her mind's eye that day's parting scene, quiet tears of mourning streaming down her cheeks and drenching her pillow.

Three days later, Eva was sitting in her office marking student papers. She was forcing herself to concentrate, brows furrowed, chewing on the end of her pencil, determinedly pushing away any random thoughts. After twenty minutes she gave up, pushed the stack of papers away, and rested her head on her clenched fists, closing her eyes tight as if to avoid seeing something.

The Jews are a smart people, she thought. They give you a week of formal, ritualized mourning to cry yourself out, to detach yourself from everyday preoccupations, to accept your loss, to find your bearings. A loss involves a redefinition of self, a forced acceptance of your new status as orphan, widow, or bereaved parent, as a person alone. She wondered whether there was a name for the kind of person she had now become. A woman grieving over a lost lover. Lost. Not dead, but gone just the same. She certainly could not make any outward show of mourning. She could continue to feign illness—she certainly looked ill—but the hours in bed gave her too much time to think and to hurt.

Keeping busy was the only solution—always had been for her—and she hunkered down with the single-mindedness that had always worked for her before. Only it wasn't working this time. The adrenaline high usually achieved by running, or in this case, running away, wasn't happening. Eva grimaced, then proceeded to tidy up her desk, resigning herself to the fact that she would get no more work done today. Just as she locked the door of her office, the phone rang inside and her heart gave a wild thump. Maybe it's Rob, she thought, holding the key aloft. She quickly unlocked the door and picked up the phone on its sixth ring.

"Hello?"

"Eva! I'm so glad I caught you before you left for the day," said the fruity voice of the dean. "Can I see you in my office sometime soon to discuss some academic matters?"

"Yes, yes, of course." Disappointment washed over her like a wave. She hoped it wasn't reflected in her voice. "I was just on my way out. Do you want to see me now?"

"No, no, my dear. You run along. Tomorrow is soon enough. Would 10 a.m. be convenient?"

Fool! Eva chastised herself harshly as she hung up the phone. You know he won't call you, just as you won't call him. Come to terms with reality and act your age, Eva. You're a grown woman, a mother. You had an affair with a married man. It was wonderful, but it's over. You've gone home, he's gone home. Put the whole year out of your life. Pretend you're tough and sophisticated. Pretend you do this all the time. Pretend you didn't love him. Pretend it doesn't hurt. She took a deep breath and mentally reviewed the list of things she had to do before going home. She *would* keep busy and it *would* work for her. It had to, and it would.

She looked at the stack of papers on her desk and proceeded to place them neatly in her briefcase. She'd mark them at home that night, and would not go to bed until they were done. Dan had left that day for a ten-day buying trip; he wouldn't be there to nag her that it was too late for her to be working. Eva would do what she had done when her father died: make sure that by the time she got to bed at night, she was too exhausted to think and to feel.

She'd get started on the articles she had been asked to write for several literary journals; she'd accept out-of-town speaking engagements again. She had agreed to do only a few of those in the past year. Once in San Francisco, when Rob arranged to be with her, they spent three full days together at the Mark Hopkins, rarely leaving what they laughingly dubbed their "suite"—two adjoining rooms with the door between them kept open. The unused room became the living room; the bedroom was the one that had seen all the action. Three days of incredible, repeated lovemaking, of exploring each other's bodies and minds, of lying in bed together and watching TV like an old married couple, of sleeping curled up in each other's arms. Eva wrenched her thoughts back to the present. She was defeating her own determination to put all that behind her.

I'm sorry, Rob, she apologized mentally. Your *Shiva* was only three days long. I have to find my way back to where I was before I met you. My life has to get back on track and I have to get back into my old groove. I hope you're doing fine. Miss me always and don't forget me. But don't remember too often, either, and please understand why I must do the same.

TWENTY-TWO

By the time Dan got back from his trip, everything was outwardly normal. He was relieved to see Eva looking better than she had in weeks, her peaked, wan demeanor replaced by a new energy, though her eyes still looked tired.

"I missed you," he said, nuzzling the back of her neck as she brushed her teeth that night.

Eva rinsed her mouth and gave him a playful shove. At least, she hoped it seemed playful. "After all the gorgeous geisha girls, you don't expect me to believe that."

"Mmm…believe it," he whispered, burying his face in her hair. "You're the only geisha I want. Come to bed."

It had to happen sooner or later, Eva thought unhappily, forcing herself to respond, wishing she had an excuse to delay what was bound to happen. She couldn't help flashing back to the last time she and Rob had made love, three weeks earlier. No one had touched her since, and she should be craving sex by now. But she wasn't. Not with Dan. He was insistent and there was no point in saying no. She closed her eyes as he caressed her, remembering the feel of Rob's skin. Dan was an adept and experienced lover, and he knew every nuance of her body—what worked and what didn't. He sensed her initial reluctance and was determined not only to ignore it, but to make her enjoy their lovemaking—there had been a certain flatness to it lately that he couldn't define, over and above the reserve that had been there since the Barbara episode, a flatness that would probably never go away.

He smiled to himself as Eva began to respond. Her eyes were still tightly shut, but the familiar signals were there. What Dan did not realize was that mentally, Eva wasn't with him; she was in a small apartment a few miles away, and the man thrusting into her with the urgency born of a long separation and absence was not her husband. Eva was making love to Rob; Dan was only his surrogate. The two men were different in build and in texture, in taste and in smell, but no matter. It was Rob's hardness that Eva felt and Rob's skin and hair that she stroked with roving hands. As the thrusts grew harder and faster, she felt herself reaching the very height of arousal that came before a climax, gasping as she went right over the edge in an orgasm the likes of which she had never experienced with Dan. But it wasn't Dan she was responding to; it was Rob who was exploding inside her with rhythmic spurts of ecstasy as her vaginal muscles contracted and grabbed and squeezed, demanding that he give her his all.

Eva's eyes remained shut until Dan's quiet breathing beside her assured her that he was fast asleep. She slipped quietly out of bed and got into the hottest shower she could bear, scrubbing herself with a rough sponge until her skin tingled. I have just been unfaithful to two men, she thought as she lathered her hair briskly, and I don't even care.

She'd always managed to keep Dan and Rob separated in her mind. Her hours with Rob were his alone. If Dan's persona intruded, it was never in the lovemaking, only in the talking that came after. And she had never allowed herself to think of Rob while Dan made love to her. She'd gone along with her husband's desires, faking when necessary. But even when there was no need to fake, the intensity of whatever sexuality she experienced with Dan was a pale shadow to the intense, all-encompassing passion that Rob evoked in her.

Tonight she'd managed to synthesize the two men into one. She'd used Dan's body to materialize her fantasy about Rob, and that had worked. She'd never lost control, acknowledging the reality that it was Dan in bed with her. But all the while Dan was making love to her, in her mind, she'd been making love to Rob, feeling him erupt inside her, seeing behind her closed eyelids the awed expression on his face as he climaxed, feeling the shudders of his body against hers as he reveled in the smoothness and warmth of her skin.

She smiled as she wondered whether what had happened in her imagination could actually be called a ménage à trois. She'd been hoping she'd be in the middle of her period when Dan got home from his business trip—that usually held him at bay—but now she was glad it was late. She had found a way to satisfy her yearning for Rob, the physical ache of wanting him that had been with her for over a year and had only been satisfied for a few brief hours every week, while their affair lasted. As she stood under the shower, the soapy water cascading down her body, she realized with a start that her period was more than a week late. It's the stress of the past few weeks, she assured herself. Late periods had happened before.

She stepped out of the tub and wrapped a towel around her hair, then dried herself, inspecting her body carefully. At thirty-four, she was probably at her peak. A little too thin, she noted critically, turning around several times in front of the full-length mirror, but looking good. Her breasts were still firm; her ass was tight and undimpled. Those thighs could use a little toning, she thought as she pinched them. Time to start jogging or biking. All in all, though, not a bad specimen.

Dan was sleeping deeply as she tiptoed out of the bedroom wrapped in a fluffy white robe, her damp hair spread out over her shoulders. She quietly checked on Sharon, then went down to her den, poured a generous cognac into a large snifter, and raised it in a silent toast. To you, Rob, may you be with me always. And you will be. She took the old leather-bound volume from the corner of a bookcase and settled down into one of the big armchairs to read Shakespeare's sonnets until her hair was dry.

TWENTY-THREE

The nausea hit her two weeks later. Eva dreamt she was bobbing up and down on a stormy sea in a lifeboat and woke up to find her gorge rising. She just made it to the bathroom, retching continuously until nothing remained in her stomach but bile.

Oh, shit! she thought as she brushed her teeth and rinsed her face; it can't be. It must be a flu bug.

Dan was awake when she crawled back into bed, eyeing her with a worried expression.

"Are you all right?"

"Sort of. I must have eaten something last night that disagreed with me." She grimaced, feeling suddenly cold. "Well, whatever it was, there's nothing left of it in my stomach! What time is it?"

Dan glanced at the clock radio. "Almost seven. Do you want me to bring you some tea?"

"No, thanks, I'm okay. I feel better now. I'll just lie here quietly for a bit until the alarm goes off."

Dan looked at her doubtfully. Her skin had a greenish cast and she was shivering, but he knew better than to argue with Eva when she insisted she was well.

Eva lay back with her eyes closed, the shivers gradually subsiding as the warmth of the bed enfolded her. Her mind was racing. Today is November 15th, she calculated, one month since Rob and I made love. My last period was October 1st. Dan made love to me right after my period was over, then not again until he got back from his trip, on November 1st. It's more than six weeks since I've had my period. I can't be pregnant; the coil is so safe. But what if I am? If I am, the baby is Rob's! she realized with exaltation. She curled up in a ball, her back to Dan, as if to shield

123

the tiny living thing that might be growing within her. You're not pregnant, Eva, she told herself sternly, you're grasping at straws. You can't have Rob, so you're imagining having his child. Being late or skipping a period means nothing, so cut it out. Her mind went back to the beginning of their relationship and she remembered Rob's expression as he lay next to her, on his side, his finger tracing the faint stretch marks left on her flat stomach by Sharon's birth.

"How come you stopped at one child?" he'd asked. "Your body is made for having babies!"

Eva had blushed at his question. It was one of the sore points between her and Dan, who'd wanted a large family.

"Well," she paused, "after Sharon was born, I wanted to complete my Ph.D. By then, Dan was involved with Barbara, and then my father died. Then came the split, and I was a very reluctant partner when we got back together again. If it hadn't been for Sharon, there wouldn't have been a reconciliation—it was as much because of her as for her. Dan wanted us to have another child, but I held out. I wasn't sure of him, I guess, and I didn't want to become more vulnerable or dependent." She crinkled her forehead in thought. "I think having another child was the kind of affirmation I wasn't prepared to make. I never met Dan halfway once we 'reconciled.' He's made a total commitment to me, the kind of commitment people are supposed to make when they fall in love and get married. But Dan wasn't ready for that commitment when we were first married, and by the time he was ready, I'd gone away…"

"…'And it is but a child of air/ That lingers in the garden there,'" he quoted softly.

Eva nodded, her eyes suddenly smarting with inexplicable tears. *A Child's Garden of Verses*—it's one of the ones Sharon and I still read and re-read. I should have figured you'd know it. We're such kindred souls!"

"I learned to speak English from that book—it was one of the first books my mother got me when we came to the States. I've always loved it."

Eva nestled closer, treasuring every moment, knowing she'd have to leave soon.

"I'd like to have *your* baby," she said softly, caressing his mouth with her finger. "A little boy with soft brown curls and big brown eyes."

Rob's eyes glistened with unshed tears, which belied his light tone. "No! He can have my hair, if you insist, but I want him to have your eyes. Can't let such fine genetic material go to waste."

Eva had said no more.

We already knew then, she thought, the sound of Dan and Sharon's morning preparations impinging on her reveries. We knew it couldn't last. That's why we never talked about a child again. A child implies a future, and we must have known all along that we couldn't have one together.

Eva reluctantly wrenched her thoughts back to the present. She was feeling almost fine, slightly green but basically okay. I'll wait a week or two, she decided as she went through her morning routine mechanically. Then if I don't get my period, I'll check it out. It's probably too early to tell anyway, and I'm probably not pregnant. But what if I am?

When four more weeks had passed without her period, Eva was certain. She finally called Dr. Wilkes' office and spoke to the nurse.

"Is it possible to get pregnant on a coil?" Eva demanded.

"It sure is, honey. Happens all the time! Why don't you come along tomorrow with a first morning sample and we'll check you out."

By the time she had dressed after her check-up and was sitting in the doctor's office, the urine test confirmed what she already knew. Sharon was more than ten years old now, but Eva's symptoms were all-too-familiar—the nausea, the fatigue—they were all a repeat of her first pregnancy. Only the father is different, she thought wistfully.

Dr. Wilkes was delighted.

"Well, dear, Nature has done it again. Your coil either came out, possibly during your last period, or it's still in there, with a little fetus thumbing its nose at it!"

"Isn't that dangerous?" Eva asked, her expression concerned. There were a lot of decisions to make and bridges to cross in this complicated situation, but one thing she knew: She wanted this baby.

"No, not really. If the coil is there, it will come out when you give birth. It's outside the pregnancy, and won't affect it. Now," he added, his soothing tones turning more businesslike, "let's get some facts down—when was your last period?"

"October 15th," Eva lied, moving up the date two weeks. She had not decided what to tell Dan, but her gut feeling was to pretend the baby was his. What other option was there?

"In that case, the baby should be born around the end of July."

Middle of July, Eva corrected him mentally. But who would quibble over two weeks if the baby came early? The due date was nine months after Dan came home. He'd remember making love that night. It was only fair.

The doctor went on about diet and appointments, but Eva wasn't listening. She wanted to be alone, to fully come to grips with something she'd known for a while, but which had now been confirmed beyond a doubt.

We're having a baby, Rob, she announced to herself as she got into her car. She drove around aimlessly for a while, trying to collect her thoughts; she had to decide on a plan of action. A little boy with brown hair and—all right, we'll have it your way, Rob—gray eyes.

For the first time since the last time she'd seen him, Eva drove to Rob's apartment, knowing he wouldn't be there, that the apartment was no longer his; she wanted to make some sort of connection with the past. She parked across the street alongside the park, which was desolate and covered with snow.

She wanted to call Rob. No, not call him, she wanted to see him. To see his face when she told him the news. She tried to envision his reaction, then stopped. No, she couldn't do that to him. It would not resolve anything. Jeannie's needs would still be the same; the same choice would still have to be made. Only instead of leaving behind the woman he loved, Rob would also have to abandon a child knowingly. His child, Eva's and his child, conceived from a depth of loving neither of them had ever known before, or would ever experience again.

I'll have the baby and he'll have the anguish, Eva thought. I can't do that to him. She looked up at the corner window of the apartment where they'd briefly shared their lives. The blinds were drawn, the apartment probably unoccupied. Rob was gone, gone for good. But he'd left behind a part of himself, a legacy that would be hers to nurture and cherish for the rest of her life.

"Thank you, Rob," Eva whispered hoarsely, her voice sounding strange in the empty car. "I wish I could share this child with you, but it would hurt you so much."

She turned the key in the ignition and slowly drove away. Eva now knew what she had to do, and she would do it. And do it right.

TWENTY-FOUR

Dan was ebullient at dinner that night, smiling like the cat that swallowed the canary. He would only admit that he had a surprise for his wife and daughter, but refused to divulge what it was until dessert was over.

"Okay, Daddy, that's enough!" Sharon declared authoritatively as she pushed away the rest of her apple pie. "The suspense is killing me! What's the surprise?"

"This!" said Dan with a flourish, as he produced a thick manila envelope and placed it in the middle of the table.

Sharon and Eva sat quietly, waiting for him to continue.

Dan opened the envelope and extracted an airline folder.

"Three tickets to Florida for Mummy, Daddy, and Sharon for two weeks, and two tickets for a one-week Caribbean cruise for Mummy and Daddy, while Sharon stays with her grandmother... We leave in one week—how's that for a Christmas vacation?"

Eva had to smile at Sharon's reaction. The child let out a yell of excitement, then hugged her father ecstatically.

"Oh, Daddy, that's terrific! Wait till I tell my friends! Can I be excused, Mummy? I have loads of phone calls to make!"

Eva's smile broadened. Sharon and her friends had discovered the telephone.

"Not so fast, young lady! Since this seems to be the Goodmans' evening for surprises, I have one of my own. Sit down, please!"

Dan and Sharon looked at her expectantly and Eva took a deep breath.

"This is a bit early, and I really should wait before making an official announcement—but what the heck!" She paused for dramatic effect, looking from one curious face to the other, wondering how their lives would change as a result of her news.

"I went to see Dr. Wilkes today—I've been feeling kind of green the last month or so and I wanted him to check it out…" She stopped again, noting the flicker of excitement in Dan's eyes. She met his gaze and nodded. His face lit up.

"Dr. Wilkes confirmed what I suspected. Sharon, you're going to have a baby brother or sister at the end of July."

"Oh, Mummy!" Sharon exclaimed in awed tones. "That's so cool! A baby! A little baby! I won't be an only child any more. We'll be a *real* family—oh, wow!"

Dan said nothing. He sat rooted to his chair, staring at Eva with a look in his eyes that she had never seen before, not even when she'd announced her first pregnancy.

"Eva!" he finally said, his voice thick with emotion. He got up abruptly and scooped her into his arms, holding her tightly as Sharon skipped around them in excitement.

Eva closed her eyes, suddenly disoriented. We're all happy for the wrong reasons, she thought. I'm happy because I'm hanging on to Rob. Dan is ecstatic because he thinks I'm having his baby. Sharon is thrilled because her family is finally getting to where she's wanted it to be for years. This is crazy!

But looking around her, Eva softened. The baby would be a source of joy to the three people here. The reasons didn't matter. The one person whose joy would be mingled with anguish, if he were to know, would never know. Rob had gone back to his family. It was a choice he'd had to make, and he'd made it. Eva had her life to live, a life she had thought would be empty and hollow without Rob. Now she would have a part of him, and that would be her consolation. And if Dan and Sharon benefited as well, she thought—well, they deserve it. Nothing would be gained, and much would be forfeited, by telling them the truth. The baby—she was sure it would be a boy—would be a Goodman. Dan's son. Sharon's brother. The baby's real father had never been a part of their lives, only hers. He would now become a part of their lives, but only she would know it. And she would never tell. That knowledge was to be hers alone. She only prayed that she would have the strength to deal with the whole situation.

Later that night, when Sharon was tucked in and finally settled down, Eva and Dan had the first real talk they'd had in years.

They were sitting in the den in the big armchairs, sipping tea, when Dan said, "I know I'm going overboard and that I'm reading more into this pregnancy than it really is, but I can't tell you how happy I am. I have been dreading the possibility of losing you for so long…I guess that's one of the reasons I wanted more children—to bind you to me. I feel like a condemned man who just had his sentence commuted. I know that's crazy, but it's as if this unborn child is telling me that things will be okay from now on."

Eva's voice was low, but gentle. "Dan…I…this baby was an accident. I didn't plan it. Nothing was farther from my mind. Don't read into it what isn't there."

"Oh, I know that, Eva. I'm not a fool. I know you didn't wake up one morning with your mind made up that you loved me again and that you wanted to have another child with me. But you could have made other choices. You could have aborted and told me later—no, that's too cruel, you wouldn't do that. You could have had an abortion and never told me. I know the baby is an accident. But your choice to keep it isn't, and I appreciate your making that choice more than you'll ever know. I know how much I've hurt you—probably more than you're even ready to admit to yourself.

"And I know I can thank Sharon—and your own innate sense of loyalty to the idea of a family—for the fact that we're together at all. I know how you feel about me. If not for Sharon, you would have walked out of my life five years ago—and you'd have been right. Thank God for that tenacious, stubborn, determined little girl—she forced you to give me a second chance to win you back, with all her scheming and plotting. This baby will give me yet another chance, and I mean to use it well. I know you'll never feel the kind of love you once felt for me—that's the price I have to pay for my own stupidity and insensitivity. I had something wonderful, and I threw it away…for what? Nothing really, in the beginning, and a lot of pain at the end. But I'll make it up to you, Eva, if it takes the rest of my life to do it. I promise you that."

He got up and bent over her chair to touch her face, then sat at her feet and buried his head in her lap, holding back his sobs. Eva sat back, her face registering sorrow mixed with compassion, as she stroked his thick blond hair, noticing the silvering temples.

"Shhh," she murmured soothingly. "You don't have to 'make up' for anything. Things happen to people. Life happens. You do things and make choices and they're not always the right ones— and if they're right, they're not always easy…"

"Just don't ever leave me, Eva. I know you can't love me, but please stay and accept my love for you. That's all I ask."

Eva bent forward, holding his chin in her hand, her eyes inches from his.

"Dan," she said with feeling, "there's something I want to say to you and I won't say it again, so please listen. I *do* love you. Not the way I used to. Not the way you want me to. But I do love you, in my own peculiar and probably limited way. Just accept that without wanting to know the reasons and without trying to change me. Don't try to woo me or win me over, or do anything but be yourself. It's not necessary. I'm here, and I'm staying. What could have been and should have been and would have been is behind us. Let's forget it. We have Sharon, we have a good life together, and we're having a baby. Let's accept those givens and take it from here and see where we go. You don't 'owe' me anything, and I don't owe you. You're you and I'm me—and we always have Sharon to keep us in line," she added with a chuckle, changing the mood. "Now come to bed; I'm falling flat on my face and I can't keep my eyes open."

"Enough drama, Dan," she added quietly as they went up the stairs arm-in-arm. "Let's just take things a day at a time—that's the best way."

TWENTY-FIVE

The pregnancy was harder than Eva had expected. Not the physical part—that was normal for her: three months of nausea and fatigue, three months of insomnia and superabundant energy, and three months of relative normalcy hampered by constant backaches and by the weariness of carrying a big bump in front of her. She was enormous! The thirty pounds she gained all seemed concentrated in front—from the back, you could hardly tell she was pregnant. Dr. Wilkes predicted a large baby and was toying with the idea of a Caesarean section.

Eva wanted natural childbirth. She took the Lamaze classes at Dan's insistence, but was skeptical about the method's ability to override the pain of childbirth. Not that she was looking for ways of avoiding the pain. With a streak of masochism that surprised her, she *wanted* to feel the pain, as a physical catharsis to the emotional pain she experienced throughout the pregnancy. It was as if one kind of pain would take away the other.

The problem was still Rob. Her need for him haunted her. She dreamt of him constantly during her sleepy months and he was in her thoughts all through the nights when she lay awake, or paced up and down the house when lying down became uncomfortable. When the baby first kicked, she cried, wanting his father, Rob, to be there, to put his hand on her distended belly, to feel *their* child kicking, making his presence known.

She was tormented by doubts. Had she done the right thing by setting up a network of lies that would determine the course of the rest of their lives? Would it have been better to tell Rob about the pregnancy, to insist he leave his wife, to leave Dan? She badly needed to talk to someone about all this, but who? Eva had not made any really close friends since coming to Minneapolis, preferring to keep to herself as a student, and she'd never felt comfortable with Dan's old friends, whose wives were much older than she and who had teenage children, while Sharon was a toddler.

If my father were alive, he'd understand, Eva thought, grief adding to her sense of loss and isolation. He would probably have advised me to do exactly what I'm doing. To put the past behind me, to live for Sharon and for the baby, to accept that a life with Rob was not to be, to be grateful for Dan's devotion and love. But talking to her father would make things so much easier.

Eva agonized over whether she should call Rob, or write to him. Not to tell him about the baby—just to touch base, to find out whether he was all right, to find out how he was coping. She actually did start to write him a few times, knowing she could not trust herself on the phone; knowing, too, that he would sense from her voice that all was not well. A letter could be bright and chipper. Words on a page could be rewritten, reconsidered, controlled. The few attempts she made sounded banal and trite and stupid. She tore the letters to bits and flushed them down the toilet, realizing the futility of attempting any contact, knowing it would only add to the pain.

She was also terrified at the prospect of the baby being less than perfect. She wished she had asked Rob more questions about Jeannie. It was such a painful topic for him, and she had been reluctant to dwell on the subject during their precious hours together, hours when they'd lived only for each other. What was the nature of Jeannie's disability? Was she a Down Syndrome baby? That could hit anyone, at random, and had nothing to do with genetics.

No, that couldn't be it, thought Eva, remembering the beautiful sculptured face in the photograph. She didn't have the distinctive features of a child with Down Syndrome, just that frightening blankness in her eyes. Had the brain damage occurred during the birth process, or was it a genetic defect? Did her size have any-thing to do with it? Eva remembered Rob telling her that Jeannie had been a big baby, and how his mother had commiserated with Rhoda, as Rob, too, had been huge at birth.

"Is there any danger because the baby is big?" she demanded anxiously when she saw Dr. Wilkes. Her "due date" was just three weeks away. The baby might even be born next week, she thought, suddenly panicking.

She was lying on a special table, a television monitor close by, looking at what seemed to be a perfectly formed baby in the ultrasound image.

"No, I'm not as concerned as I was before," the doctor replied soothingly, moving the disk on her stomach to another location, to view the fetus from another angle.

"He's a big baby—you can see that it's a boy, so I won't bother being coy about it—but the head should fit comfortably into the birth canal. You may not make it to your due date, though—he's big for 37 weeks, and he's already turned head down. He's either impatient or ready to go! Are you sure about the date of your last period?"

"Pretty sure," said Eva shakily. "Is it very important?"

"Not really, dear," Dr. Wilkes said patting her belly and motioning her to get up and dressed. "Nature has a way of getting things done when things are ready. You've had a normal pregnancy and I don't anticipate any complications. Just make sure to have your suitcase packed, and tell Dan to be available at all times. This little tyke's not planning to hang in there for too much longer!"

Eva went into labor on July 22—forty weeks to the day from the time the baby was conceived. Her water broke as they were sitting down to have dinner. An hour later, her contractions were five minutes apart and Dan called Dr. Wilkes.

"Meet me at the hospital in fifteen minutes," the doctor told Dan. "I'll phone ahead and tell them to expect her."

Sharon clung to Eva. "I know I'm supposed to wait at home," she said, crinkling her forehead, "but can I come, too? I'll sit quietly with Mary and wait—I promise I'll be good."

Eva's eyes sought Dan's and he quietly nodded his assent.

"All right, Sharon," he agreed. "I appreciate your wanting to be there, honey, but please understand that I'll be with Mummy and that it could take a long time. You'll have to be prepared for a long wait."

Sharon beamed, as did Mary, who had not been relishing the thought of staying at home, waiting for the phone to ring. Waiting in the hospital would be easier somehow. And she was worried about Eva. She'd noted the haunted look that sometimes surfaced in Eva's eyes and she knew, as only another woman could, that despite the outward calm, this pregnancy had not been easy for Eva.

They all quickly bundled Eva into the car. It was a glorious warm July evening, but they were all too preoccupied to notice the sunset or the scenery. Eva's contractions were becoming more frequent, and Dan kept glancing at her anxiously, hoping they hadn't waited too long. Everything was happening so quickly. Sharon's birth had seemed to move at a slower pace.

Dr. Wilkes met them at the admitting office and had Eva whisked upstairs while Dan completed the formalities. He chuckled as he checked her.

"Seven centimeters dilated—I told you this tyke was in a hurry! Just ride with the contractions, Eva, breathe deeply. Dan will be here in a minute and then the show can begin—if the baby waits that long!"

When Dan dashed in a few minutes later, scrubbed and robed, there were almost no intervals between contractions. Eva was panting, trying to remember the Lamaze instructions, squeezing Dan's hand when the pain became unbearable.

"You're getting there, Eva," Dr. Wilkes said excitedly. "When the next contraction hits, bear down, don't hold back, help the baby out—I can see the top of his head!"

The next contraction was endless. Eva moaned softly as she pushed with all her might. The baby's head was out, a mop of dark hair covering its perfect roundness; then a shoulder popped into sight and the doctor eased the baby out, as smoothly and expertly as a wine steward uncorking a bottle of vintage champagne. The rest was a blur for Eva. She could only stare in awe as the nurses busied themselves with all the usual birth routines. At the baby's first cry, she had started to weep, the tensions and fears of the last few months bursting out of her like a dam out of control; sobs of relief and joy and wonder racked her body. Dan gently dried her face and smoothed her hair.

"Relax, baby. It's all over. He's a beautiful boy. Don't cry. Everything is fine…"

"You did beautifully, Eva," Dr. Wilkes said, patting her and smiling from ear to ear. "The baby is fine—a handsome specimen, if I do say so myself."

Eva smiled back through her tears as the nurse placed the baby in her arms. He'd been washed and wrapped in a receiving blanket, but he wasn't about to lie still. She touched her finger to one flailing little hand and the tiny fingers promptly grasped it. Like every mother from the dawn of time, Eva quickly counted fingers and toes. The baby was perfect. He was large—almost ten pounds, the doctor said—beautifully formed. Too early to tell about the eyes—they were still that undefined newborn slate blue that could turn into any color, fringed with thick dark lashes.

He looks like my baby pictures, Eva thought with relief. She looked in vain for any resemblance to Rob, but could find none. Just as well, she thought with a frown; it would make the duplicity she had opted for that much easier to carry out.

"Hey!" Dan said chidingly, noting her frown. "Don't tell me you aren't pleased with the product! He's a work of art!"

She smiled up at him, consciously shaking off any doubts about the choices she'd made up to this point.

"Yes he is, isn't he? I guess all babies are gorgeous—he just seems more so than most."

Dan stroked her cheek gently, the pride and joy in his eyes laying to rest any fears she'd had. She'd given Dan the son he'd always wanted and she herself now had a tangible, living reminder of the only great love she'd ever felt for a man. That will do, she thought numbly. As long as the baby grows up healthy and strong and happy, that will do. She squeezed the baby gently, before surrendering him to the nurse and said to Dan, a twinkle in her eye, "Don't you think you should go out and inform Sharon that she has a brother? The poor child is probably pacing the corridors!"

Sharon was euphoric. She wasted no time while Dan and Eva were in the delivery room and had called both her grandmothers. Dan's mother was on her way; Eva's mother was waiting by her phone and had already booked a seat on the earliest morning flight. Dan let Sharon break the news.

"Oma, he's here! The baby came! He weighs nine pounds twelve ounces and Daddy says he's gorgeous. Mummy's fine. Here's Daddy."

Dan assured his mother-in-law that all was, in fact, well, and promised to pick her up at the airport the next day. Next, he had to contend with his own mother, who had just arrived at the hospital, delighted that all was well but miffed that she hadn't been called right away.

"Don't be angry at Daddy," Sharon soothed her grandmother. "Everything happened so fast, if he'd called you from home, Mummy would have had the baby in the car!"

She'll be a diplomat yet, Dan thought as he tousled Sharon's curls and exchanged a conspiratorial look of thanks with his eleven-year-old spokesperson.

"I'm going to wait until they get Mummy settled into her room, Sharon. I want you to go home with Mary and get to bed at a reasonable hour. There'll be plenty of time to stay up once the baby gets home. I'm going to put you into a cab, and I'll be home in a couple of hours. Mother," he added in a solicitous tone of voice, "do you want to stay at our house tonight, or shall I get another cab to take you home?"

"I'll go home with Sharon and Mary, Dan," Mrs. Goodman replied, recognizing from her son's tone that offering to stay with him in the hospital would be the wrong move. He wanted time with his wife, and she knew better than to intrude. He really adores Eva, she thought. I never expected that he'd feel that way about a woman for any length of time. He used to discard women like used Kleenex.

"Congratulations again, Dan," she said, her eyes soft. "Give Eva my love and tell her I'll see her tomorrow. No need for you to come down, we'll get a cab at the entrance. Come along, ladies," she added briskly, as if going home had been her idea all along, and Dan, Sharon, and Mary all smiled.

It was close to midnight before Dan left the hospital. He would have stayed longer, but the nurse shooed him out, assuring him with an indulgent smile that they could handle Eva and the baby without him. Eva smiled at him sleepily when he left, glad of his presence and his joy, but happy to see him go. She was exhausted, not only from the sleepless nights of the past week and from the sheer physical effort of the birth, but from the emotional drain of the past nine months—the grief over losing Rob; the unavoidable anger at the choice he'd made; the strain of the charade she had opted to live by; and the terrible fears she'd had about the baby being born with any abnormalities. She'd carried it off, though. No one had suspected that anything was amiss, and the baby was fine. She grilled Dr. Wilkes after Dan left the delivery room and he gently, but firmly, laughed away her fears.

"He's a fine boy, Eva," the doctor said. "Reflexes all check out, he's fully developed, and you have nothing to worry about. Go home and enjoy the next few months—once that little devil starts to crawl, you'll be too busy keeping him out of mischief to worry! He'll be an active one!"

"I know!" Eva declared proudly. "He certainly kicked enough! I still feel black and blue inside!"

"Well, he'll make quarterback on the football team yet, but that's a long way to go. You look after yourself now, and get your beauty sleep. I'll see you in the morning."

For all her exhaustion, though, Eva could not fall asleep. She would doze briefly, then wake up with a start. Her body felt strange. She'd grown used to the enormous bump in front, but that was gone. She felt the flatness of her stomach, still a bit distended and flabby, but no bump—and no kicking inside her. She dozed again—that strange, unquiet sleep when bodily functions slow down but the mind keeps racing. At one point she opened her eyes slowly, or dreamt she did, and noted with no surprise that Rob was sitting in the armchair near her bed. They looked at each other silently for a long moment. Her eyes were expressionless, his were infinitely sad. With the slow-motion movement that dreams sometimes have, she saw Rob getting up from the chair. He bent over her and gently kissed her lips, stroking her hair and her cheek with a familiar touch.

"Goodbye, Eva, I love you," he whispered.

She nodded mutely, then watched him walk away. He paused at the door, giving her one last long look, then stepped out, gently closing the door behind him.

Eva closed her eyes. He's never walked away from me before, she thought. He's always been carried away—by a boat, by circumstances. But this time he walked away. She snapped awake again, noting the empty armchair in the streaky light of the dawn, feeling the familiar pain followed by the familiar resignation. The sounds of the hospital slowly filtered through her consciousness, shifting her thoughts away from Rob and toward the nursery where their child lay sleeping.

"…He can have my hair, if you insist, but I want him to have your eyes…" She could hear Rob's voice, see his smile, feel the warmth of his skin.

"…Goodbye, Eva. I love you…"

"I love you too, Rob," she whispered. "Goodbye."

And then she let go. She could feel her muscles and her mind relax as she consciously let go, falling into a deep, relaxed sleep; finally at peace with herself, finally accepting, finally casting aside all doubts and questions, finally ready to move on.

TWENTY-SIX

Jonathan completely changed their lives.

He was a magnificent baby. Plump and round and easy-going, with a mop of soft, dark curls and enormous gray eyes fringed with thick, silky lashes.

Sharon adored him. All the maternal instincts that she had lavished on the dolls she had outgrown were now directed at her baby brother. She helped bathe and feed and diaper him. She played with him, taught him his first words, read him her favorite nursery rhymes and poems, and watched over him like a jealous mother hen.

There was no trace of sibling rivalry or animosity. Rather than fighting to retain the limelight, Sharon insisted on sharing it, sometimes demanding that they include *her* Jonnie in outings of dubious suitability for a baby his age. Her only rivalry was with Mary. She accepted the fact that Eva was Jonathan's mother, and, as such, was entitled to a few choice perks and privileges. But Mary was a *helper*, as Sharon explained patiently to her obviously obtuse parents, not the mother-replacement she'd been when Sharon herself was little and Eva was at the university.

"It's not the same, Mummy, can't you see that?" she exclaimed impatiently when Eva gently tried to explain that Mary was doing her job in caring for Jonathan, just as she'd done when Eva went back to work after Sharon was born. "I didn't have a big sister, so Mary had to do more than just take care of me. But Jonnie has *me* and Mary shouldn't spend so much time playing with him. I want to do that! And besides," she added, muttering sullenly, "he loves me more than her, and he's *my* brother."

Eva's eyes met Dan's and they both smiled as Eva said gently, "Sweetheart, this isn't a competition to see who Jonnie loves more. You're his only sister and he adores you in a very special way. That doesn't mean he can't love Mary, too, or me, or Daddy, for that matter. Mary's work is to take care of him when Daddy and I are at work and you're at school, and taking care of him includes playing and cuddling, not just seeing to his physical needs. We're lucky to have someone like Mary who sort of decided she's a mother to all of us. She mothers you, too, honey, and you like it—don't begrudge Jonnie the same kind of care."

Sharon had to concede that her mother's points were valid, but she wouldn't admit it outright.

"Well, okay. I suppose he needs Mary, too, but *I* want to be the one to read him a bedtime story. He *is* my brother."

"Fair enough," Eva smiled, giving Sharon a friendly pat on her bottom. "And now to bed, young lady. Just because you intend to be a full-fledged certified mother by your teens doesn't mean you can stay up till all hours. Tomorrow is a school day."

Sharon kissed both her parents and skipped off to bed. She paused at the den door and surveyed the domestic scene with tremendous satisfaction. Her mother was curled up in one of the big armchairs by the fire, with one of her zillions of books, wearing a soft, long, deep purple robe that made her gray eyes seem violet-colored, her hair gracefully gathered at the nape with one of Sharon's hair clips. Her dad, still in his office clothes except for his jacket and tie, was sitting at the antique desk with a million papers strewn in front of him. She liked it when he looked like that—hair rumpled, collar button undone, a look of concentration on his face. He brought work home most weekday evenings, but that was better than staying at the office the way he'd done when she was little.

It dawned on her that her parents were both spending a lot more time at home in the year and a half since Jonnie came along and she, for one, thought that was great. They went out sometimes—usually to a concert or a ballet, or just to the movies—but they weren't party or country club people like some of her friends' parents.

That's probably because Daddy is so old, she thought, and because Mummy is so serious. But I'm glad they're like that. Old-fashioned and a little bit fuddy-duddyish. *Staid*, she thought, remembering a new word she'd recently picked up. Daddy is staid and so is Mummy. And she's also sad sometimes, but that's since Papa Hermann died.

Sharon had been an insatiable, keen-eyed people-watcher ever since she was small. Her parents especially were objects of scrutiny, more so since they'd separated and gotten together again. That was an awful time, and Sharon prayed nothing like it would ever happen again. She wasn't clear on the details, she'd been so young at the time, and her parents never spoke of it—certainly not in her presence, and not even when she eavesdropped, which she did whenever she got the chance. Not that she got the chance too often. Her mother seemed to have a sixth sense with regard to Sharon's presence, and invariably threw open the door Sharon was lurking behind and sent her off to bed.

As if reading her thoughts, Eva lifted her eyes from her book and stared at Sharon, who was still standing there motionless, her hand on the doorknob.

"Are you still here!" Eva exclaimed, feigning anger, but Sharon could hear the chuckle in her voice.

"I was just leaving—g'night!" she answered hurriedly and dashed upstairs before she could be chastised further.

As she did every night after taking her bath and brushing her teeth, she checked in on Jonathan, covering him with the blanket that he'd thrown out of the crib, as he always did, arranging the teddy bear in the center of the crib.

"You're so beautiful," she whispered, gently touching her brother's soft curls, running a finger on his round, rosy baby cheek, then across his chubby, dimpled hand. "And you've made us all so happy. Even Mummy is hardly ever sad anymore. G'night, baby." She bent over the crib and brushed the sleeping child's cheek with her lips, then went off happily to her own room.

TWENTY-SEVEN

Eva continued staring at the den door long after Sharon had gone, lost in her own thoughts and oblivious to her husband's watchful look.

Jonathan was the best thing that could have happened to Sharon, she thought. And to the rest of us, for that matter. He had filled a void for each of them, she realized, and by doing so, had brought them closer together, made them more of a family.

For Dan, although he knew the pregnancy was unplanned, the baby symbolized a second chance. Jonathan was a living omen that things could still be put right between him and Eva, and he intended to make the best of that opportunity. He became a family man to a degree he'd never imagined possible, spending every free minute with his wife and kids, working as hard as ever, but staying away from home as little as possible.

And if things will never be perfect between us, Eva thought wistfully, it won't be for Dan's lack of trying. He knew better than to shower her with gifts and flowers—those were objects, and not the stuff of which commitment was made. But now he took an active interest in her work and discussed his own problems and dilemmas at the office with Eva whenever he could. He became more involved in the upbringing of his children than he'd ever been before. Eva had to chuckle when she heard him discussing with Sharon, with total seriousness, what Jonathan should be when he grew up.

And then there's me, Eva thought. Sharon and Dan have found their niches. They are where they want to be. And where am I?

One part of me is rooted firmly here, involved in the day-to-day of raising the children, running the house, teaching yet another generation of semi-literate students to appreciate Jane Austen and George Eliot. She conceded that, by and large, she was content. The children were wonderful. Sharon was developing beautifully. She was a straight-A student, popular with her friends and classmates, and gorgeous as well. She seemed to have none of the awkwardness that some adolescent girls have and none of the moodiness that Eva remembered from her own teenage years. Maybe that's just around the corner, Eva thought with dismay, but thank God she's so easy now.

Jonathan was a model baby, but even if he hadn't been, she would have felt the same fierce, protective love for him. Sharon and Mary could quibble over who would read him a bedtime story, but Jonathan was hers in a way nothing else ever had been. Beside the normal mother's love she felt for him and the tenderness he awoke in her with his softness and baby warmth, he had somehow helped to fill a void that she knew deep down would never be filled. Sharon had done that, to a degree, after her father Hermann died. But that death had been more natural, and in retrospect, easier to accept.

More than two years after their separation, she still grieved for Rob. That familiar pain that never totally left her always accompanied her thoughts of him. The anger was gone, as was the guilt she had initially felt at not telling him that she was pregnant with his child. He'd made the choice he had to make and she had accepted what she had to accept. Initially, she had hoped that he would call or write. She'd played out scenes in her imagination of a chance encounter, what she'd say, what he'd say.

And then she'd accepted that he was gone. Just as gone as her father was. Just as inaccessible. She was, despite the pain, grateful that Rob hadn't tried to contact her. It would have resolved nothing, only opened up wounds that had never, and would never, fully heal. That was why she gave up any thoughts of writing to him. She knew instinctively that his pain was, if anything, greater than hers. Although he was in a catch-22 situation, he was the one who made the choice to part. And he had no Jonathan. No Dan or Sharon, either, for that matter. Just Jeannie, with the beautiful face and empty eyes. Jeannie, whom he loved dearly and who loved him back but could never give him the kind of joy and pride and satisfaction that Eva got from Sharon's accomplishments, from the thrill of watching Jonathan's body grow and his mind unfold. Eva sighed, then gave a start as Dan's voice cut into her reverie.

"A penny for your thoughts," he said lightly. "Although that seems to have been quite a marathon, judging by the length of time you've been staring at a totally uninteresting door! Probably about five dollars' worth!"

Eva blushed, embarrassed at having forgotten his presence in the room.

"No," she paused, at a loss for words for a moment, and then went on. "I was thinking about the kids and about how lucky I am…they really are terrific, both of them."

Dan put down his pen and said quietly, "Not a day goes by when I don't thank God for the two of them, or for you…" He got up abruptly, walked around the desk to her chair, and pulled her up into his arms.

"I don't think I've told you lately how happy you've made me," he whispered gruffly in her ear, unfastening the hair clip and running his fingers through her hair. "I wish I could show you so you'll know how much I love you."

Eva extricated herself from his embrace and went to stand by the fire, stretching her hands toward the blaze, feeling suddenly cold.

"You don't have to 'show me' anything, Dan," she said, an acerbic undertone tingeing her voice, though she didn't want it to. "I wish you wouldn't feel that you have to keep proving something, over and over again."

He came up behind her and wheeled her around to face him, his hands on her shoulders, his eyes a blazing, angry blue.

"I'll stop feeling that I have to prove something when that look disappears from your eyes. You don't know what it does to me!"

"What look?" Eva asked, startled. She'd kept such a lid on her emotions for so many years now. What was it in her eyes that she was unaware of?

"That sad, forlorn look of a child who's lost everything and everyone that matters. That look!" he said fiercely. "The look I first saw when you found out about Barbara, the look that resurfaces every once in a while, when you're deep in thought and you think no one's looking."

"That's water under the bridge," Eva scoffed defensively. "*Long* under the bridge. I've told you that a thousand times."

She tried to pull away, but his large hands remained firmly pinned on her shoulders. He towered over her, the difference in their heights accentuated by the fact that he was wearing shoes and she was barefoot.

"Then what is it?" he demanded. "Why are you sad? Is it something I'm doing, or not doing? *Tell* me, for heaven's sake!" He shook her until her teeth rattled. She angrily pushed his hands off her shoulders, her eyes blazing now.

"Stop it, Dan!" she raged. "Stop looking at me through a magnifying glass and analyzing every nuance of my expression. I'm not a butterfly in a glass showcase. I'm a person! I laugh, I cry. I have happy thoughts—I even have the occasional sad thought. Imagine that, Dan Goodman! I, your lawfully wedded wife, am not ecstatically happy twenty-four hours a day, seven days a week! If that's a blow to your manhood—too bad! I can't smile and simper all the time so that you can consider yourself a roaring success as a husband. It's your ego that's giving you problems, not me!"

She turned to face the fire again, her arms tightly clenched around herself, still shaking with anger, taking deep breaths to regain her composure.

Eva rarely exploded; her deep passions and emotions were usually kept in check by her tremendous need to be in control. But when she did explode, she was a fireball, a mass of seething emotions that Dan found strangely exciting. She was only really outwardly emotional when she was deeply angry.

It hadn't always been like that. He could remember her abandon when they'd made love, early on in their relationship, before he'd lost her trust, and her love. He looked at her rigid back, knowing she was fighting for control, and realized that he found the sight incredibly erotic.

"You are so beautiful when you're angry," he murmured, pulling her toward him without turning her around, cupping her breasts in his hands, nuzzling her neck and ears.

She could feel his erection against her back and she leaned against him, willing her anger to disappear and her lower lip to stop trembling. The best way to stop a fight with Dan was through sex. She'd learned that years before and so she went along with him as he unzipped her robe and tossed it aside, then ripped off her lace panties. She stood naked in front of the fire, the flames giving her skin a burnished hue, her face impassive.

He quickly removed his shoes and pants, his erection springing at her, throbbing, demanding access. He was larger than usual, his arousal heightened by anger—both his and hers. He sat on one of the large armchairs, pulling her toward him, spearing her on his manhood, then guiding her slowly down his shaft until he was fully inside her. Eva closed her eyes. Too much was showing in her damn eyes anyway. As always at times like this, Rob's face floated in front of her. She was straddling him, moving up and down, gyrating her hips to increase their pleasure, meeting his thrusts. She could tell from Rob's expression on the face imprinted in her mind that he was about to come—the look of near-pain that marked the height of his ecstasy—and she could feel the ripple of her orgasm imprinting its own rhythm on their lovemaking.

Dan exploded inside her with a low moan of pleasure, semen bursting forth in uncontrollable spurts. Eva opened her eyes as she collapsed on him. He was still inside her. Dan, not Rob. But it didn't matter. This is where she was, and this was what she could and would have. She'd come to terms with that a long time ago, and she'd made the best of it.

TWENTY-EIGHT

This is becoming a terrible drag, Eva thought as she filled in forms with her students' final marks for the year.

She put down her pencil and rubbed her temples to ease some of the pressure building up in her skull. It wasn't a headache yet, but she could tell it would become one. She'd been having these headaches often lately, and the symptoms were becoming familiar—the slight ache in her temples, the invisible band tightening around her brain, the throbbing pain when it reached the back of her neck.

Classic tension headaches, the doctor had said, asking whether she was under a lot of pressure lately.

Eva had smiled wryly at the question. "Pressure? Yes, I would say I'm under some pressure."

The head of the department was about to announce his retirement and there was a mad political scramble for his position, of which Eva wanted no part. But it was more than that, she knew. She'd been with the department, in one capacity or another, starting with her student days, for more than fifteen years. She was comfortably ensconced, her tenure and position assured by her years of teaching experience, the success of her one book and many articles, and the popularity of her courses. Her undergraduate courses were always packed, even though English literature in general and the 19th century in particular were suffering a fall from grace in these task-oriented, career-seeking '70s.

Eva was a superb teacher. She had a way of generating excitement in a class, of giving the characters and situations not only life—Austen and Dickens did that on their own—but present relevance. She communicated her love of the language to her students. They would leave her lecture appreciating the fact that a thirty-page scene in a Henry James novel could be thrilling—even if it described "only" an outing on the Seine with lunch at a riverside café.

Eva herself was popular. Her students liked her, finding her accessible and interested, not only in their literature courses, but in themselves as people. Inevitably, there would be the odd male student who fell madly in love with her, but she could, and did, handle these cases with tact and ease. It was flattering, at age thirty-six, to have a man years younger pursue you, but she was never even tempted to follow that path, though many of her male colleagues did, with younger female students.

Eva's grip tightened on her pencil as she recalled an incident that had happened earlier that year. That damn Andrew Harper, she thought with distaste. Fifteen years later and he's still at it, the old satyr. Not that she kept tabs on Andrew. They had been cordial enemies for years, not because of the affair they had when Eva was still a student. He'd been a cad, and she'd been, in her own estimation, a fool; but she'd long since chalked up that one to experience. He had never touched an emotional depth in her and her anger, when he'd dropped her, had been directed at herself, rather than at him.

What Eva could not tolerate was his behavior since then. He'd known when her marriage was in difficulty—it was his wife, after all, who'd been busy spreading rumors and stories to anyone who would listen. He should have said nothing, or expressed his sympathy if he had to open his mouth at all. Instead, he had figured that this would be a grand opportunity to get Eva back into his bed. Eva smiled as she remembered his chagrin—and his total disbelief—at being spurned. When she and Dan separated, he'd gone after her with increased determination and no small degree of obnoxiousness. He found it truly hard to believe that she did not find him irresistible, and Eva still chuckled when she remembered the scene in her office when he'd virtually tried to rape her. She had kicked him in the balls—literally—and the look of pain and total amazement on his face was one she would never forget.

"I'll get you for this, you bitch!" he swore when he could finally hobble to the door.

"You make one more move in my direction, Andrew Harper, and I'll sue you for sexual harassment!" she shot back at him. "*I* don't care about the publicity and about what people will say about me—or about you—but your wife might care. She might even care enough to dump you. You couldn't afford your country club—or your womanizing—on a professor's salary, so think very carefully before you come near me again."

The steely coldness of her eyes had more than matched her tone and he backed off. And then, this year, she'd had to confront him again.

Margery Dale, one of Eva's brighter undergraduate students, had made an urgent appointment to see her a few months earlier. She seemed distraught and frightened, and Eva offered her a cup of tea before they sat down to talk.

Sipping tea in the coziness of Eva's book-lined office, the girl calmed down enough to start speaking.

"I'm sorry to bother you, Dr. Goodman, but I didn't know who else to turn to. The only people I know in the city are here at the university, and I don't know any of them well enough to ask them for help."

Eva nodded, encouraging her to go on.

Margery took a deep breath, then blurted out, "I'm pregnant. I don't believe in abortions, but I don't have much choice. The father of my baby is married. I don't expect him to leave his wife. There was never a question of that. But he won't help me, either. He threw me out when I told him. I...I don't have any money. My parents have a farm in Kansas and they couldn't even afford to help me go to university. I'm working my way through, and I have a scholarship that covers part of my tuition. One of the girls in the dorm had an abortion last year...she bled for a week and she probably won't be able to have children. I...I'm afraid to do that. I found out where to go, but I can't pay for it... This is terribly presumptuous of me, I know, but you're the only person I know here who could probably afford to help me... I'll pay you back, I promise..."

Eva stopped the flow of words with an impatient flick of her hand. She had an idea who the father was. She'd seen Margery with Andrew Harper a number of times—in the cafeteria and at a few of the student hangouts around the city. She had wanted to say something, to warn the girl, but felt that she would be making a fool of herself. I should have listened to my instincts, she thought in hindsight.

"Of course I'll help you, Margery, you don't have to worry about that. Is it just a matter of money? Are you sure you know where to go?"

The girl took a deep breath, her face awash with relief.

"I have the name of a good doctor, at a clinic. But it's $500, and I don't have that kind of money."

Eva nodded, frowning. "Is there a reason for the father of the baby refusing to help? A financial reason, I mean. Is he a student?"

"Oh no, Andr—I mean, the father, could afford it, but he won't help me. He was livid when I told him. Said it was my responsibility. And besides, he refuses to concede that the baby is his—just that it *might* be." Her eyes filled with tears. "It's his baby, Dr. Goodman. I haven't been with anyone else."

Eva looked at the girl with narrowed eyes, seemingly weighing something. She hesitated for a moment, then spoke.

"Margery, I don't want to pry, and I wouldn't ask this question under any other circumstances, but please answer me truthfully. Is Andrew Harper the father?"

The girl nodded mutely, then noting the hard expression on Eva's face, asked hesitantly, "How did you know?"

"Because I was in your shoes once, a long time ago, and it was also him. I didn't get pregnant, so I escaped with only a bruised ego. Thank you for telling me. I'll see to it not only that you get the money, but that you never have to pay it back. Get on that phone and make all the arrangements. I'll be back in five minutes. Don't go before I get back."

Leaving Margery behind, Eva marched down the hall to Andrew's office and rapped sharply at the door. She winced at his fruity "Come in," wondering how she could have ever found such a creep attractive.

"Why, Eva!" he exclaimed with phony delight. "What an honor! What brings you to my little domain? What can I do for you?"

"You can cut the bullshit, for starters, Andrew," she replied tersely, her eyes narrow slits of steely gray. "What I want from you, by tomorrow morning at 9 a.m., is an envelope, with $500 in twenty-dollar bills. This is the 20th century, Andrew. Men who want to play squire and have their way with naïve country girls have to at least pay the price of the abortion."

"I don't know what you're talking about," he replied, his friendly tone changing to ice.

"You may not know, but Veronica will, by 9:05 tomorrow morning, if you don't come up with the cash. I'll be in my office waiting. Don't be late. Dean Williams is next on the list, after Veronica, then the local gossip columns."

He said nothing, but the deflated expression on his face told her all she needed to know. He would come up with the money.

"It's all arranged, Margery," Eva said when she re-entered her office. "The money will not be a problem. Did you get hold of the doctor?"

"Yes—tomorrow afternoon at 2."

"Good! Be here at 1:30, and I'll take you. Bring an overnighter with your stuff. You'll stay at my house for a few days until you're better." She smiled at her and Margery smiled back, through a haze of tears.

"I...I can't tell you how grateful I am. I don't know why you're doing all this for me." She burst into tears.

Eva put her arms around the sobbing girl and quietly handed her a tissue.

"I'm doing it because you need help, and because I like you."

And because there but for the grace of God go I, and because you look like an older Sharon, and because some men deserve to be hanged, she added to herself. "Andrew Harper is a prick and if he so much as looks at you again, you come and tell me."

Eva knew she had deepened an enmity. Harper had powerful connections at the university and he could—and would—look for ways to hurt her.

Her anger grew at that thought and her tightening grip on her pencil snapped it in two, bringing her thoughts back to the present. As usual, she tried to analyze her feelings. Work had always been her salvation and refuge. Why was it becoming such a tedious chore? Departmental politics had never interested her. Her advancements had always been based on merit, not on connections. No university could afford not to acknowledge talent, and she'd been that from very early on.

Nor had she needed to indulge in the one-upmanship that so many of her colleagues used to bolster their egos. Her work had always been top-quality, solidly rooted in painstaking research, enhanced by her unique literary insight and her ability to write in an articulate, thought-provoking, and totally unpompous manner. One critic had called her style "Churchillian," which had amused her to no end; all had cited her lucidity, logic, and ability to make a point. Eva now admitted that she had not written anything of consequence in three years, hadn't even wanted to. Not since Rob, she thought, wondering whether she would always count time in terms of before and after Rob. She had devoted more time to teaching than to research of late, needing the human contact that forced her to maintain a certain façade, and consumed hours that she would otherwise have spent with her thoughts and her memories. Especially the memories.

She wondered how much of her present attitude had to do with the emotional upheavals of the last two years, and how much was simple burnout.

I've been studying and teaching for about twenty years, she thought. No wonder I no longer care about what Jane Austen's heroines wore to dinner....

TWENTY-NINE

"You look thoughtful," Dan said that evening. "Is everything all right?"

Eva smiled inwardly. He's become such a Jewish mother, she thought, so worried if anyone shows a sign of fretfulness or concern.

"I think I'm having a career crisis," Eva replied lightly. "I'm even thinking of asking for a sabbatical, but I'm not quite sure what I'd do with it."

"Write another book?" Dan asked anxiously. He remembered her total immersion when she'd written her first book and he dreaded a repeat of that.

Eva laughed, reading his unspoken thought. "No, don't worry. I don't think I have another book in me. My problem isn't that I want to write. I don't even want to read lately!"

"Why don't you just take the year off and do nothing? You didn't miss so much as a day when you had Jonathan. Why not stay home for a while?"

Eva grimaced. "Mrs. Daniel Goodman, hausfrau? No, that's not me. I would die of boredom. Of course I could always join the Veronica Harper bridge and tennis set," she added with distaste.

"Is Andrew giving you any problems lately?" Dan asked with a flash of perception. "Because if he is, I'll break his neck!"

Eva laughed again. "No, he's too scared of me. Thinks I'm a real ball-crusher!"

Dan smiled in response. He'd been proud of the way Eva handled the incident with Margery, though he'd objected when she brought the girl home, feeling that was going a bit too far. But he backed off at the ferocity of Eva's response to his mild remonstrance. It was a touchy area with her—men's responsibility to their unborn children—and he hadn't wanted to stir up long-buried feelings. Besides, Margery had turned out to be a honey. She and Sharon had become fast friends and Jonathan toddled after her wherever she went. The Goodmans had "adopted" Margery, and she became a frequent guest at their house. What a shit Andrew was to treat her that way, he thought.

"Is Andrew in a position to hurt you?" Dan asked, his businessman's instincts taking over.

Eva considered his question.

"No-o," she said eventually, "not at this point. We're equals, in terms of position. Of course, if he becomes head of the department, that could change drastically. He couldn't touch my tenure, but he could make my life miserable."

"What are his chances of getting it? Does he want it?"

"Oh, he wants it, all right. Crowning glory and all that. He might even do a good job—he's a better administrator than a scholar. But I sure don't relish the thought of working under him!"

They both smiled at the pun, their eyes meeting with the camaraderie of the shared joke. It was a warm early summer evening; they were sitting on the porch swing on the patio, reveling in the warmth.

She's so lovely, Dan thought, giving the swing a gentle nudge. Eva was wearing a pair of old faded Levis—they'd been old when he met her—and a University of Minnesota T-shirt that was miles too big. Her hair was swept back in a ponytail and in the soft light of dusk she looked fifteen, not thirty-six. He suddenly had a vision of what she would look like in thirty or forty years. The eyes and the cheekbones would always give her face a special beauty, even when the youthfulness faded.

"Why are you looking at me like that?" she asked.

"I suddenly realized that you are going to be one very sexy old lady! I hope I'm around to see it!"

Her heart gave a lurch. Eva rarely thought of the future, and when she did, it was always in terms of the children, not of herself and Dan. Not that she considered leaving him. There was no reason to leave. Not anymore. Since Jon's birth they had become closer—capturing the friendship that had eluded them in the early years; and if they didn't share a grand passion, it was at least a very comfortable relationship. They would never have had this conversation ten years ago, so it was nice to be having it now.

But I never think of the future in terms of the two of us, Eva thought with a pang. I wonder what it will be like. She smiled at her silliness, and got up as the kitchen phone started ringing.

"Don't push it, buster," she kidded, "and don't make us old before our time. We have a two-year-old sleeping upstairs, for goodness' sake!"

Dan smiled and remained on the patio, while Eva talked on the phone inside. He couldn't hear what she was saying, but sensed agitation in her voice. She stepped outside a moment later, her face white as a sheet.

"What's wrong?" he jumped up, startled.

"They want me!" Eva said, her voice muted in shock. "That was Dean Williams. They want me to head the department! I have a meeting at his office tomorrow morning, when they'll make a formal offer. He called me to 'warn' me, so I could get my thoughts together in terms of what I want to say!"

She lowered herself into a lawn chair, staring at Dan without really seeing him, her thoughts turned inward.

He remained silent for a few moments, sensing that she needed time to mull over the offer.

"What *do* you want to say?" he asked gently, breaking the silence. "It's an incredible offer. It's crossed my mind that you would jump at the opportunity if it were offered to you."

"Has it?" Eva asked, surprised. "I mean, did you really think I was even in line for the job? I didn't."

"That's because you underestimate yourself—or maybe you overestimated the competition."

"No, really, it's not that. I never thought in terms of comparing myself to the competition because I wasn't competing. You can't imagine the maneuvering that's been going on, but I've had no part of it."

Dan smiled. "A babe in the woods!" he admonished with a chuckle. "Maybe that's what they want. Someone who *hasn't* pulled strings or finagled, and who is every bit as capable of doing the job—probably more capable—than all the others. Your track record is phenomenal, Eva. You're a scholar's scholar and a gifted teacher, as well."

She warmed to his praise. He'd come a long way in his appreciation of her career. Her eyes twinkled humorously and she said in a self-deprecating tone, "And you're not biased at all, I suppose!" Her voice turned serious. "That's not the issue, anyway. A job like that is a challenge, but I know I could do it. The question is whether I really want it."

"But…"

"Oh, I know it's a big step up," she interjected, cutting him off by echoing what he'd been about to say. "I just honestly don't know whether taking that step appeals to me. Here I've been debating with myself about leaving the university altogether, then all of a sudden I'm shifting gears, figuring out what changes I'd like to make in the department. It's crazy!"

"No, it's not," Dan argued. "It's normal. You've been doing the same thing for years and you're getting bored. You've made a name for yourself and it's no longer a challenge or a climb, and you're vegetating. The new position is a whole other ballgame. It'll be another mountain to climb. And you'll be fantastic. I say, take it!"

Eva looked at him with a bemused smile.

"You've really changed, Dan," she said quietly. "I can't believe you're actually pushing me to undertake something that will take time away from you and the kids."

"But it will give you something *you* need," Dan said in low tones. He looked at her intently, then added slowly, "You know, the first time we visited your parents, your father and I had a discussion about your independence. He told me about your paper route and your need to be 'financially independent,' even at that young age. It took me years to realize that he was giving me fair warning and a good piece of advice—not to try to curb or compromise that independent spirit in any way. It was a hard lesson for me to learn, male chauvinist that I am. But I did learn—and I can't believe that you'd be happy settling into the rut you're already in, or copping out altogether." His eyes narrowed and he looked at her appraisingly. "You're not a quitter, Eva. Why are you contemplating quitting? You'd hate yourself for doing that."

She lowered her eyes, tapping a slim, sneaker-shod foot on the cement patio floor, engrossed in thought.

"You're right," she said finally. "If I turn this down, I'll always wonder whether I was afraid of the challenge. But I won't box myself in, either. I'll take it for just one year, if they let me. Then we'll see where it goes."

"Atta girl," Dan said with pride in his voice. "I know you'll be great!"

Eva's face screwed up in a goofy grin. "I'm glad I have your support," she laughed. "A lot of people are going to be mighty surprised—and mighty angry. I hope Williams has his raincoat ready, because a lot of shit is about to hit the fan!"

"You conniving bitch! You did this to get even with me!" Eva looked up from her desk, her eyes registering mild surprise. She'd been expecting an outburst of some sort, but Andrew's absolute fury as he bounded into her office was over the top.

Her appointment as head of the department had just been announced, quashing the wild and mostly inaccurate rumors that had kept the campus on its toes for weeks. There was no mention of the appointment being for one year only, although Eva had insisted that both she and the department have the option of taking stock after a year and then making a final decision.

The announcement stunned a lot of people—there had been so much politicking going on, and Eva had not been considered a serious contender, mostly because she showed no inclination to go after the job. The general reaction, after the initial surprise, had been largely positive. Eva was liked and respected by her colleagues, and the caliber of her work was well-known. A few of the older male faculty members were miffed—both because of her age and her sex—but they could not make complaints on such grounds in the last quarter of the 20th century. Those who had vied for the position and lost, for the most part, accepted their loss with good grace.

Andrew, it seemed, was going to be the exception. He stood there glowering at her, his arms akimbo, his hair wild, and his shirt and tie in disarray.

"Won't you sit down, Andrew?" Eva asked politely, with just a tinge of amusement in her voice. "Would you like a cognac? You look as if you could use one."

"Don't condescend to me, you whore! Who did you sleep with to get the appointment? Was it Williams? He goes for blow jobs, I hear. You always were good in bed, if memory serves me, but even I didn't think you'd stoop so low."

Eva's expression closed up tight and her voice was cold.

"You'd better leave right now, Andrew. And don't you ever walk into my office for so much as a paper clip without making an appointment first. You might also consider asking yourself whether all the students you did sleep with helped you to be passed over for the position, but that's not my business. I have no intention of being a heavyweight and exercising my authority— unless I have to—so watch your step and don't tangle with me. Now get out before I call the security guard to throw you out!"

He glared at her, but she met his look with icy eyes and a cold demeanor that told him she meant business.

Damn that woman, he thought as he turned to go, regretting his outburst, realizing that it wasn't the politically savvy thing to do. I can never get the better of her. The thought riled him and he left quickly before his temper got the better of him once more.

Eva slowly exhaled, realizing that she'd been holding her breath. That's one bad enemy, she thought. Not that that was anything new. But she'd have to watch her back as long as Andrew Harper was around. And he'd probably be around for a long while.

THIRTY

Dan had been right.

The challenge of the new job revitalized her and charged her up with all her old energy and fervor. Eva spent the first three months learning everything there was to know about the department in particular and about the university's administrative procedures in general.

"Hey, slow down!" Dan protested laughingly when she brought home mountains of files and documents to read well into the night. "You only took over the department—they're not expecting you to run the whole university—yet!"

Eva smiled back. "It's interesting. I'm discovering a whole new world—government grants, foundations, alumni, public relations… They'll soon need M.B.A.s to run university departments—not mere Ph.D.s in the Humanities."

"Just don't feel you have to do it all at once; they don't expect you to set the world on fire in one year—just to show that you can run a smoothly functioning department. I don't think anyone has any doubts on that score."

If anyone did have doubts, Eva dispelled them quickly. She streamlined departmental bottlenecks and broke down the cumbersome and inefficient faculty meetings into smaller, more frequent, more task-oriented sessions of four to five people dealing with similar issues. Within three months of taking over, she was able to get back to her literary work. She was teaching only one graduate course—one she had given before, for which little additional preparation time was required—and she suddenly had time to catch up on her professional reading and to sketch out drafts for a number of articles for various scholarly journals.

But I'm still bored, Eva admitted to herself grudgingly. There was only so much she could do as head of a department and she truly had no aspiration to move up higher in the university bureaucracy. Mastering the intricacies of the new job had been interesting and challenging, but by the Christmas break, the challenges facing her had been met and Eva found herself asking the same question she'd posed the previous summer: now what? Is this what I want to do with the rest of my life?

Dan sensed her unrest and suggested a family vacation in Florida as a change of pace.

"One of my clients has offered us the use of his house at Delray Beach," he told Eva one evening after Jonathan had been put to bed. "It's right on the ocean, apparently, and has every convenience you could dream of—what say we take a two-week break? It'll be great for the kids—and you're starting to look peaked again!"

Eva agreed readily. Minneapolis was already buried in several feet of snow, and the winter promised to be a difficult one. Maybe a spell in the sun would snap her out of the doldrums she seemed to be in, even if only temporarily.

"This was a great idea, Dan," she said a few weeks later as they sat by the pool watching Sharon patiently teach Jonathan to swim. A week in the sun had obliterated their northern pallor. Sharon and Dan were turning honey-colored, and Jon and Eva with their darker skin tones were well on their way to deep brown.

Dan joined Sharon in persuading Jonathan to put his face in the water and blow bubbles and Eva watched the three of them from her deck chair through half-closed eyelids. For the thousandth time, she noted what a beautiful family grouping they made as they cavorted at the shallow end of the large pool. Dan's looks belied his fifty years. He still had the physique of a college quarterback and whatever silver was in his hair only enhanced the golden-blond. Sharon, at thirteen, had none of the gawkiness usually associated with puberty. Taller than her mother, but with the same slim and graceful build, she looked stunning in a simple one-piece bathing suit, her honey-blonde mop of hair pulled back into a ponytail. Her features were a copy of Eva's, but she had Dan's startling cornflower-blue eyes, thickly fringed with long brown lashes. Eva's gaze switched to Jonathan and, as always, she felt her heart expanding in the warm glow that his baby softness always evoked. Holding on to a small flutter board and buoyed up by a set of bright yellow arm floats, Jonnie was earnestly making his way across the width of the pool with strenuous kicks of chubby baby legs, encouraged by Dan and Sharon.

"Atta boy!" Dan exclaimed as Jonathan reached the other side. He scooped up the boy and squeezed him tight, nuzzling Jonathan's neck, and being nuzzled in return. With his dark hair slicked down by the water, Jonnie looked like Eva's baby pictures. Dry, she knew, his hair would spring back into Rob's soft curls. That and his dimples seemed to be the only physical attributes he'd inherited from Rob. Not that it really matters, Eva thought drowsily, he's Dan's son.

The familiar pain engulfed her and she closed her eyes. It's more than three years, she thought, marveling at the passage of time but fully cognizant of the fact that the hurt had not really diminished. Nowadays, Eva rarely permitted herself the indulgence of thinking about Rob. He was somehow always there though, on the periphery of her consciousness, but the pain of focusing on his image was something she generally was able to avoid. Now, almost masochistically, and in direct contrast to the warmth of the sun and the idyllic family scene in front of her, she closed her mind to her surroundings and looked inward, recalling Rob's soft brown curls—so similar to Jon's darker ones—the twinkle of his dark eyes, the sound of his voice, and the feel of his large masculine hands.

There had been no contact since they'd parted. Not a note or a phone call. He had dropped out of her life completely, almost as though he'd never existed, except for the profound change he had wrought in her internal life—and, of course, Jonathan. There was always Jonathan to remind her, to hold on to, to evoke Rob's memory. Eva let her thoughts rove to Jeannie, the little girl who had come between them and whose needs had proven stronger than Rob's love for the woman he'd never expected to find. The china-doll face with the vacant eyes. She'd hated Jeannie for a while—hated her for depriving Jonathan of his real father, for depriving her of the only man who had ever fully captured her heart.

But Jonathan has another father, Eva thought, recalling the scene at the pool—the man and the boy hugging each other in a mutual outpouring of love. Jeannie has no one else, only Rob. Eva had stopped resenting Jeannie long ago, when her anger at Rob's decision had also abated. Yes, he'd hurt her. But he had no choice, and he'd hurt himself more. She had Sharon, and now Jonathan, and she had the love of a good man who would stick with her through thick and thin, who was tuned into her moods, who cared. She often wished she could reciprocate in kind, but knew she never would; not beyond the point where caring and concern and friendship and respect became the one thing she could not offer Dan—real love.

When she opened her eyes, the sun was low in the western sky and the pool was empty. She must have slept for a good two hours. Dan had taken the children inside, letting her sleep, sensing she needed the rest and the escape that sleep afforded.

Eva Goodman, she chided herself as she stretched her stiff limbs and felt the first chill of the evening air, you are an idiot! Stop your pining and get on with your life. You have more than most people, and if it's something less than Utopia, so be it!

In all fairness to herself, she conceded that pining and yearning for something she could not have was not her normal emotional state. The sun and warmth and total relaxation had lulled her into letting down her usual guard, allowing to surface feelings and thoughts that she normally kept tightly bottled up.

Back in the bottle! she commanded, grabbing her beach towel and walking slowly up the steps to the patio and into the house to rejoin her family.

THIRTY-ONE

"I'm leaving the university, Dan," Eva announced one winter evening. "I'm finishing the year and handing over the reins to whomever they choose."

Dan looked startled, but he wasn't overly surprised. The vacation had been a rest, but it hadn't solved the problem of Eva's growing discontent.

"Don't burn all your bridges," he advised, trying not to show his hurt at not being consulted on such a major decision.

"I haven't. Officially and as far as they know, I'm taking a year's sabbatical and resigning the chairmanship of the department. But I know I'm not going back. What's the point, when getting up in the morning to go to work becomes an intolerable chore? When nothing I do during the longest part of the day gives me satisfaction anymore?"

"Would one of the Ivy League colleges be better?" Dan asked slowly, realizing he might be pushing an option fraught with personal perils for their family. "You've had offers from Harvard and a few others."

Eva smiled, reading the thoughts behind his words, noting his understandable apprehension.

"No, that wouldn't make a difference; it would be more of the same in a more prestigious environment. It isn't prestige I'm looking for, it's change. That I'm sure of. What I don't know—yet—is what to do with next year—and with the rest of my life, for that matter, in regard to a career. I'd like to run something. If I've learned anything this year it's that I have a knack for ad-ministration and for working with people—I think I'd like something along those lines—but I don't want to go back to get

164

another degree. I want to do something in the real world—I've really had enough of academia."

Dan looked at her appraisingly, weighing the idea that had just popped into his head, assessing the pros and cons with his usual incisive business sense.

"Come work with me," he said, smiling at the shock and surprise registered on Eva's face. "I'm not kidding. My office manager is leaving. She's a bright, capable lady, but her husband is being transferred to the West Coast and she's looking for a job out there—she'll have no problem finding one, but I'll have a problem replacing her. The job involves a lot of areas you don't know—secretaries and keeping tabs on everything from marketing to manufacturing to bookkeeping, though each of those departments has a person in charge. Think about it."

Eva nodded mutely, then finally found her voice. "But wouldn't that look funny? I mean, my being your wife. Doesn't that smack of nepotism or favoritism?"

Dan laughed. "You know," he responded with a chuckle, "for a bright lady, you can be really obtuse sometimes. It's my company—something I built up from the small jewelry store my father left me to a nice, medium-sized business. I did it for myself initially—to prove to myself that I could, and to finance the lifestyle I wanted—which once included a fancy apartment and a sports car. But for the last fifteen years, it's all been for you and for the kids. Don't think for a minute that I would compromise what I've built just to give you a job. It's something I know you could do, and do well—and I think you might enjoy it, too. Nepotism!" he hooted. "What's wrong with nepotism, as long as you keep it in the family!"

Eva smiled back. "I'm sorry—I didn't mean to be unappreciative or ungracious—and it does sound interesting. I'd like to try it, but only on the condition that my being your wife doesn't hamper you in any way. In other words, feel free to boot me out if you think I can't handle it."

"Don't worry," he said seriously. "You and the kids have shares in this business. Do you think I would let anyone jeopardize that just to give them a job? Now sit down and let's talk business!"

They agreed that Eva would start in July, spending the first month with Katherine Brice, the present manager who was leaving in August. That would give Eva a chance to get to know the people and learn the ropes. She would start at 80 percent of Katherine's salary, working her way up to 90 percent after six months, and the full salary at the end of one year, if she proved herself. Her hours, benefits, working conditions, and advancements would be the same as for anyone else. Dan knew better than to offer anything more generous, and he wisely made no concessions based on the fact that she was his wife. Everyone in the office was on a first-name basis anyway, and he knew that within a few weeks no one would even think of her in terms of her being Mrs. Goodman. She would be Eva and she would carve her own niche, as she'd done with anything else she had ever undertaken.

Eva tackled the job with her usual zeal for challenges. She spent the first two weeks following Katherine like a shadow, steno pad in hand, taking notes. She also took files and ledgers home to read in the evening in order to familiarize herself with all aspects of the business while Katherine was still available to answer questions.

"Your new boss must be quite a slave-driver," Dan grumbled one evening when she refused a night out at the movies, pleading a stack of work as her excuse.

"Oh, he is!" Eva replied with mock solemnity. "And I'm scared he'll tell my husband if I fall down on the job!"

Delving into the workings of the business, Eva came to realize the tremendous amount of growth and progress that Dan had quietly but tenaciously brought about. He had turned a small retail jewelry shop that had provided a comfortable income into a wholesale business that supplied hundreds of stores throughout the Midwest with gold jewelry imported from Italy, pearls and jade from the Orient, diamonds from Brussels and Amsterdam, and semi-precious and precious colored stones from South America. She was able to appreciate, really for the first time, the importance of the personal contacts he'd established in each of those places and the importance of the frequent buying trips that the business entailed. She also realized how much effort and extra work Dan had expended into keeping those trips as brief as possible, giving him more time with his family than he would have otherwise had.

Eva enjoyed the innate beauty of the merchandise they dealt with. Selling was selling, but pork bellies were one thing and jewels were another. She found herself thinking in terms of doing more with their merchandise than buying, importing, and selling—there was so much that could be done with design. But there would be time for that. First, she had a business to learn.

Eva proceeded with caution initially, acutely aware of her own inexperience in the field and sensitive to possible resistance based on her being the boss's wife. Whatever changes she initiated were carried out with full consultation and consideration of the people they would affect. Katherine had run a tight, well-managed ship and many of the changes were not of substance, but rather reflected a different working style that was more typically Eva. By and large, the people working under her and with her responded favorably to her presence.

As Dan had expected, the employees soon stopped thinking of her as Mrs. Goodman. She was Eva, and she pulled her weight and was nice to work with. She also did her homework, and wasn't shy to ask questions when she encountered an aspect of the business with which she wasn't familiar.

Goodman's had started out as a family-type business—a few of the older employees still remembered the store and had known Dan since his childhood—and although the business had expanded, something of the old camaraderie and sharing still remained. Within a few weeks, Eva was accepted on her own terms and as her own person. She assumed that any jokes or complaints regarding "The Boss," as Dan was affectionately known, were curtailed in her presence, but she decided that there were probably few of either. Dan was a fair employer, liked and respected by his staff, and responsive to any valid complaints or issues that were directed his way.

Eva found, to her chagrin, that she could not avoid bringing one unpleasant issue to his attention, though she held off as long as she could.

It involved the head of the bookkeeping department, Anne Masterson, a bright, fairly attractive woman in her early thirties who had done a good job of running her department and meeting the changing needs of the business in the seven years she'd been working for Goodman's.

That Anne didn't like Eva was apparent from the first day, but Eva had expected resistance and attributed it to the fact that she was Dan's wife, hoping that time would resolve the matter. It didn't. Anne's attitude was barely civil, despite Eva's attempts to be friendly. She asked Katherine about it, hoping the more experienced woman could offer some advice on how to handle the situation. Katherine was vague and brushed off Eva's questions with a flick of the hand.

"Don't pay it any mind, Eva," she said. "She'll get over it when she gets used to the fact that you're here to stay, and when she comes to terms with the fact that being married to the boss doesn't mean you're a flighty society lady who's doing this job for a lark."

Eva smiled at that. Society lady, indeed! She, of all people! She also resented the automatic assumption on Anne's part that being well-off meant she was a lightweight.

Anne was a conscientious worker, but Eva wondered whether she'd ever spent night after night reading and researching and writing; whether she could match her own meticulous perfectionism and capacity for sheer hard work.

She finally confronted Anne. Katherine was leaving in a week and Eva wanted to clear the air and get all the issues on the table before she took full charge.

She could have summoned Anne to her own office, but opted to visit Anne's office instead, relinquishing the "edge" it would give her. She was not looking to score points or pull rank—just to clear the air.

Not much chance of that, she thought with a sinking feeling as she noted the tight, closed expression on Anne's face when she walked into her office.

"Yes?" Anne said flatly. "What can I do for you?"

"You could offer me a seat, for starters," Eva responded with an attempt at a friendly smile.

Anne shrugged her shoulders and waved her hand in the direction of one of the chairs facing her desk. She herself remained seated, keeping the barrier of the desk between them. Eva sat down and spent a few seconds surveying the office. She'd seen it the first day on the job when Katherine gave her the "grand tour," but hadn't been in it since. It was small, but extremely neat and well-organized. She looked at Anne and was taken aback at the anger in the woman's eyes.

"Would you like to inspect anything? I can assure you everything is in very good order."

Eva chose to ignore her tone. "No, I haven't come on an 'inspection'—although it is part of my job to oversee your department." She kept her tone neutral, biting back a sharper retort. "What I would like to do is resolve the working relationship between us. You've been very hostile since I started working here, and things don't seem to be improving. I find the situation very unpleasant and I'm sure you aren't enjoying it, either. We're both intelligent women and I'd like us to try to resolve whatever it is that's creating this hostility. We could start by your telling me what the problem is."

Anne's eyes narrowed. "And if I don't? I suppose then you'll cozy up to the boss one night and ask him to have me fired in return for your favors! Is that what you're trying to tell me?"

Eva was shocked at the venom, but maintained a cool façade.

"Is that what's bothering you? That I'm married to the boss? I don't see why it should. It has no bearing on what goes on in the office, and certainly not with regard to your work. You seem to know your stuff and you're running an important department efficiently. I know Dan has always been very satisfied with your work. Why am I a threat?"

Anne looked at her probingly, seeming to weigh her words. "Because," she finally replied, "I am determined to do everything in my power to get your husband away from you, and if you think coming here to keep an eye on him is going to stop me, it won't."

Eva sat rooted to her chair. Oh, shit! she thought. Here we go again! Poor woman—I wonder if Dan knows how she feels.

She rose slowly, really looking at Anne as a woman for the first time, wondering how Dan saw her, responding to the hurt in Anne's eyes.

"I'm sorry you feel that way, Anne," she said, choosing her words carefully. "It must be very difficult for you, feeling the way you do. I do have to tell you, on a personal level, that you are on a very painful course. Dan is a devoted husband and father, and this business means a lot to him—almost as much as his family. I don't think he'll do anything to jeopardize either. I think you really have only two options—to come to terms with reality and continue working here, or to leave and go elsewhere, where you can make a new beginning.

"I can promise you that Dan will not let the office be a personal battleground for anybody. I'm prepared to work with you if you're prepared to meet me halfway, but I won't tolerate your present attitude and behavior. Please think about it. There's room for both of us here—but only if we can work as part of a team. You can be infatuated with my husband and you can hate me all you like—but if it interferes with your work and creates friction or tension in the office, your job *will* be on the line. Not because you are a threat to me—you're not—but because you'd be a threat to the business. Think about it."

Eva walked out of Anne's office with the same calm demeanor, but she was trembling inside.

"What's wrong?" Katherine asked sharply as Eva walked into the office they were sharing for one more week. She had already moved out her personal effects and Eva was starting to bring in her own plants and photographs. The basic office would remain the same, but the atmosphere created by the personality occupying the office was changing gradually.

Eva sat down in one of the armchairs, her knees shaking. She hesitantly related the scene that had taken place in Anne's office and noted the sympathetic expression in the older woman's eyes.

170

"Well," Katherine sighed, "I guess it was bound to come out sooner or later. I was hoping Anne would control herself, or get over this crazy crush she has on Dan—she's good at her job and she'd be hard to replace, but if this gets out of hand, you'll have to do just that."

"Is this 'crazy crush' common knowledge throughout the office?" Eva asked with concern.

"Why?" Katherine replied, meeting Eva's eyes with a level gaze.

Eva smiled. "Don't get me wrong, Katherine. I'm not concerned with gossip—I've lived through it and survived, and it really doesn't affect me." Katherine started working for Dan long after Barbara had left their lives, but there were still a number of old-timers around and Eva was sure Katherine had heard the gossip.

"What concerns me is the possible perception of Mrs. Boss as dragon-lady, slaying any damsel in her path who dares to look at her man. I'm prepared to work with Anne if she'll work with me—but not if she lets her personal emotions get in the way. If she does, there won't be room for both of us here—and I don't think I'm about to leave. I'm enjoying this job too much."

"Then you'll have to fire her, Eva, no matter what people's perceptions are. There'll be talk—a number of people know how she feels—but talk of that nature is something you'll have to learn to live with if you're going to work in a management position. Give her another week or two, for form's sake, though I don't think it will make any difference. Then take the matter to the boss. He'll see it your way, never fear," she added, answering the unspoken question in Eva's eyes. "This company means too much to him to allow a moony-eyed employee to make trouble."

Eva nodded, grateful for Katherine's hardheaded advice and cool objectivity.

"Does Dan have any idea about all this?" she asked tentatively. "I mean, about the way Anne feels about him?"

Katherine smiled broadly. "Hell no, honey! The man is moonstruck! He has a stunning wife and two gorgeous kids and that's as far as he sees. The Queen of Sheba could throw herself at his feet and he wouldn't even notice!"

And then, in response to a strange look of pain in Eva's eyes that disappeared an instant later, Katherine patted the younger woman's arm and said in a gruff voice, "Dan doesn't even look at other women, Eva. He may have been a swinging bachelor and it may have taken him a while to grow up, but he's madly in love with you, and the kids run a close second. Don't ever have a doubt on that score."

THIRTY-TWO

"Are you going to fire her, or do you want me to do it?" Dan asked, his eyes blazing with anger. Eva had finally come to him with her problem with Anne, and he was livid. Since the affair with Barbara and all the attendant pain and heartache, Dan had been scrupulously careful with women employees, treating them no differently than he would a male, curbing the natural openness and flirtatiousness that was such an integral part of his social manner. Business was business, and his company was going to be run in a professional manner at all times. That Anne had the audacity to even think of him in personal terms—and that she'd had the gall to make no bones about it to Eva—positively enraged him.

"I think we'd better do it together. There's going to be talk no matter how we handle it, but at least let it not be perceived that one of us is hiding behind the other." Eva looked glum. She had hoped it would not come to this, but Anne's manner had gotten worse. Computer printouts and weekly reports that were supposed to cross Eva's desk before going on to Dan somehow managed to bypass her, and getting information from Anne was like pulling teeth.

"It's part of the game, Eva," Dan said, echoing Katherine's words. "You can't manage a business and be nice to all the people all the time. Sometimes you have to pull rank, and this is one such occasion."

He buzzed his secretary on the intercom.

"Please ask Anne to come to my office immediately." His tone was brusque, but controlled.

Anne walked in three minutes later, a smile on her face that faded as soon as she saw Eva sitting in one of the armchairs.

Dan motioned her into the other chair.

She already realizes, Eva thought, noting the look of defeat in the woman's eyes. She was looking at Dan, ignoring Eva as best as she could.

Dan came straight to the point.

"Today is Wednesday, Anne. I'd like you to spend the next two days clearing out your office. Leave any pending matters with the junior bookkeeper and anything of a more complicated nature with Eva. You'll be getting two months' pay in lieu of a month's notice, which I feel is fair considering the caliber of your work, and I'll be happy to give you a positive letter of reference. Let me recommend to you that in the future you keep your personal feelings as much out of your work as possible. Very few employers will tolerate that kind of nonsense, especially if it interferes with the smooth running of their operation. If you have no questions, you may leave now."

Anne's eyes were angry, but she knew better than to add fuel to the fire. Dan was furious under his calm demeanor. She'd miscalculated badly in thinking she'd intimidate Eva, but she'd erred even more with regard to Dan. She thought he was ignoring the very obvious signals she'd been sending for months as a concession to office decorum, but that he'd come around sooner or later. She was an attractive woman and any man she'd ever wanted, she got. Anne now realized that Dan hadn't been ignoring her signals—he hadn't even seen them. The office was the office, where he functioned on a purely professional level.

Oh, well, there were other fish in the sea, and she'd hook the next one, she thought. True, not too many of them were as good-looking or as young as Dan Goodman, but most of them weren't married to a knockout like Eva, either, and as a result they were easier game. Eva *was* beautiful, bright, and hardworking. She'd do her job well, but Anne would not be around to see it. She'd blown this job, but she'd go on to another one. She was good at her work, and in the long run, that's what counted.

Anne nodded curtly in response to Dan's dismissal, looked coolly at Eva's impassive face, then turned on her heels and marched out of the office, almost slamming the door behind her.

Dan and Eva were silent for a moment. Then Dan left his seat and perched at the front of his desk, near Eva's chair. He held her chin and looked straight into her eyes.

"I just want you to know something, Eva," he said quietly. "I had no idea that Anne had any kind of feelings for me, and I did nothing to encourage them."

Eva smiled up at him. When would he ever feel that she did not need his constant assurances of fidelity and love?

"I know that, Dan. With your looks, you don't need to send encouraging signals—women flock to you anyway! I'm just sorry there was no other way to deal with Anne, but I suppose it's just as well. Meanwhile, I'd better get back to work—I have to see about replacing a bookkeeper."

She still doesn't care, Dan thought with a sinking feeling as Eva left the room. He was used to women throwing themselves at him. They'd been doing that since he turned sixteen and his tall, skinny boy's frame had turned into the American ideal of male good looks. It started with the salesgirls in his father's store and con–tinued with almost every woman he'd met—including the loving wives of many of his married friends. Eva was one of the few women who hadn't gone into a swoon over his looks from the minute she met him, maybe because she elicited the same kind of response from men and found it somehow distasteful. They joked about it when they were first married, with Eva insisting that he had the edge over her in breaking hearts.

"You're smart and successful," she had teased. "Women like that in a man, even if he isn't so good-looking. Add to that your Paul Newman looks, and it's a lethal combination. With me, the smart and successful turns off a lot of men. Thank God for small favors! And a female Ph.D. is an ultimate turnoff for a lot of men."

"I'm lucky you didn't have a Ph.D. when I met you!" Dan teased back. "God knows you were bristly enough without it! It took some doing to notice your looks through the thorns, let me tell you!"

They both laughed at the time, sharing the intimacy of a mutual problem—a spouse overly attractive to the opposite sex. But they'd been sure of each other then. That was gone. Even if he remained totally faithful to Eva for the rest of his life—and he fully intended to—she would never be sure of him again. Nor he of her, for that matter. He'd wondered at times whether there had been another man in her life since they had reconciled. At one point he had thought there might be someone—Eva had seemed remote and distracted for a while some years back. But then they had Jonathan and she seemed much more contented since. Damn "contented," he fumed inwardly; I want to see her happy, ecstatic, roaring with laughter, hot with passion, or livid with anger.

She'd become placid, creating an atmosphere of warmth and calm that attracted adults and children to her, but had no room for highs and lows of feelings. As if she'd had too many of those highs and lows, and had purposely eliminated them from her life. He almost ached for a fight with her, just so he could see once again the depth of emotion he knew was in her but that she'd covered up so assiduously since Barbara. It was still there, he knew. One doesn't lose the capacity to feel deeply. But it wasn't there for him. He could not plumb the depths of her anger, just as he could not scale the heights of her passion, not because they had disappeared, but because she'd shut him out of both those emotions.

And it was all your own doing, you *schmuck*, he chastised himself for the millionth time, then sighed deeply and returned to the work piled up on his desk.

THIRTY-THREE

"Smart move, Mrs. G. Anne should have been fired months ago, but Katherine felt she'd get over her *shtick*. I knew better—those types never do!"

Eva looked up from her work and smiled warmly as Bernie Schwartz sauntered into her office and plunked himself down in an armchair facing her desk. He'd just gotten back from a trip to Japan and must have heard the news.

"I'm glad you approve, Bernie—there really wasn't much choice. I just hope it hasn't aroused too much resentment among the rest of the staff."

"Naah—don't worry about that. Most people didn't much like her—and the gal you hired to replace her is a honey. Too bad she's married!"

Eva smiled and sat back in her chair. Bernie had become her ally, and she liked him. A fellow uprooted New Yorker, raised in Brooklyn and as Jewish as his name sounded, he nonetheless looked like the stereotype of an Ivy League WASP—tall and slim, with straight honey-blond hair that always fell over his tanned face and baby blue eyes. Bernie loved women and they loved him, and, at thirty, he saw no reason to settle down with one when he could have his pick of as many as he wanted.

"That's why I left New York," he told her soberly the first time they shared a coffee break.

"There weren't enough pretty women in New York!?" Eva had asked in amazement.

"No, sweetie! Too many! My mother was always after me to get married and settle down. Especially after my sister got married."

177

Bernie decided to move to California and got sidetracked before getting there when a mutual business acquaintance introduced him to Dan, who was looking for a sales manager. He came to work for Dan around the time Jonathan was born, and the two men hit it off from the beginning, becoming fast business friends. Bernie, however, had refused to extend the friendship beyond the parameters of the business and, as a result, only met Eva for the first time when she started working at Goodman's.

"Imagine!" he said to Eva as she wordlessly handed him a cup of steaming black coffee. "I never wanted to accept any of Dan's invitations to dinner because I was terrified I'd meet a stereotypical suburban Jewish wife who would right away make like a *shadchen* and start matchmaking…so I screwed myself out of knowing you all these years!"

Eva grinned at him. "Well, we can make up for lost time…do I have a girl for you! As a matter of fact, she's coming to our house for dinner on Friday night—wanna come?"

Bernie groaned and Eva laughed. Then they settled down to business and spent an hour going through customer accounts, orders, suppliers' letters, and other aspects of Bernie's work with which Eva gradually was becoming familiar. Bernie was her most valuable mentor and, as Dan's right-hand man, knew the intricacies of the business as well as his boss did. Eva was a quick study, grasping the abstracts as well as the day-to-day nuts and bolts of the operation, and he enjoyed showing her the ropes. Eva, for her part, was reveling in every aspect of the business—especially liking the speed and ease with which decisions were made and implemented. After her years at the university, where getting a new filing cabinet could take anywhere from months to years, it was refreshing to work in a milieu where needs were answered almost as soon as they were articulated, and where decisions to buy or sell were made within hours—or sometimes minutes.

At 5 p.m., Eva's secretary buzzed to say she was leaving and to ask whether there was anything else they needed. A half hour later, Dan sauntered in, delighted to see both Eva and Bernie poring over a draft of an enormous contract their lawyers were in the process of drawing up with a big pearl dealer in Japan.

"Time to go, Eva—the kids will be waiting," he reminded her. "Bernie, join us for dinner if you're free—then we can continue this discussion over cognac and coffee." Bernie looked at Eva questioningly and she nodded with a smile. "The only girl I can introduce you to tonight is fourteen…but you're more than welcome to join us."

Bernie accepted with alacrity. He'd known Dan for years and Eva for a few weeks, but he suddenly wanted to know them better. He followed them home in his bright red Corvette and Dan grimaced as he watched in the rearview mirror.

"Young Jewish playboy with a 'vette," he said with a wry smile.

Eva chuckled. "I seem to remember a young Jewish playboy with a Mercedes who was very upset when a certain date made absolutely no comment about it!"

"You noticed that, did you? That was when I decided I'd better change my tactics." He frowned. "I hope Bernie has the sense to find someone who isn't impressed by his Corvette and who sees beyond that prickly Brooklyn exterior. He's really a fine person."

"How about Margie? Should I get them together?" Eva asked.

Dan wrinkled his brow.

"I don't know. For all his complaining about his mother, I don't think Bernie would get seriously involved with a non-Jewish girl. Let it be, for now."

The evening was a delight. Bernie loved the house with its comfortable, lived-in warmth and he and Jonathan hit it off immediately—the Corvette had something to do with that, Bernie suspected.

When Sharon finally came down the stairs—she'd been on the phone with a friend, for a change—Bernie gave a long, low wolf whistle and Sharon blushed furiously.

Bernie immediately looked contrite.

"I'm sorry, Sharon. That was very rude of me. Your mother talked of a fourteen-year-old and I expected a little kid in pigtails—not a blonde beauty who looks at least eighteen." He extended his hand for a grown-up handshake. "Please say you forgive me. I won't be able to eat a thing if you don't."

Sharon giggled and shook hands, won over by anyone remarking that she looked older than she really was, then gave

Dan her usual "welcome home" squeeze—much more reticent and lady-like than Jonathan's bear hug.

"Go see if Mary needs you in the kitchen, honey," Dan said, giving her rump an affectionate thwack. "Bernie and I will have a drink in the den until dinner's ready."

Eva disappeared—first to say hello to Mary and then to change out of her business clothes—and the two men had the room to themselves. Bernie looked around appreciatively, noting the hundreds of volumes in the bookcases as he settled into one of the leather armchairs.

"That daughter of yours is a knockout," he told Dan seriously. "You'd better watch out and not bring home too many old lechers like me. It might prove dangerous."

Dan warmed to the praise and handed Bernie a tumbler of Scotch.

"She is something, isn't she? We forget, seeing her every day and all that. But if you want her to be your friend, forget the looks and concentrate on the brain—she's one bright kid!" He chuckled and went on. "When she was about six, one of my mother's friends was gushing over how pretty she was and Sharon looked her straight in the eye and said, 'You know, Mrs. So-and-So, it's not important that I'm beautiful. What's important is that I'm smart!' She had us all in stitches."

"Well, she certainly is beautiful and that's a wonderful addition to being smart. It's the combination of your coloring and Eva's features, topped off by those eyes. She'll be breaking hearts all over the place, mark my words."

Bernie would have raved on, but the call for dinner came in the form of a yell from Jonathan. They all trooped into the kitchen for one of Mary's specialties, accompanied by a lot of laughter and lively conversation.

After dinner, when the kids had gone upstairs and the three adults were back in the den sipping coffee, they got down to business and discussed the contract with Kobe Pearls at length. They hammered out suggestions for changes to the few clauses that were not beneficial to Goodman's, then called a moratorium on business for the rest of the evening.

Over cognac, Bernie looked around appreciatively.

"You know, Eva," he said in surprised tones, "this family could make me change my mind about getting married. Looking around the dinner table at the four of you...you're such an ideal all-American family and there's such a feeling of harmony and accord and...contentment is the word, I guess. It makes marriage seem very attractive all of a sudden."

He noted a flash in Eva's eyes, a look that disappeared almost instantly, replaced by a slow smile. Contentment was a good word, she thought. Happiness...well, happiness was something else.

"We're lucky, Bernie," she said seriously, "but there's a lot more to raising a family than a Norman Rockwell exterior. We look better than most because we're financially comfortable, we live in nice surroundings, and our kids are beautiful—but that's just the outside. There's a lot of coping and compromising and commitment that you need in a family situation, so do it when you're really ready—not before. Get all your wild oats sown before you decide to settle down, and when you do, let it be for real, not just to play house because your mother wants you to, or all your friends are doing it."

Dan gave Eva a piercing look, but said nothing, and Bernie, suddenly sensing a minefield, said in a bantering tone, "You're right, Eva. And overgrown child that I am, I'm probably not ready yet anyway. Then there's the problem of actually finding someone to share the rest of your life with. Most Jewish girls I've met are spoiled princesses...maybe I'll stick around and wait for Sharon to grow up—she'd certainly be a refreshing change!"

Dan chuckled. "Forget it, Bern! Marrying the boss's daughter is not the way to move up in this company. You'll just have to keep on working your tail off!"

"Speaking of which," Bernie said, looking at his watch in mock horror, "it's past 11 and we all have a busy day tomorrow, so I better move along. Thank you for a great evening—I'll see you guys tomorrow. Tell Jon I'll come by one of these weekends to give him a spin in the Corvette. And give my love to the heartbreaker—brains or no brains, I still think she's a knockout!"

Dan was turning off lights as the sound of Bernie's Corvette faded away. He joined Eva in the kitchen, where she was stacking coffee cups and brandy snifters in the sink, and came up behind her, wrapping her in his long arms and nuzzling the back of her neck.

"Do you think I'm still 'playing house'?" he asked gravely, "or do you realize how 'for real' this is for me?"

Eva shook her head ruefully. She'd inadvertently stepped on an eggshell, hitting a sore spot without intending to.

"I must have sounded very pompous back there! I didn't mean to. It's just that I really like Bernie. I wouldn't want to see him rushing into something he's not ready for—and he's not ready to settle down, as far as I can tell."

She turned to face Dan, their eyes inches apart.

"You know what it took for us to get where we are now," she added. "People look at us and see some sort of ideal. They don't realize that we too have had our ups and downs and rough times, and that we've both had to come to terms with each other's shortcomings and flaws and... 'shtick' is the best word, I guess. I'm not complaining—don't get me wrong. I know I'm not everything you thought I was or hoped I would become, and you know where and how you've let me down. I'm just saying that that's part of any human relationship, no matter how wonderful it may look to outsiders. We all hurt, and disappoint, and fall short...the trick is to accept it and go on anyway..."

She shook her head and extricated herself from being caught between Dan and the sink.

"There I go again, waxing philosophical! I'm sorry. Let's go to bed—it's really getting late."

"Is 'contentment' enough for you, Eva?" Dan asked as they settled into bed.

Eva stretched out her arm and switched off the lamp on her night table.

"Contentment is perfectly fine, Dan—let's not start that conversation now."

"Okay," he agreed, molding his body to her curled-up form, "I won't. And you're right—contentment *is* fine." But I want more, he thought, I want so much more.

THIRTY-FOUR

Sitting on the patio on a warm, sunny fall Sunday, Eva took stock of her life and she liked what she saw.

Jonathan recently had turned four. The baby chubbiness had disappeared completely, to be replaced by a skinny, boyish toughness that she and Dan found hilarious. A bright, active, curious child, with a mop of dark curls and his mother's unusual gray eyes. At this early stage in his life, Jonathan was interested in cars, planes, and anything mechanical; dismantling and assembling clocks, small appliances—anything with nuts and bolts in it. He took himself very seriously and even Sharon had stopped babying him and playing mother. She was now teaching him to read, despite Eva's protests that Jonathan would be bored silly by the time he got to school.

"You'll just have to send him to a more challenging school," Sharon insisted. "It's not fair to hold him back. He's really bright, Mummy," she added soberly. "Much more advanced than I was at his age. We really have to start looking for a suitable school—he'll be starting kindergarten in a year, and I really think you and Dad should consider sending him to Drake. He's too good for a regular school."

Eva smiled indulgently.

"Don't you think you're being a bit biased, honey? Jon is bright, there's no doubt about that, but aren't you overestimating him? Don't forget that he's living in a household full of adults, so he's not as babyish as a lot of kids his age, but that doesn't mean he's a genius."

"Trust me, Mother." Eva noted the switch from "Mummy"—part of Sharon's determination to be considered an adult. "I do a lot of babysitting and he's really not like other kids his age."

Eva sighed. Sharon was probably right. She usually was about most things. Genetics count after all, she thought. She'd always been smarter than her peers but Rob, though he'd always been self-effacing about it, was near-genius level and it was possible that Jonathan had inherited his IQ. If he had, it should be nurtured by the mental stimulation of a top school. Yes, Sharon was right, and Eva would start researching special schools as soon as possible.

Then there was Sharon, going into her sophomore year in the private girls' school that she'd opted for and insisted upon for herself. She's no slouch, either, Eva thought. In any department. At fifteen, Sharon was nothing short of stunning, her inherited good looks enhanced by a special glowing luminescence that was all her own. She was a person who truly cared about other people, outgoing and fun-loving without a hint of the snobbery or aloofness that was often characteristic of girls her age. She was class president, co-editor of the school newspaper, active in a million and one committees, popular in a school of girls that at times had a deserved reputation for cliquishness. She consistently refused to be identified with one group or another, or to have any part in the backbiting or bitchiness that privileged teenaged girls could so often display.

Work was good, too, Eva thought. It had been the right decision to leave the university and to go to work in Dan's business. She knew the ropes now and enjoyed the job immensely. She and Bernie had proven to be a good team, bouncing ideas and innovations off each other, then "selling" them to Dan, who was more conservative and cautious. Both of them felt that the retail aspect of the business should be phased out, or at least changed, and that Goodman's should expand its turf and act as importer and supplier to some of the more exclusive department stores chains. That would take some convincing. Goodman's had been around for a long time and had a loyal clientele who wouldn't dream of going elsewhere. Dan was loathe to give that up, or even to give over the reins to a manager. But Eva and Bernie would keep trying.

As if on cue, Bernie's Corvette pulled into the driveway, right behind the more conventional sound of Dan's new Jaguar. Not the car for Minneapolis winters, he'd agreed, but something he'd always wanted, and it had been a good year. He could always ride to work with Eva or take a cab when the weather was really bad.

Everyone congregated on the patio and Sharon went inside to make lemonade. After a desultory hour of small talk, they all agreed on pizza for dinner. Bernie and Sharon would make the salad, Jonathan would help set the table and Dan and Eva would drive into town to Rossini's to get a couple of his extra-special pizzas—the ones available from the fast food places that delivered were simply not up to the Goodmans' standard for fine Italian food, nurtured by years of being pampered by the Rossinis.

"I'll take your car, Bernie," Dan said. "It will save moving cars around."

"Sure," Bernie retorted, digging into the pocket of his jeans and tossing the keys to Dan. "It will also save getting tomato sauce all over your precious new Jag! Just in case you thought we weren't on to you!"

The children giggled as Dan caught the keys and gave Bernie the finger. "Don't worry, Bonzo! Eva will hold the pizzas straight—just make sure you do a good job washing that lettuce."

"He's not wrong, Dan," Eva said, still smiling as they backed the Corvette out of the driveway. "You are a bit of a nut about your new car."

Dan grinned in agreement. "Damn right! Besides, I haven't driven one of these toys in a long time. Since my profligate youth, in fact; and there's this date I'm trying to impress who isn't bowled over by my Jag. My Mercedes didn't wow her, either, come to think of it," he continued clowning.

"Damn right!" Eva echoed, picking up his mood and enjoying the banter. "She doesn't give a hoot for your cars! It's your sexy looks that wowed her."

They drove on in a companionable silence, Dan busy with the gears as they stopped and started at the many stop signs that dotted the quiet residential neighborhood.

They chuckled at one corner as a small tow-headed boy on a shiny new two-wheeler with training wheels waddled across the intersection, to their right, his path paralleling their own.

"Reminds me of Jonathan," Dan smiled, edging the car past the stop sign.

The next few seconds would always remain vivid in Eva's mind. The shriek of a sports car's wheels to their left as a young driver came barreling down toward the intersection, oblivious to the stop sign; to the red Corvette beginning to edge out, crossing his path; and to the child on the bike a few feet ahead of the Corvette's nose.

Dan reacted instinctively, as if the child were, in fact, Jonathan. He shot the Corvette forward, into the path of the oncoming car, shielding the bicycle from certain annihilation, praying the car would hit the Corvette's rear left side. Instead, it hit the driver's door head-on in a sickening crunch of metal and glass; the impact turned the Corvette ninety degrees to the right. The windshield shattered and, through a curtain of falling glass, Eva saw the child shoot forward to the safety of the opposite sidewalk. Her head hit the side window, and she blacked out for a few seconds. When she could see again, the silence was as loud as the noise of the impact had been. Dan was slumped forward, not moving, his head at a funny angle. Then people began running toward the car, tugging her door open, trying to pull her out.

"Dan!" she screamed, touching him gingerly. His body was slumped sideways, his head now resting in her lap. His forehead was cut, she noted numbly, a trickle of blood running down the side of his face from his left temple. There was no other sign of injury, just the deathly pallor of his face, the closed eyes. Instinctively, she touched the artery on the side of his neck, feeling the faint fluttering of a weak, irregular pulse.

A sob broke from her throat. "Help me, help me! Please! He's alive!" She resisted the person trying to pull her out, then realized there was no other way to get Dan out of the car. Vaguely she could hear sirens, hoping it was an ambulance.

Orderlies and police officers moved in, doing their duty methodically and efficiently, sitting her in a special seat in the ambulance alongside the stretcher on which Dan was now laid out. Events overtook her and she moved mechanically, numbly doing as she was bidden by the white-uniformed people who seemed to know exactly what to do.

"Is he all right?" she asked the doctor bending over Dan in the emergency room, fighting down the hysteria she felt creeping into her throat, her eyes huge with fear.

"He's alive," the doctor said crisply. "We'll see more in surgery. Is there anyone we can call to be with you?"

She nodded mutely as the nurse stuck a phone in front of her and she quickly punched in the number.

"Sharon, honey…Daddy and I have been in an accident. We're at the General Hospital. Please stay with Jon and ask Bernie to come right away. I'm fine. We don't know how badly Daddy was hurt, but he's alive, that's what counts. I'll call you as soon as I know, honey. Stay with Jon! I'll call you soon."

THIRTY-FIVE

When Bernie came tearing in, Dan was already in surgery. Eva had refused adamantly to be admitted and the doctor conceded that since all she seemed to have was a large bump on the side of her head, she could sit in the waiting room outside the O.R. Bernie found her there, looking beaten and fragile, her eyes stricken.

"There was a little boy," she told Bernie numbly. "He would have been hit...Dan shot the car forward to shield him...Your car—it's a mess. I don't know what they did with it."

"Shhh," Bernie soothed, smoothing her hair back, noting the bump on her temple and the spreading blue mark. "Are you all right?"

"Yes—I was on the other side. I only bumped my head. But the other car plowed right into Dan. He was going so fast." She closed her eyes, reliving the horror of the moment.

"Stay here, Eva. I'm going to find out what's going on and call Sharon. She'll be frantic with worry."

He came back a few moments later with a steaming cup of black coffee laced with sugar, which he forced her to drink, and a blanket and pillow he'd conned from a nurse, who had assured him that this was highly irregular.

"I spoke to Sharon. Everything is fine at home. She gave Jonathan some dinner and is putting him to bed, and she called Mary at her sister's house and asked her to come back right away. I promised her everything would be all right," he added solemnly. "I hope I won't turn out to be a liar."

They sat quietly for a few minutes, although Bernie was thoroughly prepared to barge into the O.R. to find out how things were going. At one point, a nurse came out looking for Eva. The doctor had sent her out to tell them that it would be a while yet.

"How does it look, nurse?" Bernie asked anxiously.

She shrugged her shoulders noncommittally, but her eyes misted up and her expression looked stricken.

Eva clutched Bernie's hand, watching the nurse retreat. "It's not good," she said, her voice breaking. "I can tell by her face that it's not good."

The half-hour that followed felt like a year. They talked of small things, but their eyes kept returning to the swinging doors of the operating room. The hospital was relatively quiet on Sunday eve-nings, with none of the bustle and movement of daytime rounds and routines.

The surgeon finally came out, slowly, his gown spattered with blood, pulling off his green cap and shaking his head in resignation.

"I'm so sorry, Mrs. Goodman. There was nothing more we could do, though God knows, we tried. There was a tremendous amount of internal damage and bleeding—the pancreas, the left lung…"

Eva nodded mutely, then found a semblance of her voice. "Thank you, doctor," she whispered. "I'm sure you did everything you could."

"Those damn drunken kids!" the doctor raged, his anger fueled by the sheer waste of it all. The beautiful young woman standing before him was now a widow. The magnificent physical specimen of a man in his prime, broken beyond repair, was now a sheet-co-vered corpse who would never again laugh or cry, feel joy or pain. There were probably children, too. "Will you be all right?" he asked Eva gently. "Do you want me to get the social worker to accompany you home?"

"She'll be fine, doctor," Bernie said gruffly. "I'm a close friend of the family, and I'll see to all the arrangements. Thank you for your concern."

He led Eva outside as though she were a fragile doll. She hadn't cried yet, but the dry-eyed grief registered on her face was somehow more devastating. They sat quietly in Dan's car for a few minutes before starting for home. Eva looked around the interior of the car, then shook her head ruefully and said with a strange, tight smile, "It makes you wonder. Had we taken the time to juggle cars and take ours, we wouldn't have been at that particular intersection at that exact moment. Dan would be alive, and a little boy would be dead." She shook her head and grimaced. "It makes you wonder if somebody up there is controlling things. It's so scary."

Bernie put his arm around her, the lump in his throat threatening to dissolve into tears. "Don't think about it, Eva. There's nothing we can do to change anything now. We have to concentrate on making it as easy as possible for the kids. Come, let me take you home."

She nodded, still dry-eyed, still numb. Bernie carefully fastened her seat belt, then put the car in gear, driving slowly, his eyes constantly shifting from the road to the woman sitting so quietly at his side.

Sharon was standing at the front door as they slowly walked up the steps of the porch. She noted her mother's faltering walk and Bernie's solicitude—and she knew.

"He's dead, isn't he?" she asked as Eva reached her, enveloping her in her arms. Eva nodded and held the girl tighter as her keening cry of anguish broke the dam of grief that Eva had been holding in.

Bernie's eyes misted at the tableau of the two sobbing women, each propping up the other; black hair intermingling with gold curls as they shared their sorrow. Out of the corner of his eye he noted a movement and realized that Jonathan was slowly creeping down the stairs, one step at a time, his gray eyes opened wide, the look in them reminiscent of Eva's at the hospital.

Bernie was up the steps in a bound, scooping up the child in his arms, bringing him to where Eva and Sharon were, signaling to Mary to stay away.

They instinctively avoided the den and gathered in the more impersonal living room. There was too much of Dan in the other room. This was somehow easier.

Eva sat on the sofa, with Sharon next to her and Jon in her lap. When the tears subsided, they talked softly, remembering Dan, their life with him suddenly becoming a closed chapter, something that would continue only in their memories; no new events or memories would ever be added.

Bernie and Mary were in the background, making the necessary phone calls and arrangements, giving Eva and the children the time and space they needed to make the first steps of the enormous adjustment to this sudden change in their lives. Bernie left them at one point to go and break the news to Dan's mother. He brought her back to the house and Eva's heart broke to see the terrible pain etched on the older woman's face. She tried to imagine the grief involved in losing an adult son, and found that she couldn't. The children hovered over their grandmother, sensing her need for them, finding comfort in the contact with someone who had been a part of so much of their father's life. Eva had never liked her mother-in-law, finding her to be a shallow, social woman who cared for appearances more than for essentials, but her heart went out to her now.

"You'll stay with us at least until the *Shiva* is over, Mother," she insisted quietly but firmly. "I don't want you to be alone right now." Millie Goodman nodded mutely, appreciating the gesture.

Bernie took over all the arrangements. At midnight, with the children, Mrs. Goodman, and Mary all tucked into bed—Jonathan in bed with Sharon, at both their insistences—he handed Eva a stiff cognac, poured himself a Scotch, and sat down with a weary sigh.

"I think everything that has to be done is done. We'll have to go to the funeral home in the morning to finalize some arrangements. The funeral is scheduled for 2 p.m. tomorrow. The police still have to talk to you, but I told them you need a few days to recover. There'll be a notice in tomorrow's paper, and Mary and I have called most of the people whom we felt should be informed right away. I spoke to your mother, Eva, though I didn't call you to the phone. She's flying in tomorrow on the first flight out of New York and I've arranged for someone to pick her up and bring her here. The rabbi will meet us right after we come back from the funeral home. He knew Dan pretty well, but he'll want to talk to you and the kids and Mrs. Goodman before preparing his eulogy. Is there something I've forgotten? Can you think of anything?"

Eva put her hand on his, and said softly, "You can slow down now, Bernie. You've been more than wonderful…like a brother. I know you're hurting, too. Stop running for a moment and let the hurt take over. You'll feel better if you do."

Bernie looked at her, the tears he'd intermittently pushed back throughout the long evening now welling up, unchecked. Eva had already cried—first with Dan's children, then with Dan's mother. She now cried with Dan's friend, somehow sensing that this grief was more like her own than the pain of the others had been.

She had known Dan for more than sixteen long and formative years, and their relationship had covered the gamut of passion, love, hurt, anger, pain, resentment, guilt, apathy, warmth, affection, and ultimately, deep friendship. They had been at loggerheads over the different demands of their respective careers, yet they'd become close business associates, working toward common goals in running and expanding the family business. They'd raised children together and laughed and cried over their mishaps and tribulations. They'd shared joys and sorrows, moments of pride and moments of fear, and if much had been lacking in their love for each other—on his part initially, then later on hers—they had almost always managed to be friends, with the kind of caring that takes the rough along with the smooth. Watching Bernie's grief dissolve in the tears he finally permitted himself, Eva knew that, more than anything else, she would miss Dan's friendship. She had lost a husband, a partner, a father to her children. But more than that, she'd lost an old, close friend. Her best friend.

THIRTY-SIX

Jewish tradition ensures that you have very little time for wallowing in grief, Eva thought grimly as the *Shiva*, the week of ritual mourning following a death in the immediate family, came to a close. The house had been full of people for days, especially in the evening when the men participated in the prayer service, shooing out the women. The traditional seven-day candle in its red glass container burned on the mantelpiece, behind the row of low chairs set out for the mourners—spouse, parent, and children, there being no siblings, in Dan's case. There were times when the evening became almost a social gathering, with people chattering after the service, exchanging gossip and trivia after the requisite "Isn't it terrible? Such a tragedy!" Eva's instinct then was to take a broom and chase people out, but she realized she couldn't, and even had to admit that in some strange way, the tumult and noise were helpful.

The children were the focus of everyone's attention, and they seemed to need the extra human contact, the many quasi-strangers telling them what a wonderful person their Dad had been, what a great football player he'd been in college, and how he bowled over all the girls with his movie-star looks.

Millie Goodman also needed the hustle and bustle. Her friends turned out in droves, clucking and cooing over her misfortune. Many of them had lost husbands—one had even lost a daughter to cancer—and they somehow had the capacity to soothe their friend that Eva, and even the children, lacked.

Eva could have done without all of it, but recognized that tradition, social mores, and the needs of her children and mother-in-law came first, in this case. She longed for the quiet and privacy of her den and would spend long hours there, nursing a cognac, after the house had emptied and the callers had gone. Bernie stayed with her until the house settled down, making sure the children went to bed and that Mrs. Goodman was safely en‐sconced in the guest room. It was a quiet time, with everyone generally too exhausted to stay up much beyond 10. That, too, was the purpose of the tumult, Eva realized, to make sure you were too tired to brood. Bernie was more tired than they were, spending hectic mornings and afternoons at the office, then joining the family for a quiet early dinner before people began to arrive.

"Everything is under control at work," he assured Eva. "You don't have to worry about rushing back right away."

Eva shook her head. "The kids go back to school tomorrow, Jonnie till 1 and Sharon till 4. We all have to get back into a normal routine as soon as possible. I'll leave early for the first few days, but I'd like to get back to a full-time schedule as quickly as I can. We have to meet with the lawyers about Dan's will, and there will be a lot of reorganizing to do."

She noted the worry in his eyes and smiled reassuringly.

"Don't worry, Bernie, I'll be all right. It's the kids I'm most concerned about right now. They've been taking it almost too well."

Bernie nodded in agreement. The children had been phenomenal. They had sat quietly at the funeral, flanking Eva, listening solemnly to the rabbi's words, holding their mother's hands. Both had come to the cemetery, at their own insistence and at the recommendation of the rabbi, who had much experience in such matters.

"It makes it more real for them," he had told Eva, "and somehow it reconciles them to the loss more easily. There is the physical act of burial to relate to, a coffin being lowered into the ground—not just a father being there one day and gone the next."

Eva had drawn the line at their viewing the body; the coffin was closed. She had seen Dan laid out in the plain oak casket, looking waxen and unreal; but she wanted the children's last memory of him to be as he'd been that Sunday afternoon, dressed in jeans and a red plaid shirt, his hair rumpled and his eyes laughing as he kidded around with them.

Watching the three of them during the funeral, Bernie felt an indescribable grief. Eva, in a simple black linen suit, black straw hat hiding her hair and shading her face, her eyes enormous in a face suddenly grown smaller; Sharon, in a pleated gray skirt and white blouse, her hair pulled back in a ponytail tied with a black velvet ribbon, looking like a young, vulnerable schoolgirl, not the sophisticated teenager she liked to consider herself. And little Jonathan—knee-high to a grasshopper, holding his mother's hand with a newfound manliness, so touching at the age of four. He'd been good, controlling his tears during the funeral service and sobbing quietly into his mother's skirt as the coffin was lowered into the earth, picking up a handful of dirt to throw gently on the grave as it was being covered. He'd insisted that Bernie teach him how to say *Kaddish*—the prayer for the dead traditionally recited by the son after the death of a parent, and he'd practiced the strange-sounding Aramaic words extolling the glory of God until he could recite them without stumbling.

The children had clustered around Eva during the past difficult week, drawing strength from her presence and her calm. But they would now have to pick up the threads of their own lives, going back to school, to their friends, resuming a routine of day-to-day life in a house suddenly bereft of a beloved parent.

Bernie raised his eyes as a noise from the door of the den aroused him from his reverie. Jonathan, oblivious to anyone but his mother, who was curled up in the old leather armchair, climbed into her lap wordlessly and snuggled. Eva looked over the dark curls and met Bernie's glance, signaling him not to say anything.

She sat quietly, stroking Jon's hair, nuzzling his neck, until he finally broke the silence.

"Mummy," he asked in his clear, still babyish voice, "Daddy isn't ever coming back, is he?"

"No, sweetheart," Eva answered quietly. "When you die, you don't come back."

"Where is he now? Is he still in that big box, or did he go to heaven?"

"His body is in the box, Jon, but that's only his body. We don't know what happens to the part of the person that you can't see, the part that makes the body a person—the part that thinks and laughs and loves. That's called a soul, or a spirit. Some people think it goes to a place called heaven, but we don't really know."

She smiled, touching the boy's cheek. "You know, Jon, my father, your Papa Hermann, died a long time ago, even before you were born, and I sometimes have a feeling that he never went away, that his soul is somewhere around, watching me and caring about me. That's just a feeling of mine. It's not that I've ever seen him, though I dream about him sometimes; but I think when somebody loves you and is very close to you, they never go away—they stay in your memories and in your thoughts and in your heart, and that way the soul stays with us. But I may be wrong. Nobody knows for sure."

"I like that. That means I can say goodnight to Daddy when I go to bed and I can tell him that I'm learning to read and what happens in school."

"Mmm…" Eva agreed, too choked-up to reply. Jon seemed to relax after that, his curled-up body relaxing in her arms as he fell asleep, comforted by his mother's physical proximity and by a sense that, in a different way, his father too was nearby.

THIRTY-SEVEN

The will was a surprise to them all. It had been drawn up only months before, when Dan realized that Eva's involvement in the business should change the disposition of his estate. All personal assets and investments were left to Eva, with a special trust fund set aside for the children. The business was left one-third to Eva, one-third to the children, and one-third to Bernie, the children's share to be administered by Eva and Bernie until such a time as the children might decide, once they reached the age of twenty-one, to either sell their share or become active partners. There were complicated clauses and provisos ensuring that, should either Bernie or Eva decide to sell their own shares, the other would manage the business, with provisions made for the children's share in any eventuality that might ensue.

"As you can see Mrs. Goodman, Mr. Schwartz," the lawyer said when he finished reading the will, "this is not the will of an old man leaving behind an elderly wife and grown-up children. Dan was adamant that his will reflect the present reality; that it should be effective, should he die in the near future. He planned to revise and amend it annually to accommodate circumstances.

"He was very realistic in terms of the various options that would be available to you. What remains to be determined is what you plan to do about the business, as certain aspects of the will are contingent on that. Otherwise it is quite straightforward, and the paperwork involved should not be too onerous."

Eva and Bernie both nodded, then Eva asked softly, "Mr. Rainey, did my husband have any kind of premonition or feeling that he would die young?"

James Rainey removed his reading glasses and began polishing them with a white linen handkerchief, pondering Eva's question.

"I can't really answer that, Mrs. Goodman. I myself was somewhat taken aback at the detailed disposition of the estate of so young a man, and I queried him about it; but he had been revising his will at regular intervals over the past fifteen years and this really wasn't out of character. Unlike most young men, Dan Goodman seemed highly aware of what would happen to his dependents should anything happen to him. That's an extremely commendable and most unusual trait, I might add."

Eva nodded. "Yes, that fits. When he was building up the business, years ago, we used to fight over the long hours he spent working, and his rationale and excuse was always that if anything happened to him, we'd be well looked after."

She wrinkled her brow, thoughtful, apparently debating with herself whether to ask the next question. She looked at the lawyer with a determined expression and asked, "In any of the previous wills, were any provisions made for a Barbara Wallace? I ask not in order to pry, but because given Dan's nature, I find the omission in this will somewhat surprising."

James Rainey cleared his throat in discomfort and squirmed in his chair.

He knows all about that chapter in Dan's life, Eva thought, feeling guilty at making this soft-spoken and somewhat old-fashioned gentleman uncomfortable.

"Well, um…yes. I may as well be candid with you, as you will have access to all the financial records. There was a provision in earlier wills for an annual stipend, first to a Miss Wallace and a child she was expecting; then just to her, as I gather the child died either at birth or at a very young age. Mr. Goodman had set up a fund from which Miss Wallace drew an annual income, but that was dissolved some years ago when her attorney approached him with a request for a lump sum amount, in lieu of the annual stipend. I believe Dan was quite pleased to do that and to…um, sever any ties with the person in question."

Eva smiled at the old man's obvious reticence and tact, and at the look of total confusion on Bernie's face.

"It's a long story, Bern. I'll tell you about it someday." She turned back to the solicitor and said drily, "It was a fairly substantial lump sum, I would imagine, was it not?"

"Well, yes…" Rainey answered. "It was not ungenerous. But I believe Dan was glad to be rid of a situation that had become an emotional burden."

Poor Dan, Eva thought, realizing the full extent of the burden of guilt he'd carried with him—not only toward her, but toward a woman he'd used callously, and toward an innocent child who'd never even had a chance at life.

She said nothing, but nodded curtly, signaling an end to that part of the discussion.

"There is one additional matter, Mrs. Goodman, if I may." Rainey was polishing his glasses again. "Your husband left a personal letter to you with us, to be given to you in the event of his death. Needless to say, I have no idea what is in it, but my experience has taught me that people tend to be morbid when they write letters they know will be read once they are gone. I am almost reluctant to give it to you, should it cause more grief and pain than you've already experienced; but, of course, I must fulfill my mandate and my obligations to a client." He looked at her unhappily. "I just want you to know, whatever is in the letter, that I've been your husband's personal solicitor for many years, and I have rarely seen anyone more devoted to his family or more caring of their welfare." He paused. "What I am trying to say, rather ineffectively, I'm afraid, is that your husband loved you very much. I…I thought I would like to say that to you."

Eva reached across the desk and covered his old, gnarled hand with hers.

"I know that, Mr. Rainey, but I appreciate your kind words. Don't worry about the letter," she added softly, "I think I know what's in it. Dan and I had our ups and downs over the years, but we had a good marriage for all that, and I know how he felt about me and about the children. Nothing can take that away. Thank you for your concern."

Rainey nodded mutely, her solicitude touching him strangely. What a fine woman, he thought, after Eva and Bernie had left. Even with all his inborn reticence and his years of training in being discreet and circumspect, he could not help wondering about the contents of the letter Eva had tucked efficiently into her briefcase.

Dearest Eva—the handwriting was Dan's familiar scrawl in heavy-nibbed black pen on thick creamy paper.

I've never written this kind of letter before and I must confess I feel sort of foolish—like a teenager writing his first love letter to a girl, not knowing what to say. The strangeness is compounded by not knowing whether you will ever see this letter—I may decide to tear it up at some point in the coming years, or I may outlive you, or we may split yet…who knows.

It's the "who knows" that is the compelling force behind this crackpot idea. I'm haunted by the thought that our lives will pass and that you will never know how I feel about you, about the kids, about us…

I can see you shaking your head impatiently at this point with that special expression you get when I try to tell you I love you. It's as if you're saying, "I know, I know—now let's get on with life and not dwell on emotions." I'm writing his letter because you won't let me dwell on emotions—with me not around, you can't shut me up and change the subject—but knowing you, I can't imagine that you would leave anything you've started to read, unread…

I'm rambling. Let me get back to what I wanted to say.

I looked back on all the times I've said "I love you" since we met and I realized that, no matter what the circumstances, that was always the truth. I can see the skeptical look in your gray eyes, the left eyebrow slightly raised—but you're wrong to doubt. I know that in the course of our years together, I've been everything from a demanding lover to an adoring husband to a total shit; but no matter what stage I was at—that statement was always true. It was true from the night I met you at that dumb party. You looked so…luminous—simply dressed, with no jewelry except your eyes—among the peacocks and the social butterflies. You were bored to tears and you were angry at yourself for being there in the first place. Then I came along—I'd been watching you for half an hour—and did my knight-in-shining-armor bit and you were supposed to fall for it—but you didn't. What a challenge that was! But I'm digressing again. Almost as if I'm afraid to get to the point.

The point is, Eva, that I love you, that I've loved you since the moment we met, and that I will always love you. I once had a vision of what you would look like when you were old—with a pang, when I realized that I probably wouldn't be around to see you; and I wondered whether that magnificent old lady would ever realize, once and for all, how much I loved her. I hope she does—I hope she realized it long ago.

My deepest regret, Eva, is what happened with Barbara all those years ago. I know that from that point on, your love for me changed irrevocably and I mourn what could have been, had I only been more mature and more aware of what you had to give and how much pain I was inflicting. I'm sorry for Barbara. She suffered because she loved me and I never loved her. She was devastated when the baby died and when she realized that, even if you left me for good, I wouldn't marry her or live with her. I used her, as I've used other women in my long and checkered career, and I'm ashamed of the way I behaved. I tried to make it up to her by giving her some sort of financial security, but that, too, was a bond and I wanted no permanent bonds with her. I was relieved that she felt the same way. I "paid her off," to be crass about it, a few years ago, and there is no longer even any indirect contact, through lawyers. I don't know where she is or what she is doing and that's fine. I hope she never touches my life again, or yours.

I know what you're thinking, and you're right. In a way I got off easy because a little girl died. Had she lived—God knows what would have happened. You wouldn't have come back to me; Jonathan wouldn't have been born...I don't even want to think about it...

The price I paid for my stupidity has been high—but I know how much higher it could have been.

What I regret most of all—and regret is too light a word, but I can't think of a better one—is what it did to you. Not just the pain I put you through then—that's in the past and I know you've gotten over it, to the extent that anyone gets over pain—but in terms of what I did to your capacity to love me. I blame my emotional immaturity, my acute lack of sensitivity, and my total inability to fathom the depth and intensity and quality of what you could have felt for me, had I not screwed up so terribly.

I know you lost a huge measure of respect for me and I know how much justified anger you felt at the time. But the real loss is those areas of yourself that you blocked off from me, that you barricaded behind the walls of the bloody medieval fortress that is now at the core of you. They were there before I came along, those walls—but they weren't that high—they could have been scaled and breached, and maybe torn down completely. And I could have done it. But I didn't. Instead I helped you build them higher and stronger, and we are both the worse off for it. I, because I will always stand outside looking in, and you, because you could be giving everything you have to offer to someone *who has earned the right to get it. And that person will never be me... You can't imagine how painful a realization that is.*

There was a while when I almost hoped that you would meet someone and really fall in love—if only so you would realize what I realize—that you have the capacity to love to a far greater degree than you love me. It was almost a masochistic thing to wish for, because then you would have left me for good. I know you too well to think that you would have stayed with me if there had been someone else whom you really loved. I kept waiting for the shoe to drop. It hasn't, so far, and I should be happy. But I feel a nagging sense of guilt—guilt that I could not be the man for whom you feel the kind of love that I feel for you; guilt at being happy that you haven't found someone like that, because his gain would be my crushing loss...it's very complicated, isn't it?

I don't know if there have been other men in your life since we got married. You are a beautiful woman and, contrary to what you believe, not all men are turned off by brains. I'm sure you've had opportunities to have flings and affairs—I've seen the look in men's eyes when you walk into a room. I don't know if you've ever availed yourself of such opportunities, but if you have, I'm glad that there hasn't been an involvement serious enough to make you decide to abandon what we do have together. And don't think, Eva, that I don't cherish what we do have, just because I know how much better it could have been. When we sit around the dinner table and I look at you and the kids, or when I walk into the warmth and coziness of our home after a hard day's work—I count my blessings, as corny as that sounds. Things are good between us and our family is probably one of the best around. I don't often dwell on what's missing. It's only when I sometimes see a fleeting look of sadness in your eyes, for no apparent outward reason, that I know that you too know that something is missing.

What is that line from T.S. Eliot that you've always liked...?

"I have heard the mermaids singing, each to each,
    I do not think they will sing to me."

That's what's missing, Eva... The mermaids singing.

There is one more thing I want you to know before I end this letter—and that is how grateful I am that you had Jonathan. I know you were angry when I saw his birth as an affirmation of something between us that I wanted affirmed. "Don't read into it something that isn't there," is what you said. But it was an affirmation of something—of us as a family, of a commitment to maintaining that family, of a future together. And if the conception was one of those wonderful fluky accidents—the pregnancy wasn't. You could have ended it—but you didn't, just as you could have terminated our marriage—but you didn't. And for both those things, I thank you.

Please understand me, Eva, though I'm not doing a great job of explaining myself. You are the most wonderful thing that has ever happened to me. Because of you I learned to love, and to give, and to feel depths of emotion I never believed existed. My sorrow is at not having given you the same measure of everything that you've given me. That was and is my greatest inadequacy. Maybe somewhere out there in the big world there's a man who could have given you that—for whom you could have felt what I feel for you. If you find him after I'm gone, don't let the walls keep you back. Let yourself experience the joy of giving what I've learned to experience with you—and thank him, from me, for not showing up sooner...

I love you, Eva. I wanted you to hear it one more time, though I'm not around to say it anymore. Go on with your life. I wish I could be there to share the rest of it and to savor every experience that is still left to savor. Never let the kids forget how much I love them. Sharon is a unique person—she has in her the best of you and whatever is good in me. And Jonathan... Jonathan was God's gift to me—almost as though, because I could never have all of you, I could have him as my consolation and my joy. No matter what you do with the rest of your life, please let no one replace me in his.

I love you, Eva.
Yours always,
Dan

THIRTY-EIGHT

The year following Dan's death passed quickly, but not without pain. Business adjustments were more easily made than personal ones. Bernie and Eva worked well together and had similar ideas on how the business should grow and which areas needed development. They expanded the wholesale aspect of the business, with Bernie scouring the Far East, Europe, and South America for new sources of gems, pearls, and gold jewelry. Eva took the shorter hops, on the selling end, traveling to New York, L.A., Dallas, Houston, Chicago, Miami—the large population centers that contained luxury stores catering to the rich and famous. She proved to be a persuasive salesperson and the business flourished, to both her and Bernie's delight.

The children had a harder time adjusting, Sharon more so than Jonathan. She had been very close to Dan and he'd adored her. At fifteen, suddenly bereft of the person she'd most loved, Sharon turned inward, avoiding friends and social contacts beyond the barely essential minimum. Her grades in school didn't suffer. Like Eva, Sharon was the type who drowned her sorrows in her work, but the long talks on the phone ceased and the house was no longer filled with chattering teenaged girls, trying on clothes and experimenting with makeup.

Eva spent as much time as she could with Sharon, but sensed after a while that what the girl really needed was the company of her peers. The two of them were having dinner at Rossini's one night when Eva finally took the bull by the horns.

"Sharon," she began tentatively, "how come your friends don't come to the house anymore? Have you dropped them, or are they avoiding you?"

Sharon didn't reply right away, tilting her head to one side as she thought about Eva's question.

"Well, it's not either of those things, Mom. It's just that suddenly Marsha and Anne and all those girls…they're just so empty and…*childish*! All they care about is boys and clothes and makeup and the latest *Seventeen* magazine—they bore me. And I guess I bore them, too—they figure I'm way too serious."

Eva smiled. Sharon was describing Eva's own teenage years. She, too, had been aloof. But not as aloof as Sharon had become.

"But you enjoy all those things, too—you just have more interests than some of the girls. That doesn't mean you have to cut yourself off from them," Eva said gently.

Sharon sighed. "I know, Mom. But it's hard. I see them at school all day and I try to be sociable, but by the time I get home, I've really had it—I just want to read, and do my homework, and play with Jon." Her eyes lit up as she mentioned her brother. "Do you know that he's reading all the easy Dr. Seuss books by himself, and he's starting to tackle the harder ones!?"

Eva smiled and added, "With you around, he won't have to go to school. He'll be doing Shakespeare by the time he's ten!"

"Oh, but it's so much fun to teach him. He catches on so quickly. And I like being with him. It's rough to be a little kid without a father." Her lower lip trembled as she spoke, fighting hard for control.

"Sharon, baby," Eva soothed, cradling the girl's hand in her own. "You can't replace Daddy in Jon's life. We all have to adjust to life without him."

Sharon swallowed back her tears. "I know. But you have your work and I have school—Jon is so little. And he's a boy; he needs a father—someone to throw a ball with or to teach him to skate—or just to toss him up in the air and rough-house, the way Daddy used to do with me." Memories overcame her and she covered her face with her hands, trying to hide her emotions.

Eva gently reached across the small table and stroked Sharon's long blonde hair, so much like Dan's in texture and color.

"You can cry if you want to, sweetheart. Don't try to keep it all bottled in. But don't make the mistake of trying to become a substitute parent. I'm here to mother and you're here to be a caring big sister, but Jon will learn to manage without a father and we'll both see to it that he isn't deprived. We can't replace Daddy, but we can make sure that Jon's life is full of all the activities he would have had if Daddy hadn't died. Bernie is anxious to help, too. I had to talk him out of getting Jon a ticket to the hockey game. Four and a half is a little young for that—even Bernie had to agree!"

Sharon laughed, picturing Bernie's chagrin at being blocked by Eva.

"He's such a nice person, Bernie, and he's been so good to us. I think he likes you a lot, Mom," she added shyly. Eva looked at her sharply, then smiled. "Sharon Goodman!" she exclaimed, glad to see a smile on her daughter's face again, "Don't go hatching any plots or schemes! I love Bernie—he's like a wonderful younger brother, which is how your father regarded him—and he and I make a great business team. But don't start spinning any romances in that imaginative little head of yours…"

"Okay, Mom, I won't," Sharon agreed sheepishly, then added with defiance, "But if you ever get serious about a man, he better be a lot like Daddy or Bernie, or else Jon and I will give him—and you—a hard time!"

Eva stared at her daughter with amazement, sensing that she'd hit on another cause for Sharon's introspection.

She spoke slowly, weighing the words before articulating them. "Sharon, are you worried that I'll become involved with someone you won't care for, or that I'll get involved with someone at all? Is that what's troubling you?"

Sharon blushed. "Well, I guess I don't want anybody taking Daddy's place," she said defensively. "Men must make passes at you all the time—you're so pretty, you know. And women aren't supposed to like being alone."

Eva laughed, then chucked Sharon under the chin. "Don't worry, sweetie," she reassured her. "I don't *like* being alone—but then, I don't feel that I am alone. I like my work and I like coming home to you and to Jon. I may go out on an occasional date once in a while, though I have to confess that doesn't particularly tempt me right now, but I'm not looking for any serious involvements. Really, I'm not."

"That's because it's still too soon," Sharon answered soberly. "It isn't even a year since Daddy died. But you'll feel differently as time goes by. You'll see…"

Eva was determined to maintain a note of levity, but could not ignore the real concern Sharon expressed. She kept her tone light, but her words were dead serious.

"I'd like to tell you something, Sharon, and to make you a promise at the same time. You and Jon are the most important people in my life. Not the only people. But by far the most important. Everything I've done and will do is measured by the effect it will have on you two. I don't know what's down the road. Nobody does. So I can't make you promises of what I will or won't do, or what will or won't happen. But I *can* promise you that you two will always come first, before anybody else, and that I won't make any changes in my life that would hurt you or harm you or exclude you."

Sharon looked relieved, and Eva patted her hand briskly. "There! Now that I've signed my life away to you two monsters, let's eat our lasagna! Mr. Rossini has tried to approach this table three times and has gone back with our portions each time because he felt he shouldn't intrude. He's always had that knack!"

She caught the old man's eye and he quickly trotted over with their steaming plates of pasta. He pinched Sharon's cheek affectionately—this beautiful young woman who had been coming to his restaurant with her parents since she'd been old enough to sit. She had grown into a beauty—even lovelier than her mother, whom he'd always adored. *Poverina*, he thought, losing her father at such a young age. But she'd get over it. Young men would soon be swarming around her and she'd learn that her father was not the only one. It was the mother he was concerned about. Knowing her, she would try to be mother and father and business tycoon all at once. It was too much for one person, especially a woman, even one of her strength and resiliency. But she would never admit that, he knew. She'd grit her teeth and go on. He only hoped she'd have the strength and that she wouldn't lose her softness and warmth, and that she'd find a man worthy of her. A woman like that should not live out her life alone. But a woman like that would do what she pleased, he admitted to himself, and she'd laugh if he expressed his concern. Better to keep quiet and keep a fatherly eye out. So far she seemed to be coping well. He'd be around to offer his help and friendship if a time came when she needed them.

THIRTY-NINE

SFO was bustling, as always, as Eva waited at her gate before boarding her American Airlines flight from San Francisco to Hawaii, then on to Tokyo. It wasn't "her" route—Bernie had been doing most of the buying trips during the past three years. He had the experience and the contacts, the time, and the freedom. Eva traveled too—quite extensively of late, as the business had grown, but she tried never to be away from the children for more than three or four days at a time, and her trips had been limited to the U.S., with only an occasional short European jaunt. And even then she called home every night, always conscious of the fact that she was an only parent and that both Sharon and Jonathan worried about her—especially when she was away. If anything happened to her, they'd be alone.

Children their age should not even be thinking along those lines, she knew, but hers did. Sharon was also worried about leaving home to go to school. She'd be graduating in the spring and she could pick and choose from among the best colleges in the country—her marks ensured that, and money was no object. But Sharon worried about leaving her mother and Jon behind, clinging, as she always had, to the warmth and security of the family.

Eva sighed. She hadn't given up yet on encouraging Sharon to go to Harvard or Columbia, or any of the better colleges where she could explore the many facets of her natural talent for almost anything she set her mind to doing. And Sharon needed the independence—needed it even more than the academic challenge. She was too attached to Jonathan, and to Eva, too, for that matter, too involved in their lives for a girl of almost eighteen. Her own life should now be the center of her attention.

Jon was fine, and it would do him good to be the oldest and only child around. In the second grade, at a small private school for boys that offered special programs for gifted children, he was mature and precocious beyond his years.

The Jewish mother's dream, Eva thought, a fond smile touching her lips. Two beautiful, talented children who did well in school and in sports, who had lots of friends, and who were attached to their mother. Her lot wasn't too bad, either, to be honest. She loved her work, enjoyed her children, and was too busy to be lonely. There were nights, she admitted to herself, when she awoke with a start, often from a deep sleep, overcome with an aching, haunting sense of loneliness that sometimes took days to shake off. She missed Dan terribly. With all that had been lacking in their marriage, they had been close, caring friends. The warmth of his presence—both emotional and physical—was something she had taken for granted. Bernie filled part of the gap, but not the dark, gaping emptiness that enveloped her on those long nights when she woke up feeling overcome by a familiar, haunting, bittersweet sadness that she usually managed to keep at bay.

It didn't usually affect her during the day, as it seemed to be doing now. She put down her unread book and looked around her at the teeming crowd scene—people and bags and porters, each intent on their own activity and their own destination. She still had an hour before her flight would be called and if she couldn't read, she'd better keep busy until then.

Eva took the escalator down one flight to the coffee shop, had a cup of black coffee, then looked for a magazine stand. God, I hate airports, she thought, trying to calculate the number of useless hours lost yearly by all the people waiting for delayed flights, as she was waiting now.

She quickly scanned the colorful magazine covers, then gasped audibly as Rob's smiling face suddenly confronted her from the cover of the latest issue of *BusinessWeek*. She had no recollection later of picking up the magazine, of paying for it, or of sitting down numbly in a relatively quiet corner to read the article about him, after first staring long and hard at the still-familiar lines of his face, at the brown eyes, crinkling at the corners, smiling up at her.

The article described him as one of the budding young stars of the computer revolution that was sweeping the American business world. Rob had been busy in the years since they'd parted. He had left the company he'd been working for to found his own consulting firm, catering to small and medium-sized companies who could now, with the dropping costs and increasing capa—bilities of small computers, afford to computerize. Robert Miller showed them how, offering them experts who knew every computer and every item of business software on the market and could determine, given the needs and budget of a specific company, what hardware and software that company should buy. The client paid a consulting fee, the computer company paid a commission on sales. It was a simple concept and it had worked. CompTech had opened branch offices in the major cities after the success of its initial Silicon Valley operation, and had now gone public, its shares trading on the New York Stock Exchange.

The article went on, describing the stages of CompTech's development, touching here and there on the personality of the man behind it. The interviewer had spent a week dogging Rob's footsteps, and had glimpsed personal aspects of the man, in addition to the plethora of business details. "Robert Miller has a mentally disabled daughter, twenty years old," the article read, "who, according to him, is one of the driving forces in his success."

"'There are no public provisions for children like Jeannie,' he told us, 'yet they will require care and supervision for the entire duration of their parents' lives...and beyond. When you have a child like that, you have a responsibility that extends far beyond the normal twenty- to twenty-five-year span when we support and nurture and provide for our children emotionally and financially. They remain children forever, and your life is forever bound up with theirs. They come first—they have to—and they become the only personal focus of your life, one that takes precedence over everything and anyone else, often at tremendous personal cost.'"

The article went on to describe Rob's involvement in charities and institutions catering to children with mental and emotional disabilities, but Eva could read no further.

Almost in a daze, yet calmly and methodically, she dug out a quarter from her purse and went to the nearest pay phone. The number was easy to find and she only panicked when the call was answered by a crisp, efficient receptionist: "CompTech. May I help you?"

"Mr. Robert Miller, please," Eva swallowed to get rid of the sudden tremor in her voice.

"One moment please, I'll connect you with his secretary."

The next voice was equally efficient, but somewhat warmer.

"Mr. Miller's secretary. May I help you?"

"I'd like to talk to Mr. Miller, please."

"I'm afraid he's out of town for the week. Can someone else help you, or would you like to leave a message?"

"No, no—I'm an old friend and I'm just passing through San Francisco. I saw the article in *BusinessWeek* and I thought I'd call him to congratulate him." Her voice was controlled now, but her heart was still racing.

The voice at the other end warmed up some more. "It *was* a great article, wasn't it? A lot of people have been calling. If you'd leave me your name and number, I'm sure Mr. Miller will be happy to call you back."

I'm not so sure, Eva thought, suddenly fearful of the Pandora's box she had been about to open, impulsively, without thinking it through.

"No, it's all right. He probably wouldn't even remember me. I'm just happy to learn he's done so well and since I just saw the article, I thought I'd call. Thank you for your time."

Eva hung up quickly before the woman could insist that she leave her name, before she might be tempted to do so. She stood leaning against the curved Plexiglas wall of the phone booth, her mouth suddenly dry and her hands clammy, shocked at her own action, relieved that Rob hadn't been there, wondering what she would have said or done if she'd reached him.

She suddenly realized that her flight was being called and hurried to her gate, wanting to get out of San Francisco as quickly as possible.

She left the magazine in the phone booth. Unintentionally—but it was just as well. She hadn't finished reading the article, but that didn't matter. She'd read enough to reinforce what she had long known—that Jeannie would always come first in Rob's life, just as her children would in hers. What was harder to accept was the effect that seeing Rob's picture and reading about him could still have on her. She'd buried his memory a little bit deeper each year and the preoccupation with her work and her children had made it easier to do so. She truly thought she'd gotten over him. But she hadn't. She'd still felt the need to reach out to him, to make contact. And she could not, and should not! What had been complicated before Jon was conceived was even more complicated now. Better to bury it. Better to start working, again, on forgetting. She obviously hadn't done it successfully the first time around.

I did what I had to do, Eva told herself as the plane began to taxi down the runway. Closing her eyes and gripping the seat handles tightly, as she always did on takeoffs, she allowed herself to remember her first meeting with Rob, his droll comments about her fear of flying, the warmth of his smile when she'd opened her eyes in response. The same warm smile that had grabbed her attention at the magazine counter. A smile she had trained herself not to think about, a memory she had been trying to avoid and evade for the last seven years.

FORTY

For the first time since Dan's death three years earlier, Eva questioned the course of action she'd followed since Jonathan was conceived, since she and Rob had parted.

There was no doubt in her mind that the total break she had opted for had been the right thing to do. Had there been no Jonathan, her resolve might have weakened, she might have called, or written, or at least inquired indirectly about Rob, if only to know how he was and what he was up to. Maybe even to resume their love affair, or to meet him, however sporadically, when opportunity allowed. Rob and Eva, as lovers, as friends, as a totally separate entity from their "other" lives, might have been, after all, a scenario they both could have handled. It would have been painful, but doable. Rob as the father of her child, a child she was raising to regard another man as his father...that she would not have been able to deal with. It would have meant hiding the truth from Rob and at the same time calling him her friend. Or telling him and watching him suffer. No, she'd chosen the right route. The decision she'd made that morning in bed, when she first realized she was pregnant and that the child could only be Rob's, was a decision she would make again today.

But things have changed for you, said the nagging voice in her mind. The voice she always argued with when answers weren't clear-cut. Her alter ego or her built-in devil's advocate. She wondered if everybody had one.

Eva's usual method of tackling a problem was to lay out all the facts, examine and analyze each one in turn, then see what order or process could best be made of them. She did that whether analyzing a business problem or writing a critique of a novel, and she now used it to try to resolve her personal situation.

My life *has* changed, she answered the voice. There is room in my life for a man. I'm a young, eligible widow. Successful, wealthy, still attractive, and in the fairly unique situation of not needing a man for the usual reasons of financial support or social status. There has only been one Rob in my life. One man to whom I gave myself totally—heart and body and soul, as the cliché goes. Do I look for another man like him? Do I explore the possibility of resuming the relationship with him—any relationship? And what kind? What did I want when I picked up that phone to call him? What would I have said if he'd been there?

Hi, Rob. This is Eva. I'm now a widow and I wondered whether you and I could be lovers again. And, oh yes, we have a wonderful seven-year-old boy I never told you about. I thought you might want to be a father to him and experience the joys of having a normal, healthy child….

And what about his life? It was his situation, not hers, which had made their relationship a dead-end one. She'd been ready to leave Dan. It would have been hard on Sharon, but other kids have lived through divorce and survived. Sharon had had a taste of it when Eva and Dan were separated and it hadn't spoiled her—if anything, it had made her stronger and better and more sensitive. She would not have adored Jonathan less, and, possibly, she would have accepted Rob more readily as the father of her adored brother. It was Rob who couldn't or wouldn't change the realities of his life. He was the one tied down to a beautiful little girl with empty eyes and whose needs came first.

And if that hasn't changed, nothing has changed, Eva admitted to herself. I'm not really more available than I was seven years ago. It's just simpler and less messy in my case. But what about you, Rob? She hadn't read the article to the end, but the part she'd read about Jeannie didn't make it seem as if he were a single parent. He'd spoken of parents, in the plural. And if things had changed in his life—if he *was* available and free—why hadn't he contacted her?

No, Eva, she told herself with an inward sigh, nothing's changed. What you had to do then is what you have to do now.

215

Put him out of your mind to the extent that you can—and do a better job of it this time, she added chidingly. You have Jonathan and you have some beautiful memories. Enjoy the former and try to forget the latter. There's no happiness there for you.

A long-forgotten memory of her father suddenly surfaced in her mind. She had come home from school terribly upset about a math test she'd flubbed. The grade was barely a passing one, and her exam results were always stellar. She'd cried bitterly as her father tried to comfort her, spilling out, between sobs, the reasons she'd done so poorly.

"It's all my own fault," she'd anguished. "I really didn't study and I thought I could wing it. Oh, I wish it was last week and I could do it over again!"

Her father laughed and dried her tears with his monogrammed linen handkerchief. Then he looked at her soberly with that special expression he saved for Big Truths.

"You have to learn one very important lesson, *Leibchen*," he said soberly. "You can't go back. You can change and alter and sometimes undo—in this case, you'll do so well on other math tests and projects that the effect of one low mark will be diluted. But you can't go back. Learn that and you'll be spared a lot of pain in the future."

He was right, Eva thought. He's still right. And I'd better get down to work or I'll blow my first big buying trip just like I blew that math test.

She pulled out her briefcase and got out the contracts she had to peruse, rang the flight attendant for some black coffee, and settled down to her reading.

I'm doing my Scarlett O'Hara routine, she admitted to herself as she sipped the hot bitter fluid. Even in first class, airline coffee was awful. But what the hell, it will take me to tomorrow.

FORTY-ONE

Tokyo was a combination of dream and reality. Hard-nosed business discussions and negotiations with suppliers, juxtaposed with incredible sights and smells and sounds and the serene, almost too fragile, beauty of the cherry blossoms at their peak.

John Yamamoto, their Japanese-born, American-trained lawyer, acted as her host, picking her up at the Imperial Hotel each morning and making sure that the business day was interspersed with sight-seeing and fine dining and time for personal shopping. His American wife, who'd been raised in Japan, was a warm, bubbly person, a refreshing contrast to the Japanese reserve that Eva encountered in her business dealings.

"The pearls we chose are magnificent, John. I think we'll do well with them. Americans are discovering pearls and the prices will be up 20 percent by the time this shipment reaches the States."

"Show Diana the ones you got for yourself. I think you just blew all your profits on the one strand!" John chuckled.

Eva took the flat velvet box from her purse and looked at Diana sheepishly. "He may be right, but I'm not sorry. I've never bought myself anything really outrageous, but these were irresistible."

She opened the large box and took out a magnificent seventy-two-inch strand of enormous rose-colored pearls that not only reflected their three awestruck faces, but seemed to glow with an inner light of their own.

Diana gasped as Eva looped the pearls twice around her neck, the heavy double strand hanging to her waist.

"Nobody will believe they're real!" she exclaimed. "I've never seen anything like them."

Eva smiled in delight, like a little girl with a new doll. "Aren't they something?! Mr. Katsura was saving them for last, after we'd looked through and chosen hundreds of strands of different sizes and lengths."

She described the scene to Diana.

"He's a tough old bird, Mr. Katsura. Bernie warned me about him, though I suspect he didn't warn Mr. Katsura about me! He haggled and negotiated like the most hard-nosed Wall Street businessman—thank goodness John was there to back me up—but when all the business was over, he suddenly became the most charming elderly Japanese gentleman you could hope to meet."

"That's when he pulled out the family heirloom," John interjected drily. "He figured that Eva wouldn't be able to resist!"

"What woman would?" Diana laughed. "The problem isn't resisting—it's affording."

"Considering their size and color, and the length of the strand, it wasn't bad," Eva said, looking down at the cascade of rosy luminescence on the plain background of her creamy silk blouse. "He said it took twenty years to put the strand together, culling millions of pearls for ones just the right shape and size and color."

"And what you paid could support a Japanese family for over twenty years," John added with a broad smile, "but they really are beautiful, enjoy them!"

Eva looked at the two of them soberly. "I know it's very extravagant and probably crazy, but I've never bought myself a piece of jewelry—everything I have was either a birthday or an anniversary gift from Dan. I never really appreciated jewelry until I started working in Dan's business, and I could never understand his excitement at finding a particularly beautiful stone, or a fabulous design. I've been running the business with Bernie for almost three years now, and this is the first time that a piece of jewelry actually got to me, made me feel that I had to have it. I've opened that box twenty times in the last few hours—just to look at these pearls! I think I finally understand the expression I sometimes see on women's faces when they go to Harry Winston or Van Cleef & Arpels. I never felt that way before. I'm not really a jewelry person—I'm a former English teacher!"

John chuckled. "You should have seen this English teacher handling old Mr. Katsura," he told his wife laughingly. "You must have been an ogre of a teacher!"

Eva laughed. "Not really," she said. "I was tough but I was fair, and my students actually quite liked me."

"So did your readers, of which I happen to be one," Diana added warmly.

Eva looked surprised. She'd always regarded her book and articles as scholarly, not the kind of books that normally become best sellers. The popularity of her book was a fluke of subject and timing.

"Thank you," she replied almost shyly. "My timing was right, in terms of the subject matter and the women's movement, but it's still nice to have your work appreciated."

The evening went on in the same vein of warmth and friendship. John and Diana had known Dan well and liked him, and they opened their hearts to Eva with the sensitivity of people who have known what it is to be a stranger in a strange land. Diana had spent many of her formative years in Tokyo, feeling out of place—a tall, gangling Occidental blonde amid her petite, dark Oriental schoolmates. John had known the loneliness of being an exchange student at an Ivy League college in the Northeast. His aristocratic Japanese ancestry meant nothing to the petty snobs in his law school class, and loneliness was a condition that he'd thought was synonymous with America until he met Diana.

They exchanged backgrounds and histories, finding an immediate affinity in their shared experience of cultural duality and in the constant striving for excellence that that duality had instilled in each of them, in different ways. Diana was a brilliant artist, Eva discovered, and had exhibited her oils in Japan and New York to great critical acclaim. John was a successful international lawyer, and Eva was well on her way to becoming a force in the jewelry business, first having left her mark on the academic world.

"The Unstoppables, that's what we are!" Eva summarized as the three friends sipped cognac in her suite after a delicious Japanese dinner at one of Tokyo's famous restaurants.

After the Yamamotos left, she bathed and put on a white satin nightshirt, then donned her pearls again as she curled up in an armchair with one last cognac. Tomorrow would be her last day in this exotic locale and she didn't know when she'd be back—the two weeks away from the children had not been easy, though she'd called every few days.

It had been exhilarating, exhausting, challenging—and a lot of fun. Diana and John were the first people she'd met in years with whom she could share common ground. It amazed her that there actually were people like herself out there—and in Tokyo, of all places. People whose background was different from the norm, people she could relate to. Her world of late had been confined to her children, her business, and Bernie. The people she met through business activities were not her type, and her neighbors and the parents of her children's friends were typical small-town affluent suburbanites. Nice, but ultimately boring, their interest in football scores and the pros and cons of European or Japanese cars leaving her cold.

She wondered whether she should seriously consider Bernie's suggestion of expanding the New York office and moving back to the big city. She could move into the spacious apartment on Central Park West where she'd grown up. Her mother was talking of giving it up for something smaller. Sharon would be close by and Jon could get the finest education and the advantages of a New York upbringing. Rumpelmayer's and the ballet, she remembered, smiling to herself at the vision of a little girl in white socks and a dapper European professor escorting her with all the gallantry and formality one saved for a special date.

Rob would still be able to find me, she told herself, then sat bolt upright in her chair as she realized that being "findable" had been at the back of her mind all these years. He's not looking for you, Eva, she said to herself, angry at the sudden vision she had of herself. Penelope waiting for Ulysses. Must get off that track.

People like Diana and John would be easier to find in New York. She would be able to stop living in an emotional and social limbo. You might even decide to take up with a man, she chided herself as she climbed into the big, empty bed, before you become a dried-up old prune. She thought of all the men she knew and grimaced. Maybe men are easier to find in New York, too, she thought. Minneapolis certainly didn't seem to offer any.

FORTY-TWO

"You are out of your mind, Eva!" Bernie exploded. "I've never heard of anything so ridiculous in my life and I won't go along with it!"

"Just hear me out, Bernie. It's not ridiculous at all. Look at fashion today—the hippie era is basically over and everything is going back to dressier and more elaborate. Evening gowns are coming back, for goodness' sake! And what goes with that kind of fashion? Fancy jewelry—that's what! And who can afford it anymore? Two percent of the population, that's who. And even that small group is scared to walk around with the real thing on, because it's too risky."

"Costume jewelry is something cleaning ladies and teenagers buy at Woolworth's. How can you even think of it in terms of Goodman's? Where's your taste?" he sputtered.

"But I'm not talking Woolworth's! I'm talking Saks and Neiman Marcus and Bonwit's. I'm talking gold-plated instead of gold—with real onyx and lapis and high-caliber fakes—the kind you can't tell from the real thing. Bernie—every woman today wants to look like Princess Di—and a three-strand pearl choker with a sapphire-and-diamond clasp is something very few women can afford. But make a knockout facsimile and sell it for under $200 and you'll have women buying it—that whole array of middle-class and not-so-rich women—career women who have extra money to burn, but couldn't dream of Harry Winston except over the pages of *Town and Country* at the hairdresser."

There was still a look of skepticism on Bernie's face, but Eva could sense the weakening and pressed her point.

"Look at these pearls!" she exclaimed, jumping up from her chair and perching on the desk near Bernie, holding up the heavy rosy strands. "My reaction when I saw them was that I absolutely had to have them—and I've never felt that way about any piece of jewelry before. How many women can afford such pearls as compared to how many women want them? Good fakes will be virtually impossible to tell apart. They wouldn't be cheap—scratch Woolworth's—but they'd be affordable. There are millions of women out there who'd love to play Cinderella even if they haven't met Prince Charming; and if they can't handle a glass slipper, Lucite will be just fine!"

Bernie unpretzled his tall, lanky frame and paced Eva's office. "What woman is going to wear something, even if it looks real, that everyone will figure is fake because there's no way she could afford a $60,000 item? The whole charade would be out the window."

He's starting to explore possibilities and to ask questions, Eva thought gleefully. She might convince him yet.

"That's the point, Bernie," she said, controlling her excitement. "It wouldn't be a fake masquerading as the real thing. It would be a fake saying, 'I'm not real, but I'm gorgeous!' By pricing it just right—expensive for costume jewelry but far cheaper than anything real—and by advertising in *Vogue* and *Harper's* and by selling only at exclusive stores, the stuff will acquire its own cachet. Fake will be in—and the more outrageous, the better!"

Bernie still looked dubious. "I don't know, Eva. It sounds convincing, but it's somehow so not...Goodman's, if you know what I mean. We've always dealt in the finest, and that's what our name is linked with."

"So we'll use another name! We'll create a separate division, with a different name. Bernie—do you realize what designers we can get? All the talented, creative people who have been stifled for years because they can't afford the kind of raw material it takes to create a magnificent piece of jewelry. And the quality will still be there, because we'll use good materials and because the craftsmanship will be the same as you find at Tiffany's."

She was winning him over, she could tell. There was even a reluctant spark of enthusiasm when they started batting around marketing strategies and deciding which stores should be approached.

Eva took over the new division of Goodman's. At Bernie's insistence, they used her first name for the new line.

"What could be more essentially feminine and primary than 'Eva'?" he demanded.

The advertising agency had a field day. *"Jewels by Eva—when a fig leaf is simply not enough,"* the ads declared, showing one magnificent piece in each full-page spread, placed on a bright green fresh fig leaf, on a stark white background.

The big, prestigious chains ordered tentatively at first, then flooded Goodman's with additional orders as customer demand increased. Items were sold for $100 and up, and included traditional pieces like earrings and necklaces as well as far-out belts, shoe buckles, and hair ornaments. Whatever style of dress a woman favored, she could find an appropriate accessory conceived by Eva's growing cadre of designers, whose personal mark ranged from the discreetly traditional and low-key to the outrageously ornate and flamboyant.

"I can't believe the whole thing," said Bernie, shaking his head as they sat in the large boardroom, about six months after launching Jewels by Eva, going over the accountants' reports. "And it's all your doing! It was a genius of an idea, and to think I pooh-poohed it initially!"

Eva chuckled. "It was only initially, I'll say that in your favor. Once you saw the logic behind it, you threw yourself into it with equal enthusiasm. It's like my book was—the right thing at the right time—but on a much bigger scale."

Bernie's expression was still quizzical. "I must say, I'll never understand women. Even when I saw your point of view, I never believed they'd go for this stuff in such a big way."

Eva smiled. "Remember when denim was the rage? I remember going to get a pair of pants shortened at a little tailor's shop my father used to go to on Lexington. Mr. Adler, the tailor, was a Holocaust survivor, from Poland. He took my expensive but very traditional wool crepe pants and held them up next to a pair of jeans made up of a zillion little pieces of worn denim, of all different hues. 'Can you believe this?' he asked me. 'The price tag is still on it. A woman paid $125 for a pair of pants made from *shmattes*!' That rag fad waned, and so will this one, but I don't think it will disappear. We may see another year or two like this one was and then it will drop off, until the next revival of the regal look. The bread-and-butter of Goodman's will still be pearls and gold and real gems, but that's going to remain a limited market as long as prices stay so high. And this fling with costume jewelry has been fun, you have to admit!"

"Fun!" Bernie chimed in incredulously. "Do you realize that our net profit this year was over fifty million dollars?! A bloody bonanza is what I'd call it, never mind fun!"

"That part of it is nice, too, Bernie," Eva said wistfully. "So now I have even more money than before—I already had more than I needed. And where do we go from here? What do we do next to keep busy? This division is practically running itself now. I think we should give it another year and then sell it."

Bernie looked at her sharply. "You're probably right about divesting," he said slowly. "I had the same thought, but was afraid you'd bark at me if I suggested it. But why the big rush to look for something else? You've been working like a coolie; sit back for a while and rest on your laurels—and on your profits," he added with a broad smile.

"You're probably right. I should take a month off and take the kids somewhere this summer, after Sharon's exams are over—catch up on my reading and swim and relax." She screwed up her face in a grimace. "It sounds deadly, actually! Sharon probably has other plans and Jon really wants to go to a computer camp—I'm so reluctant to let him go—he'll only be eight."

"Eva," Bernie said quietly. "The kids are growing up. Sharon's been an adult for years, and being out east at college this year has matured her even more. And even Jon's not a baby anymore. He's also going to leave the nest one of these years. Right now you're devoting yourself to your kids and to the business. The kids are growing up, and the business is running very smoothly. What are you going to do about *Eva* when neither of these two things occupy so much of your time?"

Eva's eyes misted over and she tried hard to control the quiver in her voice. "You're a fine one to talk, Bernie!" she said, tilting up her chin defiantly. "I know what you think—that I should start making an effort to find a man to share my life. Well, I'll be honest with you—I'm not averse to the idea. But the one man I really ever wanted to share my life with is not available and maybe I'm not ready to compromise and settle for just any other male. Being alone is not so terrible. You should know!"

The familiar expression of pain and sympathy crossed Bernie's face.

He thinks I mean Dan, Eva thought with a pang of guilt. And maybe I do. I could have lived out my life with him and been fairly happy. Even more than fairly, she admitted to herself, remembering the camaraderie and the warmth, the friendship and the sharing that had marked their last years together. She was surprised at the sting of tears in her eyes. This is absurd, she thought, shaking her head to clear her thoughts.

She looked up to find Bernie staring at her piercingly. "There you go again," he said seriously.

Eva looked perplexed.

"I know that look," he growled. "That shaking of the head to clear it of any unwanted thoughts, shoving them back into their little compartments so they don't interfere. You're a master at doing that. Then you can go on being bright and alert and chipper—not to mention incredibly effective and efficient. Why don't you break down sometimes?" he demanded angrily. "You *are* human, you know! You're allowed to indulge in self-pity once in a while."

Eva was angry, but she managed a sarcastic laugh. "I can just see the headline," she said dramatically. "'Lady Tycoon Breaks Down in a Fit of Self-Pity!' How can I sit around feeling sorry for myself, Bernie? I have two wonderful children, a successful business that I enjoy, more money than I can spend—and, as Dan used to say, I'm not bad-looking for an old broad! Should I be passing around a hat, asking people to drop their sympathy into it?"

Bernie's expression softened. "Don't be an idiot, Eva. And don't take me for one. There's a lot more to happiness than what you've got. I'm not saying you should make a public display of sorrow. But you don't have to hide it constantly from those of us who love you. You don't have to be superwoman all the time— even if you are one most of the time," he added ruefully. "You can allow people to coddle and pamper you emotionally from time to time. There's nothing wrong with needing someone."

"Like who, for instance?" Eva demanded defiantly.

"Like me, for instance," Bernie replied, more agitated than she'd ever seen him.

Eva softened and reached over the boardroom table to take his hand. "I'm sorry, Bernie," she said with a slow, heart-stopping smile. "I didn't mean to sound bitchy or ungrateful. You know how much I depend on you. It worries me sometimes, how involved you are with us; I'm sure at the expense of your own private life. If I don't lean on you more, it's because I feel it wouldn't be fair—not because I think you wouldn't do absolutely everything for us. You're the closest thing I've ever had to a brother—and I know Dan felt the same way—but even devoted brothers deserve a life of their own. Don't worry about my not indulging in self-pity—I do. More often than you imagine, in fact. And if I don't go running for your shoulder each time, it's because I can handle it. I know you'll be there any time I can't, and very often that's comfort enough."

Bernie looked dubious, but mollified, and Eva added briskly, "Now, what do you say to ending this discussion and getting back to business?"

He smiled and nodded. "You're hopeless, you know. Hopeless and ruthless. And way too strong! Women aren't supposed be like that!"

Eva punched his arm playfully and added, "Okay, Mr. Macho! That'll do! Now back to these numbers!"

FORTY-THREE
MARCH 1987

The cold shook Eva out of her reverie. Hours had passed since Sharon's call and her casual remark about meeting Rob, and Eva realized she'd been somewhere on the verge of sleep, in that twilight area between conscious waking thought and the hazy impressionistic imaginings of quasi-dreaming.

She glanced at her watch and realized with a start that it was well past midnight. No wonder she was cold. The heat in the building went off at ten and she'd been lying curled up on the leather couch for more than two hours, reviewing events, marshaling memories. Eva grimaced at her reflection in the full-length mirror as she opened the door of the concealed closet to take out her fur-lined coat. I look my age, she thought, surveying herself critically. There's a softening around the jaw line, the wrinkles look deeper, and the gray in my hair is becoming noticeable. She shrugged into her coat and buzzed the guard in the lobby.

"I'm through, Frank. Would you be a honey and bring my car to the front?"

"Sure thing, Mrs. G.!"

By the time she got down to the lobby, Frank had the Jag idling in the circular drive in front of the building.

"You look tired, Mrs. G. You shouldn't be workin' so late. I was startin' to get worried about you!"

Eva flashed him a warm smile. "I'll start slowing down, Frank—had a lot of paperwork to finish."

"You rich folk are sure hard to figure out, ma'am! We simple folk work eight hours and have time to play. I reckon that's got to be better for you."

"You're right, Frank. Thanks for the car."

She tipped him the usual dollar, too tired to argue about the merits of a nine-to-five existence, and drove slowly home.

What will I do if Rob does call? she wondered as she brushed her teeth.

Her mind was reeling as she slid under the covers, still replaying the scenarios of years past. Whenever her resolve had weakened or when she'd been terribly lonely, she had allowed her mind to rove, imagining chance meetings. Airports, hotel lobbies, Fifth Avenue—all had been possible sites. But things don't happen that way in real life, she thought as sleep overcame her. Only in books and movies. Her last waking thought was of Jonathan. No one must ever know about Jonathan but me, she thought sleepily. It wouldn't be fair to him, and it wouldn't be fair to Dan. Jonathan is Dan's son. And mine. Especially mine.

When two weeks had passed after Sharon's phone call without a word from Rob, Eva felt that the danger, if danger was the correct term, was behind her. She refused to examine her own disappointment, or to admit there was pain involved, but there was. Not the dramatic new-born pain of losing someone, but the old, chronic, niggling pain of knowing that nothing had changed. That Rob was either just as unavailable as he'd been ten years earlier or, what was worse, that he simply wasn't interested anymore; that their love affair, which had been the watershed of *her* life, was, for him, a warm, nostalgic memory, but no more.

Being Eva, she immersed herself in work. She was startled one gray afternoon, in what passed for early spring in Minneapolis, when her secretary knocked tentatively and entered the office.

"I know you asked not to be disturbed, Eva, but it's almost 5:30 and I have to leave. Here's your mail to sign—I held it up, figuring you'd buzz; and there's a gentleman outside who would like to see you. He doesn't have an appointment but he asked me to give you his card and to find out if you'd see him."

"Thanks, Susan," Eva replied absently, reaching for her mail but not looking up from her work.

Susan handed her the card instead—she'd already put the folder down, and Eva froze as she saw the familiar name. She was silent for a moment, and then, in what she hoped was a controlled voice, said, "Give me two minutes to finish this, then send in Mr. Miller."

The girl nodded.

"And Susan," Eva added, smiling, "don't let me do this to you again—next time let me know that it's 5. I tend to lose track of time."

Susan nodded gratefully and left the office, closing the door behind her.

Eva shoved the papers aside, ran her tongue over lips that were suddenly dry, sat back in her chair, and took a deep breath, watching as the door slowly opened.

He looks the same, she thought, hoping that the dull, almost painful thumping of her heart couldn't be heard across the expanse of carpet between her desk and the door. Grayer, but the same, a separate and strangely detached part of her mind noted. She had stood up slowly as he'd walked in, the lines of her body tensed in anticipation and—yes—fear. They both stood for a long moment, saying nothing, surveying each other, pushing back memories, trying to isolate the moment.

"Eva," he said finally, and in the two short syllables of her name she heard the longing she had feared would not be there, an echo of the pain and love and incredible sense of loss that had become an integral part of her psyche over the long years.

"Rob!" she replied, her voice a ragged whisper, husky with tears.

They were in each other's arms a second later, somewhere between the desk and the door, holding onto each other for dear life, swept by a wave of emotion neither had expected, or could cope with unsupported. His arms were around her, holding her up as her knees buckled, her face buried in his shoulder, smelling the familiar mixture of skin and aftershave as she closed her eyes, not daring to look into his until she could push back the sudden wave of longing and sorrow that engulfed her, strangely moved with an exultation she'd never known before, a joy so all-encompassing that details like marital status or availability no longer mattered. He'd come back into her life—if only for this one meeting—and at this moment she could not think of anything but the once-familiar warmth of his arms, the gentleness of his hands as they buried themselves in her hair, pulling her gently away from him so he could look at her face.

"My God, you're beautiful! I'd almost forgotten how beautiful." He touched her cheek tentatively. "It was the eyes that stayed with me all these years—they haven't changed..." His voice choked. "I've missed you, Eva. I can't tell you how much...I didn't know about Dan... Why didn't you contact me when it happened? I could have helped—you must have been so alone."

She shrugged herself loose from his embrace and led him to the soft leather sofa.

"You weren't part of my real life by then," she finally answered, then noted the pain in his eyes.

"No, don't get me wrong, Rob. I never stopped caring about you—no, *loving* you, but you were a part of me that only existed in my head—in my memories, in my daydreams. You were no longer—real—somehow. Oh, I 'called' you," she smiled. "I've been talking to you for years—you've even given me some very sound advice at times! But it was the 'you' that I created for myself after you'd gone. The you that was a part of me even when the physical you wasn't there anymore."

She looked at him with a question mark on her face. "That doesn't sound very sane, does it?"

Bitterness tinged his laugh. "It sounds right to me—it sounds very much like what I did with you." He looked at her for a long moment. "We're fools, aren't we, Eva," he said soberly, "to martyr ourselves as we have. I should have come back when I really wanted to—the moment I saw that straight, proud back of yours walking out of my life. That's when I should have run like hell and brought you back."

Eva shrugged. He was describing a scene she had imagined so many times that it had an almost tangible quality—like a memory of something that had happened, rather than the wistful daydream it had been for them both.

"You couldn't come back, given the circumstances. I understood that. Jeannie needed you more than I did, and you couldn't have both." She paused for a moment.

"How is Jeannie?" she finally added, not daring to ask the question to which she so desperately wanted an answer. How are *you*, Rob? Has anything changed for you?

He answered haltingly, his eyes focusing on the middle distance.

"Jeannie is well, all things considered. She's in an institution in New England run by a very special couple who've made adults like her their life work. They have a farm, and they take in about a dozen kids at a time—kids like Jeannie who aren't severely handicapped and who can work at simple tasks and lead a productive life and help earn their keep. They help take care of the livestock and make preserves and jams to sell. Jeannie seems happy there—it's almost like a children's house on a kibbutz in Israel—and she has friends. I see her at least once a month— sometimes more often, when I'm in New York a lot."

He looked at Eva directly now, not bothering to conceal the pain. "She's still very beautiful in a very undeveloped, childlike way. Very innocent and sweet and cooperative. And she'll never be mentally older than eight… It's something I've learned to accept after all these years. I know that the pain is mine, not hers. She's happy in her own little world and she can't miss what she doesn't know. But it's such a waste, nonetheless. All the pieces are there, except the intellect. It's so unfair."

He shook his head, as if to clear it of thoughts about Jeannie. "But I didn't come here to cry about Jeannie—what about you, Eva? I know you've done phenomenally well in business—your daughter was very proud to recount your successes—but how have you managed on the inside? Has it been very rough for you?"

Eva got up abruptly and walked over to the large plate glass wall, contemplating the view of the city in the reddish hue of the sunset. She didn't really know where to begin. There was so much to tell him and so much to find out. The empathy that had always been there was still there—she could have sat down and spilled out her life story to him without pausing for breath. That was how their relationship had begun initially—with that same ease of sharing matters neither of them normally shared with anyone else. And it had led to love, and passion, and a closeness unlike anything either had ever experienced. What if that happened again? What if it didn't? What did she really want?

Eva smiled inwardly, chiding herself. The man is asking you a simple question, and you are so busy analyzing ramifications and consequences that you don't know what to answer! She came back to the sitting area and sat down in one of the armchairs, facing Rob. He had not taken his eyes off her, trying to fathom through her expressions and body language what he feared she would leave unsaid.

Eva smiled at him, that same dazzling smile that had captivated him all those years ago, that still took his breath away.

"There isn't much to tell, really. I was a bit of a mess after you left, I have to admit, but I functioned. I don't think anyone knew that there was anything wrong."

Her smile was more of a grimace. "I felt like someone who had just had a limb amputated, but nobody else knew about it and I wasn't about to let on." She breathed deeply. "Things got easier after I…after we had Jonathan. It made things better between Dan and me—to him, Jon was the reaffirmation he wanted that I had at least forgiven, if not forgotten, the Barbara incident, and once he no longer felt that he had to spend each day making amends, the tension between us eased. Working together also turned out to be a good thing. Our lives were more in sync and there was less pulling in opposite directions in terms of career and work commitments."

"Is that why you left the university? You had such a promising future there."

Eva laughed, then quickly recapped the events that had led to her decision, making light of the hard patches, giving the frustrations and hurts she'd encountered an almost comic slant that they certainly hadn't had at the time.

Rob saw right through her.

"I'm sorry you had to go through all that. You make it sound amusing now, but I'm sure it wasn't amusing to live through."

"But in retrospect, it's good that it happened. It pushed me out into the real world, which academia is not, and I found to my great surprise—and to everyone else's, except Dan's—that I not only liked it, but that I could do very well in it. I haven't done it on my own," she hastened to add. "I walked into a thriving business and added aspects and ideas that made it better. But I had mentors—first Dan, then Bernie, my partner. They were both supportive and I learned a lot from them. I may have had an innate talent for this kind of thing, but they enabled me to develop it and to take all kinds of risks that someone else might have been reluctant to allow."

She spent some time fleshing out the details of how the business functioned now, of the roles she and Bernie played, each enhancing the other's abilities and talents. Her cheeks flushed as she warmed to the subject, her enthusiasm about her work fanned by his obvious interest and quick understanding of the intricacies.

She still has the spark, Rob noted with satisfaction, the same zest and enthusiasm she had for her writing and research with the added sparkle that business success can add.

Eva noted his look and stopped in mid-sentence, suddenly abashed. "My God, I've been carrying on and on—why didn't you stop me? I've been talking nonstop for an hour!"

He smiled. "It didn't feel like an hour! I'm intrigued by the new you—the lady tycoon, I believe your daughter called you. She wasn't wrong!"

Eva chuckled. "You haven't done so badly yourself, I understand," she retorted. "It was some shock, walking up to a magazine stand and seeing your face plastered all over it!"

Rob laughed. The laugh hadn't changed either, she noted. It was the same throaty, contagious, sexy laugh that had drawn her initially and that she always remembered.

"Don't believe everything you read in the press!" he said in amused tones. "But seriously, the past few years have been good."

He described the trepidation with which he had embarked on the new venture, the gut-wrenching fear at launching his own business at a time when his financial commitments to Jeannie's future were so onerous.

"Success tasted sweet," he admitted openly. "I'd always made a good living—not by Rhoda's standards," he added with a grimace, "but certainly by anyone else's. But making real money, and doing it by means of something I loved to do anyway, felt good. I'll be crass enough to admit that."

Eva nodded, understanding fully.

"And how is Rhoda?" she finally asked, not really wanting to hear but recognizing the opening he had just given her. Rhoda is alive and well and holding on for dear life, she answered her own question.

"I was hoping you'd ask me that," Rob said simply. "Rhoda is fine. She's living in the Bahamas, married to a shipping magnate she met on a cruise about eight years ago."

Eva looked at him, stunned, and he continued slowly. "She came to me about two years after we…after I left you, to ask for a divorce. I think I must have looked at her with the same kind of look that's on your face now. I was in total shock. She was so adamant two years earlier when I literally begged her to agree to end our marriage. But the shoe was on the other foot now. She'd met someone and was truly in love for the first time in her life—if someone like Rhoda could ever really be in love—and she wanted out—amicably, with no hassles over money or custody. I have custody of Jeannie and I was glad to give her everything else, which surprised her."

He paused for a moment, his brow furrowed. The lines were deeper, Eva could see that now.

"She really expected me to exact my pound of flesh. She knew about us, Eva. Knew that you weren't a fling, that I'd never loved anyone the way I loved you. I think foisting the choice that she did on me—you or Jeannie—gave her a perverse kind of sadistic pleasure. Maybe it was her way of paying me back for giving her a child who wasn't perfect. Whatever the reason, she figured that I would treat her the same way. I think she was almost disappointed when a battle royal didn't ensue. I gave her what she wanted and let her walk away. It wasn't the happiest day of my life—but it came close!"

"And you didn't think to…didn't want to…" She paused, finding it hard to go on.

"Didn't think to get in touch with you?" he continued her question gently, bending toward her with a look of such naked longing in his eyes that she had to lower her glance to her tightly clenched fists lest he see the same look reflected in her own.

"You said it so well earlier on, Eva. I'm surprised you can even ask. And it was harder for me than it would have been for you—because I was the idiot who let you walk out of my life two years earlier. You were ready to make changes and to turn your life upside down. I wasn't."

He caught the expression on her face and continued roughly, his voice tinged with self-anger.

"Don't say what you were about to say—that things were different for me, and that I didn't really have a choice. I had a choice. I didn't realize it at the time—or I was too boggled by the enormity of it—but I had a choice. Damn it, there's always a choice!"

It was his turn to get up and pace in front of the window, unleashing the pent-up anger and disgust at himself by pacing like a caged panther across the expanse of the office.

"And what was I supposed to do two years after I'd rejected you—and that's what I did, let's call a spade a spade. Come back and say, 'I'm free now, so even though you've put your life in order and mended your broken heart'—I knew you'd do that, by the way; it kept me going, the knowledge that you were strong enough to do that—'so now that it's convenient for me, please disrupt your life again...'? No. I couldn't do that to you, Eva. I didn't even know you'd had another child, but all the more so if I had known. It wouldn't have been fair..."

Eva got up from the sofa and stood facing him with a strange, sad smile on her face.

"Fair?" she echoed in a flat, hollow voice. Her hand reached out and gently touched a crisp salt and pepper curl in Rob's unruly hair. "We've spent all these years being fair to everyone but ourselves." Her hand moved down his face, caressing his cheek, grazing the outline of his jaw.

"I love you, Rob," she whispered. "I've never stopped loving you—and you love me—and nothing else matters. Don't you see? Nothing else matters."

She gently lifted her face to his, pulling his head down toward her, kissing his lips softly, easing the lines of tension and pent-up frustration that still tensed his back.

He responded by crushing her to him, allowing his passion for her to take over, the passion held in abeyance for so many years, afraid it would drive him crazy.

They were undressed in seconds, pressing toward each other on the soft oriental rug with an urgency born of years of pushing away the very thought of such a moment. He entered her with no foreplay or preamble, his throbbing hardness encountering no resistance, only wetness and warmth and longing. She climaxed almost immediately, the pulsations around his thrusting penis driving him to a frenzy of desire that he could not control. He exploded inside her, only to be met with the rippling of yet another orgasm as she moaned with pleasure and gasped for breath. He slowed his tempo, savoring the exquisite sensation of her throbbing, sucking sensuality, feeling himself engorging and growing within her again.

Eva held him tightly, wrapped her legs around his arched back, forcing him deeper inside her, holding back now, to prolong and slow down their pleasure in each other.

He took his cue from her, barely moving, their ragged breathing the only sound in the room. He moved in millimeters, withdrawing his full length almost completely, then slowly, agonizingly, piercing his way into her with an equally slow and sweetly tormenting thrust. By the third slow thrust, she could take it no more. "I want you," she whispered, her lips locking onto his, her hips pushing toward him, so that he was completely inside her.

"I want you, too," he whispered back, his tongue exploring her mouth as he quickened his thrusts, feeling her whole body arch into his. Their movements quickened, first to a regular, steady in-and-out beat, which became more ragged and swift as they both reached the point at which control would be totally lost. She drew him into her, body and soul, and he felt the first convulsions of her orgasm as he began to come in uncontrollable bursts of overwhelming pleasure, matched pace for pace with the sweet contractions of her orgasm.

It lasted forever, waning then quickening again; culminating in a final burst of passion that left them breathless, clinging to each other, locked together in an embrace that neither wanted to relinquish.

When their hearts stopped racing and their bodies were totally relaxed, he began to withdraw, propping himself up on one elbow so that he could look at her face, her satisfied, happy smile belying the tears misting her eyes.

She made a little wordless noise of protest, pulling him down toward her again, moving her hips in that maddeningly seductive way of hers. He stroked her breast with one hand—it was larger and more rounded than he remembered, though the rest of her body was still slim and taut. Her nipple hardened under his caress and he felt himself hardening again, inside her, all thoughts of withdrawing blown clear out of his mind.

With the initial avalanche of desire now behind them, they spent the next hour exploring every square inch of each other's bodies; rediscovering sensitive spots; exploring with eyes, hands, and tongues; rekindling and satisfying each other's needs again and again. The room was long dark, with only the light of the desk lamp and the blaze of the city's lights illuminating the reaffirmation of their love.

They showered together in the small but complete bathroom off her office, soaping each other's bodies, using the slickness and softness of their wet, soapy skins to pleasure each other some more.

They talked in whispers, like conspirators, speaking of all the things they had not been able to articulate in the formal setting of their earlier discussion. They spoke of loneliness, of the ache of desire, of the spooky sensation of years of making love to each other while each was with another person. They bared their souls to each other—Rob totally, Eva almost totally, re-establishing the unique rapport and sharing that had marked their relationship all those years ago.

"I was hoping to find you still kindly disposed to me," Rob confessed in the small enclosure of the bathroom, "but this was beyond my wildest expectations. Don't ever allow me to let you out of my sight again!"

He was sitting on the closed toilet seat, a towel wrapped loosely around his waist, watching her apply her makeup with quick, efficient strokes.

She picked up his bantering tone. "If you don't feed me soon, there won't be anything to keep in sight! I'll waste away to a mere nothing."

He laughed, surveying her naked body from head to toe yet again, still hungering for her.

"Ten years and a child haven't hurt your body any," he said approvingly. Eva's skin was glowing from their hours of lovemaking and she eyed him with a twinkle as she reached for her mascara.

"You don't look too bad yourself, for an old guy!" she laughed back, noting his muscular arms and the still-flat midriff.

"No—we're not bad for a couple of middle-aged tycoons," he grinned. "Can't do it as much as before—but not bad!"

"Ooh!" she replied tartly. "That was a challenge, if ever I heard one. Shall I make you rise to it?"

"Even you couldn't! And if you couldn't, no one could," he protested laughingly.

Never one to resist a challenge, Eva got on her knees before him and slowly pulled the towel away from his waist. She surveyed him critically, then, with a gleam in her eye, proceeded to lick the delicate skin of his inner thighs, her hands caressing the backs of his legs, moving upward with agonizing slowness. By the time she took him in her mouth, he was almost hard, and within a minute, he was pressing her head toward him in an agony of desire he would not have dreamed possible. She moved back quickly, sen—sing that he would not contain himself much longer, and in one deft motion, straddled him, directing his engorged manhood into her, kissing him deeply as her buttocks rode him, sinking into his arms as he came inside her with a moan, the ripples of her muscles around him the only movement between them.

She smiled as she slowly pulled away from him.

"Never throw me a gauntlet unless you expect me to pick it up," she said mischievously. "Now, sir, get dressed and let's go out to eat. I'm famished!"

FORTY-FOUR

The next few months were strangely reminiscent of their first time together. Eva spoke to Rob daily, no matter where each of them was or what juggling and calculating of time differences it involved. They both traveled a lot and with creative scheduling, managed to spend time together—in Los Angeles, in New York, even a long weekend in London. When Rob came to Minneapolis, Eva would go to his hotel room. If she was in San Francisco for a night or two, he would move into her suite at the Mark Hopkins. She would not set foot in his apartment and he had not been invited to her home, not even at Passover, nor had he been introduced to Bernie or to Jonathan. Eva would not discuss the future. She threw herself into every minute they had together with the abandon of a hedonist who knows or senses that this one moment of pleasure, or this one night of rapture, would be the last.

Rob said nothing at first, sensing that she needed to be sure of him before taking what for her would be the tremendous and irrevocable step of making him a formal, acknowledged part of her family's life. Whenever he broached the topic of a future together, she would change the subject. He was puzzled at first, then hurt when she did nothing to alleviate his puzzlement.

Of her love for him, he had no doubt. He could hear it in her voice when he called her from all ends of the globe; he could see it in her eyes when they met at airport lounges and hotel lobbies; and he could sense it in the hunger and desire with which she made love when they were together.

And she knows how I feel about her, too, he thought. She knew it from the moment I came back. There was no coyness or holding back at that first meeting. Just an outpouring of love and desire that would have been held in check if she hadn't been sure of me. So why the wall?

"Are you paying me back, Eva?" he asked gently, smiling down at her in the soft glow of the bedside lamp. Their lovemaking had been long and slow and gentle, then fierce and pulsating, their bodies acknowledging the two weeks of agonizing absence while Rob had been in Japan.

Her look of contentment, born of total abandon, changed to consternation, and her brow furrowed. "What do you mean? Paying you back for what?" There was an undertone of panic in her voice. He was treading on dangerous ground.

"For everything—for leaving you, for staying away for so long, for—whatever."

"Oh, God no, Rob! It was just something that—had to happen, I guess. We were the right people at the wrong time. I understood that. You know I understood."

"But it isn't the wrong time anymore," he chided her gently, "and we're still the right people... Why are we having an illicit love affair? A young, attractive widow who has behaved with tremendous circumspection since her husband died, and a not-so-young but fairly eligible, divorced businessman who has barely glanced at other women because of the torch he was carrying for his one lost love. Who are we hiding from, Eva?" he demanded in rougher tones. "Is there a secret husband or lover who would take great umbrage at my existence? Is it Bernie?"

Eva giggled in spite of the sudden tightness in her chest. "No, it's not Bernie! I think Bernie's half in love with Sharon, though he doesn't know it yet—and thank God he doesn't, because I think she considers him her old familiar uncle."

"Then what is it, Eva?" he asked, refusing to follow the new conversational path she had just opened. "Why are you keeping me out of your public life? Why won't you bring me home to meet your family? Why won't you talk about anything beyond the now? Why have you got me so scared that I'm afraid to ask you to marry me—scared that you would probably say no?" His voice was angry now. Angry and hurt.

And I have no answers, Eva thought. I knew it would come to this; I've been expecting this confrontation, and I still have no answer.

Rob noticed the stricken expression on her face and his tones softened.

"Eva, Eva...please talk to me. There is nothing you can say or do that would change the way I feel about you. You know that. All those years we were apart, you were with me constantly. Not a day, not an hour went by when I didn't think of you—anything from long, elaborate fantasies that helped me fall asleep at night to a passing thought in the middle of a business conference or a bittersweet memory triggered by the sight of a pair of gray eyes, or a mop of jet black hair. I *love* you, dammit! What I don't understand is why you're doing what you're doing when I know you feel the same about me. I'd understand it if you didn't. But you do. I know you do. Everything you do and say tells me you do. Except this—wall. This barrier you've set up between me and everyone else who is near and dear to you. Why, Eva? Why?"

He'd been pacing up and down the room and was standing at the foot of the large bed, looking down at her. Eva was sitting up in bed, hugging her knees, wrapped in the sheet she had gathered about her to retain his warmth when he left the bed.

She'd been expecting this outburst, in one form or another, but although she had racked her brain to come up with the proper response, had rehearsed God knows how many possible scenarios, she still wasn't sure what to say or how to say it. But she could no longer hold him off. It wasn't fair and she'd always—almost always—played fair. That's why this is so hard, she thought sadly.

"Sit down, Rob," she said finally. "I guess we still have a lot to talk about. You'd think we would have talked about everything already, the way we go about it when we're together," she added with a wistful smile. "But we haven't. You're right. And you deserve an explanation."

Rob wrapped the hotel's terry robe around him and sat on the dressing table chair, to the left of the bed, facing her, steeling himself for he knew not what.

Eva was silent for a moment, then began talking in level tones. "When Dan died, his lawyer gave me a letter that he'd written a couple of years earlier, to be given to me should he die before me. He was fifteen years older than me, so it wasn't an unreasonable expectation, but it was spooky nevertheless, because there was such an aura of premonition about it, and because he wrote it when he was still so young—younger than you are now.

"What he said doesn't matter now—it had to do with the past and what he'd learned and how he felt about me. What matters is what he asked at the end of the letter and what I promised myself—and him—that I would do."

Rob interjected, his voice ragged with anger and pain. "So he asked that there not be another man in your life, or that you not remarry, never dreaming in a million years that he would die so young; and you are going to sacrifice your future happiness to a promise you made to a dead man at a time when your whole life was turned upside down!? That's absurd! It's morbid. I won't let you do it!"

Eva's hand motioned him to let her continue. "It has nothing to do with me. On the contrary. He hoped I would meet someone I could love the way I love you, so that I could experience what that kind of love felt like. He knew I didn't feel it for him and he blamed himself for that, though I really wonder if it was his fault…but that's beside the point."

She'd been looking at some invisible point in the center of the room, but she now focused on Rob's face, her eyes holding his, their grayness darkened to charcoal by the turmoil in her mind.

"The point isn't me. It's Jonathan. *No matter what you do with the rest of your life, let no one replace me in his.*' That's what Dan asked of me, and I owe him that. You see, he died thinking he owed me— thinking that whatever was missing between us was his fault— because of Barbara and because of the way he felt about my work, at least initially. And I thought so, too, until I met you and realized that I'd never felt the same way toward Dan, even at the beginning. Maybe Barbara happened because he sensed that lack—I don't know, and there isn't much point in speculating now."

"So you're afraid that if I come into your life—officially, that is, and especially if we got married—that I would somehow take Jonathan away from Dan? That I would make him forget his own father? That I would insist, perhaps, on his changing his name? Is that what you're afraid of?" He spoke slowly, trying to follow the logic of what seemed to be her fears and reservations, not succeeding because he could find no real logic to follow.

Eva looked at him mutely, feeling cornered. It really didn't make much sense, and Rob was right to shake his head, but he didn't know the whole story, and she had promised herself that no one ever would, never imagining that anyone would ever need to.

Rob moved to the edge of the bed and sat facing her, taking her hands in his. Her hands were icy, though the room was warm. The warmth of their lovemaking had long since evaporated for her.

"Eva, Eva, you fool!" he said gently, stroking her fingers, trying to get some warmth into them. "You don't understand, do you? You think I'm looking for a ready-made family to step into and take over—a daughter, about the same age as Jeannie, whose mental development didn't stop at age eight, and a son to fill the empty slot of the son I never had…"

He shook his head slowly. "There are lots of things I wish for, Eva, when I can't sleep at night. They all boil down to one wish, when you stop to analyze it—I wish I'd met you before Dan did, before I married Rhoda. Then there would be no problems of my kid and your kids, and my wishing that you hadn't had your tubes tied and that we could still have a child—all that wouldn't matter in my make-believe. We'd be celebrating our God-knows-what anniversary and we'd have umpteen kids who would all look like you with maybe a touch of me… But I know that's a fantasy. In fact, it was one of my favorite ones for years."

He smiled. "I know the realities—and if they're not what I would have wished for, they're a heck of a lot better than I expected a year ago—and that's enough for me. Don't you understand that? *You're* enough for me—everything that comes with you is wonderful. Sharon is great—and I'm sure Jonathan is, too. But they have nothing to do with my love for you or with my wanting to spend the next hundred years with you."

Eva shook her head ruefully, her eyes glistening with unshed tears. "It's not so simple, Rob. It really isn't."

"Yes, it is; it's very simple and it happens all the time. Children lose parents—to death or divorce—and the parent they live with remarries and continues his or her life—and the kids adjust—they're even happier sometimes, because a step-parent can be better than no parent—especially in Jonathan's case, where there is no contest. I'm not the man who took his mother away from his father. He must know how alone you've been all these years. And maybe he'd like to have a stepfather, if that man were someone he could relate to. There doesn't have to be a conflict, Eva," Rob continued insistently, making his case. "Jonathan would continue to be his father's son—I would never do anything to interfere with that. My God," he added bitterly, "it would be poetic justice, wouldn't it, giving you up once because of my daughter, and having to do it again because of your son."

He noted the sudden flash of pain in her eyes and drove his point home. "That's what you're saying, Eva, if you follow your convoluted logic to its logical end. You have to realize that we can't go on like this forever—we couldn't ten years ago, and we can't now. You have to bring me into your life—as a friend, at first, if not as a husband. You have to see how I fit into your life—as a part of it, an open part. Not the way it was ten years ago when neither of us could be open, when we couldn't be seen together, when our lives only touched at one corner of our existence, without overlapping. Let me be part of your life, Eva. I won't take advantage of it, and I won't usurp anyone's place or take anything that isn't rightfully mine."

He stroked her hair, pushing it back to reveal her face, his eyes pleading.

"Only you, because you *are* mine—as much as any human being can be another's—but nothing else, I promise."

Eva lay back, drained, her eyes closed. He was right. And he merely was articulating what she knew would be the simple reality of the situation—if the situation had, in fact, been as simple as he thought it was. She was boxed in, first by her decision to keep Jon's paternity a secret, a decision made when she was sure she would never see Rob again, and then by her commitment to the last request Dan had made of her. If she and Rob made a life together she would have to tell him about Jonathan. And once he knew, would he be ready to play the role of stepfather to a child who was, in fact, his own son? Would he ever forgive her for having kept the truth from him? She had no answers.

She opened her eyes and met Rob's piercing stare, his dark brown eyes looking right into her, trying to fathom the reasons holding her back, trying to understand why she couldn't see it his way.

Eva felt she could not stand it any longer. The subterfuge, the covering up, the deeply buried secret she had been carrying for so many years, hidden from all those she loved and from those who loved her. It hadn't been that difficult, until Rob's return. No one else *needed* to know. But this man did. He had a right to know, and she was torn between her recognition of his right—and of his need—and the promise she had made to herself, and to Dan, so long ago. Looking into Rob's eyes, she knew that she could not withhold the truth from him for much longer, not unless she was prepared to give him up again.

And I'm not, she thought fiercely. I'm not!

"Say something, Eva!" Rob begged. "I've been talking my heart out—tell me that I've convinced you. Invite me to Minneapolis for the Fourth of July. You said Sharon would be home then. I'd like to see her again. Tell me you'd like that. Tell me you're ready for me to meet your son."

"Yes," Eva responded faintly. "I *would* like that. We usually have a barbecue on the Fourth of July." Her glance turned inward, picturing the patio, smelling the steaks and baked potatoes, seeing the hot apple pie with a little American flag stuck into it.

She sat upright on the bed, her hands clutching Rob's. "And I'd like you to see Sharon again—she's been very curious about you, and I've been evasive." Eva took a deep breath. "And yes, I would like you to meet Jonathan, Rob. I've been putting it off for too long."

The words she wanted to say next would not come out... I wasn't putting it off because I was afraid that you would try to take him away from Dan and make him yours, she thought, but because I was afraid of what could happen when you looked at him and spoke to him. You see...he looks a lot like me, just like you wanted; he has my eyes and nose and mouth, but he has your hair—just like *I* wanted, when we talked about having a child—

and he has your personality and your brains. He's so much like you, Rob, that he made missing you so much harder on the one hand, and so much easier at the same time. Jonathan is your son, Rob. Our son.

Eva took a deep breath, wondering if the words seared in her brain should have been said aloud. "And it is time you met each other," she finally said, as an extension to her thoughts. "High time."

FORTY-FIVE

Eva looked around the tidy kitchen with satisfaction. The steaks were marinating on the counter, the potatoes were scrubbed and ready to bake, the corn was peeled, the salad was washed and dried and ready to be dressed, and the crisp Italian rolls needed only a few minutes in the oven to warm.

She took stock quickly and efficiently as she reached for her mug of coffee. Dishes and cutlery were piled on the tray, ready to be set out, the gas barbecue needed only minutes to heat up, and the garden looked lovely in the bright light of what promised to be a gloriously sunny Fourth of July.

Sharon walked into the kitchen and looked at her mother in amazement. "How long have you been here?" she demanded. "It's only 9 o'clock and no one is arriving till 3!"

Eva grinned mischievously. "I couldn't sleep, so at 6 I gave up trying and came down here to get organized."

Sharon rolled her eyes in mock horror. "That should be your motto—'get organized!' What are you going to do now that you're all organized and have six hours to kill?"

"I don't know," Eva answered, suddenly serious. "Worry, I guess."

"You're really keen on this guy, aren't you?" Sharon asked probingly.

Eva nodded mutely. Keen, she thought sardonically. I wonder if she knows how inadequate that word is in this situation.

Sharon noted her mother's expression and sat down at the kitchen table, taking Eva's hand in hers.

"Don't worry about it, Mom! We'll behave and we'll be nice to your friend. I've met him and I liked him right away, and I'm sure

Jon will too. Bernie might give you a rough time, but that's only because he's so overprotective of all of us. That seems to be his mission in life," she added bitterly.

Eva looked at her sharply. "Do I detect a note of resentment? Has there been any problem with him?"

Sharon nodded, her eyes suddenly brighter than they should have been. "I was at a club with some friends last night and Bernie walked in with one of those tarty types he likes to date—you know, the bleached blonde 'fuck 'em and forget 'em' kind. He almost flipped when he saw me there and stopped just this much short of making a scene and demanding that I leave. He thinks I'm still fourteen," she continued resentfully.

Eva smiled. "He knows you're not fourteen. He's just having a hard time coming to terms with the fact that you're a full-grown woman." And with the fact that he feels about you the way he does, and that he's too scared to admit it to anybody, most of all to himself, she added silently.

"Well, don't let him boss you around," Sharon replied. "You're allowed to go out with men—you're even old enough to go to bed with one, if you like," she added with a laugh.

Eva blushed, the memory of yesterday afternoon rising to the surface of her consciousness, and Sharon looked at her with a sudden flash of insight.

"You're really serious about Robert Miller, aren't you?" she asked in a subdued tone. "He must be really special. I don't think anyone has gotten through to you since Daddy died."

Then she smiled, tossed back her blonde mane, and carried her coffee mug to the sink as she prepared to leave the kitchen to get dressed. "Don't worry, Mom! I'll warn Jon—*and* Bernie—to be on their best behavior. We won't spoil anything for you. I promise!"

Sharon walked out of the kitchen, leaving Eva's emotions in a turmoil—turmoil that Rob's lovemaking and her constant busyness had been able to subdue, but not to erase.

Despite Sharon's assurances, Eva was nervous and scared. What if Rob took one look at Jon and realized he was his son? They were so alike...their similarities had been a source of comfort for Eva all those years. But could anyone else see it? Jon looked like his mother. Except for his hair, which grew in soft curls, whereas hers was straight. But her father had curly hair and Dan had often commented how much Jon looked like Hermann. Like one of the old sepia-colored photographs from Hermann's childhood that Eva's mother had taken with her when they left Germany; as if, since she could not have her dead baby, she would at least have an image of what he might have grown up to look like.

The similarity is more of character and talents, Eva admitted to herself, if it's there at all. Maybe it's only something my mind created as a way of holding on to Rob.

And what if Rob realizes that my eight-year-old son is almost nine and starts to calculate dates. Jon was born nine months, to the day, after…but maybe Rob doesn't remember the date, she added to herself, knowing full well that he did—that the date would be etched in his memory as clearly and as vividly as it was in hers.

Eva sighed, mentally throwing up her hands in defeat. I have to tell him, she thought, and I have to tell him soon. How and when she would do it was another matter.

As if on cue, Jonathan walked into the kitchen, still in his pajamas, hair tousled from the night's sleep. He poured himself a glass of orange juice, drank it, then blinked a few times.

Eva smiled. He wasn't a morning person, her son, and she knew he'd been reading till all hours, knowing that he didn't have to get up early the next day.

"Morning, Mummy," he finally said when the cobwebs cleared, reaching for the cornflakes.

"Morning, Jon. Did you have a good sleep?" A pro forma question, she thought. The boy always slept like a log.

"Mmm," he responded noncommittally, heaping sugar, blueberries, and milk on his cereal. Eva watched silently, waiting for him to start talking, knowing better than to chatter at him before he was fully awake.

"What's your friend like?" Jon finally asked, his overly casual tone betraying some anxiety.

"You'll meet him in a few hours, and you'll be able to judge for yourself. I like him. I think he's nice."

"Mmm," Jonathan said again, looking at her from the corners of his elongated, half-closed gray eyes, under thick dark lashes. "Sharon said I have to be nice to him or she'll clobber me. She says this is serious and I'd better not be a brat. Are you gonna marry this guy?"

Eva smiled in spite of herself. "Nobody is marrying anybody at this point, Jon. Rob Miller is a very good friend whom I hadn't seen or heard from in years and years. He met Sharon at Harvard and sent regards, then looked me up, and we discovered we still like each other. He'd like to meet the rest of my family—so I invited him to come to our barbecue."

It's so straightforward when you take away the complicated details, Eva thought.

"Did he know Daddy?"

She'd expected that question and she fielded it in the same way. Less is more. "No, no, he didn't. Rob is from California and he never lived in Minneapolis."

"Oh, so he knew you when you were young."

Eva smiled. Young, to Jon, was anything under fourteen, but she had been young, so she merely nodded her assent.

"What does he do?"

Oh, my, Eva thought, Rob is in for the third degree if this is what *I'm* getting.

"He has a computer business. Something to do with getting companies the right kind of hardware and software—but you can ask him when he gets here."

"Okay," Jon agreed, taking his dishes to the sink. He looked out the window with approval, then turned to face her.

"Can I tell you something? But it's a secret."

Eva nodded.

"Bernie is in love with Sharon."

Eva's jaw dropped. "How do you know that?" she finally asked. "Has he said anything?"

"No, of course not!" Jon replied scornfully. "But I saw him looking at her funny. You know, the way they do on TV in the mushy movies. I wonder if they'll get married."

"Whoa, Jonathan! You're marrying off a lot of people in a big hurry. Of course Bernie loves Sharon. He's known her since she was a little girl, and he's very proud of her success at school and of how pretty she is—but that doesn't mean he's in love with her, the way people are when they decide to get married. I think you're seeing things. How come, Jonnie? It's not like you."

To her surprise and chagrin, he burst into tears.

"I'm *not* seeing things," he protested. "You'll marry your friend and Sharon will marry Bernie, and I'll be all alone." He started to run out of the kitchen, somewhat ashamed at his outburst, but Eva intercepted him and held him tightly in her arms.

"Oh no, Jonnie! No, no! No matter what happens, that is one thing you never have to worry about. Sharon will always be your sister, though eventually she *will* get married and have kids of her own. And I will always, always be your mother, and that comes first, before anybody or anything else."

She wiped his tears with a tissue and gave him a fond thwack on the rear, eliciting a reluctant, but relieved smile.

"Now go upstairs and get cleaned up. Our guests are going to be here soon."

Problem number one, she thought grimly, watching Jon's slender form go up the steps. He hasn't even met Rob, and he's already feeling threatened.

Eva wondered again about telling Rob. She had toyed with the idea of telling him that night, after Bernie left and Sharon had gone out and Jonathan had gone to bed. But it might be too soon, she thought. What if he and Jon don't get along? Whatever I do with my life, Jon is a central part of it, and he has to be com—fortable. She wondered if she was simply procrastinating. Delaying the inevitable so as not to confront it now. Doing her Scarlett O'Hara bit. She smiled, recognizing the futility of trying to find all the answers, then followed her own advice to Jon and went upstairs to get ready for her guests.

FORTY-SIX

The afternoon just missed being a disaster. Eva had been worried about Rob, but she hadn't bargained on Bernie. Bernie, usually so easy-going and friendly, was in a foul, bear-like mood, ready to snap off anyone's head.

He was the first to arrive and asked Eva if he could talk to her privately for a few minutes. She nodded and led him to the den, concerned that it might be a business matter, but suspecting it was Sharon. She wasn't wrong.

Bernie poured himself a drink, then paced angrily, unable to find the right words.

"Well?" Eva finally prodded gently.

Bernie exploded. "You have to do something about Sharon, Eva! I bumped into her last night at a club where she has no business hanging out. It's a fast-action pick-up joint, and a girl like her shouldn't be there!"

Eva raised one eyebrow, suppressing a smile. "Was she picking up guys?"

"Don't be ridiculous! She was there with a bunch of her friends, but that's beside the point. The point is that she shouldn't hang out in places like that. She's just a kid."

This time Eva laughed outright. Bernie was taken aback.

"Your daughter hangs out in a...a hooker joint...and all you can do is laugh! I don't understand you...!"

"Bernie, Bernie," Eva said consolingly, patting his arm. "Sharon has just turned twenty. She's been living on her own for the last three years and she's a responsible adult. She wasn't doing anything wrong—merely going out with some of her friends—and she doesn't drink; soda or Perrier is about as far as she goes. And the Shangri-La isn't so bad; I've been there myself a few times… This is Minneapolis, Bernie," she added with a smile, "not Bangkok."

Bernie had the grace to blush. His memories of Bangkok *did* make the Shangri-La seem tame by comparison.

"That's not the point! The point is that a girl that age shouldn't be hanging around such places, and if you won't tell Sharon that, I will!"

"Tell me what, Bernie?" Sharon asked coolly, walking in. "Mom, Mr. Miller is here. I intercepted him in the driveway and took him to the patio; do you want me to tackle Bernie while you go to greet him? Bernie obviously needs some tackling."

"I don't know about tackling, but you might care to discuss a few things with him—please make it snappy, both of you. I'd like you to join us as soon as you can."

Eva rushed out, hoping the potential fireworks she was anticipating wouldn't erupt too spectacularly.

Rob was sitting in one of the patio chairs when Eva dashed out. He rose and pecked her cheek discreetly, his eyes flashing approval at the way she looked in jeans and a pink oxford shirt, her hair held back with a large pink barrette.

"You look terrific, Eva. I just realized that I've never seen you in anything less formal than a skirt and blouse. You look about eighteen."

Eva smiled. "You've seen me in a lot less than a skirt and blouse," she teased, "but I guess that doesn't count. I do thank you for the compliment, though! They get harder and harder to come by."

He smiled back at her. "Given the way you look, I find that hard to believe, but I'm ready to keep you supplied, if you'll let me."

They both beamed with the warmth and confidence of two people whose attraction for each other is well beyond the doubting stage.

"Shall I call Jonathan? He's probably at his computer," Eva said, hoping her nervousness was not as evident to him as it was to her. "Bernie and Sharon are in the den hammering out their relationship." She grimaced. "We may never see Bernie again—Sharon might just kill him; she's angry enough, God knows."

"If you like," Rob answered her. "Or show me the house first. Is it as nice as the garden?"

Eva showed him around the house, trying to see it through his eyes. Though rooms had been repainted and some furniture and draperies changed, the house still maintained the rambling but cozy charm it had when Eva and Dan moved in as a young married couple. The large formal living room was their last stop on the main floor and Eva looked around it critically.

"This room was my pride and joy when I was busy nest-building. The antiques are real and the carpet is a very fine one—but we never use this room. The kids use the family room in the basement and the den is my favorite hangout—but we can't go in there until Bernie and Sharon iron out their differences."

She grimaced and Rob grinned. "Maybe they'll find out that they agree on a lot more than they realize," he said.

Eva cocked her head in the direction of the angry sounds emerging from across the hall.

"I hope you're right. Doesn't sound like it right now."

He followed her up the wide curving staircase with its turned oak banister.

"I can't vouch for the kids' rooms—especially not for Sharon's, though Jon is usually neat. That's the guest room, which my mother uses when she's here. This is my room…" She led him into the large master bedroom, which had been completely redone since Dan's death. It was a tasteful, quiet blend of soft peaches and off-whites, with black Oriental lacquer adding touches of drama. A black parson's table was the only cluttered surface, with a bonsai tree in an off-white china container at one end and an array of family photographs in a variety of frames at the other.

Following Rob's glance, Eva picked up a family portrait in a heavy hammered silver frame.

"This was taken a few hours before Dan was killed," she said quietly. "Bernie had just picked up a new camera in Hong Kong and he was busy experimenting. We all forgot about it until he had the film developed months later. Most of the photos he took were of Dan and the kids, and they finally convinced me to get into the act."

She handed the picture to Rob, watching his face.

"I envy you and your kids—having had this," he finally said, emotion clogging his voice. "It's such a beautiful family portrait."

Eva took back the photo. It showed the four of them on the back lawn, the flowerbeds blazing with color behind them. Dan was in the center of the picture, squatting on the grass with the athletic ease that had marked all his movements, Jonathan on one knee looking at his father with a smile of adoration. Sharon was behind Dan, her head resting on his right shoulder, hand reaching forward to tickle Jonathan, and Eva was to Dan's left, kneeling in the grass, her face in profile to the camera, hair streaming down, a mischievous smile playing around her mouth, anticipating Jonathan's squeals when Sharon's hand reached him.

"We *were* a good group," Eva said, suddenly somber, as she carefully placed the photo in its spot. "Oh, we always looked the part—ideal suburban American family and all that. But at the time that picture was taken, I think we were actually getting there. Dan and I had both made some sort of peace with what had been and what wouldn't be. I think he'd accepted the fact that I was what I was, and that what we had was good, even if it didn't fulfill his ideals."

"And you?" Rob asked quietly.

"Me?" She tilted her head and looked at him squarely. "I was...quiescent. I had buried my dreams and come to terms with reality. You were gone, and though I used to daydream about unplanned meetings, I don't think I ever expected to see you or hear from you again. I wasn't in pain anymore. That part of me had gone numb. Sometimes I'd wonder if you had ever really been part of my life or if it had all been a dream...I..."

A sudden triumphant war whoop emanating from Jonathan's room put an abrupt end to what she'd been about to say, and the expression on Rob's face changed from sadness to surprise.

Eva smiled knowingly and led Rob to the next room, knocking softly on the door before opening it.

"Did I hear the distinct sounds of a breakthrough?" she asked teasingly as she opened the door.

"Yeah, Mom—I did it! I got the whole program right this time. It really works."

Jon started to explain the technicalities of the program he'd been copying from a magazine when he suddenly noticed Rob standing behind his mother in the hallway and stopped in his tracks.

Eva stepped in smoothly. "Jon, this is my friend Robert Miller; Rob, this is my son Jonathan."

The two shook hands, studying each other, ignoring Eva for the moment.

"Nice to meet you, Mr. Miller," Jon said politely but warily.

"Please call me Rob, Jonathan, everybody does."

The boy nodded.

"What program did you just finish? Sounds like it was a toughie," Rob asked easily.

Jonathan's face lit up. He started explaining the steps of the program to Rob, then quickly realized that this man really understood what he was talking about, not like his mother or Sharon, who nodded and said "um hmm" politely, or even Bernie, who knew a bit more but wasn't really interested.

Rob asked more questions, and Jonathan answered with enthusiasm. Before they knew it, they were both at the keyboard, going through the program, Rob showing Jon what changes he could make to expand its capabilities.

Eva remained standing at the door, leaning against the doorpost, her knees suddenly rubbery. She'd been dreading this meeting, dreading Jon's reaction to her having a male friend important enough to bring home, wondering whether Rob would know how to deal with the boy, not knowing yet how to deal with the problem of telling Rob that he was the boy's father. And here they were, busy chatting away in a language she barely understood, as if they had known each other for years.

Rob shot a glance in her direction and asked meekly, "Is it okay for us to stay at the computer for a while?" There was a twinkle in his eye meant only for her. A "see, there was nothing to worry about" kind of twinkle. She smiled weakly and nodded.

"I'll call you two when it's time to start the barbecue," she answered faintly.

The two heads of curly hair—both brown but one generously laced with gray—turned back to the computer terminal, her existence peripheral at the moment.

They *don't* look alike, Eva thought yet again, except for the hair. But they are so similar...

FORTY-SEVEN

She quietly closed the door and walked slowly down the stairs, wondering what had transpired in the den.

She found Bernie sitting there alone, brooding. Sharon was nowhere to be seen.

Eva silently poured him a Scotch and took a cognac for herself. Bernie looked at her in surprise. "Isn't it a little early for you?"

Eva made a face at him. "I needed this drink four hours ago," she shot back, "but at least it's already afternoon. Here," she added, handing him his drink, "you look like you need it more than I do! Did Sharon make mincemeat out of you? You were asking for it, you know."

"I know," Bernie responded glumly. "I was, and she did. She was furious that I was trying to mix into her life, told me she was perfectly capable of taking care of herself, and that where she goes with her friends isn't my business. She's right! And I really blew it—she'll probably never talk to me again."

Eva laughed outright. "I'd say you overdid it somewhat, but I don't think you blew it forever. Sharon has her father's temper—she explodes easily, but she forgives quickly, too. Where is she, by the way?"

"She went out on her bike and said she'd be back—I think she had to do something physical to get the anger out of her system."

"Yes, that sounds like Sharon. She'll be fine when she gets back."

"Yeah," Bernie agreed, "and I better keep my big mouth shut. It was that guy she was with, too; he kept putting his arm around her shoulder, like she was his property. That really got to me."

"Why?" Eva asked conversationally.

"What do you mean 'why'?" Bernie retorted.

"Just that. What's wrong with a guy putting his arm around her shoulder? Why does that bother you? People do it all the time—it isn't even a particularly intimate gesture. You do it all the time."

"What are you saying, Eva?" Bernie asked shakily.

"I'm not saying—I'm asking. Why do you feel so overprotective when it comes to Sharon? Ask yourself that."

"Eva, for Chrissake! I've known that girl since she was a child. I'll never forget the way she looked when I first saw her walking down the stairs. Her parents were my closest friends for years; her mother still is—how would you expect me to react when I see some sleaze putting his arm around her?"

"How do *you* expect to react? Fatherly? Avuncular? That's not how you're reacting, you know. You're behaving like a jealous boyfriend, and I suspect that's what Sharon is having a hard time handling."

Bernie looked at her dumbfounded. "Oh my God, no wonder she's angry! If that's how she thinks I feel, she must be totally disgusted!"

Eva's laughter rang out. "I don't think she's the one who's disgusted, Bernie, I think you are—with yourself—because you find Sharon attractive, as a woman, not as a little girl you saw growing up; and because you find that attraction wrong. Almost incestuous, maybe. So you're angry at yourself—and you're taking out the anger on Sharon."

Bernie stared at her for a long time.

"You're a very astute woman, Eva," he said finally. "You should have gone into psychology, not literature, you know."

"There's a lot of psychology in literature," Eva said lightly, "not to mention in real life…"

"And you're not angry at me?" he asked anxiously.

"Angry? Why should I be angry? Sharon is a magnificent woman. She's bright and fun and beautiful—and she's a *mentsch*! I expect she's broken more hearts than you or I—or even she—will ever know."

Bernie was lost in thought, obviously exploring an avenue that previously had been closed off.

"How does she feel about me?" he asked suddenly.

"I don't really know, Bernie," Eva answered. "I don't think you've given her time to even find out. Why don't you give her a chance to get to know you as someone other than her tyrannical Uncle Bernie? The outcome may surprise you both…"

The back door slamming signaled Sharon's return, and she marched into the den, flushed and hot, bathed in perspiration and looking absolutely stunning.

"That was a good bike ride—do I have time for a quick shower?"

"Go ahead, sweetie," Eva replied. "Rob and Jon have discovered they have computers in common and the longer we give them, the happier I suspect they'll be—so we'll just wait a little while longer before we start."

Sharon smiled, her eyes including Bernie, signaling her for–giveness.

"I suppose Rob and Jon are talking Basic and Fortran to each other—I kind of expected that to happen—but you were nervous, Mom, weren't you?" Her blues eyes narrowed as she examined her mother's expression closely. "Don't you worry about Jon, Mom. He's scared of you getting involved with anyone because of how it would affect his place in your heart. Once he gets to know Rob, he'll want him in the family."

With this declaration, she sprinted out of the den to head for the shower, leaving Eva and Bernie sitting in the den agape, each for their own, separate reasons.

The rest of the afternoon and evening were relaxed and almost anti-climactic. The fears that had tormented Eva were at least partially laid to rest by the easy relationship that Rob seemed to be establishing with Jon. And Bernie was on his best behavior, with only Eva noticing that he was somewhat subdued. He'll go home, she thought, and mull over his relationship with Sharon and he'll make one of two decisions—either to pursue the attraction he feels for her, to see where that leads; or to keep on playing the role of Sharon's uncle and to torment himself whenever she goes out with another man. Eva shrugged inwardly. Bernie is a big boy and he'll have to find his own way. In some ways, Sharon is more grown-up than he is.

The food was delicious and Rob had volunteered to help clean up while Sharon and Bernie took Jon to the park to see the fireworks. It was strange to be standing in her own kitchen, methodically loading the dishwasher, with Rob bringing in the dishes from the patio, straightening out chairs, and efficiently wrapping leftovers in Saran. They were both quiet, aware that the scene they were playing was the most domestic one they had ever been in, each wondering how this would feel on a permanent basis.

At one point Rob had come up behind Eva, nuzzling her ear and the soft stray hairs at her nape, cupping her breast in his hands.

"They shouldn't allow women like you to wear jeans and ponytails," he whispered gruffly, pressing against her, feeling her nipples harden through the soft cotton shirt.

Wordlessly she turned off the tap and turned to face him, placing her mouth on his, feeling his manhood harden and bulge against her.

Still silent, she led him back to her room, unbuttoning her shirt and peeling off her jeans, then turning down the bedspread as he quickly undressed.

Her breasts sprang at him as he unhooked her lace bra and he paused to caress them before reaching under her silk panties, feeling the heat and wetness of her desire.

He entered her with no further ado and she was ready for him, meeting his thrusts and the shudders of his almost instantaneous orgasm with the contractions and ripples of her own.

"I feel like a teenager," Rob finally said with a grin. "I have no self-control when I'm with you. I even find the way you wash dishes irresistible!"

"How about the way I do this?" Eva asked huskily. He was still inside her as she slowly rolled them over until she was on top of him, rubbing her body slowly against his, fondling him until she could feel his semi-hardness grow into a full-blown erection, filling her completely. He moaned softly.

"It's not fair," he whispered.

"I never promised you fair," she whispered back, grinning, "just fun."

She played with him for what seemed like hours, though it wasn't, bringing him to the verge of orgasm, then stopping and holding back just as he was about to come. Finally she could not bring herself to stop, craving his release as much as he did. They clung to each other as the waves of passion rolled over them, mouths locked, groaning in mutual ecstasy, each wondering why sex had never been this way with anyone else.

An hour later, when Bernie and Sharon came home with a tired but happy Jonathan, Eva and Rob were sitting sedately in the den armchairs, sipping cognac and talking like old friends. Jonathan said goodnight to everyone and went upstairs to get ready for bed. About fifteen minutes later, Eva left the other three talking animatedly and went upstairs to kiss Jonathan goodnight. She smiled as she walked by her own bedroom. The bed was neatly made, the room in perfect order, in total contrast to the earlier disarray of clothes strewn haphazardly all over the room and bed sheets tangled with the frenzy of their passionate lovemaking. She wondered if she should feel guilty. If I should, I don't, she thought, while recognizing the complexities and subtle ironies of the situation. Dan's picture, Jonathan's paternity, and the supposed decadence of bringing her former and present lover into her late husband's bed...

Jonathan was reading in bed when she tiptoed in. She tucked in his covers and stroked the silky curls as he smiled at her sleepily.

"Goodnight, sweetie," she whispered as he put aside his book and put his arms around her neck.

"G'night, Mummy. I like your friend. He's nice and he sure knows a lot about computers."

"That's good, Jonnie. He likes you, too."

"He likes you even more, Mummy. I saw him looking at you all mushy."

Eva laughed. "Aren't you the expert on love and romance, my little eight-year-old!"

"I'm almost nine," Jonathan responded indignantly, then smiled as he realized his mother was teasing him.

"I'll miss you when I'm in camp," he added.

"I'll miss you, too, baby—but it's just for two weeks and you will have a ball—unless you want to stay home, of course!" she added wickedly. The computer camp in Maine had been Jon's idea and he'd pestered mercilessly until she had agreed to send him.

"No, no—I'll be fine," he added quickly. "I really want to go!"

"I thought as much," Eva said drily, a smile curling the corners of her mouth. "Now go to sleep—we have to start getting you organized tomorrow and you've had a busy day."

Jonathan curled up into a ball and Eva switched off his light. She stood in the doorway for a moment, watching the boy drift off.

It's a good beginning, she thought. Now where do I go from here?

FORTY-EIGHT

Rob met them at Logan Airport. They were spending a day in Boston sightseeing, seeing off Jon at his camp bus, and then Eva and Rob were going on to visit Jeannie before spending two weeks in a seaside cottage north of Kennebunkport that Rob had borrowed from a friend.

That's when I'll tell him, Eva thought. It would be their first real time together, and it will be "kosher" and above-board, she realized, with everyone knowing where they were and that they were together.

Sharon was delighted. She liked Rob and she liked what his being around was doing to her mother. There was a sparkle in Eva's eyes that Sharon had never seen before, and she wasn't driving herself as hard as she usually did at work. It would have been easier had they both lived in the same city, and Sharon wondered how they would solve that problem if they decided to marry—each had a business firmly established in their respective cities and she could not see either of them, and especially not her mother, giving that up.

Jonathan liked Rob too, but wasn't yet prepared to consider the possibility of his mother marrying anyone. He had friends who had stepfathers, but that was different, somehow. He didn't mind her spending a vacation with Rob while he was at camp—as long as she went back to being his full-time mother at the end of the two weeks.

He clung to Eva before boarding the big yellow bus, and she hugged him tightly, burying her face in his soft curls.

"Have a good time, Jonnie. I'll miss you."

"I'll miss you, too, Mom—enjoy your vacation too. Bye, Rob." He waved to both of them from the bus window, the excitement of the moment overcoming his fears of the strange new adventure he was embarking on.

Rob watched Eva's face as the bus drove away. "You're very attached to him, aren't you?" he asked softly.

Eva looked at him, her eyes glistening with held-back tears. "He's a very special child," she said slowly, "and he came at a time in my life when I most needed him…" She broke off, not wanting to discuss the subject further. Not here in the dusty parking lot of a deserted Boston school.

Rob sensed her mood and didn't pursue the matter further. "Come," he said, taking her hand and leading her to the car, "we'd better get going if we want to make it to Bakers' Inn by this evening. Then we can visit Jeannie tomorrow morning and get to the cottage by the afternoon."

They spent that night at the small New England inn, not far from Jeannie's school. The proprietors, Mollie and John Baker, knew Rob from his earlier visits and were thrilled that he was there with a woman friend. He'd always come alone, or with Jeannie, and they'd seen the sad, quiet, and lonely side of him that few people ever glimpsed. He was still quiet and somewhat tense—he always was before visiting Jeannie, never knowing what to expect—but there was a glow of contentment about him now that had never been there before.

"I like the way she looks at him," Mollie declared when she marched into the kitchen from the small intimate dining room where ten or twelve couples were eating the gourmet dinners for which her inn was renowned. "I think he means business—he's never taken anyone to meet his daughter before. And this one is a real lady—not like that snooty one he was married to before."

Rhoda had stayed at Bakers' Inn once, at Rob's recommendation.

"I should have known better than to suggest this place to her," Rob laughed as he recounted the story to Eva. "She took one look at the braided rugs and wood-burning stoves—not to mention the bathroom down the hall—and hightailed out of here to the nearest Howard Johnson!"

"The Bakers are wonderful people," he added. "I've brought Jeannie here for meals and visits a few times, and they were really great with her."

"You're worried about my meeting her, aren't you?" Eva asked perceptively, and he smiled sheepishly.

"I'm terrified—and I don't really know why. I guess I want her to like you—and you to like her. I know it doesn't really matter, but the two of you are the people I care about most."

"I felt the same way when you first visited my house," Eva admitted. "Sharon was already accounted for. She liked you from the moment she met you, but I was petrified that Jon would decide he couldn't stand you—I'm glad the two of you have hit it off so well."

"He's a terrific boy, Eva. I don't know if you realize how bright he is—his grasp of math is uncanny."

He comes by it honestly, Eva thought, wondering whether this was the time and place to tell Rob the truth. No, she added to herself. Let me meet Jeannie first and alleviate Rob's fears about my acceptance of her. And her acceptance of me.

Their lovemaking that night was gentle and subdued, the soft light of an antique kerosene lamp their only illumination. Rob was tense, and would continue to be, Eva realized, until the encounter between Jeannie and her was behind him; and she herself was distracted, wondering how Jonnie was coping in the new and strange milieu of a camp full of boys his age. He was used to not having her or Sharon around—but when Eva traveled, he stayed at home with Mary and spent weekends with Dan's mother. This was different.

"He'll be okay, Eva," Rob whispered, caressing her face and reading her thoughts at the same time.

"So will she," Eva replied with a smile. "I promise you we'll get along."

"Tit for tat," he answered. "Don't you know it's dangerous to read minds?"

"Umm," Eva said. "If you read mine too often—especially when I'm thinking about you—you might not consider me a fit stepmother for your daughter!"

"Just keep thinking those thoughts—as long as they're reserved for me only!"

Eva curled up against him, feeling the warmth of his arms around her, reveling in the familiar smell of his skin.

"Only for you," she murmured sleepily, overwhelmed by a sense of well-being she could not remember feeling before. "Only for you."

FORTY-NINE

Nothing, not Rob's descriptions, nor the picture of Jeannie that he carried in his wallet, could have prepared Eva for the breathtaking beauty of the girl who now ran to greet them.

For years she had carried in her mind a picture of Jeannie as she had looked in the photograph Rob showed her when they first met—a lovely china doll in a velvet dress, posing sedately for the photographer, looking like a child from a Reynolds portrait, a product of another age.

Somehow that portrait never changed with the years, leaving Eva totally unprepared for the magnificence of the young woman who now came charging down the path calling "Daddy! Daddy!" in excited tones.

Rob ran to her and Eva watched, with a pang of jealousy that took her by surprise, as the two embraced in a massive bear hug.

Jeannie was tall—almost as tall as her father, and even the big denim overalls and plaid cotton shirt did not hide the slim yet curvaceous lines of her voluptuous, long-legged twenty-two-year-old body. But it was the face, more than anything else, that drew the eye; the long mass of soft dark curls framing magnificent thick-lashed blue eyes, a small straight nose, a saucy chin, and a soft, full-lipped mouth. Sharon is lovely, Eva thought, but this girl is dazzling. She hung back, letting Rob have his meeting with the daughter he had not seen in more than two months, feeling guilty at being the cause of his paternal neglect.

Rob laughingly disentangled himself from his daughter's embrace, took her hand, and walked her down the path toward Eva.

"Jeannie, I want you to meet a very special friend of mine—Eva Goodman. Eva, this is Jeannie." He looked expectantly at Jeannie as Eva smiled warmly and stretched out her hand.

"Hello, Jeannie. I'm happy to meet you—your father talks about you a lot."

Her smile was met with a stony countenance and no hand forthcoming to press hers.

"I don't like your friend, Daddy. Tell her to go away."

Eva could suddenly see the eight-year-old coming through. The woman in front of her was not a woman; she was a young, insecure child in the body of a woman and the gap between the two was disconcerting.

Rob started to remonstrate but Eva signaled to him to stop. She dropped her hand but kept a pleasant smile on her face.

"Don't worry, Jeannie. I only came along with your Dad because I wanted to meet you. I know you haven't seen him for a while and you probably want to spend time with him. I'll go visit with Mrs. Meredith and ask her to show me the farm. You two run along and have your visit."

Rob started to protest but Eva's frown and Jeannie's hostile stance convinced him otherwise.

"Wait for me at the main house," he said to Eva quietly. "Jeannie and I have to have a talk."

"Go easy on her," Eva said in broken German, surprised that she found the words, but not wanting Jeannie to understand. The girl's hostility was palpable.

Rob nodded seriously as he watched Eva turn and walk slowly away. He'd seen that view of her before, the head held high, the pace steady, the determination not to look back etched into every line of her body. She'd walked out of his life once, because of this same child, and he'd let her go. He would not let her do it a second time.

Eva's stride may have seemed determined and confident to Rob, but she was shaking inwardly. She approached the rambling farmhouse, but then, unable to face Mrs. Meredith's kind chatter and tea and scones, she decided to go exploring instead. A walk would give her a chance to think and to get her emotions under some semblance of control.

She hadn't expected Jeannie's reaction. Some hostility and suspicion, yes. She'd expected the same from Jonathan, and was relieved that it hadn't materialized, but not this out-and-out rejection, the verbal slap in the face that stung more than a physical slap ever could.

She's only a child, Eva told herself over and over, and an emotionally disabled one at that. Her emotions and thought processes are not like Jon's or Sharon's. She wondered suddenly if she was biting off more than she could handle. Merged families were difficult enough under normal circumstances. Was she making a terrible mistake in thinking that she and Rob could have a happy and relatively carefree future together? The problem of geography was the least of it. They had talked about it and a solution, tentative as yet, was possible. They both had substantial branch operations in New York City and each had considered moving their respective head offices there, leaving San Francisco and Minneapolis as major branches. Eva had been toying with the idea for quite some time, even before Rob's reappearance in her life. Sharon already was on the East Coast and she had wanted better schools for Jon and possibly a less lonely social life for herself.

I'm avoiding the issue, Eva thought, forcing herself to consider the problem of Jeannie.

She had been walking along a path that marked the perimeter of the farm and found herself near a picturesque little waterfall created by a small brook cascading over granite-like rocks. It was an idyllic country scene, the hot sun dappling the treed landscape with warmth and soft light.

Eva took off her jean jacket, rolled it into a pillow, and propped herself against a warm boulder overlooking the brook.

Jeannie had always been the problem. No, not Jeannie per se, but Rob's relationship with her. Eva knew full well that the stab of jealousy she had felt was not unfounded. He gave me up for her once, she thought, I wonder if he'll do it again. She realized how much that old rejection still rankled and wondered if the contentment and warmth and ease that she and Rob had together could counterbalance it and overcome it.

The well-being of the previous night had dissipated completely and Eva wondered if she could find it again, if Rob's feelings toward her would be the same after this visit with his beloved daughter, who was refusing adamantly to have anything to do with the woman he loved.

"The two of you are the people I care about most." Eva could still hear the words, but the comfort they had instilled in her the night before was gone.

And what if you have to choose between us, Rob, or if you think you have to choose? Who will it be?

She realized from the sun's position that it was well beyond noon and began to retrace her steps. Hopefully, lunch would be over. Rob had described meals around the big refectory table in the large farmhouse dining room—everyone ate together and meals were boisterous, cheerful, and very social occasions. Eva didn't think she could face that. Nor did she want to cause Rob any discomfort at having to tackle the problem of having Jeannie and herself in the same room. The girl's animosity had been so intense and so palpable.

Rob was waiting for her on the wide steps leading up to the veranda of the farmhouse. Lunch was over and the kids had all gone for a hayride. He'd said his farewells to Jeannie, promising her to stop by again in two weeks on the way back to Boston. He had watched Eva turning away from the house and figured she'd gone for a walk, but she'd been gone for some time now and he was somewhat worried, so he was greatly relieved to see her walking back toward the house, her jacket slung over her shoulder, her chin tilted high in the manner she had when confronted with an adversarial situation.

"Hi, Rob, where's Jeannie?" she asked, her voice light, the tone conversational.

"She's gone for a hayride with her friends. She'll be gone for the rest of the afternoon, so we can leave whenever you're ready. Want something to eat before we go? Mrs. Meredith is saving you some lunch."

Eva shook her head. Food and emotions didn't mix in her book, and she was too tense and—yes, frightened—to eat.

"How was your visit?" she asked noncommittally, sitting on the step next to him.

He grimaced and said nothing, and Eva probed no further. Their silence, usually so companionable and comfortable, was an uneasy one.

"I guess I'll go in and say goodbye to the Merediths, and then we can leave if you like," she said.

Rob nodded and Eva headed for the front door, pausing to look back at him. If he'd been anxious before the visit, he was miserable now—head bent forward, back muscles tensed, hands clenched into fists.

Eva said her goodbyes and followed Rob silently to their rental car. The silence grew somehow heavier as they left the farm behind, picking their way down the bumpy road to the highway.

FIFTY

The beach house was magnificent. An expanded A-frame, on a low bluff overlooking the ocean, with twin skylights built into the tall sloping cathedral ceiling to catch the sun. The back wall was warm red brick with an ample fireplace, and the furniture was simple and austere—some good Shaker pieces combined with Italian leather sofas and armchairs, with hand-woven rugs and bright pillows adding warmth and softening the simplicity.

The dining room contained an old refectory table, with eight ladder-back Shaker chairs around it. The small modern kitchen was compact, clean, and extremely functional. The refrigerator and larder had been stocked with enough food for at least two weeks and a note from the housekeeper, who came in once a week, was prominently displayed on the fridge, asking them to call her should they require anything.

The bedrooms comprised the southern ell of the house—a large master bedroom with its own bathroom occupied the front of the ell and two smaller guest bedrooms, divided by a shared bathroom, faced the woods in the back. The front wall of the house, the wall facing the ocean, was almost entirely of glass, bringing the ocean right into the house, almost making it part of the décor.

"This looks like something from *Architectural Digest*," Eva murmured in awe as they finished exploring.

"It is!" Rob chuckled. "It took up almost a full edition when it was first built. Bill always nags me to use it, especially since I come up to New England so often, but it never seemed to make sense to come here alone, and there was no one I really wanted to spend all that seclusion with—it's off the beaten tourist track and literally no one ever comes here unless it's by invitation."

"Let's hope two weeks of seclusion with me won't be more than you can handle!" Eva said in a light tone.

They had exchanged almost no words at all during the drive to the house. Rob had been engrossed in his own thoughts and concerns, and Eva's few attempts at small talk had been countered with monosyllabic answers. She'd given up after a few tries, deciding to let him work out his emotions without interference from her, but the insecurity she'd felt at the farm had increased, and with it her annoyance at herself for allowing him to make her feel so vulnerable.

Her attempt at a humorous response was both a cover-up for her own emotions and an attempt to ascertain what Rob was thinking and feeling.

His response surprised her. She'd expected a humorous riposte, and was unprepared for the violence of his sudden anger.

"Don't ever make jokes like that, Eva," he replied, his face tight, his dark eyes furious and stormy. "And don't ever doubt what I feel for you or how lasting it is. I want to spend a lifetime with you, not only two weeks, and nothing and nobody, *nobody*, is going to interfere with that—not our work, not your children, and not my daughter. Do you understand that?"

Eva nodded mutely, her eyes stinging with unshed tears.

Rob's eyes softened and he reached for her as she went into his outstretched arms. Their lips met in a long explosive kiss, tongue seeking tongue, hands caressing wherever they could reach.

They undressed each other slowly and agonizingly, mouths never parting. His erectness pulsated against her as he ran his hands down her bare back, caressed her buttocks, and slowly parted her trembling thighs. He picked her up bodily and lowered her slowly onto his throbbing phallus, his strong hands kneading her inner thighs. She exploded as he slowly entered her, rocking her softly up and down as she clutched him to her, wrapping her legs around his lower back.

"Not so fast," he murmured huskily as she groaned, the waves of her orgasm encompassing his manhood. "I have plans for you."

He carried her slowly into the bedroom, her arms and legs still locked around him, her still-throbbing slickness increasing his hardness and size, heightening his desire for this one woman he had ever really loved.

He sat on the edge of the large bed, still inside her, adjusting her in his lap, probing her with long, measured thrusts, as she groaned softly. She unlocked her legs and pushed him gently back; then, straddling him, she met his thrusts with longer, deeper ones until it was his turn to groan.

She watched his face as he closed his eyes. It was contorted with an ecstasy that was almost pain as he pulled her buttocks to him in a rising crescendo of thrusts. When she sensed that he was about to explode, she slammed into him, his engorged shaft entering yet deeper, then stayed perfectly still as he spurted into her in a never-ending orgasm that fueled her already-heightened desire.

She felt her insides convulse as muscles contracted and throbbed to meet his pulsations, and she moaned softly as she bent over him to meet his waiting arms.

They lay still for long minutes, savoring each other, exchanging feather-light kisses, not wanting to break the magic between them with a spoken word.

The room darkened as the sun slowly set, its last rays still touching the surface of the ocean with an occasional sparkle. Eva rose slowly, still not saying a word, and went into the bathroom to fill the large oval tub with hot water and fragrant bath oil that bubbled softly.

He watched her through the open door, too exhausted to move. He noted again how little her body had changed in the intervening years. There was a roundness to the belly, which had then been flat as a board, and her breasts were rounder and fuller. Everything else was still as slender and youthful as before—the slim legs, the smooth arms that drove him to distraction, the creamy skin and the V of soft black curls, the rounded buttocks and small waist...he was not surprised to feel himself hardening again. Looking at her glorious nudity had that affect on him.

Eva beckoned him to join her, and smiled when she saw his budding erection. Bathing together in the enormous tub was an erotic experience in itself. Wordlessly, they soaped each other, fiercely concentrating on every inch of each other's body, starting at the neck and working their way down. She soaped the tight dark curls on his chest, paused to caress the indentation of his belly button, then brazenly reached under the bubbles and grabbed hold of his now full-blown erection. Not one to be outdone, he reached for her, finding her clitoris and stroking it in time to the piston-like strokes of her clenched hand. The bath oil made their skin slick and both reached orgasm within minutes of the other's ministrations. Rob then led Eva out of the tub and into the large stall shower. She yelped as he turned on the water full-blast, then reveled as he shampooed her hair and soaped her from head to toe, holding her close as the stinging spray removed bath oil, soap bubbles, and the last traces of their lovemaking.

Her skin tingled as he wrapped her head in a large towel and enveloped her in one of the two fluffy white terry robes hanging behind the door, wrapping the other one around himself.

They were lying on the bed, the light from the bathroom and the phosphorescence of the ocean their only illumination, when he finally broke the silence between them and spoke.

"I love you, Eva," he said in a whisper. "I'm sorry about the way Jeannie reacted to you—but that will change, I promise you."

"And if it doesn't?" she asked slowly. "Or if it gets worse...what then?"

"It won't," he answered quickly, not willing to consider such an alternative.

Eva smiled enigmatically. His assurances that nobody would come between them didn't seem as fervent anymore, now that the passion was slaked and only the sweet aftermath of lovemaking remained. But they had these two weeks together. Come what may, they had that, and it would be wonderful for both of them, regardless of what the future held.

Her smile broadened as she wriggled out of his arms.

"I beg thee, sire, now that our sexual appetites are satisfied— for now—allow me to tend to our stomachs. Unhand me and allow me to prepare us some supper."

Eva unwound the towel from her head and quickly ran a brush through her hair.

"You must be starving!" he exclaimed, remembering with a pang that she had eaten no lunch. "I'll give you a hand."

They puttered around the kitchen, preparing a simple dinner—broiled veal chops and a leafy salad, with crisp fresh country bread and some Vermont cheddar for dessert.

They ate on the large deck at the front of the house, talking little, enjoying the roar of the surf and each other's company.

"I'm too tired to walk on the beach right now," Eva said, "but I'm game for a long walk first thing in the morning if you are."

He smiled at her as he poured the last of the burgundy into their wine glasses. "As long as you don't keep making those insatiable physical demands on me—if you do, I won't have the strength to manage the steps going down to the beach, let alone a long walk."

Eva threw her napkin at him and screwed up her face at his. "I fully intend on making all kinds of demands!" she declared. "We have a lot of years to catch up on, Rob," she added soberly. "And we've never had this kind of time alone together. Let's enjoy it."

He nodded, then got up and kissed her gently.

"Come on, woman," he said, his voice husky with emotion. "Let's throw these dishes in the sink and go to bed like an old married couple."

As if they were an old married couple, he was asleep before her, breathing deeply almost as soon as his head touched the pillow.

Eva lay awake for a long time, trying to analyze the situation, to figure out where their relationship was going and what effect Jeannie's hostility would have on it.

For all the intensity of their lovemaking and the lightness of the evening that followed it, she was scared. As scared as she'd been during that long and painful week years ago when Rob had made his choice to break off their relationship for Jeannie's sake.

There was no question now of telling him about Jonathan. That would box him into a corner and she'd never know whether he'd opted for her or for fatherhood. Possibly to make up for the first time around, Eva needed more than anything to have Rob choose a life with her because of *her*, not because her son was his child. And it isn't as if I'd be depriving Jonathan of anything, she rationalized. He's never been Jonathan's father and if he walks out of our lives again…well, nothing will have really changed.

But she knew deep down that that wasn't true. That Rob's leaving now would be the hardest loss she'd ever had to face. Harder than before, harder than her father's or Dan's deaths. And just as final.

She also knew that postponing telling him about Jon was risky. The longer she kept the truth from him, the harder it would be to justify or explain the delay. It was a double gamble. She might not lose out to Jeannie, and then lose Rob after all because she hadn't been honest with him.

But if I tell him now I'll never know, she argued with herself. If he knows about Jon, there will be no question—and there will be no answers for me, either. I'll never know whether it's me he really needs and wants—only that I need and want him more than I've ever needed or wanted anybody.

She looked at Rob's sleeping face, almost childlike in repose, the dark curls falling over his brow, just as Jonathan's did. I'll do my Scarlett bit, Eva thought as she settled herself down for the night, snuggling against Rob's warmth, his familiar scent sending a tremor of desire through her that took her by surprise. I'll worry about it tomorrow.

In his sleep, Rob wrapped his arm around her, gathering her curled-up form closer to him. Her last sensation before falling asleep was the monotonous roar of the ocean and Rob's even breathing as he held her in his arms, the only place she wanted to be.

FIFTY-ONE

The days passed quickly and gloriously. Rob and Eva took long walks along the beach, sometimes venturing into the ocean, which was really too cold for swimming. They lounged and swam in the heated salt-water pool at the back of the house, usually in the nude; ate and slept when they felt like it; talked and laughed and cried together, recounting childhood memories and adult pains. But, more than anything else, they made love—spontaneously, often, anywhere, and at the slightest instigation on the part of either one. She was always ready for him, wanting him even within minutes of a bout of lovemaking that left them breathless. His virility and desire for Eva amazed Rob himself. The years with Rhoda had been sexually arid but he'd remained more or less faithful, straying only occasionally, usually in far-flung cities when an opportunity presented itself. Eva had been the first woman to kindle his desire to such an extent, but the intensity of their affair had been confined necessarily, both in time and in space. Since resuming their affair, even with both of them freer than they'd ever been, their meetings had been limited by geography, time constraints, and familial and business obligations.

Now, for the first time, they found themselves truly free and truly alone, in an idyllic setting, with no business or family demands, with nothing to do but relax and explore each other's minds and bodies to a degree they had never done before.

They were floating on a double-sized air mattress in the center of the pool when Eva started to giggle, almost flipping them over.

Rob opened a baleful eye and stared at her. "What's so funny?" he demanded.

"We are!" Eva retorted between chuckles. "We're both workaholics and we're vacationing with the same intensity that we work! Milking every minute for all it's worth."

She sobered up suddenly. "It's almost as though we're afraid this will never happen again—it's like a swan song," she whispered hoarsely.

Rob flipped over, onto her, upsetting the mattress and dunking them both. When she came up sputtering he dunked her again, pushing her head under water with a firm hand. He then pulled her up by her hair and held her face level with his, their noses almost touching, wiping the salt water off her face with his hand.

"Don't ever think that, let alone say it," he said sternly, with none of his usual playful warmth. "This is *not* an ending; it's a beginning, a beginning of the best thing that has ever happened to either of us."

He knew instinctively that some of the salty drops pouring down her cheeks actually were tears and he gently led her out of the pool, wrapping her bronzed body in a big beach towel with the gentleness one would use in handling a newborn. He spread another towel on the grass near the pool and sat her on it, kissing her softly, settling himself down next to her.

"What are you afraid of, Eva? You know me like a book— better than I know myself, I think. You know how I feel about you—and how I feel about the fact that after all the years and all the pain, you just opened your arms and your heart and let me back in. Everything has changed since the first time around—and everything is so much better than I expected it to be."

He shook his head ruefully. "When I came back to Minneapolis to look for you, after I met Sharon, I did it with my heart in my mouth. I hoped that you'd at least agree to see me—but I wasn't sure you would. Then when your secretary said to go in, I figured I'd get a polite reception at best. You bowled me over with that first kiss. I think I must have been hoping it would happen that way, but I wouldn't let myself think about the possibility or it would have been too painful if you'd been cold…Eva, Eva—I adore you, I love you, I want to marry you—tomorrow or sooner, if you'll only agree. Why are you so fearful? Why don't you believe this is for real?"

Eva's face tightened. "What about Jeannie?" she asked in a low voice. "We've talked about almost everything under the sun except Jeannie. What if there's no room in your life for both of us—if she continues rejecting me the way she did at the farm? Who gets dropped then—Jeannie or me?"

She raised her gray eyes to meet his dark gaze, defiance and misery intermingling in her glance and in the tilt of her chin.

Rob looked at her in amazement. "That's not even a question that merits an answer!" he exclaimed, then reconsidered as he saw Eva's eyes narrow ominously.

"No—no, I'm wrong. Anything that's troubling you to that degree begs an answer—and then some!" He took a deep breath, choosing his words carefully.

"The situation is very different now, Eva," he began slowly. "Jeannie is no longer an eleven-year-old living with a mother who can't handle her and who doesn't love her. She's as grown-up as she'll ever be and she's in a wonderful setup that is worth every one of the many dollars it's costing because she's basically happy and well cared for. I would love for her to like you—and she probably will when she gets used to seeing you—her reaction was fairly typical for her, and I was a fool not to anticipate it and warn you. I thought you understood that when you told me not to push her and when you went off on your own."

He saw the pain on her face and it cut him to the quick.

"Eva, Jeannie is secondary! You come first, don't you understand? There's room for both of you, whether she likes you or not. She will get all the love and attention from me that she needs—but not at the expense of you, not by me giving you up. Do you understand that?!"

Eva nodded mutely, her eyes glistening with tears, too overcome to answer.

"I love you, Rob," she said thickly, stifling a sob. "I couldn't bear to lose you again—you don't know how much that would hurt."

"Yes, I do know," he whispered in her ear, caressing her damp hair, kissing her eyelids, then her cheeks, and finally her waiting mouth.

They made love slowly and tenderly, almost sedately, as if they found each other's fragility and vulnerability a precious trust, clinging to each other as though the intensity of their joint orgasm could blow them both away. Rob remained on top of Eva, his face nestled in the thick fan of her hair. She lay listening to the evenness of his breathing, once his heartbeat resumed its normal pace, with a heightened awareness of her surroundings—of the small high clouds moving at a leisurely pace across a bright blue sky, of the birds chirping in the woods behind them, of the hum of insects predicting another long, hot day.

"Rob," she said quietly, "I... There's something I have to tell you...something important."

Her only answer was his steady breathing and she realized that he had fallen asleep. She extricated herself slowly, so as not to disturb him, covered him with a towel, and touched his sleeping face with the back of her hand, a soft smile lighting up her face and her eyes. Her fears assuaged, Eva could finally allow herself to give in totally to the feelings that overcame her as she looked at Rob's peaceful sleeping face. Feelings of love and desire, coupled with serenity and calm, with a sense of security and well-being she had never known before.

There'll be time to tell you when you wake up, my love, she thought as she left him to sleep, going inside to shower and dress. She looked down at her totally tanned body as she emerged from the shower. With the complete seclusion of the place and their total ease with each other, Eva and Rob had virtually stopped wearing clothes.

She'd never had an all-over tan before, and she liked the way it looked in the large mirror that covered one of the bedroom walls. She'd stopped wearing two-piece bathing suits after Jonathan was born and it had been years since her stomach—still firm, though slightly rounder—had been this shade of mahogany brown. The ass isn't bad either, she thought as she turned in front of the mirror, searching for telltale bumps of cellulite.

Eva jumped with a start as the phone on the night table rang loudly. She had never heard it ring before. Only Bernie, Sharon, Rob's executive assistant, Jon's camp, and Jeannie's school knew where they could be reached—and all had been instructed only to call in case of a real emergency.

She picked up the phone with trepidation, her mouth suddenly dry as she said, "Hello?"

"Hello, Mrs. Goodman?"

"Yes?"

"This is Dr. Foster, from CompuCamp. I'm afraid Jonathan has been involved in a riding accident. We don't know how badly hurt he is, I'll be honest with you, but I don't think there is any serious danger. We just admitted him to the Memorial Hospital in Derry—it's the nearest one to the camp. The doctors are checking him over for internal bleeding and he may require surgery. We feel you should get down here as soon as you can."

Eva felt the blood freeze in her veins and forced herself to remain controlled. She got exact directions to the hospital, but could not learn any more about Jonathan's condition. He was unconscious and had a broken leg, and possibly a broken shoulder, but that was all Dr. Foster could tell her at the moment. She suspected he knew more than he was telling her, but was not about to waste precious minutes arguing with him on the phone.

She dashed out to get Rob and collided with him coming inside in search of her.

"Eva, what's wrong?" he exclaimed, noting her pallor under the deep tan, and the fear in her expressive gray eyes.

"It's Jonathan," she replied urgently, "he's been hurt. We have to get to the hospital. Let's go quickly, and I'll tell you more in the car."

They were heading for the highway in record time and Eva recounted her conversation with Dr. Foster, her voice controlled but her clenched hands trembling.

Rob reached over and took her hand in his. It was icy cold, despite the warmth of the day.

"He'll be okay, Eva. Kids are incredibly resilient. And it will be better when we're there and know exactly what's what."

She nodded mutely, unable to talk, remembering another harrowing ride to a hospital, and its tragic outcome.

Rob broke every speed limit, hoping to get stopped so that he could ask for police assistance in making good time to the hospital.

After an hour of driving, as they were nearing Derry's city limits, he heard the welcome siren. Eva looked up, startled.

"Don't worry," he assured her, squeezing her hand. "This is what I wanted."

He pulled over to the shoulder as a burly Maine state trooper strode toward the car.

"Officer," Rob explained before the trooper had managed to open his mouth. "We need your help! Our boy has been hurt in an accident and we're rushing to the hospital in town. Do you think you could escort us in? The boy's mother is beside herself. We don't know how badly he's hurt."

The trooper looked skeptical until he saw Eva's face. The fear in her eyes was palpable.

"Sure thing," he said quickly. "Just follow me and step on it. We'll get you there in no time."

Eva was unaware of the stir their little motorcade created as it sped through the sleepy streets of the small New England town. Her hands still clenched in tight fists, her face drawn, she looked ahead with an unseeing stare, fighting the hysteria she knew could overcome her if she let go.

Rob was silent, concentrating on sticking close to the police car, casting a concerned glance in Eva's direction every few minutes. He knew how close she was to the breaking point and what a tremendous effort her outward calm entailed, but he knew better than to try to comfort her with what might be empty words. The best thing he could do for her right now was to get to the hospital as quickly as possible.

The trooper pulled up at the emergency entrance in a screech of rubber, with Rob right behind him.

"You folks go on in," he said in a kindly tone. "Leave the keys in the car—I'll park it for you and bring them in."

"Thank you, officer," Rob said gratefully. Eva could only nod her thanks.

Dr. Foster was waiting for them.

"You must be Mrs. Goodman," he said, rushing to greet them. "Your son looks just like you."

"How is he, doctor? Is he okay?" Eva asked in a low voice.

The doctor's expression was sober. "It's too early to tell," he admitted, realizing that the person in front of him needed straight talk, not platitudes. "There's definitely internal bleeding and we're prepping him for surgery. The only delay is his blood type—he's an O-positive and we have virtually none on hand—it's an uncommon blood type, and there's always a chronic shortage—but we have a few local donors we're trying to reach and Boston General is rushing some over, which should get here soon." He stopped suddenly. "What's your blood type, Mrs. Goodman?"

Eva shook her head in misery. "A-positive," she answered glumly, and began to ask a question when Rob interjected, "I'm O-positive, doctor—how fast can you take my blood?"

The relief in Dr. Foster's eyes was measurable as he hustled Rob onto a bed in the emergency room and summoned a nurse to begin the procedure. He quickly punched the O.R. local on the bedside telephone.

"This is Foster. I have a blood donor for the Goodman boy. Tell Dr. Grant to start scrubbing. We'll get the blood up to him as quickly as possible."

He turned to Eva. "They'll be taking him up to surgery. You can see him very briefly just before he goes in, if we hurry."

Eva nodded mutely, then looked at Rob, hooked up to all the paraphernalia, his dark red blood already beginning to fill the plastic sac.

He waved her out with his free arm. "Go, Eva! I'll join you as soon as I can. Stay calm. He'll be all right."

Eva nodded again and rushed out after the doctor. They got to the corridor leading to the operating room just as Jonathan's bed was being wheeled out of the elevator. Eva swallowed back tears as she saw the pallid, unconscious face. She stroked Jon's curls gently, the soft brown curls that she would have known anywhere as his. The boy's eyes were closed, his long thick lashes resting on high cheekbones so like her own.

Foster, looking on, could not help responding to the poignant tableau in front of him. She knows how bad it is, he thought as he looked at Eva's expression and realized she was saying goodbye to her son. The nurse wheeled the bed through the wide swinging doors. Foster grabbed Eva as he saw her knees buckling, and led her gingerly to one of the sofas in the adjacent waiting room.

"My husband died the same way," Eva said dully, shaking her head as though to separate the two images, the five intervening years suddenly bridged by the familiar antiseptic smell and the pale green walls. Why were hospital walls always painted that bilious shade of green? "It was a car accident. A drunken kid smashed into him. There was so much damage inside they couldn't put him back together. The other driver got off without a scratch."

"This is a little different," the doctor said sympathetically but cautiously. In truth, they did not know how badly hurt Jonathan was. He'd been thrown off his horse but he'd landed on his head and shoulders and then rolled quite a distance down a rocky slope. There was no paralysis, they'd ascertained that, but God only knew how much other damage had been caused.

A nurse came in at that moment, her arms full of forms. "I'm sorry to bother you at a time like this, Mrs. Goodman," she said, "but I'm afraid I have to get some information from you and get your signature on a few forms."

Eva nodded, almost glad of the diversion that bureaucratic procedures injected, even into life-and-death situations.

Foster watched her as she quietly answered the nurse's questions, and then scrawled her bold, distinctive signature in the appropriate spots. She was a widow; he'd known that from Jonathan's file at camp. Her hands were devoid of any rings and her fingers were evenly tanned. He wondered why she hadn't remarried, and who the man with her was. Lucky break, his being the same blood type. That had saved time and improved the boy's chances.

When the nurse finished, he silently handed Eva a cup of hot coffee from the vending machine. "I don't know what you take in your coffee, so I got it with cream and sugar—is that okay?"

Eva smiled at him gratefully, and reached for the hot liquid.

Dr. Foster was at a loss for words. This temporary summer position was his first real job after finishing his residency. He'd be starting at Boston General in the fall. "I wish I knew what to say to make you feel better," he told Eva candidly.

She smiled at him, but the smile never touched her eyes. "I guess we just have to sit and wait and pray," she said quietly. "I remember that part, too…" She stopped, unable to go on, her hand trembling as it held the Styrofoam cup.

"I'll go and see how your friend is doing, and I'll tell him where to find you. Are you okay on your own?" he asked, wondering whether he should leave her, yet truly sensing that his presence was intrusive.

"I'm fine, thank you, doctor. If you could just let me know how things are going, I'd really appreciate it."

Foster nodded and rushed back down to Emergency.

Eva put down the untouched cup of coffee and walked over to the window. The day was just as glorious as it had been earlier, the sky becoming a deeper shade of blue as dusk approached. People were moving about outside, getting in and out of cars, chatting in the parking lot, driving by en route to other places. Life was going on normally all around her, just as it had on that fateful Sunday when Dan was killed.

Eva tried to picture what life without Jonathan would be like— and she couldn't. She could see his lanky eight-year-old form clattering down the stairs for breakfast. Nine, he'll be nine in a few days, she thought, if he lives… She found herself shaking uncontrollably as she envisioned Jon's ninth birthday—with Jon not there.

No, you can't let yourself think that, she commanded herself, wrapping her arms around herself to control the shaking, resting her forehead on the cool glass, her memories leaping back and forth over the past nine years, recalling scenes from Jon's life in no particular order or sequence. Like a jumbled-up photo album with the pages gathered at random. The first moment she had held him in her arms, looking in vain for a sign of Rob in the round baby face…Jonnie's first steps, on waddling chubby legs…Sharon teaching him his first words…Dan dunking him in the pool in Florida…Jon at his father's funeral, clutching her hand tightly, then burying his face in her skirt as the simple oak coffin was lowered into the ground.

Eva pushed away the image of a smaller coffin, refusing to let her thoughts move in that direction. She wondered, not for the first time, whether she was being tested in some fashion or whether the losses she'd experienced during the past years were a normal part of life. First, her father's death, then Dan's affair with Barbara, which had left her emotionally bereft, then losing Rob, then Dan's accident...and now this.

Eva was aware that many of the people who knew her envied her looks and success; that they even saw the tragedy of her widowhood as something that added an aura of glamour to a woman whose name had become synonymous with glamour in the fashion world.

I wonder if they envy the pain, she thought, stepping outside herself, seeing Eva standing in the austere severity of a hospital waiting room, her forehead resting against the cool window, her hair a glossy halo around her face as it caught the golden rays of the now-setting sun.

Still no word from the doctors.

Eva looked up to see Rob standing in the doorway, watching her quietly and thoughtfully.

"Are you okay?" he asked softly.

Eva nodded, not trusting her voice. She walked over to him, touching his bronzed bare arm, noting the small Band-Aid at the crook of his elbow.

"You?" she asked.

"I'm fine. They took a double portion of blood, at my insistence, and the blood from Boston arrived—so they're fine on that score. He'll pull through, Eva. I'm sure he will."

Eva nodded mutely, not finding words, and he wrapped her in his arms, holding her close to give her whatever strength and comfort he could.

"Rob, there's something I have to tell you—I tried earlier, at the pool, but you were asleep..."

Rob sat her gently on the vinyl sofa, holding on to her still-icy hands.

"Is he my son, Eva? Is that what you wanted to tell me?"

She looked up at him, her gray eyes startled.

"Yes…yes, he is your son, Rob," she finally said, her voice unsteady. "I got…It happened the last time we made love, the week before we parted…before I forced you to make a choice…"

The look on his face was one she would never forget, a mixture of joy and sorrow, of happiness and pain. They said nothing for a long moment, until Eva finally broke the silence.

"I've been wanting to tell you for a long time. When did you figure it out? Or was it a shot in the dark?"

Rob spoke slowly. "When Sharon told me about her brother, the thought crossed my mind for one brief moment, but I dismissed it as wishful thinking. Then, when I met Jon, I really wished he had been mine—he's everything I would have wanted in a child, and I wanted to have a child with you from the first time we met. But I never really considered it seriously until now— I knew that you were taking precautions and you're so efficient at everything you do…" He couldn't help smiling at that. "It was also in keeping, somehow, that once you gave up on me you would make a total commitment to where you felt your responsibilities lay—you don't do things by half-measures and I thought you might have decided to have another child with Dan to cement a bond that had more duty than love as its basis… It was the blood type that set me thinking again—thinking and hoping."

And then Rob started to cry. Quietly at first, with no sound or motion, just large wet tears coursing down the cragginess of a face suddenly grown older. Then, as she reached over to wipe his tears with the back of her hand, in large, heaving sobs that shook her to the core as he held her tightly in his arms with a quality of desperation she had never seen in him before and could not understand.

"Don't be angry at me," she whispered, wondering if he could hear the slow thumping of her heart as he buried his face in her bosom, the sobs still racking his body. He shook his head, still unable to talk, and she felt compelled to explain, to make good all the years he hadn't known, to justify her actions and to assuage her own guilt.

"I…I found out after we…after you…left. That's what kept me going those first weeks and months, knowing that I was carrying a part of you inside me. That you hadn't left me completely. That I would have more than a memory. I couldn't write to you or call you," she added, answering the unasked question in his eyes. "What would I have said? 'I'm pregnant and you'd better come back and make an honest woman out of me!' You didn't leave me because of me and a baby wouldn't have tipped the scales. You had to go back to what you had to go back to…I understood that. And I felt that the extra wrenching—the knowledge that you weren't leaving only me, but also a child—was something you didn't need or deserve. It wouldn't have changed anything—only made things so much harder for you. Was I wrong?" she asked in a quaking voice. "Did I do the wrong thing? Are you furious with me?"

Eva was now on the verge of tears herself and he held her head, then hugged her close.

"No," he said, his voice finally controlled, but barely. "I'm not angry or furious at you. How could I be? At myself maybe, for making the choices I made, but once I made them, what else could you do?" He paused. "I'm such a fool, Eva. Things could have been, should have been, so different for us…all these years…we could have been together…I could have been Jon's father…"

He shook his head as if to clear it, and she sensed his anguish. It was palpable. A presence that permeated the room. Anguish at the lost years they could never recapture, at Jon's babyhood and early years that he would never share, at the possibility that the boy would not survive the accident that threatened to end his young life before Rob could really know him.

They sat quietly for what seemed like forever, holding hands, not talking, but drawing comfort and strength from each other's presence.

They both jumped up when Dr. Grant walked into the waiting room in blood-spattered O.R. greens, his eyes tired but a look of guarded optimism on his face.

"Your boy is a fighter, Mrs. Goodman," he said, smiling in spite of himself. "I don't like to give people false hopes, but I think he'll pull through—the next twenty-four hours are crucial, but he's young and healthy and strong and I think he'll make it. We stopped the internal bleeding, and fixed him up as best we could…I won't trouble you with technicalities for now. He's in the recovery room and his vital signs are strong. He has a concussion, but it's not as severe as we feared, thanks to his riding helmet, and there's no paralysis or neurological damage. I'll take you in to see him soon—I'll go clean myself up, then I'll come back for you."

"Thank you, doctor," Eva said in a hoarse whisper, but Dr. Grant dismissed her gratitude with a brusque gesture. Life and death on the operating table he could deal with, but the joy and warmth that blazed in the unusual eyes of the woman in front of him made him uncomfortable.

"I'll be back soon," he said gruffly as he turned to leave. "Keep praying—he's not totally out of the woods yet, but he's well on his way."

Eva swayed as she felt her knees turn to rubber, and Rob caught her and hugged her tightly, as overcome by relief and gratitude as she was.

To his surprise, Eva started to cry. Deep, racking sobs that caused her body to shake uncontrollably. The outward calm that she had forced herself to maintain during the long drive to the hospital; the control she had exercised in the waiting room during the interminable wait for the surgery to end; the strength she had displayed during Rob's emotional reaction to learning that Jo—nathan was his own son—all these were now swept away in a torrent of gratitude and joy and emotion that could only manifest itself in a river of tears.

Rob shook his head ruefully as her sobs slowly subsided. He wiped away her tears and made her blow her nose, marveling at the strength of the dam that had enabled her to hold back her emotions during the past hours, allowing them to be vented in a storm of tears only once the initial danger was past.

"You are one heck of a lady!" he said as she emerged from the small bathroom off the waiting room. She'd washed her face in cold water and only the puffiness of her still-pinkish eyes betrayed the ordeal of the past few hours. Other than that, she looked tanned and fit and hale.

She smiled at him, thanking him wordlessly for his support and acceptance. But it was not her full real smile. That would light up her face only once Jon was completely out of danger.

Dr. Grant walked in briskly.

"I just looked in on Jonathan, Mrs. Goodman. He should be waking up soon. Let's see if we can have you there when he does—it's a lot less frightening that way, for youngsters."

Eva scrambled to follow him, then paused. "Can my...can we both go in together? I think Jon might like that."

Dr. Grant started to protest, but something compelling in both Eva's and Rob's faces stopped him.

"Well," he considered in a doubtful tone, "it's highly irregular. Ah well, what the hell! I'm the boss around here anyway—sure you can. But it will have to be brief, and very low-key. Don't get my patient all worked up!"

Eva paled discernibly when she saw Jon, looking tiny in the large hospital bed, a tangle of tubes and wires attaching him to an assortment of machines and bottles.

"He'll be off those in a few hours," Grant explained, noting her expression. "Don't let it scare you—it's not as intimidating as it looks."

Rob scrutinized the child's pale face, searching for the first time for some resemblance, trying to assimilate the fact that the small still form on the bed was his son, not only Eva's but also his. The child he had fantasized about. A tangible product of a love he thought he'd lost and then miraculously regained.

Eva bent over the child, touching his curls, bouncing them gently with her hand in a gesture that was heart-stoppingly familiar to Rob, brushing his soft cheek with her lips.

Jon's heavy eyelashes fluttered, then his gray eyes opened, staring straight into his mother's. He looked blank at first, then a faint smile touched his lips.

"Mummy!" he murmured, and Eva shushed him gently.

"Don't talk, sweetie," she said gently, her hand still stroking his curls. "You've been in an accident but you're all right."

Jonathan's smile deepened as his eyes closed again. Dr. Grant motioned Eva and Rob to follow him out. "He'll be in and out of sleep for the next few hours and we'll gradually unhook all the monitors and tubes, except for the I.V."

He looked at Eva and Rob sternly, not allowing them to see the warm chord they had both struck in his heart, cutting off Eva's attempts to thank him again in mid sentence.

"Sir!" he said to Rob in authoritarian tones. "This young woman needs a meal and a long, relaxing bath. I had my nurse arrange accommodations at the Holiday Inn down the street—take her there, see that she eats, bathes, and has a good night's sleep. Don't bring her back before tomorrow morning. We're going to give the boy something to make him sleep all night, and there's no use in pacing the halls."

He paused and answered the unasked question in Eva's eyes. "Yes ma'am, now I'm sure he'll be fine—you should be able to take him home in a week or so."

He looked from one to the other. Dr. Foster and he had discussed the details of the case and had speculated on who Robert Miller was, but Dr. Grant had drawn his own conclusions.

"That's a fine family you've got there, Mr. Miller. See you take good care of them."

FIFTY-TWO
AUGUST 1987

Eva sat with her back to the enormous desk, chair swiveled to face the plate glass wall, drinking in the view of the city. She would never see this particular view again, from this particular angle, and she let her eyes rove over the familiar landmarks and lights, remembering the night of her birthday five months earlier, when she had felt like a lonely queen ensconced for life in the hub of her little empire.

So much had changed. Rob had come back and the last missing piece in the jigsaw puzzle of her life was now in place. Sharon and Bernie had discovered each other and tentatively were exploring a very different relationship than the one they'd had before. Jonathan was alive and well, as excited as she was about the impending changes in their lives. And he now had a father. After years of making do with Bernie's sporadic attempts at playing an avuncular role, Jonathan had discovered the wonder of having a man in his life—someone who took him to ball games and spent hours with him at his computer and tousled his hair in a manner so different from his mother's gentle caresses.

Rob had unabashedly neglected his business to spend as much time as he could with them until the move—moves—to New York were finalized. The house was sold and the penthouse apartment on 73rd, overlooking Central Park, was almost ready. Goodman's and CompuTech would occupy the same floor in the Park Avenue office tower where one of Rob's branch offices had been housed. They were both relocating their head offices to New York—a sensible move for Goodman's and one Eva had been contemplating in any event, and one equally logical for Rob's company.

So many changes…so much had happened in so short a time…

Eva turned back to face the office. The rug was rolled up and tied, the paintings and the more delicate antiques were crated, ready for the movers, who were coming tomorrow. The only item still out was a silver-framed picture—that would go with her in her briefcase. She picked it up, a smile lighting up her face, and looked at the three happy faces—Rob, Sharon, and Jonathan. It had been taken a week after they'd come home with Jonathan—the day all these changes had been resolved…

Rob had not left her side during the week after Jonathan's accident, except for the half-day he took off to go visit Jeannie. He returned grim-faced and subdued, refusing to talk about it, saying only, "She'll come around. And if she doesn't—she won't."

Jon's progress had been miraculous, and the distance he put between himself and death's door in that one week surprised even the doctors.

They'll never know how close it was, Eva thought as she watched Jonathan and Sharon embracing at the airport, the day they brought him home.

Sitting in the kitchen after one of Mary's incredible meals, Eva and Rob watched Jonathan's animated face as he recounted the story of Rob having the same blood type. He'd heard the story from one of the nurses and thought it was definitely cool.

"Does this make us blood relatives?" Jon had demanded, turning to Rob in mid story. "Does this mean that if you marry my mother, you can be my real father?"

Eva held her breath. Rob shot her a keen glance, then answered Jon with all the seriousness he felt that the boy's question deserved.

"Jon—if you can help me persuade your mother to marry me, you will not only be the realest son I ever had, but you will be my pal and my ally for life!"

Eva blushed and Jonathan looked at her in amazement.

"You mean he asked you, and you said no!? But you love him—we all know that. So what's the problem?"

Sharon saved the day by interrupting at that point. "I don't think there will be a problem if we let these two people talk about it some more—I think Mummy may have been worried about how you'd take it, Jon. But now that she knows, I think we'd better get out of here and let them talk—or better still—we'll stay here and clean up and you guys go to the den and decide your future there! Remember, Mom—say whatever you want, as long as it's yes!"

Words had long been Eva's forte, but she was tongue-tied and speechless as Rob led her laughingly out of the kitchen. Sharon's and Jon's giggles were drowned out by Rob's firmly shutting the door. He sat her down in one of the armchairs with equal firmness and, with mock seriousness, got down on one knee in front of her, holding her hand as if he'd never let go.

"Now that we have the permission and approval of both your children, though only of one of mine, will you do me the honor of marrying me?" A crooked smile almost slipped out, but Rob squelched it, seeing Eva's face and tense demeanor.

"What about the child of yours who doesn't approve?" Eva asked gently.

"What about her? She will either learn to accept it or she won't. If she doesn't, she won't have less of me—I'll visit with the same regularity and all the love that was always there for her will still be there. If she does learn to accept it, she'll have the benefit of you and Sharon and Jonathan making her part of their lives, and she'll gain immeasurably. But Jeannie, at this point, is not a factor, Eva. The time when I had to choose between you and her is over. Circumstances have changed. And even if they hadn't..." he added softly, noting the fleeting look of pain that crossed Eva's face and quickly disappeared. "I'm not sure I made the right decision then—in fact, I'm pretty sure I made the biggest mistake of my life at that point—and I won't make it again. So please say yes and let's get on with our lives—we have so much lost time to make up for."

Eva nodded mutely, acknowledging the truth of his words, finding no more strength to resist what she wanted as much as he did; her last fears about a tug-of-war between Jeannie and herself laid to rest by Rob's total commitment to their future together, an unwavering commitment no one else could shake.

Enveloped in Rob's arms, breathing in the fragrance of his aftershave and skin, his face buried in her hair, then nuzzling her ear and neck until mouth found mouth in an endless kiss that only enhanced her longing, Eva knew that, finally, she'd come home…

A noise in the outer office startled her out of her reverie as Rob's voice called out, searching for her.

"I'm here," she called, surprised to find her voice thick with emotion. This office, now packed up and bare, represented a period of tremendous significance in her life, a chapter that was now ending, as a new one was about to begin. Within its four walls she had reached a pinnacle of business success that few women ever dared to strive for, let alone realize. True, she'd had a great head start—Goodman's had been a thriving enterprise before she took over—but she had turned it into a small empire, making her name famous across America and beyond, turning what could have been an empty life bereft of the love of one man and the life of another into a dazzling success.

"Finding it hard to extricate yourself?" Rob asked gently.

"Yes!" Eva answered, surprised at her reply. "I never expected it to be hard, but so much of me went into making Goodman's what it is today. Everything that was left over after Jon and Sharon's needs were attended to went into these four walls and what they represent—all the loneliness and fears and ambitions and drive and energy. That's never going to be the same."

"No," Rob agreed seriously, "especially with Bernie and later Sharon taking over as much as they will in the coming years. Then, with any luck and judging by the way he's going now, maybe Jonathan will be able to take over a lot of my work at CompuTech, and we two old fogies will be able to travel for pleasure, spend weekends in the country making love, and find time to spend some of the wads of money that we've both made. I see at least a dozen gray hairs amid the ebony, and I have a few dozen myself."

Eva laughed. "If you're suggesting retirement, forget it! I love this business. I'm relocating, not quitting."

"Exactly," Rob agreed complacently. "I'm merely suggesting that there's no cause for mourning; you're not quitting—merely making some long overdue changes. They won't detract from your ability to run a business—I promise you!"

Eva smiled. As always, he'd zeroed in on her fears and concerns with uncanny accuracy.

"What else do you promise me?" she demanded with mock solemnity.

Rob looked at her. "I promise you the best damned years you've ever had in your life."

Eva looked at him long and hard, knowing he meant it, and knowing he'd deliver.

Her expression was serious for what seemed to Rob an interminably long moment. Then her face broke into the same luminous smile that had captured his heart all those years ago.

Rob smiled back. "I'll give you a few more minutes to tear yourself away while I bring the car around. Meet me in the lobby."

It's time to start my life again, Eva thought as Rob left, her emotions a jumble of joy and anticipation, trepidation and excitement. Everything that's happened to me has been leading up to this.

She was startled by the unexpected sound of a strangely ethereal melody and wondered where it was coming from. It was at once new yet hauntingly familiar, like a fragment of a dream from long ago. It was only when she realized that the melody was reverberating in her own head that she recognized it for what it was.

"It's the mermaids singing," she whispered, awestruck. "It's the mermaids singing..."

ACKNOWLEDGEMENTS

My heartfelt thanks to the people who made the publication of this book possible: my son David, whose technical and publishing expertise was invaluable; my "critical readers"—Naomi, Tamara, and Miri—who read the manuscript and made valuable suggestions; Lisa Beres of MindHive Design for her brilliant creation of the cover; Palmer Gibbs for her diligent proofreading; and all those who encouraged me to keep writing throughout the years.

ABOUT THE AUTHOR

Esti Jedeikin lives in Montreal, Canada, and has a B.A. and M.A. in English Literature from McGill University, specializing in the 19th century novel. Her love of fine jewelry is an extension of her love of the craftsmanship of words. Esti divides her time between her business concerns in Montreal, her writing, and her bi-coastal family, but still finds time for gardening, music, and the movies. *The Mermaids Singing* is her first published work.

www.ingramcontent.com/pod-product-compliance
Lightning Source LLC
Chambersburg PA
CBHW070304260626
47160CB00003B/712